Praise for
Sue Margolis's Novels

Apocalipstick

"Sexy British romp ... Margolis's characters have a candor and self-deprecation that lead to furiously funny moments.... A riotous, ribald escapade sure to leave readers chuckling to the very end of this saucy adventure."—*USA Today*

"[An] irreverent, sharp-witted look at love and dating."
—*Houston Chronicle*

"Quick in pace and often very funny."—*Kirkus Reviews*

"Margolis combines lighthearted suspense with sharp English wit ... entertaining read."—*Booklist*

"A joyously funny British comedy ... a well-written read that has its share of poignant moments ... There are always great characters in Ms. Margolis's novels. With plenty of romance and passion, *Apocalipstick* is just the ticket for those of us who like the rambunctious, witty humor this comedy provides."
—*Romance Reviews Today*

"Rather funny ... compelling ... brilliant send-ups of high fashion."
—*East Bay Express*

Spin Cycle

"This delightful novel is filled with more than a few big laughs."
—*Booklist*

"A funny, sexy British romp ... Margolis is able to keep the witty one-liners spraying like bullets. Light, fun ..."—*Library Journal*

"Warmhearted relationship farce ... a nourishing delight."
—*Publishers Weekly*

"Margolis does a good job of keeping several balls in the air at once."
—*Southern Pines Pilot*

"A nice, refreshingly funny read."
—America Online's Romance Fiction Forum

"Satisfying … a wonderful diversion on an airplane, poolside, or beach."—*Baton Rouge Magazine*

Neurotica

"Screamingly funny sex comedy … the perfect novel to take on holiday."—*USA Today*

"Cheeky comic novel—a kind of *Bridget Jones's Diary* for the matrimonial set … Wickedly funny."
—*People* (Beach Book of the Week)

"A fast and furiously funny read … Scenes that literally will make your chin drop with shock before you erupt with laughter."
—*Cleveland Plain Dealer*

"Taking up where *Bridget Jones's Diary* took off, this saucy British adventure redefines the lusty woman's search for erotic satisfaction. … Witty and sure … A taut and rambunctious tale exploring the perils and raptures of the pursuit of passion."
—*Publishers Weekly*

"Splashy romp … giggles guaranteed."
—*New York Daily News*

"A good book to take to the beach, *Neurotica* is fast paced and at times hilarious."
—*Boston's Weekly Digest Magazine*

"This raunchy and racy British novel is great fun, and will delight fans of the television show *Absolutely Fabulous*."—*Booklist*

"A lusty laugh-out-loud tale about adultery."
—*Woman's Own*

Breakfast at Stephanie's

Sue Margolis

DELTA TRADE PAPERBACKS

BREAKFAST AT STEPHANIE'S
A Delta Book/June 2004

Published by
Bantam Dell
A Division of Random House, Inc.
New York, New York

This is a work of fiction. Names, characters, places, and incidents either are the product of the author's imagination or are used fictitiously. Any resemblance to actual persons, living or dead, events, or locales is entirely coincidental.

Book design by Patrice Sheridan
Cover art by James Dignan
Cover design by Lynn Andreozzi

Delta is a registered trademark of Random House, Inc., and the colophon is a trademark of Random House, Inc.

Library of Congress Cataloging-in-Publication Data

Margolis, Sue.
Breakfast at Stephanie's / Sue Margolis.
p.   cm.
ISBN 0-385-33733-7 (cloth)
1. Women musicians—Fiction.   2. London (England)—Fiction.
3. Jewish women—Fiction.   4. Pianists—Fiction.   I. Title.
PR6063.A635B74 2004
823'.914—dc22
2003064603

Manufactured in the United States of America
Published simultaneously in Canada

10 9 8 7 6 5 4 3 2 1

BVG

To Gay
with love, thanks, hugs and kisses
for always being at the other end of the phone

Breakfast at Stephanie's

Chapter 1

"Elizabeth Arden?"

It was the third Saturday before Christmas and Stephanie Glassman, resident pianist at the Oxford Street branch of Debenhams, was sitting at a white baby grand on the ground floor, playing "Winter Wonderland." She couldn't have looked less Elizabeth Arden–like if she'd tried. Unless, of course, Miss Arden used to celebrate the festive season by dressing up in a tacky Mrs. Claus Christmas outfit, which included a fur-trimmed thigh-high skirt and Teutonic blonde wig with plaited Alpine shepherdess-style earphones.

As she carried on playing, Stephanie looked up from the keyboard and saw a bulky, tweedy woman standing at her side. She was weighed down with carrier bags, and her face exuded faint desperation and the urgent need of a large gin. Stephanie had been at Debenhams for two weeks now and the haunted, get-me-out-of-here Christmas shopper look was one she had come to recognize only too well.

"I'm looking for her Perpetual Moisture," the woman

panted, desperation rising. "It's for my sister-in-law in Stoke
Poges. She swears by it. Lord knows why she bothers. Got a
face like a fossilized custard skin. Harrods and Selfridges have
both run out. Of course, if I had my way the poisonous old
boot would get a box of Newberry Fruits and a Jamie Oliver
video and be done with it."

While the woman paused for breath, Stephanie gave her
a warm, sympathetic smile.

"The Elizabeth Arden counter is just over there." She
nodded. "Behind Dior."

"Right, well, if they haven't got it I think I'll plump for
a foot spa. That way I can always live in hope she might
electrocute herself." Stephanie thought it best to remain
noncommittal—at least regarding the electrocution bit. "A
foot spa's always useful," she said. "Or gardening gloves and a
pair of pruning shears, maybe."

With that the woman huffed off toward the Elizabeth
Arden counter and Stephanie segued into "Have Yourself a
Merry Little Christmas."

Being Jewish, Stephanie's family didn't do Christmas—
something for which she knew her mother, Estelle, had always been eternally grateful. The spring cleaning, shopping,
baking and fish frying frenzy of Passover was enough to send
her racing for the Valium—without having to cope with
Christmas as well. Stephanie, on the other hand, had always
rather resented the family's lack of Christmas celebrations.

Traditional as they may have been where Passover was
concerned, her parents weren't particularly observant. For a
start, they ate nonkosher food. When she was a kid they went
out for Chinese dinner nearly every Sunday night. Her father
was a ferocious advocate of cha siu pork, believing its medicinal
qualities to be infinitely greater than those of chicken soup. Her
grandmother, who usually accompanied them on these jaunts,

2

refused to touch the pork. On top of this she always insisted on going through what Stephanie called her preening ritual, whereby she painstakingly picked out all the pork and prawns from her yung chow rice and piled them up in her napkin.

Christmas was like pork. You could "have it out"—like the turkey lunch at the Finchley Post House, even the midnight carol service at The Blessed Virgin down the road (her mum loved the tunes)—but on no account was it to be brought into the house.

As a child, Stephanie ached to take part in all the Christmas excitement and always felt jealous of her non-Jewish friends. Each year at junior school, just before they broke up for the holidays, all the kids in her class (except her, David Solomons and the Qureshi twins) would stand around in groups, busy competing about what they were getting for Christmas and having impassioned debates about whether Father Christmas really existed or whether the fat old bloke who delivered presents was just your dad dressed up.

She could still remember walking home from school on those dank December afternoons. It was teatime and in all the non-Jewish houses, the tree lights were being switched on. Every so often she would stop and stare at the twinkling windows, feeling she was peering into a never-never land. Ordinary houses, with their boring tarmac drives and UPVC window frames, became enchanted fairy grottoes. Her eight-year-old heart quite literally ached not just for Santa and the pillowcase of presents, but for the tinsel, the Christmas tree baubles, the crackers, the ritual of leaving mince pies outside for the reindeer—the sheer wondrous, sparkling magic of it all.

Of course she had Hanukkah, which happened around the same time as Christmas, but it wasn't the same, lighting a few pathetic candles and getting a fiver pressed into your hand by some whiskery old aunt.

When she gave birth to Jake, two and a half years ago, she promised him three things: her unconditional love and support, that she would never allow him to own a motorbike while he lived under her roof, and that he would have a childhood full of brilliant Christmases. Although this was his second, it was the first he was old enough to appreciate. As a result, Stephanie's living room ceiling was thick with paper chains, streamers and balloons. In the alcove next to the fireplace stood a garish, overdressed, six-foot-tall Norway spruce, which—since there was no husband or boyfriend to do it for her—Stephanie's father, Harry, had insisted on schlepping back from the greengrocer's around the corner, on the strict understanding it was to be referred to as a Hanukkah bush. Deciding that she shouldn't look a gift horse in the mouth, Stephanie agreed.

She looked down at her watch. Almost three. Time for her break. Although she loved Christmas, she loathed her Mrs. Claus getup. What she hated even more was walking through the store wearing it. She didn't mind the short skirt so much because it showed off her long—and even if she did say so herself—shapely legs, as did the long stiletto-heeled boots she'd been given. No, what she loathed was the earphones wig. It made her look like that woman in *The Sound of Music* who, having been handed second prize at the Salzburg Music Festival, refused to stop bowing.

Women who noticed the earphones tended to smile in sympathy, but blokes always made some kind of smart remark. "Can you get the football on 'em, then?" Yesterday a shaven-headed youth in a Manchester United football shirt, loitering suspiciously with his mates by the watches, had yelled out: "Whassit like shagging Santa, then?"

4

"Not that good, actually," she'd replied, grinning. "He only comes once a year." Ho bleeding ho.

What worried her most about being Mrs. Claus was the thought of being seen by somebody who knew her, such as her parents' rabbi, or an ex-boyfriend, or perhaps some girl from school she hadn't seen for years and who now looked like Gwyneth Paltrow and was in mergers and acquisitions. It wasn't just the costume she would have to explain away. Far more important was why, more than ten years after leaving university (English, honors) and a successful stint at drama school—not to mention her great singing voice—she could aspire to nothing more elevated, careerwise, than a temp job as a cheesy, piano-playing Mrs. Claus in a middle-market chain store.

Stephanie finished with a quick burst of "Jingle Bell Rock" and then stood up. The place was teeming with the fraught and the frazzled. A few feet away, a middle-aged couple seemed to be having a major fight about driving gloves. Then: "Coooeee."

Her heart sank to her stiletto boots. It had finally happened. Somebody had recognized her. OK, she could always say her dad played golf with Mr. Debenham and she was just helping out because the store's regular piano player had come down with Ebola.

She turned toward the voice. Instant relief. It was only the tweedy woman bent on electrocuting her sister-in-law in Stoke Poges. She was holding up a Debenhams carrier bag.

"Mini carpet bowls," she cackled. "Byeee. Merry Christmas!"

"You too."

Stephanie gave her a small wave and watched the woman disappear into the crowd. She was just trying to work out whether she had time to go to the loo and get to the toy department to buy Jake his main present—a Bob the Builder tool belt, on which she was entitled to a 20 percent staff discount—when she saw someone even more embarrassing than Rabbi Nodel.

She recognized Frank Waterman at once. Dark, swept-back hair, eyes the color of conkers, just a hint of well-tended stubble. They'd been in *Cabaret* together at the Nottingham Playhouse, six or seven years back. Stephanie had been in the chorus and he'd played Cliff Bradshaw, the romantic lead. During their time together, she developed *the* most almighty crush on him, but nothing ever happened between them. They exchanged hellos at rehearsals, went drinking with the same gang after the show, but since he was so resoundingly A-list to look at and always had stacks of women (not to mention a couple of blokes) sniffing round, she'd never plucked up the courage to flirt with him.

The show had been on for a couple of weeks when the message filtered down to London that the production was particularly excellent and a theater critic from one of the broadsheets turned up. He raved about the show and Frank's performance in particular, saying he possessed that indefinable quality common to all great actors and that celebrity undoubtedly beckoned. Frank had never looked back. These days, he was the Royal Shakespeare Company's rising star— and she was Mrs. Claus with earphones.

Now he was coming her way, but since he was busy chatting to the woman with him, Stephanie was pretty certain he hadn't noticed her. Plus it had been years since they'd last met and it wasn't as if they'd had much to do with each other back then. Chances were that even if he saw her, he wouldn't recognize her. Nevertheless she sat back down on the piano stool and buried her head in her music book.

"Steph?" Bugger. OK, play it cool. Do not let him see you're flustered. She looked up and forced her mouth onto full beam. "Frank? Frank Waterman?"

"I don't believe it," he said. "I knew it was you. I said to Anoushka"—glorious cheekbones, Fulham highlights— "I'm sure that's Steph from *Cabaret*. God, it must be what, four, five years ago?"

"Nearly seven."

"No. As long as that?"

"Yup. Time flies."

"God, doesn't it? So, you're Mrs. Christmas."

He was looking at the wig and smiling. Her hand sprang self-consciously to her left earphone. "A bit Heidi, I know." A smirk of agreement from Anoushka. "Still, it's only until Christmas Eve. Pays the bills."

"But what about the singing? Don't say you've stopped. You had such a fantastic voice. You were into blues and jazz, if I remember. Ella, Peggy Lee, that sort of stuff."

"That's right." She was gobsmacked. Utterly astounded that he remembered. He turned to Anoushka. "One night in the pub when we were touring, Steph got up and sang 'My Melancholy Baby.' She was outstanding. Had us all in tears."

"Really?" Anoushka said with a brief, polite smile.

There was a moment's silence. "Wow, stunning earrings," Stephanie said to Anoushka, noticing the glistening pinkish-red stones. "I love rubies."

"They're pink diamonds, actually."

"Anoushka designed them herself," Frank said. "She runs her own jewelry business."

"Oh, right." Stephanie nodded. Then the penny dropped. Anoushka didn't run a mere business. It was a full-frontal corporate empire. "God, of course, you're Anoushka Holland. I read that piece about you in last month's *Vogue*. Didn't your company just get bought out by Theo Fennell for eleven million quid?"

"Eleven point five," Anoushka corrected. Having been put in her place, Stephanie didn't quite know what to say next. Frank picked up on her awkwardness.

"So," he said to Stephanie, "are you still singing?"

"Yes. I do a couple of gigs a week at the Blues Café in Islington. And I've had the odd bit in *Chicago* and *Les Mis*. Nothing major, though."

"Oh, it'll happen one day," he said. "With a voice like yours, it has to."

"But what about you? The critics loved you in *Othello*."

He blushed ever so slightly. Before he had a chance to reply, Anoushka broke in: "We really ought to be going, Frankie. I need to pick up a few bits at the General Trading Company." She put a proprietorial arm through his. "We only popped in to buy that Dustbuster thingy your grandmother was after." That last remark was clearly for Stephanie's benefit—to explain why the likes of Anoushka, her highlights and her eleven point five million, were slumming it at Debenhams.

"And don't forget," she went on, "we're due at the wedding planner's at six."

"Tying the knot in the spring," Frank explained.

"Wow, congratulations."

"Thanks. We're off to discuss harpists and doves. Bit bloody camp if you ask me. Plus I've got visions of two hundred guests turning up to the reception covered in bird turd."

"Frankie," Anoushka said, laughing, but Stephanie could tell she was cross, "how many more times? Otto has promised faithfully they don't feed the doves for three hours before the ceremony. Now then, we really must get going."

"Yes, we must," he said. "Sorry, Steph. It's been great seeing you."

"You too."

"Sweetie," Anoushka simpered.

"Perhaps Anoushka and I could catch you at the Blues Café one night?"

Anoushka had already started walking away. "Yeah. That'd be good," Stephanie said.

"Catch up on old times."

"Excellent."

He gave her a soft smile.

"Bye," she said. A moment later he had caught up with Anoushka, who turned her head and gave a little wave. "Bye Beth, lovely meeting you."

Stephanie arrived home just before seven. She rented the house—a large four-story Victorian terrace in Muswell Hill—from Jimmy, who was best mates with her friend Cass. He was also filthy rich. In November, having been dumped by his lover, Brian, he decided to take off to Phuket for six months "to heal myself." He had simply wanted somebody to look after the house and feed Liberace the cat, a Persian with a coat of the palest peach. Stephanie had to persuade Jimmy to take any rent at all. In the end he asked her what she was paying for her flat round the corner—which was so small it would have virtually fit into Jimmy's living room. She told him and he said she might as well pay him the same.

Since Jimmy was a film set designer as well as gay, the place had been totally decorated when she moved in. With its overstuffed sofas, chandeliers (in the bathroom), swags and tails curtains—not to mention the Cath Kidston cowboy ironing board cover—it was just a bit too camp for her taste. She was more of a black-leather-sofas-and-white-walls-covered-in-huge-abstracts sort of a person. But since she could barely afford the Habitat catalogue, let alone buy anything from it, she wasn't about to get picky. Stephanie had been there eight weeks and still couldn't believe her luck. Even now she was still pinching herself whenever she walked through the door.

"Hi, Mrs. M.," she called from the hall. "Sorry I'm late. Had to let three trains go at Oxford Circus, they were so packed. God, I forgot, it's your darts night tonight. I haven't made you late, have I?"

"Don't worry, darlin'," Mrs. McCreedy's voice came from the kitchen. "Doesn't start until eight. I've got loads of time."

She hung up her coat and went into the kitchen, where Jake—aged two and a half—was sitting astride his red plastic road digger, eating Marmite soldiers. His face—what she could see of it under his rather too-big policeman's helmet—was smeared in a crust of dried-up baked bean sauce. The moment he saw her he jumped up and came charging toward her.

"Hi, poppet," she said, scooping him up and kissing him on a patch of bean-free face. "So, how are you?"

"Better."

Jake didn't really understand the question. A couple of months ago, when he was getting over chicken pox, he'd overheard people asking Stephanie how he was. She'd said, "Oh, much better." This had led him to believe that "better" was the correct and only response to the question. "That's good," Stephanie said. "And what did you have for lunch?"

"Chickens." For some reason Stephanie had yet to work out, Jake only ever ate meat in the plural. "Hard noses, Mummy. Hard noses." Before she'd had a chance to protest, Jake was pressing his nose against hers with all his might. She tried to give as good as she got, but Jake's tiny young nose was

10

so soft, he felt no pain. "Enough. Enough," she cried out, eyes watering.

"Now then, Jake," Mrs. McCreedy said, closing the dishwasher and wiping her hands on her tabard overall, "will you stop hurting your poor mammy when she's just come in exhausted from work."

"Me won! Me has won!" He wriggled down and got back on the digger.

"How's he been?" Stephanie said to Mrs. McCreedy.

"Not a moment's trouble. He slept until four, though. He's not going to be ready for his bed in a hurry."

Poor Mrs. M. sounded so apologetic—she must have seen Stephanie's face fall ever so slightly. She adored Jake, was always desperate to see him when she got in from work, but what she wanted more than anything right now was a long soak in the bath and an early night.

"Now then," said Mrs. McCreedy, "how's about a nice cuppa?"

"No, you sit down. You've been on your feet all day. I'll get it. On second thought, I think I'd rather have a glass of wine. What about you?"

"Ah, go on, then." Mrs. McCreedy smiled, pulling out a kitchen chair. "Twist my arm. It is the festive season, after all." She landed heavily on the chair. Then she leaned over to where Jake was sitting on his digger and gave him a gentle, conspiratorial nudge in the ribs. "But you're not to go telling on your mammy and me. Understand?"

Jake gave a solemn shake of his head and Mrs. M. rewarded him with another Marmite soldier.

"So," Stephanie said, pulling the rubber wine stopper out of a half-finished bottle of Jacob's Creek, "the darts team in good shape for tonight?" She was referring to the Duke's Head pub ladies' darts team. Mrs. M. had been a member for fifteen years. Tonight they were taking on the team from The Crooked Billet.

"The best we'll ever be. Not that it'll get us very far. That other lot—crooked by name, crooked by nature." She lowered her voice. "Two of them are bloomin' whatyoumacallits. Trans something. That's it, transsexualists. Apparently they look like women, but according to my friend Audrey, they've still got their willies and everything. I always say, live and let live, but what chance do we stand with them and all their male hormones still raging?"

"I get the point," Stephanie said, battling to keep a straight face. She handed Mrs. McCreedy a glass of wine and sat down next to her at the long kitchen table. Whenever Stephanie thought about Mrs. McCreedy, she couldn't believe her luck. She was *Ballykissangel* meets *Mary Poppins*—except she had a good fifty years on Ms. Poppins, couldn't sing a note and had a dodgy hip. She was, however, magic. At least where Jake was concerned. Nobody could bring him down from a tantrum like Mrs. M. Or get him to eat like Mrs. M. Her methods would have caused Penelope Leach to take a Valium and lie down in a darkened room, but they worked. Mrs. M., who had raised nine children of her own back in Cork, was a firm believer in bribery. This took the form of cakes. Mr. Kipling Fondant Fancies.

"Eat your dinner, Jakey," she would say, "and I'll see what I can find." He would clean his plate and she would pull a Day-Glo pink Fancie out of her handbag the way Mary Poppins produced a hat stand. Stephanie suspected he had already developed a three-a-day habit.

On the one hand, Stephanie lived in fear of Jake starting school with a full set of dentures; on the other, she was loath to confront Mrs. M. in case she got offended and left.

Jake adored Mrs. M. as much as he adored his grand-mother. In fact, they adored each other. It was true love. Stephanie couldn't risk losing her. Plus she was cheap. On what Stephanie earned a month, she couldn't begin to afford a proper nanny.

Mrs. McCreedy always said she didn't look after Jake for the money, she did it for the company. After her husband died, she moved to England to live with her widowed sister. When the sister died a couple of years ago, she realized she needed something to fill her days. She refused to go back to Ireland to live with her children because "they had their own lives" and it would mean leaving her friends on the darts team. Stephanie knew she would have to say something about all the sugar, but not just yet.

Of course, there was a much more serious issue with Mrs. M.: her arthritic hip, which had gotten much worse over the last few months. It had been barely noticeable two years ago when she first came to look after Jake, but now she walked with a heavy limp and Stephanie could see how she struggled to chase after Jake. Suppose she slipped on the stairs? At least Jake did the stairs on his own these days, so she didn't have to carry him. She also insisted on a leash when Mrs. M. took him out for a walk, but this didn't stop Stephanie having nightmares about Jake running into a busy road and Mrs. M. being too late to catch him. Something had to be done. But sacking Mrs. M. was unthinkable. She lived for the time she spent with Jake. Stephanie took a huge glug of wine. She would think about it again after Christmas.

"Right, I'll be off, then," Mrs. McCreedy said. As she stood up, they both noticed Jake over by the kitchen cupboards. He had poured half a packet of flour onto the floor and was jumping up and down in it. "Oh, darlin'—not the flour."

"Jakey! No." Jake hated being shouted at and burst into tears.

"Oh, now then, now then," Mrs. McCreedy soothed, limping over to him. "Stop your tears. Let's see what I've got in my bag, shall we?"

Jake sniffed and took Mrs. M.'s hand and the pair of them proceeded back to the kitchen table, Jake leaving a trail of floury footprints. Stephanie looked on as Mrs. M. said the magic words: "Issie wizzie, let's get busy."

"Ooh, I know," Stephanie said, attempting to interrupt, "why don't I—" She was about to suggest reading him a story to calm him down, but she was too late. Mrs. M. had already dug into her bag and, with a flourish, produced a fluorescent yellow Fondant Fancie. Jake yelped with delight.

While he sat on his digger demolishing the Fancie, Stephanie swept up the mess, but not before Liberace had come mincing in. Before she could stop him he'd walked through it and left a mixture of wet mud and flour prints all over the floor.

In the end it needed a complete mop and Mr. Clean. Then, because it was an expensive wood floor, she had to get out Jimmy's electric polisher, which was huge and unwieldy, the kind that required wearing a sports bra to operate. It was well after eight by the time she'd finished. She decided they might as well take their evening bath together. Jake laughed to the point of hiccups as she deposited clusters of bubbles on his nose and head and made shampoo horns with her hair.

As they played, she found herself thinking about Frank and Anoushka—how hugely successful they were and how she longed to be part of some smug self-satisfied couple with their own Web site. Since having Jake, she'd had a couple of short-lived relationships, but nothing serious. The last one had ended just before she moved into the house. She was getting to the stage when, hard up as she was, she would hand over a winning lottery ticket for one single night of passion. The last time she'd slept with somebody had been after her fat cousin Miriam's wedding. At the reception she'd been put next to a bloke called Lewis, who was in dried fruit. She could tell he fancied her because all through dinner he kept on and on about how a cross section of a dried pear resembled a vulva. He was cute enough, but much as she tried to steer the conversation off dried fruit, somehow they always came back to the pear thing or to EU fig quotas. The only light relief came when they spent half an hour discussing the ins and outs of his impending laser eye surgery. Apparently he was blind without his lenses.

That night she went home with Lewis. It was more to end her sexual drought than anything else. Jake was spending the night at Stephanie's friend Lizzie's. Normally, she never slept with men she had just met, and it occurred to her that Lewis might be some mad pervert. She decided it was unlikely, though, since he was cousin Miriam's boring, straight-as-a-die husband's best mate.

She'd expected him to be from the "brace yourself" school of foreplay, but he wasn't. He spent ages getting her warmed up. Finally he suggested getting some K-Y jelly. She insisted she didn't need it—what was it with this bloke and the dried pear metaphor?—but he insisted. He returned from the bathroom, said he'd run out of K-Y jelly but had found a jar of Vaseline. Then he asked her in a rather naff, doctorish way, which she found herself rather enjoying, to open her legs. She let her knees fall apart and waited, heart thumping. A moment later she was screaming, but not with delight. It wasn't a jar of Vaseline poor, myopic Lewis had found in the bathroom, it was Vicks VapoRub.

As well as sex, she desperately wanted a decent singing

gig. When she left drama school her mates and her tutors all said that if anybody was destined to make it in musicals, she was. But it just hadn't happened. There had been the small solo part in *Chicago,* but mainly all she got was chorus stuff. Occasionally she was called in to do a TV advertising jingle, which was always good news because ads paid top dollar. What with that, the theater and the odd stint playing the piano in hotel lounges and department stores, she just about managed to pay the bills. The Blues Café paid virtually nothing, so it didn't count. She did it for pleasure and in the hope that one day she might get discovered by some hot impresario.

The Billie, Ella and Peggy stuff was in her soul. Her dad was a fanatic and their music—those melting, melancholy melodies—formed some of her earliest memories. She'd lacked confidence as a child, and her parents thought singing lessons might help. Not only did she find her confidence, she found her voice—a deep, velvet, practically black voice, her singing teacher said. Had she ever thought of singing blues? The first time she sang in public—"Summertime" at a school do—and she felt the adrenaline, saw how she could touch an audience, she knew she wanted to do it for a living.

Her parents and teachers urged caution and she did the sensible thing and went to university—Leeds—and carried on singing in local clubs. Then she joined the drama society and discovered that she could act too. After she graduated from university, three drama schools offered her a place. These days, plenty of people—apart from her mum, dad and grandmother, who were clearly biased—said she should be doing better professionally. Nobody could understand why she hadn't landed a lead part in a musical. Sheer bloody bad luck, they said. But she could understand it perfectly. She knew the way show business worked, and that it was perfectly possible her luck might never change. She was thirty-two.

When she went back to work six months after Jake was born, she gave herself two years to land a decent part in a musical or get some kind of recognition as a solo jazz singer. Her time was up. For weeks now she'd found herself looking at courses in teaching English as a second language in *The Guardian*.

From time to time she'd thought about changing agents. Eileen Griffin, who was in her sixties, had represented her for years and was starting to lose her edge. Not that she'd ever had much of one. The booze had seen to that. Two or three years ago Stephanie had even made a demo CD to send out to other agents. Then just as she was about to do the deed, Eileen would get her six weeks in *Chicago* or *Les Miz* and she would put it off. Maybe the time had finally come to send out that CD. If nobody else was interested, then she would think about giving up. At least then she could say she'd tried everything.

Of course Jake wasn't remotely tired even after the bath and they had to go downstairs to make Play-Doh green eggs and ham. Then he had a tantrum because she put the eggs and ham on the same plate, when he had apparently made it abundantly clear that they were to go on separate ones. By nine she insisted they go upstairs to his brand-new "big boy's bed" and read stories.

"Do Fatapillow," he shouted, bouncing on the *Thunderbirds* duvet. "Do Fatapillow."

This meant she should sit on the bed reading *The Very Hungry Caterpillar*, Jake's all-time favorite read, over and over again while he lay in bed and "zizzed" his label. Other kids went to bed with bits of smelly old blanket. Jake had a grubby Mothercare label torn out of an old T-shirt, which he rubbed, or, in Jake argot, "zizzed," between his fingers. Every time her voice faltered or her eyes started to close he would prod her.

17

"Read, read. Read, read." Four rounds of Fatapillow later and he was still wide awake. "Sing, sing. Sing, sing."

"Jake, Mummy's totally knackered," Stephanie pleaded, virtually on the point of offering him an entire box of Fondant Fancies if he would only go to sleep and let her go to bed with the telly, the wine bottle and a Be Good to Yourself lasagna.

"Sing, sing. Sing, sing."

"OK...Your baby has gorn down the plughole / Your baby has gorn down the plug..."

"Not that one. Not that one." She looked at her beautiful, innocent child and felt instantly guilty.

"Say night-night Daddy now," Jake said. He picked up the picture of Albert from his bedside table and licked it. "Jake, you know that's not a kiss. Now I have to clean all your slobber off Daddy." She wiped the glass with her sleeve.

"My daddy come for Christmas from 'merica?"

"I hope so, darling, I hope so."

Albert had this habit of saying that he was coming for a visit, then a job would come up and he would cancel at the last moment. To give him his due, though, he always turned up eventually, laden with guilt presents. Of course, the timing never mattered much when Jake was a baby, but now he was old enough to understand about daddies and to be hurt by broken promises.

"Come on, Jakey, sleep time." She pulled the duvet up over his shoulders.

"Sing, sing, Mummy. Sing, sing."

"All right." She turned off the bedside light, slipped in bed beside him and began stroking his head.

"There were birds, on a hill / But I never heard them singing...Till there was you."

18

Chapter 2

Stephanie went back downstairs to the kitchen and topped off her wineglass. She was pricking the cellophane film of her microwave lasagna when the phone rang.

"Hello, darling." It was Grandma Lilly—her mother's mother. She was seventy-nine and lived at The Haven, a small complex of warden-assisted flats in Hendon.

"Hi, Gran. How you doing?"

"Oh, you know. Can't complain." She sounded down, which was unusual. Despite her age, Grandma Lilly was one of the most energetic and upbeat people she knew.

"Gran, is there something the matter?"

"No, not really."

"Come on. There is. I can tell by your voice."

"Well, it's a bit difficult. You know, a bit personal."

"It's OK," Stephanie said. "You can tell me."

A pause. Then: "I'm seeing a man."

"Wow, Gran. Good for you."

"Anyway, the point is, I've had to give up sex."

Stephanie nearly choked on her wine. "Omigod." She hoped it hadn't come out as "Omigod, do people of almost eighty actually still have sex?"—which is what she meant, of course. What she vainly hoped it sounded like was: "Omigod, what a shame."

Lilly said her chap's name was Maury, that he was eighty-three and had made a fortune in vacuum-packed matzo balls. "You must have heard of him: Maury Silverstone. His balls are massive." Lilly chuckled at the joke. "And it's not just his balls that are big. He's also got a great body and this absolutely huge—"

"No, Gran. Stop! Too much information."

"I was going to say," Lilly said, "he's got this absolutely huge villa in Marbella."

"Oh, right. I see," Stephanie replied. "But what's happened? Why have you had to give up sex?"

"Why do you think? The pacemaker." Lilly's heart rate had become a little irregular lately, and she'd had the pacemaker fitted at the Charing Cross hospital a couple of weeks ago. "I don't understand," Stephanie said.

"I'm frightened—you know—that when I reach the moment of ecstasy, I might overload the circuits and electrocute myself." Hang on. Her seventy-nine-year-old grandmother was not only still having sex, she was having "moments of ecstasy"? "The thing is," Lilly went on, "I can't talk to your mother about this. She wouldn't approve. She thinks I spend my spare time playing board games. But there's more to life than a triple-word score in Scrabble. You're young and modern, though. Your generation is much more open about these things. I feel I can talk to you. I didn't want to mention it to the doctor. He was some old fuddy-duddy in his sixties."

Stephanie hadn't the foggiest idea what to say. She was

still processing "moment of ecstasy" and trying to rid her brain of the picture of her grandmother and her herring breath, writhing naked on her orthopedic bed. Did she keep her teeth in? "OK, Gran. Look, don't worry. I'll check it out with a doctor friend of mine, but I'm pretty sure you're safe to carry on life just as you always have and I'm certain you can't possibly electrocute yourself."

"You reckon?"

"I'm certain. But I'll double-check, OK?"

"Thank you, darling. I appreciate it. Look, I haven't said anything to your mother about Maury. You know how she likes to interfere. I know she wouldn't approve, particularly if she knew I was still, you know, active in the bedroom department." That was probably an understatement.

"Promise. I won't say a word," Stephanie said.

No sooner had she put the phone down than it rang again.

"Hi, it's me." It was Stephanie's mother, Estelle. She was phoning to check that Stephanie was still bringing Jake over in the morning.

"Course, he's really looking forward to it." Every other Sunday, her parents would look after Jake, and Stephanie's two best friends, Lizzie and Cass, would come over for one of her famous fry-ups.

"Oh, by the way," Estelle said, her tone low and conspiratorial, "I think your grandmother is seeing somebody."

"What? As in a man?"

"Yes. I bumped into that Pam the other day, you know, the warden at The Haven. Nothing gets past her. Anyway, apparently your grandmother's got 'a gentleman caller.' Been seeing him for quite a while."

"Really? Good for her," Stephanie said.

"No, don't get me wrong, I totally agree. Your grandfather's been gone three years and it's companionship for her. Somebody to play Scrabble with, or to sit in the other armchair and watch *Countdown*. I mean, it's not as if they get up to anything at that age. God, can you imagine?"

"No, not really," Stephanie said.

"Look, you won't tell her I know, will you? She'll be on the phone telling me I'm interfering before I've even said a word."

"No, Mum, I won't say anything. Promise."

$\mathcal{S}$tephanie laughed quietly to herself and at last put the lasagna in the microwave. As she sat looking through the TV listings in the paper, her thoughts returned to Albert, Jake's father, with whom she'd had a brief fling in Italy over three years ago. It sounded appalling, she always thought, to describe Jake, whom she loved more than anybody in the world and without whom life would be totally meaningless, as the result of a brief fling, but it was true.

Albert lived in L.A. He'd always helped support Jake financially and he came over as often as he could. But his visits were erratic. Stephanie knew there was nothing to be done. They lived on different continents. Albert had a living to earn. But Jake wasn't a baby anymore: he was a little boy and he needed a daddy in his life to do boy stuff with. He needed somebody constant—somebody who would play kick-around in the garden with him before bed, who would be there when he woke up in the morning. The only person he had at the moment was her dad. Harry did his best, but he was pushing seventy and he just didn't have the energy to keep up with a toddler. Unlike her mother, who as a result of hormone replacement therapy, not to mention her congenital neurosis, was positively brimming over with energy. Naturally, she worshiped her only grandchild and had taken it as a personal slight that Stephanie had employed Mrs. McCreedy instead of asking her to look after Jake. The reason was simple: like Grandma Lilly said, Estelle interfered too much.

"Of-course-you-know-best-darling-but..." had become her mantra since the day Jake was born. This was followed by one or a combination of the following: "don't you think he might be too hot/cold/uncomfortable in that? Or perhaps he's hungry/tired/wet, has an infection/a virus, needs more Infants' Tylenol/less Infants' Tylenol/the doctor, just to be on the safe side. I mean, God forbid. You'd never forgive yourself. Stay where you are, I'm phoning an ambulance...."

OK, the ambulance bit was an exaggeration, but not much of one. Had Estelle come to look after Jake it would have taken all of Stephanie's strength to hold on to her sanity. Love Estelle as she did, her interference and general neurosis drove Stephanie round the bend. Over the years she'd tried talking to her, and discovered Estelle wasn't without personal insight.

"I know I'm annoying. I know I interfere too much, but I can't help it. You and Jakey are so precious and I worry about you all the time. Sometimes I lie awake at night worrying."

It was clear that Estelle would never change. But Stephanie had begun to. These days she was getting much better at letting her mother's behavior wash over her. Her friend Lizzie, who watched a lot of *Oprah,* said visualization was the key. Whenever her mother started to annoy her, Stephanie had to imagine her irritation was a balloon. Then, in her mind's eye, she had to visualize it floating higher and higher into the sky until it finally disappeared. Of course Stephanie scoffed at first, but she agreed to give it a go. A year later, Estelle still drove her mad with her constant interfering, but now when

23

she put down the phone from her mother, Stephanie was just that bit less inclined to want to eat her own head.

Of course, when she was a teenager, Stephanie and Estelle had had the most spectacular set-tos. The ear-piercing one was the worst. At fourteen, Stephanie was desperate to wear gold hoops in her ears. Her mother refused to allow this, on the grounds that a) it was common, and b) there wasn't an establishment on the planet that performed ear piercing to the Estelle Glassman Gold Standard of Hygiene. Stephanie would get a gangrenous infection in both earlobes. This would spread to her brain, cause meningitis, and she would end up a vegetable—or worse. Since they would have nothing left to live for, her parents' lives would be over too. In other words, Stephanie's getting her ears pierced was certain to bring about the complete destruction of the Glassman family.

But Stephanie refused to let the matter drop. After months of verbal battles, she finally wore her mother down and she gave in. Stephanie could have her ears pierced, as long as it was done at Harrods. Afterward, when gangrene and meningitis failed to set in, Estelle took the credit. What Estelle didn't know to this day was that Stephanie never went to Harrods. Instead she got her friend Natalie Finkel to come round when Estelle was out, and she performed the ear piercing with a needle that they sterilized on Estelle's gas stove. The two girls then went to Top Shop and blew the Harrods money on tube tops.

Stephanie had met Albert in Verona. It was September and still baking hot. Back in London, she'd just finished recording a ridiculous jingle for men's briefs: "Ground control to Major Thong." Since her bank account was now in the black for the first time in ages, she decided to take a break and spend some time with her friend Lucy. They had known each other since school, and Lucy, who was studying postgrad art history in Verona, had been nagging her for ages to come and stay. Stephanie decided she would stay in Verona as long as her money held out.

It turned out that Paramount, which was doing a remake of *Spartacus* with Chris Eagle in the lead, was filming at the city's Roman amphitheater. Lucy, who practically swooned at the mention of the star's name, happened to have a contact at the Paramount press office. He managed to wangle them onto the set one afternoon to watch the filming.

They spent the morning visiting the *Romeo and Juliet* balcony and wandering from one street café to the next, getting high on the glorious espresso. After lunch they decided to hit the posh shops for an hour. Not that either of them could afford anything. In the end Lucy made her buy a black Versace G-string with a scarlet sequinned pubic heart, just for a laugh and to say she'd gotten something.

Stephanie had imagined that the amphitheater would be in the middle of a field somewhere out of town, but it wasn't. It sat there, a vast, squat, wondrously preserved stone ruin in a piazza right in the middle of the city. Encircling it, fifty or so yards from the walls, were low metal police barricades. This created an off-limits area, which was crowded with Winnebagos, trucks full of equipment and catering vans. Then there were the film people: darting women with headsets and clipboards, sweating, jelly-bellied blokes lugging gear or standing around drinking from liter bottles of water.

Stephanie and Lucy showed their press passes to one of the darting women who appeared to have momentarily stopped darting in order to be chatted up by a severely cute Italian policeman. She barely glanced at their passes.

Lucy asked around and soon located Chris Eagle's Winnebago. According to a couple of Italian tabloid photographers, he was inside giving an interview and was due out at any moment. Lucy decided to hang around and wait. Since Chris Eagle had never done a lot for her, sex god–wise, Stephanie decided to go into the amphitheater and take a look around.

She walked through one of the arches and climbed the steps. Inside—apart from the lake of equipment and film people—it was exactly like the picture in her first-year Latin textbook: a central stadium the size of a football field. Then, fanning up and out perhaps two hundred feet, a circular auditorium was made up of row upon row of gnarled gray stone. Of course, these days the theater put on operas, but this afternoon the stage and stadium seats had all disappeared. From what Stephanie could tell, any minute now there was about to be a chariot race.

She strolled over to a trestle table, opened an icebox and helped herself to a bottle of water. A large open truck stood at one end of the stadium. The director and cameraman sat on it, on specially mounted seats. They were surrounded, on the ground, by more camera people and sound and lighting engineers. Near one of the exits stood a posse of paramedics in blue jumpsuits.

Stephanie took a swig of water and watched two utterly authentic-looking charioteers in helmets and metal breastplates climb into their equally authentic wooden chariots. "Stuntmen," said a woman carrying a black plastic sack full of paper plates, cups and bottles. "Apparently Chris was meant to do the dangerous bits himself, but he chickened out. Not that he'd ever admit it."

"Really?" Stephanie said, wondering what the hacks outside would give for this piece of information.

The director picked up his megaphone. "OK, let's go for another take. Quiet, please." A darting woman appeared with a clapboard. The truck moved off and began to pick up speed. Then the two charioteers cracked their whips in the air and the horses were off, thundering around the stadium, throwing up an enormous, dense dust cloud. The truck maintained its position, just a few feet in front. Stephanie watched with her face screwed up as the sides of the chariots came closer, until they were touching and sparks flew between the wheels. Then one charioteer leaped from his vehicle onto the other one. Having grappled with his enemy for the reins, he then managed to keep control of the chariot while at the same time engaging in a wondrously choreographed fight, which ended in his thoroughly convincing mortal wounding. Stephanie let out a gasp as he fell from the chariot and hit the ground with a series of somersaults.

"And cut," the director shouted through his megaphone. The horse pulling the empty chariot slowed to a trot and allowed one of the technicians to take his reins.

The dead guy, who was wearing remarkably little padding, Stephanie thought, got up and removed his helmet. She watched him as he ran his fingers through his wavy collar-length hair. The next moment, somebody came running up and handed him a can of Coke. He walked toward a couple of chairs. The other charioteer—shorter, stockier, nothing like the handsome dead guy—was already sitting on one of them. She watched the pair of them as they started laughing, backslapping and generally joking around. She got a bit nearer. As Dead Guy took off the padding on his arms and legs, she could see his tight muscular body. Then he sat down and put on a pair of wraparound sunglasses. It shouldn't have worked, this bloke in a breastplate and tunic, drinking Coke and wearing sunglasses, but somehow it did.

"Hey, Steph." Stephanie jumped and turned round. It was Lucy. She'd come running in from the piazza and was panting. "Chris Eagle's due out of his Winnebago any minute. You coming?"

"No, you go. I think I'd rather hang around here." Lucy shot her a puzzled look, but was in too much of a hurry to argue.

A few minutes later the director decided to go for a second take. In the end it took five or six until he was satisfied. Each time, Dead Guy got up without a scratch on him. "OK, that's a wrap. Good job, everybody."

Stephanie couldn't help herself. She just had to tell him how wonderful she thought he was. She ran to catch up with him. She was a few feet away, when she tripped over a cable. The next thing she knew she was lying on the ground, flat on her face. There was a sharp stabbing pain in her knee. Dead Guy put down his Coke and came running toward her.

"It's my knee," she said, wincing. "I've pulled it or something."

"Let's take a look," he said. Soft, sexy voice. American accent. He bent the knee gently, making her wince. "So, what's a nice joint like you doing in a girl like this?" And that was pretty much it. Maybe it was the romance of Verona, that carefree holiday feeling, or even too many espressos before lunch, but she couldn't fight it. In a moment she fell for the body, the cheesy charm.

"Oh, for God's sake, stop beating yourself up," her friend Cass would say a few weeks later, when Stephanie was trying to make sense of it all. "Look, you'd been working hard, you were in the market for some fun. So when you discovered this great-looking bloke, you just knew you had to have him. I've done it loads of times."

The paramedics said she ought to get the knee checked out at the hospital.

"Let me take you," Albert said. "It's no problem. We're finished here for the day." Since Lucy's car was parked miles away and Stephanie couldn't bear to ruin her friend's chance of meeting Chris Eagle, she agreed. While one of the paramedics went off to find Lucy and tell her what was happening and that she shouldn't worry, Albert scooped her up and carried her to the parking lot. He put her down gently in front of a silver Audi convertible. She leaned against the door while he produced his keys from under the leather tunic he was still wearing.

"OK, let's go," he said. The next moment she was being hoisted onto the back of a shining BMW motorcycle. She looked back at the car. "Oh, sorry," he said, clearly seeing the horrified expression on her face. "You thought..."

"I've never ridden on the back of one of these," she said.

"Look, I'll take it real easy, I promise."

"But what about helmets?"

"Hey, this is Italy. Who would buy Armani and then spoil it with a helmet?"

"Er, me?" Stephanie said.

"Don't worry, you'll be fine. The best hospital is only a few minutes out of town."

The force of the air rushing past quite literally took her breath away. For the first few minutes she buried her head in his back. Then, bit by bit, she lifted her face to the sun and the wind. At one point they stopped at a traffic light. He turned round and smiled. Then he started singing. "Take it easy, take it easy / Don't let the sound of your own wheels drive you crazy."

29

His voice wasn't half bad. "You OK?" he said.

"Fine."

"Not going too fast?" She shook her head. He smiled again and turned away. He carried on singing. His voice wasn't half bad, she thought again.

After a few minutes they hit the autostrada and he really picked up speed. Suddenly they were overtaking everything in sight. She could see drivers staring at Albert in his short charioteer's tunic and breastplate. Heart pounding, she held on to him for dear life. She realized she'd never felt so much fear or exhilaration. Until they reached the hospital, she completely forgot the pain from her knee.

Leaning heavily on him, she hobbled up to the reception desk. "It's OK," he said to Stephanie. "Leave this to me." By now the woman at the desk had noticed his centurion costume and was giggling. He ignored her.

"La mia amica si è fatta male a ginocchio," he said, his accent faultless. *"Le fa molto male. Dovrebbe visitare un dottore immediatamente."*

The woman at the desk, still looking at him warily, as if she thought she was about to spot a hidden camera from some terrible Italian reality TV show, took Stephanie's name and told the two of them to take a seat. Albert turned to Stephanie.

"I told her you've hurt your knee and that you're in pain and need to see a doctor quickly."

"Wow, where did you learn to speak Italian like that?"

By pure coincidence, Albert was half Italian. He'd been christened Alberto, surname Rossi. His father had died a few years earlier and his mother ran a tiny Italian restaurant in Venice Beach, California.

The doctor said it was only a sprain and gave her an elastic knee support. A week later she was walking normally again. Albert sent her flowers, and three days after they met he took her to dinner. The day before, she'd gone hobbling back to one of the posh shops in town and blown a fortune on the sexiest dress she had ever owned.

It was a beautifully cut silk shift with spaghetti straps. The pale blue matched her eyes perfectly. When he saw her he whistled. "Wow, *principessa*."

That first evening they drove a few miles down the autostrada—this time with helmets on—to eat at a fish restaurant in Sirmione, an exquisite medieval town on Lake Garda. They sat at a table a few feet from the water's edge and drank delicious thick red wine as the sun went down. Afterward they strolled along the narrow cobbled streets. As they reached the bike he stopped, pulled her gently toward him and kissed her.

They went out practically every night for the next two weeks. Lucy didn't mind, since she'd only been expecting Stephanie to stay for a few days anyway and had already made plans to go to Milan for a couple of weeks to see her boyfriend.

Stephanie accepted Albert because they were never going to be serious and because he made her laugh until she wept. He also made her come with more skill than any man she had ever slept with.

The memory of the first time they slept together—she held out until the fourth date—would stay with her until the day she died. She was at his flat, leaning against the balcony rail in another obscenely expensive silky shift thing she couldn't really afford. This time it was backless and in the palest of

31

pinks, which looked glorious with her tan. As she stood there watching a sun as big and red as a medicine ball sink behind the cypress trees, he came up behind her and ran a cold champagne glass very lightly down her spine. She gave a shiver and turned to face him. He put the champagne glasses down on the small garden table. As he cupped her face and kissed her, she felt her insides melt into soft warm molasses. As he started kissing her neck, she threw back her head, holding on to him to steady herself. She felt him begin to unzip her dress and pull down the shoulder straps. Now he was kissing her shoulders, the tops of her breasts. She could feel his erection hard against her. By now she was letting out little sighs, kissing and nipping his face. She felt his hand go up under her skirt. In a moment he had slipped his fingers inside her panties and was feeling the moisture seeping from her.

"Oh, boy," he whispered, parting her and caressing her gently, back and forth, back and forth.

He led her to the bedroom, where he finished undressing her as if he were unwrapping the most precious, delicate object in the entire world. He stood gazing at her for what seemed like an eternity. When he laid her on the bed, gently spread her legs and opened her with his tongue, she truly thought she would die from the pleasure.

At the end of two weeks, she had to get back to London. Eileen, her agent, had rung to say she'd found her a job singing the jingle for a building society ad.

Stephanie knew it would always be just a physical thing between her and Albert. He could never be right for her. For a start he talked too much and too loudly, mainly about himself—the job, how his much-adored late father had been a stunt artist and taught him everything he knew, how he got into bikes, the stars he'd worked with, the bikes he owned, the Hollywood parties, the bike he'd like to own. On the other hand, his job was fascinating and she couldn't help finding his stories and all the gossip hugely entertaining.

Then there were the other women. He was renting a studio flat in the center of town. Once when she stayed over, she dropped an earring, which rolled under the bed. As well as retrieving the earring, she found two bras—of different sizes. His mobile rang constantly. He said it was work, but she could tell by the way he turned his body away from her and lowered his voice that he was speaking to girlfriends. After the third or fourth time it happened she was reminded of the rest of that Eagles' song—the bit about him having "seven women on my mind." She smiled to herself. There was no doubt, Alberto Rossi went through women like Pete Sampras went through tennis rackets.

Even so, there was a tearful, passionate good-bye at the airport.

"Ciao, *principessa*."

"Ciao, Albert."

They promised to e-mail. She knew they would for a bit. Then it would peter out. She would miss him—not to mention the glorious sex—for a few painful weeks, but eventually she'd get over him and the whole thing would have been no big deal. Then she missed her period.

"I can't have a baby yet," she wailed to Lizzie and Cass. "I can't. I'm not ready. There were all these things I wanted to achieve before I became a parent. I wanted to get my career off the ground, trek round India, own a Habitat sofa."

But what really scared her was doing it alone. She, Lizzie and Cass all sat on the bathroom floor, holding hands until it was time to check the stick for the pregnancy kit.

"It's pink," Lizzie whispered. "You're pregnant. Oh, Steph." Then they both hugged her, but Lizzie, who was already a mother and knew about babies and the months of sleepless nights, hugged her the hardest.

Stephanie went to her GP, who confirmed the pregnancy, along with the fact that her diaphragm, newly fitted before her trip to Italy, was "just a tad too small." Cheers, Doc.

She considered an abortion for all of two minutes. She firmly believed in a woman's right to choose, but for her there was no choice. There was no way she was about to destroy this life growing inside her. She dreaded making the call to Albert in L.A. It occurred to her he'd probably gotten women pregnant in the past and she was sure he'd be pretty dismissive and simply offer to send her a check to cover the cost of an abortion.

"*Principessa.* So, what's new?"

"Well, the thing is . . ."

"Steph, can you just hang on a minute? . . . Hey babe," he called out. "I'll be back in a second. Don't start without me." He laughed. "Steph, this won't take long, will it? You see, I'm kinda on a date here, and she's really hot for me."

She came straight out with it.

"You're pregnant?"

"Yes. Seems like my doctor fitted me with the wrong size diaphragm."

"Oh my God. Pregnant."

"Look, I know it's a shock."

"You can say that again. Are you sure?"

"Positive."

34

"Pregnant? You're pregnant?"

"Albert, please stop asking me. I've said I am."

"But that's fantastic. I'm gonna be a dad. I cannot believe it. This is so cool. I mean, this is the best news." A pause. Then: "Steph, you are going to keep it, aren't you? I mean, you're not..."

"No, Albert, I'm not."

"Oh, thank God. You know, my mom is just gonna go crazy when I tell her. This will be her first grandchild." Then he promised faithfully to be there for her and the baby as much as he possibly could. Over the next weeks and months they discussed all the practical things like how much he should pay in child support. They never discussed the possibility of rekindling their relationship. There seemed to be a silent agreement between them that this was a non-starter. Nevertheless, throughout her pregnancy he phoned a couple of times a week to see how she was doing and to make sure that she was eating properly. He even bought a book on childbirth, but said he couldn't read it because it was too gory.

"Life is a strange thing," Cass said after Stephanie made that first call to Albert. "Sometimes the people you'd least expect come up trumps. It's like the time that tax inspector let me off that huge fine because I sent in my return too late."

"Cass, you offered to give him a blow job behind the filing cabinets. He let you off because he was twenty-two, totally petrified and desperate to get rid of you."

Albert had promised to be there for the birth, but in the end he missed it because she went into labor a month early. Looking back, it was probably for the best, what with Albert's low gore threshold and her mother offending the doctor on their arrival by telling him it "might be a good idea to check

35

how dilated she is." Then there was the doula—the oh-so-fashionable "alternative" birthing coach (a present from Cass)—who ignored Stephanie's cries of agony on account of contractions not being "real pain" and skipped around in size eighteen orange silk pajamas lighting scented candles.

"So," she singsonged at one point, "are we planning to do anything festive with the placenta?"

Estelle pulled a face and muttered something about this being northwest London, not the Congo Basin. Then she handed Stephanie the gas and air. Stephanie had taken no more than half a gulp when the doula snatched it away, proclaiming that "baby would come out all tipsy." At this point Estelle suggested a temporarily tipsy baby might be preferable to a permanently traumatized mother. The doula smiled thinly.

"I'm guessing you're a meat eater," she said.

In a few minutes the two women had locked antlers and their "discussion" developed into a blazing row. Of course they both ignored Stephanie's cries of agony and neither of them noticed when the hospital midwife came in. "Epidural?" she mouthed to Stephanie. Stephanie gave her an instant thumbs-up. When the anesthetist arrived a few minutes later, the doula left in a huff.

From the moment they found out about the pregnancy, her parents' only concern was how she would cope emotionally without a partner to support her. Especially since Sylvia down the road's lesbian daughter who'd had an IVF baby was finding it a real struggle on her own.

Stephanie suspected that from a selfish point of view, Estelle was secretly pleased there was no man on the scene. It wasn't that she objected to having a son-in-law—far from it.

What she wasn't keen on was being forced to share the baby with a rival grandmother. Since Albert's mother lived six thousand miles away, this wasn't going to be an issue and she could have the baby all to herself.

After Jake was born, Estelle offered to come and look after the two of them for a couple of weeks. The offer was something Stephanie had been dreading. Then Harry's mother had a heart attack, which later turned out to be fatal. Harry wanted to be with the old lady. Estelle said she would stay with Stephanie and the baby, but Stephanie insisted that her mother's place was with Harry and that she'd be fine.

In the end Lizzie's mother came to stay with Lizzie's husband, Dom, and the twins, and Lizzie came to look after Stephanie. For ten days Lizzie was just there. She walked Jake up and down for hours at a time when he refused to stop screaming and Stephanie was desperate to sleep. She shopped, tidied up and even had cabbage leaves at the ready when Stephanie's nipples started to crack. On day four, Stephanie got a major attack of the baby blues. "I'm never going to be able to do this," she sobbed to Lizzie. Lizzie took her in her arms. "Yes, you will. And you're going to do it brilliantly."

When Lizzie left to go back to the twins, Stephanie sent up a prayer.

"Look, God, I appreciate that what with the world situation you're probably a bit underresourced right now, but if you could just see your way clear to making Jake sleep through the night, I'd be very grateful." Clearly the Almighty's mind was on higher things. Jake screamed practically nonstop for the next three months. On the rare occasions he slept, Stephanie would sleep too. Once she woke up with the words to Marianne Faithfull's "Ballad of Lucy Jordan" going round and round her head. The woman in the song has reached her late thirties and she suddenly knows she'll "never ride through Paris in a sports car with the warm wind in her hair."

"My God, that's me," she wailed on the phone to Cass. "I'm turning into Lucy Jordan."

"Don't be an arse. First, you're not in your late thirties, and second, nobody in their right mind would want to drive through Paris anyway. The Périphérique's a sodding nightmare. I should know, I got stuck on it for five hours last year."

Colic, the clinic said. He'll grow out of it. Estelle spent hours on NetDoctor and came back with countless possible illnesses and conditions. She insisted on paying for Jake to see a private pediatrician. Colic, he said. He'll grow out of it. Then, when Stephanie was virtually on her knees with exhaustion, he suddenly stopped. He began sleeping through the night and she began to believe that, one day, she might indeed ride through Paris in a sports car with the warm wind in her hair.

Albert visited every few months. He always arrived on a motorcycle, which he hired or borrowed from Tom, a mate of his who lived in Kentish Town. He was a film cameraman and often away filming abroad. Each time, Albert had a different woman with him. They were all the same: exceedingly sweet California flakes with fake tits and too much lip liner. They couldn't have been more different from Stephanie if they'd tried, and she often wondered why he had fallen for her in Verona. She'd challenged him about this several times. "I've dated all types of women," he would shrug. "You represented the height of my gorgeous, feisty intellectual phase. Right now I'm going through my Pammie phase."

Albert and the girlfriend would come straight from the airport, him carrying champagne and toys for Jake.

"*Principessa!* Let me look at you." Then, bursting with

excitement, he would charge over to Jake. "Hey, champ. How you doing? You know, Steph, he's got my dad's eyes."

He'd hold him for a few minutes, but hand him back to Stephanie the moment he cried. He would always call Stephanie if he puked or filled his nappy. She knew it wasn't Albert's fault. Most men had no idea how to cope with babies. Learning to be a dad was something they did on the job. Still, she couldn't help thinking that Albert was one of those men who, even if he'd been around, would never have wanted to be a hands-on father. This great big guy in his Levi's and cowboy boots was far too macho to change a shitty diaper. He'd tried it once, just after Jake was born, but he'd made a great show of telling everybody how he didn't inhale. No, Albert was in love with the *idea* of fatherhood, and especially having a son, but there was no way he was going to *do* it.

"Come on," he'd say an hour after arriving. "What say we all go out to eat? Chinese food good for everyone?"

"But, Albert, you've just gotten off a ten-hour flight. Don't you want to get to the hotel and sleep?"

"Nah, we're fine. We took melatonin on the plane. So, where's good to eat around here?" And they would go, Albert and the girlfriend, Stephanie, her parents, Jake in his portable car seat. Estelle, in particular, loved Albert, and no matter how often Stephanie assured her it was never going to happen, Estelle—not to mention Grandma Lilly—had never quite given up hope that Stephanie and Albert would get together.

Albert would spend the evening telling his Hollywood stories, flirting with Estelle and listening to Harry's theories about the medicinal properties of char siu pork, while Stephanie tried to pacify a colicky baby with her breast and manage chopsticks at the same time.

39

"Say, Steph," Albert said the first time they all went out to dinner, "don't they use pacifiers in this country?"

"You tell her, Albert," Estelle said. "I've been trying to get through to her for weeks. Stephanie doesn't seem to realize there's no shame these days in using a dummy."

"I know," Stephanie said, "but they become addictive and eventually all that sucking can push their teeth out of shape."

They were always short visits. After two days he would be off on the bike with the girlfriend. A few days later she'd get a postcard addressed to her and Jake from Scotland or the Lakes.

Later that night she phoned her friend Ben, who was a GP, to ask whether Lilly could still have sex now that she had a pacemaker.

"No problem," he said, laughing. "She can't possibly electrocute herself. Plus a bit of energetic sex will help keep her fit. It's important that she does some formal exercise as well, though. Something gentle, like yoga or tai chi, would be excellent for somebody her age." Then he launched into a long spiel about VD rates among the over-sixties, which rather put her off her lasagna.

Jake woke in a bad mood. Then he started coughing. "Oh, sweetie, I hope you're not coming down with any-thing." She felt his head but it was fine.

He ate his honey toast on his digger, watching his *Mary Poppins* video. He must have watched it two hundred times. Stephanie knew the entire script by heart.

Jake was going through a phase of refusing to get dressed,

and because he was in a bad mood, he was being even more difficult than usual. Then, once he was dressed, he had to decide which hat to wear to Grandma's. "Not policeman one."

"OK, how's about the pirate hat and you can take your hook if you can find it."

"No pi-wat one. Crown. No, no, no. Wolf mask. Wolf mask. To scare Gan'ma."

He ran to fetch it. Then they couldn't find his zizzing label. She looked in his bed, under it. She checked the dirty laundry basket to see if it was in there with his pajamas. Nothing. "Jake, we'll have to go without it. Or I can tear out another one from one of your T-shirts."

"No. No. No. Want my lay-a-bel. My one." Just then the doorbell rang.

"Who's that at nine o'clock on a Sunday morning? Jake, go and have one last look for the label while I answer the door." He went charging upstairs.

An elderly, rather agitated woman she didn't recognize was standing on the doorstep.

"Stephanie?"

"Yes."

"I'm Audrey. Mary McCreedy's friend."

"Oh, yes, from the darts team."

She couldn't begin to fathom what she was doing there.

"Mary asked me to pop round. I'm afraid she had an accident last night—at the match."

"Goodness. It's not serious, is it?"

"She broke her hip."

"Oh, my God."

"You see, she needed a double seven to win. There we were, holding our breath. And she did it. The landlord—who's a bit soft on her—came dashing over, picked her up and swung her round. Eventually he let her go, but she

41

landed badly and that was it. She was in real agony until the morphine kicked in."

"How long is she going to be in hospital?"

"Oh, a fair few weeks, I think. They're talking about doing a hip replacement. Don't know how long she'll have to wait, though."

Stephanie thanked Audrey and said she'd visit Mrs. M. in a couple of days.

She shut the door and went back to the living room in a trance. She was feeling a mixture of emotions. Along with the sadness she felt for Mrs. M., she couldn't suppress a feeling of relief. Relief that Mrs. M. would be out of action for Lord knows how long, which meant she didn't have to sack her. There was, of course, the major problem of who was going to look after Jake. Lizzie could probably help out for a day or two, but what then?

"Found it. Found it." Jake was standing on the sofa, waving his label.

"Good boy, Jakey. Good boy. Listen, I've got something to tell you. Mrs. M.'s had a bit of an accident. She's got a poorly leg and she can't come to look after you. That's really sad, isn't it? But the doctors are going to make her better and she's going to be all right."

"We get Mary Poppins ven, yes?"

"No, Jake, she's just pretend, I'm afraid."

"OK, Gan'ma come."

"Er, no, I don't think that would work."

He started bouncing on Jimmy's white overstuffed sofa.

"Gan'ma come. Gan'ma come. Gan'ma come."

Chapter 3

Estelle opened the front door.

"Hello, darling," she said, kissing Stephanie. "Listen, your Grandma Lilly's here. Not a word about what we were discussing, OK?"

"OK."

"Oooh," Estelle squealed in mock horror, seeing Jake's werewolf mask, "and who's a big scary monster, then?"

"My am," Jake growled, waving his plastic sword. This caused a small but significant intake of breath from Estelle. "Careful, darling. You'll have somebody's eye out. Now then, who's got a kiss for his grandma?"

"Mum, he's less than three feet tall. How's he going to have somebody's eye out?"

Her mother didn't reply. Jake delivered his kiss through the mask, and the three of them walked down the hall toward the kitchen. As they went in, a Peggy Lee CD was playing softly in the background. The large kitchen-diner with its central breakfast bar, dividing the kitchen bit from the dining bit, had the familiar smell of Glade and fried onions. But to-day Stephanie detected another smell. Fish. Estelle saw her wrinkling her nose.

"Just steaming some salmon," Estelle said.

"But the stove's not on," Stephanie observed.

"I'm steaming it in the dishwasher," her mother said with a shrug. "It's brilliant. Takes four whole salmon at a time."

"O . . . K. Assuming I can get my head round the dish-washer bit, which isn't easy, could we move swiftly on to why you and Dad need four salmon? By my reckoning that's two entire fish each."

Estelle looked at her daughter as if she had lost the plot. "For the freezer," she said. "Why else?" Estelle was a great believer in cooking in bulk—some for now, some for the freezer. As a result the freezer was always bursting with food. It wasn't so much a place to store food as another mouth to feed.

"You have to wrap it in loads of foil," Estelle went on, "but it works a treat. I'll give you some before you go. The first time I did it, the fish tasted a little bit like Rinse Aid, but I think I've got the hang of it now."

It was a second or two before she noticed her father. He was sitting at his desk in the Glassmans' pub-style conservatory, spectacles perched on his bald head, peering intently into his computer screen. Surrounded by a thicket of yucca leaves, palms and various dangling tendrils, he looked like a distinguished botany professor hard on the trail of a new genus of lupine; although it had to be said that his M&S tracksuit, instead of the botanist's regulation worn gray cardigan full of holes, did rather spoil the illusion.

Harry had been against the conservatory from the word go. He objected on grounds of heat loss and the calamitous effect this would have on his gas bills. Estelle kept nagging and eventually won him over, maintaining that the conservatory, which looked out over the garden, brought nature into the house. In fact there wasn't a great deal of nature to be found in the Glassmans' fifty-foot back garden, made up as it was of a twenty-foot concrete tiled patio and a small patch of lawn bordered by the narrowest of low-maintenance flower beds. It soon emerged that Estelle wasn't so much concerned about bringing nature inside as ensuring that visitors to the house had an IMAX view of her two-thousand-quid John Lewis patio furniture and outdoor heater.

"Penis extensions," Stephanie heard Harry mutter to himself. "What do I want with bloody penis extensions?"

"Harry! Please! Jake's here." Estelle turned to Stephanie. "It's all this junk e-mail, driving him mad." Harry saw Stephanie and Jake and his face broke into a smile. He stood up, arms open wide. "Hello, sweetie," he said, hugging Stephanie. He looked down at Jake. "And who have we here, eh? The Big Bad Wolf?" He bent down, but before he could hug Jake, the sword, which he was waving wildly, connected with Harry's eye.

"Jakey! No!" Stephanie took the sword from him. "Look, you've hurt poor Granddad. Now say sorry."

"Nobody listens to me," Estelle said in that singsong way of hers.

"It's OK," Harry said, dabbing his watering eye with a handkerchief. "No harm done."

Jake looked like he was about to dissolve into tears. Harry scooped him up and took him to the window. "There was a fox on the lawn earlier on. Let's see if it's still here."

"Look, you know best," Estelle said to Stephanie. She had lowered her voice the way she did when she talked about S-E-X, "but this monsters and carrying swords thing. It's all a bit violent, isn't it? I'm sure it must be giving him nightmares. And you read him that dreadful thing—what is it?"

"*Where the Wild Things Are.* It's a classic. He adores it."

"When you were his age you were into *Noddy*."

"Which is about a weird-looking homosexual teenager and an older man," Harry butted in, "who persecute black people. Very nice."

He winked at Stephanie, who started laughing. Realizing she'd lost this battle, Estelle shrugged and asked who was for coffee.

"Just a quickie," Stephanie said. "The girls are coming at eleven. Where's Grandma?" Estelle explained that Lilly was upstairs putting on her makeup. She was staying for lunch and then she was off to a funeral. Harry was giving her a lift to the cemetery. When they couldn't see the fox, Harry took Jake into the living room to choose a video. Her parents had practically a library of Disney films.

"Jake looks a bit peaky," Estelle said, getting mugs down from the cupboard.

"Yeah. He's got a bit of a cough. I hope he isn't coming down with something. He hasn't got a temperature, though."

"Are you sure he gets enough green vegetables?"

"Yes, Mum. He gets enough greens."

"And fruit?"

"And fruit."

Stephanie was trying to imagine the balloon of her irritation floating skyward, but today, for some reason, it remained determinedly grounded and seemed to be inflating rapidly.

"I've got some children's echinacea upstairs," Estelle went on. "I'll give him some in a minute."

Just then Harry came back in. "Look," he said to Stephanie, indicating his computer screen. "Look at all this junk I get." She followed him over to his desk. There had to be two dozen junk e-mails in his mailbox.

"God, I thought I got a lot," she said. "Still, only takes a moment to delete it."

"But I shouldn't be getting it in the first place. Nobody should. I don't need a mortgage, new golf balls or a loan. I don't require a penis extension, I don't want to see Jenny and Heather get down, and I certainly don't need Viagra."

A meaningful snort from Estelle, which Stephanie chose to ignore.

"Anyway," he went on, "what is a penis extension? Some kind of prosthesis? Do they have to operate or do you strap it on?"

"Harry, Harry. For crying out loud, give it a rest."

It was Grandma Lilly. She was tiny, with wonky blue eyeshadow and newly coiffed hair that looked like a giant auburn cotton candy. Although she was almost eighty she retained her dancer's posture. As a child she'd learned ballet, discovered she had a real talent and, before she met her husband, spent several years appearing in West End musicals. In 1945 she even went to Paris to appear in a cabaret with Maurice Chevalier. Everybody agreed that Stephanie had acquired her love of performing from her grandmother. Lilly had also been a bit of a babe. Stephanie had seen the photographs. There were still traces of it, even now—the vivid turquoise eyes that refused to fade, the high cheekbones and girlishly full lips.

"You've been going on about this all morning. You're obsessed. You sound like my friend Vera. She's got this bee in her bonnet about Ex-Lax. She thinks they add Imodium to it to make you use more." Stephanie couldn't help noticing that in the background Peggy Lee was singing "The Folks Who Live on the Hill." It seemed appropriate somehow.

"Hi, Grandma," Stephanie said lightly. She stood up. As she kissed her grandmother she got the familiar whiff of herring.

"I just said hello to Jake. He looks a bit peaky. You know what my mother used to give us children when we weren't well? Calves'-foot jelly."

"Mum," Estelle said, "don't be ridiculous. You haven't been able to get that stuff for fifty years."

"So," Stephanie broke in, taking in her grandmother's navy trouser suit with outsized seventies' lapels, "you're off to a funeral."

She nodded. "Your dad's going to drop me off."

"He's only taking you," Estelle said, "if you promise to behave when you get there. No practical jokes like the last funeral you went to."

"Sid Hirsch was ninety-three," Lilly retorted. "He had the best sense of humor of anybody I've ever known."

"Yes, but I don't think his children appreciated you and Vera sticking a 'just buried' sign on the back of the hearse."

At that moment Jake reappeared, clearly bored with the video. He climbed onto Estelle's lap. She kissed him and held him to her large bosom.

"Gan'ma come look after me at my hou-is?"

Stephanie closed her eyes and pressed the lids with her hand. Thank you, Jake.

"I'd love to, darling, but you've got Mrs. M."

"Mrs. M. bad."

"Oh, no. Mrs. M.'s not bad," Estelle said. "She's lovely."

Stephanie looked up. "He means she's got a bad hip," she explained. "She broke it last night after her darts match. She's going to be in hospital for weeks, apparently."

"So, what will you do? Who will look after Jakey when you're at work?"

"I don't know. I'll phone round a couple of agencies. I'll sort something out."

"Don't be ridiculous. Agencies. You don't have agency money. And how can you even think of having strangers looking after your child? I'll come. It's settled. I won't hear another word."

Stephanie struggled to find an excuse. "But what about Dad? Won't he mind you leaving him every day?"

"I'll come too," Harry said. "I can introduce Jake to the wonders of char siu pork." Stephanie suddenly had visions of Jake starting school with not only dentures (courtesy of the Fondant Fancies) but an appointment for an angioplasty. "Well, Mum, if you really don't mind."

"Mind? How could I mind?" She put her arms tight round Jake and kissed the top of his head. "As if I'd let my only grandchild be looked after by strangers."

Lilly insisted on showing Stephanie to the door. "I didn't want to say anything in front of your mother. Have you managed to find out anything—you know, about what we were talking about?"

"I have and it's fine. My friend Ben, who's a GP, said you can carry on doing what you've always done. No problem."

"Really?" She grinned. "I won't electrocute myself?"

"No, you won't electrocute yourself."

"Excellent." Then she gave a wicked laugh. Stephanie also told her what Ben had said about doing some gentle exercise.

"Tai chi? What's that? Sounds like one of those slimy tofu things you see on dim sum carts."

Stephanie said an old boyfriend of hers used to do it and that it was part ancient Chinese spiritual teaching, part

49

meditation and part self-defense. When Lilly said she didn't think it sounded quite like her and that she was much more of an old-time dancing girl, Stephanie took the hint.

In Stephanie's opinion, the perfect fry-up contained several key elements. For a start the bacon had to be streaky (more flavor) and done to a crisp. The sausages had to be brown but not burned and preferably the cheaper, fatty kind because, like streaky bacon, only they delivered that authentic fry-up taste. The 95 percent lean pork varieties were for wimps and totally unacceptable, as were fancy herbified ones. The fried eggs had to have a hint of crunch on their underside, but it was imperative that the yolks were thick and creamy and as yellow as a school bus. The best way to achieve the creaminess was to baste the eggs with the oil during frying. That way, the yolk's outer membrane turned into a smooth white cataract, leaving the yolk soft. The fried bread had to be crisp like the bacon, but not oozing fat. Most important of all were the baked beans. Under no circumstances could these be merely heated. They needed to be cooked very slowly over the lowest possible heat, until they burst their skins and turned into a congealed pinkish lump.

Stephanie had acquired her fry-up skills years ago. One summer, when she was a senior, she'd gotten a job waitressing at The Acropolis, a Greek greasy spoon in Archway. The owner, Nick, reckoned he'd been cooking all-day breakfasts since he was sixteen. He'd probably been eating them since then, too, since at the age of fifty or thereabouts, he had the figure of Baloo. He chain-smoked while he cooked, saying it improved his concentration, "and thee flavva." Then he would break into loud guffaws. Certainly most of Nick's breakfasts arrived at the table with a light ash accompaniment, but none of the stubby-fingered geezers who made up the clientele seemed to notice. Apart from his chain-smoking theory, what Nick taught her more than anything was the importance of timing.

Twenty minutes before Lizzie and Cass were due, Stephanie laid the table, squeezed the oranges in Jimmy's fabulous chrome juicer and broke the eggs into a bowl. Then she pricked the sausages and put four slices of bread in the Dualit toaster. Finally she took out his largest Le Creuset frying pan and placed it on the industrial six-burner stove, ready to go.

The women's Sunday breakfast tradition went back years. It was the one day they could always get together. The rest of the week Stephanie was working, often late, Lizzie had the twins and Cass was up to her eyes managing her advertising business, plus, of course, her unending string of blokes.

She had met Cass when they were students on another summer waitressing job. They were working at the same Hampstead coffee shop. A shared interest in insubordination had drawn them together. They'd spend their breaks in the back with the trash cans, smoking joints and taking the piss out of the customers. Cass was reed thin and pretty, but not quite beautiful. If you were being picky, you'd say her mouth was just a tad Julia Roberts and she also had a couple of slightly crooked front teeth. But even then, she was completely at ease with her body. It was this confidence that had always made her attractive to boys. Apparently she'd lost her virginity at some absurdly early age like thirteen or fourteen.

"All I can say is," she confided to Stephanie a few months ago when they were discussing their earliest sexual exploits, "thank God *Seventeen* didn't have a gossip column."

After university she worked for Saatchi and Saatchi for a few years. Then she left to set up her own advertising company. Stephanie put Cass's ballsiness down to her public school education. She was entirely without self-doubt. She simply assumed that she had the right to go out into the world and claim what was hers. Getting the business off the ground was a struggle, but she turned the corner financially just before Jake was born—which was how she could afford to hire the doula for Stephanie.

These days she was still sexy and vampy—the kind of woman who, when she got dressed in the morning, began with her Jimmy Choos.

Lizzie, on the other hand, was a real beauty. A natural blonde, creamy white skin, dazzling blue eyes. Stephanie met her on their first day at secondary school. Most of the other first-years knew each other when they arrived because they'd been to the same primary school, but Stephanie and Lizzie had only just moved into the area and knew nobody. They found each other, looked after each other and had been doing it ever since. They'd been through some tough times together: boyfriends chucking them, both getting mediocre A-level grades and having to stay at school an extra term to do retakes, Lizzie's dad dying suddenly in the middle of it all.

When they were sixteen they used to spray their hair pink and orange and go off to see the Jam or the Clash and get back at three in the morning. Neither set of parents knew because the pair had arranged to stay with another friend, a girl called Caramel, whose house smelled of patchouli oil and whose parents didn't care what time they got home.

Then Lizzie went to Bristol to study English. After a few months she had grown her hair long and was dating floppy-haired boys called Piers or Hugh and wearing their cricket sweaters. Stephanie wasn't surprised. Lizzie had never been at ease with the rebellion thing. There had always been something deeply conservative about her. For a start, she was hooked on romance. Not many people knew, but Lizzie actually had a hope chest. It was an old pine chest that sat at the end of her bed. And Lizzie never actually put anything in it. Her dottily old-fashioned mother did. Every so often she would add another set of M&S sheets or a couple of Liberty print tea towels. Even though she was embarrassed by the hope chest, Lizzie was sucked into her mother's 1960s' pearls-and-amontillado-before-dinner image of marriage. Even when she was at university, she bought a subscription to *Bride* magazine. She always knew who the most fashionable caterers were and, even though she was, under normal circumstances, the most even tempered of souls, she could get quite heated when she saw just a hint of gypsophila in a wedding bouquet.

Lizzie left university with an honors degree and got a job in the City as a trainee hedge fund manager. Pretty soon she had met Dom, a handsome corporate lawyer, and had fallen madly in love. He took her on romantic weekends to Rome and Venice, where he would present her with something understated but exquisite from Tiffany. In return she spent her Sunday afternoons in the summer watching him play cricket.

They were married on a clear, crisp winter's afternoon, just as the sun was setting. The perfect Devon village was blanketed in snow. The trees in the churchyard glistened with white fairy lights. Inside the fourteenth-century stone church, scores of tall white candles flickered in the semidarkness, casting a soft golden light onto the sea of winter roses and lilies of the valley.

Lizzie wore the simplest oyster satin gown and matching

coat. It must have cost well into four figures, since simplicity like that never comes cheap. Six tiny flower girls in ballet shoes and oyster dresses with dark green velvet sashes sat on tiny dark green velvet stools and behaved impeccably. When Lizzie said "I do," her exquisite face turned toward Dom's solid, square jaw, everybody knew it would be forever. Dom and Lizzie. Lizzie and Dom.

They started trying for a baby almost immediately. Two years later, when nothing had happened, they started in vitro fertilization. Finally, three grueling years later, the twins were born at The Portland by cesarean—squeezed in between Dom's split capital investment trust meetings.

Lizzie was so overjoyed to be a mother at last that it didn't occur to her to go back to work. These days she wore chinos and Sebagos, drove Archie and Dougal to their trumpet lessons in Dom's company minivan and went with Dom to the kind of dinner parties where people discussed loft extensions and agonized over schools. She sent handmade thank-you notes with pressed dried flowers on them, and when Dom was working late in the city, which was most nights, she went to bed with *How to Be a Domestic Goddess* and the latest Martha Stewart catalogue.

When she first introduced them, Stephanie wasn't sure if Lizzie and Cass would hit it off, but they did. Cass made Lizzie laugh and Cass, whose life was a chaotic round of work, blokes and parties, probably found something old-fashioned and comfortingly grounding in Lizzie, although she'd never admit it.

Cass arrived first, carrying a bottle of Lanson. She'd come straight from the gym and was wearing a pink Juicy Couture tracksuit. Her red curls were tied back in a ponytail. "I thought we'd make Bucks Fizz," she said, handing over the bubbly. "I need something to cheer me up."

"Wassup?" Stephanie said, fetching the jug of freshly squeezed orange juice.

"I'm manless. Virtually for the first time in my entire adult life, I have nobody." She put her gym bag down on the counter and started rooting around inside for her cigarettes.

"So, join the club," Stephanie said.

"Yeah, but you're used to it." Cass popped the champagne cork, which landed by the back door.

"Oh, thanks."

"No, God, sorry, I didn't mean it like that. But you know what I'm like. I need regular sex. Without it I get all cross and irritable."

"What happened to that Irish bloke you were seeing? Milo, wasn't it?"

She shrugged. "He just lost interest. Stopped returning my calls. Then the other night he got back in touch. We made a date and an hour before he's due to pick me up, he rings and says he has to cancel because he has a work emergency."

"Maybe he did."

"Steph," Cass drew deeply on a Marlboro Light, "he's a bloody poet."

They both snorted.

"But what about all the others? That Will, for instance. He was tall, dark, handsome. Went with everything."

"Wears corduroy."

"Trousers? What's wrong with that? Bit boring, maybe."

"No, coat. Ankle length." She flicked some ash into the ashtray.

"Christ. OK, what about Josh? You were seeing him for ages."

"Total commitment-phobe. I made the mistake of asking

him if it was OK to keep a toothbrush at his place. He virtually had a heart attack. Haven't seen him for ages."

Just then the bell went. "Lizzie," Stephanie said.

"God, you look a bit green round the gills," Cass said to Lizzie as she came into the kitchen.

Apparently one of Dom's clients, an exceedingly grand fashion designer, had had a party last night. "I don't know if I drank too much, or if it was the cod semen."

"Cod semen?" Stephanie and Cass cried in unison.

"Yeah. Apparently it's all the rage."

"So, come on," Cass said, giggling, "did you swallow?"

Lizzie couldn't face champagne and said she'd just have orange juice. She took off her fleece, which she hung on the back of a chair, and handed Stephanie a posh silver carrier bag. "It's just to say thank you for having the twins the other day." Dom and Lizzie had been to a wedding, to which children weren't invited.

"Oh, wow! Linen water."

"I hope you like it. It's sage and comfrey. I adore it."

"Oh, I'm sure I'll love it. But what's it actually for?"

"You know, your bed linen."

"What, you spray it on?"

"Yes, when you iron it."

Cass hooted. "Christ, Lizzie. Who bloody irons bed linen?"

"Loads of people," Lizzie said brightly. "You should try it. It's so soothing. You can't beat a pile of ironing and *Woman's Hour*."

Stephanie gave Lizzie a thank-you kiss and said she'd get the sausages going.

"So," Cass said to Stephanie, "Albert coming for Christmas?"

"Hope so, for Jake's sake. Still waiting to hear for definite. Actually, I haven't checked my e-mail today. There might be something." She asked Lizzie to keep an eye on the sausages while she ran upstairs. "I'll be two ticks."

There was one e-mail waiting for her and it was from Albert. The contents didn't even remotely surprise her.

Hey, principessa. Bad news. A job has come up at Universal. Won't be able to get to you for the holidays. I'm so sorry. Can you forgive me? Will definitely make it after New Year's. Say hi to Jakey for me. Tell him I love him. Will send his presents by courier to make sure they arrive in time. Have a great Christmas.
  Ciao,
  Albert.

"Huh," Cass said when Stephanie had announced what was in the e-mail.

"What does 'huh' mean?"

"I don't like the way he messes you about, that's all."

"What can I do? It drives me mad, too, but he doesn't do it on purpose. He has a living to earn. Anyway, the first week of January is so dead, it'll give me and Jake something to look forward to."

"You have to stay positive," Lizzie chipped in. "I mean, look at Dom. He's working sixteen hours a day on this new Asia Pacific merger. He'll get Christmas Day and New Year's off, but that'll be it. But I count my blessings. I have a beautiful house, two wonderful children. And Dom has promised we'll get away together the moment—"

"—this big case is over," Cass and Stephanie chanted.

They'd heard it so many times before. Lizzie and Dom never got away because the "big case" was always followed immediately by an even bigger one. Stephanie immediately felt guilty for making fun and went over to put an arm round Lizzie.

"Sorry," she said.

"Dom does his best, you know. It's just that they work him so terribly hard."

"I know," Stephanie said. "I know."

Cass gave Lizzie's hand an affectionate pat. "Tell you what we should do," she said. "Bugger the blokes and take ourselves off somewhere hot for Christmas. God, I can't remember the last time I felt the sand under my feet."

"No money," Stephanie said. "The nearest I could get to a hot sandy beach is turning up the radiator and sticking my feet in the cat's tray." As if on cue, Liberace sashayed in and leaped up onto the counter. He virtually had his snout in the bacon when Lizzie grabbed him and threw him out the back door. Stephanie told her to lock his cat flap or he'd be back in.

"You really need to think about earning some money," Cass said. "Jimmy and Brian have split up half a dozen times. They always get back together. This time won't be any different. Mark my words, pretty soon Jimmy's going to want to move back in."

"But he said he'd be away at least six months."

"Don't bank on it."

Stephanie shook her head. "God, you know, a huge bit of me thinks I should give up the whole showbiz idea and take a course on teaching English as a foreign language."

"No money in that," Lizzie said. "Tell you what, though, I'm thinking of going into business selling homemade soaps and candles. Just part-time. I really need something to keep me occupied now that the boys are at school. Martha Stewart shows you exactly how to do it. I've been practicing. They're dead easy."

Lizzie virtually idolized Martha Stewart. *Martha Stewart Living* was her bible. She kept stacks of back issues piled up in the living room. "God," Stephanie had remarked a few weeks ago, flicking through one of the mags, "how can you respect a woman who tells you that April is the time to dust your stuffed animal heads? Plus there's this whole criminal investigation going on." Lizzie got all huffy and defensive, snatched the magazine from her and said that the truth would come out about the criminal investigation and the whole thing was a despicable conspiracy hatched by jealous rivals.

Cass drained her glass, but didn't say anything. They'd been through it all before—Cass telling Lizzie she had such a sharp mind and why didn't she go back to work and start stretching it again. Then Lizzie would say that Cass hadn't given birth and didn't understand that after everything she'd been through to get the twins, she'd feel so guilty abandoning them. Stephanie tended to sympathize with Lizzie during these debates. On the other hand, although she did feel guilty leaving Jake, she wasn't sure if she could give up all her ambition to sit at home making Play-Doh green eggs and ham. Anyway, for her, staying at home wasn't even an option. Even with Albert's help, she still had to work to pay the bills and that was that. She told them about her plan to find another agent.

"Thought I'd send out my demo CD to half a dozen West End agents."

"Go for it," Cass said.

"I agree," Lizzie said. "What have you got to lose? Only blinkin' Eileen."

"You're right," Stephanie laughed, realizing the champagne had well and truly kicked in. "You're absolutely right."

59

"Right, then," Cass said, and they drank a toast to the future.

By now the sausages were nut brown and the bacon was just a couple of minutes from perfect crispness. Stephanie poured some of the hot fat into another pan and added triangles of bread. Lizzie offered to do the toast and Cass made more Bucks Fizz. On the back burner, the beans had just burst their skins.

Carefully, Stephanie tipped the eggs out of the bowl. The fat spattered as they hit the pan. She turned down the flame and began basting.

Lizzie asked after Cass's love life. She repeated the story she'd told Stephanie.

"Corduroy?"

"Ankle length."

"Blimey."

Nobody said anything for a minute. In the background the eggs were spitting.

"Of course you know the best way to find a man," Lizzie said. "Stop looking."

"What, you mean if I give up looking for Mel Gibson, he'll come and find me?"

"Well, maybe not Mel Gibson exactly, but somebody will."

"You reckon?" Cass said.

"I do. And why does it always have to be about sex? Why don't you just take time to get to know a bloke and see where it goes? Dating should lead to sex, not the other way round."

"What I don't understand," Stephanie said, "is why, when you run a successful business and make stacks of dough, your whole sense of self-worth is tied up in attracting men."

"You know," Cass announced, "you're right. I think the time may have come for me to do some work on myself."

"I agree," Stephanie said, dishing the bacon and eggs onto plates. "Therapy might be a good idea."

"No, I didn't mean that kind of work," Cass came back. "I meant maybe I'm losing my sex appeal. Perhaps I need to have some cosmetic work done."

"Cass," Lizzie said, "you look stunning. Look at you with the hair, the figure, the BMW Z4, the Joseph wardrobe."

"I agree," Stephanie said, handing round plates of fry-up.

"I was thinking about maybe having my lips done."

Stephanie and Lizzie leaned toward her and squinted at her lips.

"Your lips are great," Lizzie said.

"Perfect," said Stephanie.

"No, not those lips." She stood up and pushed back her chair. "These lips." She was pointing to her crotch. "I think they could do with plumping out a bit. You know, to give me a better contour." She sat down and began cutting into a sausage.

"I'm not sure I know what 'better contour' means," Stephanie said.

"I think she means she wants it to be more in your face," Lizzie explained.

"That's right," Cass said, chewing on a lump of sausage. "What do you think? Apparently they inject them with fat from your bum." She burst her egg yolk with a corner of fried bread and began mopping it up. "They can do your inner labia as well as the outer ones. God, Steph, this fried bread is fab. So come on, you two, why aren't you tucking in?"

Chapter 4

The doorbell rang just before nine the next morning. Stephanie was tearing around looking for her lipstick. Jake was still in his pajamas.

"Leave the front door," Estelle said, bustling in. "Your dad's just unloading the car. We popped into the supermarket to get you a few bits."

"What few bits?" Stephanie took her mother's coat. "I don't need bits. Honest, Mum, I'm fine for bits."

"Well, I didn't know what you had in for Jakey's lunch." As they walked into the kitchen, Stephanie explained there were plenty of eggs, cheese, pasta and jars of tomato sauce. "I thought, you know," Estelle said, about to launch into I'm-not-trying-to-get-at-you-I'm-only-thinking-of-Jake mode, "I'd make him something fresh. So, I bought a nice haddock fillet. I thought I'd do a fish pie."

"Gan'ma. Gan'ma," Jake squealed from his digger.

"Hello, darling," Estelle said, bending down to kiss him. "How are you?"

"Better."

"He's not dressed yet?" Estelle said. Of course what she really meant was: "Why isn't he dressed yet?"

"No. He's going through this phase where he just refuses to put proper clothes on."

"Oh, Jakey will get dressed for his grandma, won't you, Jakey?"

"Maybe. Look, about the fish. You see, Jake's not a big fish eater."

"That's because you only give him fish fingers. He'll eat my pie. Won't you, sweetie?" This morning the balloon of Stephanie's irritation had turned into a veritable zeppelin. Jake nodded.

"You look a bit pale, though," Estelle said to Stephanie. "A bit of lipstick wouldn't hurt."

Stephanie took a deep yoga breath. Let it go, Steph. Let it go. "I know. I was looking for it just before you arrived."

Stephanie hung her mother's coat over the back of a kitchen chair while her mother began gathering up the letters and days-old newspapers that littered the table. "This it?" Estelle asked.

"Oh, yeah. Thanks," Stephanie said. She stuffed the lipstick into her bag. "I'll do it on the train."

Just then Harry walked in carrying four supermarket bags. "Right, that's the lot," he puffed. "Hi, Steph." While Harry said hello to Jake, Stephanie looked inside the bags. "Mum, this is really kind of you, but I don't need any of this stuff."

"So, I'll put it in the freezer. Then you won't have to worry."

"But I wasn't worried."

"Gan'dad come read *Fatapillow*?" Jake piped up.

"In a moment, sweetheart," Harry said. "Just let Grand-dad get his coat off."

"You know," Estelle said to Stephanie, her voice lowered so that Jake couldn't hear, "this little boy needs a father. Darling, why don't you marry Albert? He's good-looking, charming. I'm sure, with a bit of persuasion, he'd move to London."

"Mum, Albert and I have never even discussed marriage. You know it was only ever a physical thing between us."

"Shh. I don't want Jake hearing us talk about the O-T-H-E-R."

"Mum, why are you spelling the word *other*?"

"You know what children are like. They pick up on things." Stephanie shook her head. "OK, well, I'm off to W-O-R-K," she said. "I'm doing my gig at the Blues C-A-F-E afterward. You two still OK to sleep over?"

"OK? It's a pleasure," Estelle said.

She supposed it was the e-mail from Albert. Today, as she sat playing the piano in Debenhams, she kept noticing the fathers with their toddlers. Presumably they all had jobs, but had taken time off to bring their children up to town to see Father Christmas. She had to keep reminding herself that for Albert, being with Jake involved taking more than the day off work and hopping a 747 rather than the tube. But it was Christmas. Jake might just about remember this one when he was older. Just for once, Albert could have turned down a job and made the effort.

After she'd finished work she realized she was starving. She decided to walk up the road to Selfridges and treat herself to a couple of dishes at Yo Sushi. As she sat down she picked up a copy of *Cosmo,* which somebody had left on the seat next to her. She sat at the packed bar, wolfing down sashimi and teriyaki and reading up on the "ten spectacular ways to make his bells ring this Christmas."

She took the tube to Islington and arrived at the Blues Café just after eight. It was a small, dimly lit basement restaurant just off Upper Street. People came to eat the vast cheapish pizzas, drink the OK Barolo and listen to the music. Most of the singers only performed one night a week. Because she was so popular, Stephanie did two: Mondays and Thursdays.

The jazz trio that accompanied the singers was the same every night. Mac, Ian and Dennis were three rather dog-eared Scottish blokes in shiny tuxes and bad comb-overs, who'd been together for forty years and had played everywhere from New Orleans to New Malden, stopping off on the way for the odd bar mitzvah and D-list crooner backing track. These days they were pretty much retired and worked at the Blues Café just to keep their hand in.

Next to the loos was a large walk-in store cupboard, which doubled as Stephanie's dressing room. Among the catering packs of flour and the giant cans of tomato puree there was a full-length mirror and an old Formica table that doubled as a dressing table. Hanging on a wire coat hanger on the back of the door was the slinky black dress she wore onstage.

Each night she sang for an hour and a half. This was divided up into three thirty-minute sets. In between she sat sipping mineral water while Mac, Ian and Dennis knocked back the house McClaren and told their stories.

"Och, aye, we've met them all. Ella, Peggy, Satchmo. Go on, Ian, tell Stephanie about the night us, Peggy and the Satch sat up drinkin' malt until dawn."

And Ian would begin.

"Of course, you know Peggy Lee wasn't her real name."

65

"I think you did happen to mention it once or twice, Ian," Stephanie would say.

"Did ah? Did ah really?" Then he'd carry on as if he were imparting his sacred piece of information for the first time. "Not many people know this, but her real name was Norma Deloris Egstrom. Aye. There's a name to go to bed wi'. Strange, isn't it, that two twentieth-century icons, Peggy and Marilyn, were both called Norma?"

"Very strange."

From time to time she changed her repertoire, but usually she kicked off with some Cole Porter or Gershwin—"The Man I Love" was one of her favorites. Then she would ease into "Summertime," "I Can't Give You Anything But Love," "I Get a Kick Out of You." Occasionally her mum and dad would pop in. Her dad in particular always ended up reaching for his handkerchief.

"That's my daughter, you know," he'd say to anybody who would listen.

Sometimes Cass and Lizzie would come by. Stephanie and the band would join them in their breaks and the night would turn into a party. But no matter how drunk Mac, Ian and Dennis got, their playing remained faultless.

Occasionally they got a rowdy crowd in off the street, but mostly they were smart thirty-somethings who sat quietly and listened.

When she sang "Fever" there was always a complete hush. She loved that. Whenever she had moments of self-doubt she thought about how people reacted to her singing that song. Singing "Fever" made her feel sexy, and she and Ian, who played drums, flirted like crazy while she performed: him winking, her thrusting her hips to the beat. The audience picked up on it and it brought the house down—

inasmuch as fifty people eating Quattro Staggione pizzas were capable of bringing the house down.

*A*s she took her place on the tiny podium, the room darkened and she felt the adrenaline kick in. She was aware that people had stopped talking. She was starting off with "The Man I Love." The band began its intro. It was slow, fluid, easy. She felt herself swaying gently.

"Someday he'll come along, the man I love / And he'll be big and strong..."

By the fourth number the applause got louder. The audience was really starting to warm up. As usual she ended her first set with "Fever."

First that drumbeat. Then the bass kicked in. Her fingers clicked to the pacey rhythm.

"Never know how much I love you, never know how much I care..." Drum. Thrust. Wink from Ian.

The applause went on and on. She even had to do an encore.

When it was time for a break, she headed off to the bar to get some water. She'd taken a couple of sips, maybe, when she felt a tap on her shoulder. She turned round. It was Frank Waterman. She blinked.

"It's me, Frank. You know, Nottingham Playhouse 1997, Debenhams last Saturday? I said I'd come and see you. Well, here I am."

"Yes, yes, I know. Sorry, I didn't mean to be rude. It's just that I, er... You were the last person I'd expected to see. You know...people say these things..."

"Just to be polite. I know." He was wearing jeans, trendy sneakers and a fabulously well-cut suede jacket. "Actually, we popped in on the off chance." He gestured to a group of people sitting at a nearby table. She noticed it didn't include Anoushka. "I wasn't sure which night you were on. Anyway, I just wanted to come over and tell you how fantastic you were."

Her face lit up.

"You know, when you sing 'Fever' you sound just like Peggy Lee."

Now she was blushing. "Yeah, everybody says that. So you're really into this kind of music, then?"

"Have been for years." He told her he had a sizable collection of old recordings and that last week he'd picked up an original 1938 copy of Ella Fitzgerald singing "A-Tisket, A-Tasket."

"No! God, I'd love to hear it."

"Of course, her voice sounded almost childlike back then. By the midforties—you know, the Dizzy Gillespie years—she'd really come on."

"Boy, you really know your stuff."

He grinned and confessed he picked up most of his knowledge from the blurbs inside CDs. "Her real name was Norma Egstrom," he said.

"Whose?" Oh, God, why did she say that? As if Ian hadn't told her seventeen million times.

"Peggy Lee's. Not many people know that."

"To be precise," she said, "it was Norma Deloris Egstrom."

"Is that right?"

She nodded. "Strange, isn't it," she went on, "that two twentieth-century icons—Marilyn and Peggy—should both be called Norma."

"Yes, I've often thought that."

"So, er, how's Anoushka? You guys all ready for the big day? When is it, again?"

"April. I guess we're as ready as we'll ever be."

He explained that he had another canapé tasting on Saturday, which would be the seventh or possibly the eighth. The next day he was driving to Gloucestershire to meet up with a local estate agent.

"He'll drag me round another load of quaint houses. Anoushka's seen them once. She adores all that Aga and pine dresser stuff."

"Gloucestershire's dead posh, though."

He grunted. "Bloody miles from the nearest kebab shop."

This made her laugh. "You'll have to get a flat in London as well. So, where's Anoushka tonight?"

"In Düsseldorf, having her teeth-to-gum ratio balanced. She's worried she's going to look like Quick Draw McGraw in the wedding photographs. All nonsense, of course. Her teeth are perfectly fine."

"Oh, well, it's her big day. Every bride wants to look her best."

"I guess. Anyway, it's been great seeing you again. I really hope things start to pick up. If anybody deserves it, you do."

She found herself blushing again. "I've decided to try and find a new agent. So you never know . . ."

"Great," he said. "Fingers crossed."

He explained he had to leave now because he was taking one of his companions to Heathrow. She felt a lurch of disappointment. She'd really enjoyed chatting with him. Yes, he was cute. OK, amazingly cute, but there was also this easy humor and laid-back charm about Frank Waterman, which she found particularly attractive. "That's OK. Thanks for coming."

"My pleasure," he said.

She watched him walk back to his table and take some money out of his wallet.

"Hey, Steph . . . Dennis to Steph, come in, Steph." Dennis was waving the back of his hand in front of her face. "Are you with us? Come on. We have a show to do."

"Oh, right. Sorry. I was miles away."

The moment she opened the front door the smell hit her. Fried onions. She went into the kitchen. Her mother was standing at the stove in her pink velour dressing gown, turning lamb chops in the frying pan.

"Fancied a snack," she said. Estelle was trying to lose weight. She'd never been slim, but neither had she been a size eighteen until now. "When a woman's bosom becomes singular rather than plural," she'd said the other day, pulling her blouse tight over her bust, "you know something has to be done." As a result she had gone on a protein-only diet.

"I knew you'd get hungry. Meat isn't a complete food. At least have some bread with it."

"No, the wheat's bloating. I'll have a couple of broccoli florets."

"Bloody hell, Mum. Onions and broccoli—you'll be farting half the night."

"Stephanie, do you have to be so coarse?"

"OK, you'll be F-A-R-T-I-N-G all night."

Estelle said there was some fish pie left in the fridge if Stephanie fancied it.

"Jakey loved it. Even had seconds."

"Brilliant," Stephanie said, forcing a smile.

"And the moment you left, he got dressed. Not a moment's trouble, bless him. You just need to be firm."

Just then Harry appeared. He, too, was in his dressing

gown (maroon, with gold crest on the breast). He had his mobile phone to his ear. "Look, I don't want one. I don't need one. How many more times do I have to tell you people?"

Stephanie shot her mother a what's-going-on? look. "Your father's talking to those people."

"Which people?"

"You know, the penis extension people." The words *penis extension* were mouthed. Apparently Harry had been e-mailing them nonstop, demanding they cease and desist harassing him, but it had done no good. The junk mail was still coming. Somehow he had managed to track down their phone number.

"But it's half past one in the morning," Stephanie said.

"It's only half past five in California." Estelle tipped the two chops onto a plate and piled on some onions. "I can't be bothered with the broccoli."

By now Harry was verging on irate. "Look, I don't give a damn if they are curved for greater sensitivity. I don't need another three inches. What is a G-spot, anyway? Is it like a liver spot?" Stephanie stood shaking her head. Her mother brought her plate to the table and sat down.

"These chops aren't bad, for the supermarket. A bit tough maybe. But they're a lot cheaper than the ones the butcher sold me last week."

Stephanie didn't know whether to laugh or cry. It was half past one in the morning. Her father was on the phone discussing penis extensions and her mother was comparing the prices of lamb chops. These people made the Osbournes look sane.

Harry took the phone from his ear and stared at it. "He cut me off."

"I'm not surprised. Dad, leave it. Just delete the e-mails like everybody else does."

"Oh, no. I'm not letting this one go. Not on your life. I

71

will not let these people win. Right, I'm off to bed. Estelle, open the window when you come up. You'll be farting all night after that lot."

"Look, for your information I do not . . . that word."

"No, my sweet," Harry said, "you gently break wind and it smells of gardenias."

Before she went to bed, Stephanie took down the list of six West End theatrical agents she'd printed out from the Internet the day before and pinned on her kitchen bulletin board. Then she went upstairs, typed out a cover letter and made copies. Finally she addressed the padded envelopes she'd bought on her lunch hour and placed a letter and a CD in each.

She fell asleep almost immediately and dreamed that Anoushka Holland caught distemper.

Chapter 5

The following Sunday, Stephanie, Cass and Lizzie got together for tea at Lizzie's.

Stephanie came straight from the Royal Free hospital, where she and Jake had been to visit Mrs. M. Jake wore his Spiderman outfit, his sword tucked down his trousers. They took her a giant poinsettia, which she loved. It was clear from the expression on her face that she was in pain, but she was in great form and let Jake climb all over her.

"Oh, I've missed you, little man," she said, giving him a cuddle. "I really have and no mistake. But I've got a surprise for you. Stephanie, darlin', open my locker, would you?"

Stephanie opened it and took out the surprise—a pack of Fondant Fancies.

"Oh, Mrs. M., you shouldn't."

"I asked Audrey to bring them in." She leaned across and took the cakes from Stephanie. "Now, Jake, what color is it to be?"

"Lellow."

"Excellent choice." He sat eating the Fancie, getting crumbs all over the bed.

Stephanie asked her if she had any idea when the hospital was going to let her out.

"Hopefully before Christmas. My kids have come over from Ireland, but Geraldine—she's the eldest—has said she'll stay on over Christmas to look after me." Stephanie and Jake got up to leave when a group of Mrs. M.'s children arrived.

"But you'll come again soon?" Mrs. M. said, giving Jake another squeeze.

"Promise," Stephanie replied.

Lizzie and Dom owned a five-bedroom Edwardian in Highgate, done in various shades of beige. When Stephanie arrived, Cass was already there. She and Lizzie were sitting in the kitchen. (Taupe Shaker units, tofu tiles.) On the kitchen table sat a dried turkey carcass. Lizzie was holding a can of spray paint. Cass had the end of a raw zucchini sticking out of her mouth.

Stephanie stood there for a moment, trying to decide if she was more interested in finding out about the turkey carcass or the zucchini. The zucchini won hands down.

"OK," Stephanie said to Lizzie. "What's she doing?"

Lizzie cleared her throat and turned to Jake. "Er, Jake, Dougal and Archie are playing in the living room. Why don't you go and show them your Spiderman costume?"

He'd known Archie and Dougal all his life and was happy to trot off. Cass took the zucchini out of her mouth. "I gave up on the lips idea and decided to get my teeth done instead. See?" She was wearing a clear, almost invisible brace over her two slightly crooked front teeth.

"OK, but where does the zucchini come in?"

"Nobody told me it would be totally impossible to give a blow job with these things on my teeth." She held up the zucchini. Along the sides, a significant amount of green skin was missing. "See, I'll never get it right."

Stephanie laughed. Lizzie picked up a can of spray paint, shook it hard, rattling the ball bearing, and pressed the nozzle. A fine mist of gold paint shot out and landed on the turkey carcass. "I'm guessing this is one of Martha's bright ideas," Stephanie said, sitting down and starting to cough. "Could we at least let some air in?"

"Oh, God, yes. Sorry." Lizzie leaped up and opened the back door, letting in a gust of icy wind. They all decided they'd rather get high than freeze. Lizzie closed it again and opened the window over the sink a crack. "Don't you think it's sweet?" she said, coming back to the table. "I got the carcass from some American friends down the road, after Thanksgiving. I picked off all the bits of dried meat. Then I blanched it. Who'd have thought that turned upside down it would look just like a sleigh? I found a lovely little Santa and some reindeer in that little knickknack shop up the road. I thought I'd fill it with nuts."

"I'm sure it's going to look lovely," Stephanie said.

Just then Dom walked in—tall, Teutonic, as square jawed as ever. He was wearing a smart navy jacket and chinos. Over his shoulder was a brown leather suit carrier.

"Hi, everybody," he said, waving and smiling at Stephanie and Cass. "Look, I really don't mean to be rude, but I've got to dash. My taxi's here."

"But you are being rude," Lizzie chided gently. "You've been upstairs for ages. You could have come down and said hello."

"Sorry. I've been on the phone to the boys in Tokyo for

the last hour. Look, I've got to go." He gave Lizzie a perfunctory kiss on the cheek.

"OK, darling. Safe journey."

"Christ, what on earth is that?" he asked, gesturing at the half-spray-painted turkey carcass.

"It's going to be Santa's sleigh. I thought I'd put nuts in it."

"Lizzie, couldn't you go out and buy a sleigh, like a normal person?" He picked up his wallet and passport off the breakfast bar. "Right, bye, everybody."

He turned to go.

"Bye, Dom," Stephanie and Cass chanted.

"Say bye-bye to the boys," Lizzie shouted into the hall.

"Already have. By the way, they've piled sofa cushions all over the living room floor. You'd better sort it out."

She ignored the last remark. "Ring me when you get in," she called out. The front door slammed.

"God," Cass said, "he seems a bit stressed."

"It's all the hours he puts in. I really worry about him. On top of that, I don't think he's been home for more than ten days this month."

Cass sat shaking her head. "It would drive me mad if I were married to him."

"Oh, it won't be forever," Lizzie said brightly. "They're bound to offer him a partnership in a year or so. In fact they've said as much. When that happens, he'll be almost entirely London based and able to dictate his hours more. Now then, who's for another cuppa?"

"That'd be nice," Cass said.

"Steph?"

She nodded.

"Ooh, I've got some homemade stollen in the cupboard," Lizzie said. "I made one for the playgroup Christmas bazaar. Then I thought, well, it's as easy to make two as it is to make one."

Stephanie and Cass exchanged glances. "You know," Cass said, "I'd never do another line of cocaine again, if I could have some of what you're on."

"Oh, you can always find the energy for the things you enjoy." Lizzie put the stollen on the table and started cutting it into slices. "So, Steph, how's it going with your mum looking after Jake?"

"Oh, God," Cass said, laughing. "Don't get her started. How long have you got?"

Stephanie explained that the house was cleaner and tidier than it had ever been and her fridge was permanently full.

"I know I should be grateful, but I feel like a guest in my own house. It can't go on. God knows how you sack your own mother. Did I tell you she's started potty training Jake?" She explained that Estelle had started a few days ago—using the method advocated by the psychologist in the *Daily Mail*. Each night when she came home, Jake would come running up to her.

" 'My got a surprise. My got a surprise,' he goes. Then he takes my hand and drags me into the downstairs loo. Sitting in the corner is his potty covered in paper towels."

"Oh my God," Cass said, anticipating the next bit of the story.

"So every night I take off the paper and squeal, 'Ooh, another big-boy poo. Oh, Jake, you are clever. Well done.' "

"Poor you," Lizzie said. "Can't be much fun coming home and being greeted by a day-old turd."

"Apparently," Stephanie went on, "this bloody shrink says the 'secondary carer' should keep the poo for the 'absent' parent—note the provocative use of the word *absent*—so that both the child and the parent remain bonded."

"Well, I can see the point," Lizzie said.

"Yes, so can I. It's just that I wanted to be the one to potty train Jake, that's all."

"But you can't," Lizzie said. "If it hadn't been Estelle doing it, it would have been Mrs. M."

"Mrs. M. doesn't believe in potty training," Stephanie said. "She reckons kids do it naturally, in their own time. I brought it up a couple of times and she told me to leave it. 'Ach, Stephanie,' she'd say, 'you're worrying about nothing. Now then, when was the last time you saw one of those punk rockers still in nappies?' "

Just then Dougal and Archie charged in, noisily demanding food. Jake was standing behind them, keeping his own counsel, but clearly in awe of the two big boys.

Stephanie offered to cut them some stollen.

"It's absolutely scrummy."

"Best not," Lizzie said. "My two have had their sugar ration for today." She went to the fridge and took out a large plastic container of ready-prepared celery and carrot sticks. She put a handful into three small bowls.

"These are poo," Dougal declared. "We want Hula Hoops."

"You know you're not allowed junk food, Dougal. All those additives make you and your brother hyper."

"We want Hula Hoops," Archie shouted. "Give us Hula Hoops." Then Jake, clearly getting into the spirit of things, threw his celery and carrot sticks onto the floor.

"Hey, look what Jake's done," Archie shouted. Then he hit him hard, on the head.

Jake started bawling.

"Archie," Stephanie cried. "Stop that. It's naughty. He's only little."

She scooped Jake up and sat him on her lap, cuddling him and rubbing his head.

"Steph," Lizzie said, "I tend not to raise my voice or use words like *naughty* with the boys. It can give them a negative self-image as well as make them reluctant to express their inner frustrations."

"God," Cass said, "you sound like you've swallowed a bloomin' psychology book."

"Maybe I have, sort of. This kids' shrink came to give a talk to the mums of the children in the reception class at the boys' school. She really made sense—particularly about the effects of food additives on children's brains."

Lizzie turned back to the twins. "Now then, boys, that wasn't very nice, was it? Say sorry to Jake." The boys mumbled their sorries. "So, boys, are you feeling a bit tired? Perhaps you'd like to go up to your bedroom and have some time out. You could lie on your beds and listen to some nice music. I bet Jake's never heard *The Nutcracker*. Did you tell Stephanie and Cass we're all going to see it after Christmas?"

"*Thunderbirds* video! *Thunderbirds* video!"

"Tun'birds," Jake echoed, climbing off Stephanie's lap.

"Dom bought the twins biscuits when they went out shopping this morning. I keep telling him that sugar and additives make them hyper, but he never listens." Lizzie paused. "All right, *Thunderbirds,* but only for twenty minutes."

"Yeah-yeah. Yeah-yeah." The twins ran into the living room, with Jake in pursuit. Lizzie followed them.

"Additives, my arse," Cass muttered. "They're just brats. I'd clout them if they were mine."

"Believe me, they are not brats." Stephanie smiled. "Correction. They are brats, but all the kids round here are the same. Proper discipline is so five decades ago."

"But Lizzie's just rewarded their bad behavior."

"I know, but it's Christmas, she has them on her own practically all the time because her husband's never here and she's knackered. You or I would do the same."

"God, I never want to be a mother. Never ever." She reached into her bag and took out a packet of weed and some cigarette papers.

"Cass!" Lizzie cried, coming back into the room. "There are children. Please."

"It was for them. I thought it might calm them down." Now Lizzie looked not only harassed, she looked horrified, too. "Lizzie, calm down. It's a joke." She put the weed back in her bag. "So, Steph, have you told Lizzie about Frank?"

"Who's Frank?" Lizzie said.

"The actor, Frank Waterman. Fancies Steph."

"Gawd. How many more times? He does not fancy me."

"Does, does, does and does."

"You're kidding, right?" Lizzie said. "*The* Frank Waterman?"

Cass brought Lizzie up to speed.

"He does not bloody fancy me," Stephanie said again. "He's engaged to Anoushka Holland. You should see her. She's totally stunning. And rich. They're buying a house in Gloucestershire. Or they may have said they're buying the whole of Gloucestershire."

"God," Lizzie said, "didn't I read she's just been bought out by Theo Fennell for eleven million quid?"

"Eleven point five, actually," Stephanie replied.

"OK, OK," Cass broke in. "This is way off the point. The point is, if he doesn't fancy you, why did he turn up at the Blues Café less than forty-eight hours after bumping into you in Debenhams?" Stephanie shrugged. "It's simple. He's got the hots for you."

"So, do you fancy him back?" Lizzie asked.

"Oh, I dunno. I did once. Big-time. But it's all academic. When he showed up at the Blues Café, he had no idea I would even be there. You're both reading far too much into this. We like the same kind of music, that's all."

"And speaking of music," Cass went on, "have you heard anything from those agents you wrote to?"

Stephanie shook her head.

"Oh, well, it's Christmas," Lizzie said. "Everything shuts down from now until the new year. You'll hear something in January, just you wait."

Stephanie had planned to work at Debenhams right up to Christmas Eve, but in the end she realized she had too much to do, since Christmas Day had now turned into more of a full-scale production than ever. In the beginning it was going to be just her and Jake, Estelle and Harry. Then Pam at The Haven came down with bronchitis and canceled the traditional Christmas Day buffet and old-time dancing. So Lilly was coming to Stephanie's, as well. Then, three days before Christmas, Dom rang Lizzie to say he was stranded in Japan because Mr. Hashimoto of Matsushita—or it may have been Mr. Matsushita of Hashimoto—had had a mild stroke on the golf range. He wouldn't now be back until the twenty-seventh.

"Right, then you're coming to my place, no arguments," Stephanie had said to Lizzie, realizing afterward how much like Estelle she must have sounded.

"You sure?"

"Of course I'm sure, silly. I couldn't bear the thought of the three of you on your own."

"OK. Don't worry about the pudding or the cake. I did

mine weeks ago. They'll be my contribution. Ooh, and I'll do some mulled wine, as well."

"You've got a deal. Mull away."

The day after the conversation with Lizzie, Cass rang to say she had meant to spend Christmas with her parents, but was having second thoughts.

"It's not so bad when it's just them," she explained, "but this year my sisters will be there. I know exactly how it will be. They'll be in the kitchen, peeling spuds in their M&S cashmere polo necks, outimpressing each other with their home improvements. Their husbands will be in the living room, skulking round each other like fighting cocks, trying to work out who got the bigger bonus. The kids will be up-stairs killing each other. About twelve o'clock, my dad's Rotary crowd will arrive for drinks. As I pass round the ham and cheese spirals, a couple of old gits in blazers will grope me and the women will want to know if I've 'found a nice young man yet.' I'll wind them up by saying 'No, a nice young woman, actually.' My mum will overhear this and it will all end in one of her lectures in the downstairs loo, about my uncouth sense of humor and how Eddie Izzard and his ilk may be popular among the Islington set, but that kind of thing just isn't acceptable in Tiverton. So," she finished, "I was wondering if I could come to you instead."

"More the merrier," Stephanie had said, not giving a thought to how much extra work would be involved.

Debenhams was fine about her finishing a few days early, since the woman who stood in for her on Sundays was des-perate for extra cash and only too happy to do some over-time.

Estelle and Harry had Jake all day on Christmas Eve. Stephanie hit Waitrose as it opened at eight o'clock. Even then, she queued for twenty minutes to get into the parking lot. By half past eight she was wandering round the super-market feeling like a worm in a tin of fisherman's bait. Even though she had a list, there were so many people, so much confusion, that she lost track of what she wanted, why she was there and very nearly who she was.

She got home just after eleven. She'd remembered the hand-cooked crisps and pistachios, the booze, the cranberries to make fresh sauce, the red cabbage, the sweet potatoes (which she would roast around the meat so that they ended up all crispy and caramelized and gloriously soft in the mid-dle), the brandy butter, the veggies, the gravlax for the hors d'oeuvres, and the mini pizzas, because the kids wouldn't eat gravlax. It wasn't until she sensed there was more space in the fridge than there should have been that the penny dropped and she realized that she'd forgotten the turkey. How it was possible to go out food shopping on Christmas Eve and for-get the turkey, she had no idea, but somehow she had man-aged it. She decided to walk to the organic butcher around the corner. She queued for another twenty minutes.

"Right, what name is it?" the butcher said, barely look-ing up from his order book.

"Ah. I didn't actually order a turkey."

"Sorry. If you didn't order one, I can't help you."

"So, there's no chance you've got one, you know, lying around."

Sharp intake of breath from butcher. "You have to be joking."

Stephanie, whose blood sugar was already low because she hadn't eaten breakfast, could feel herself about to burst into tears. The butcher clearly saw her distress. "What size were you looking for?"

"Dunno. Fifteen pounds?"

"Look, bear with me. I'll see what I've got in the back."

A few minutes later he came back with a bird. He placed it on the electronic scale.

"That's eighty-five pounds."

"Oh, no, I don't want anything nearly as big as that. It wouldn't fit in my oven."

"No. I mean eighty-five pounds in money."

"What, for a turkey?"

"It's organic."

"It should be blinkin' orgasmic for that price."

"That's the best I can do, I'm afraid." She was aware of irritable murmurings from the women behind her in the queue. "OK, I'll take it."

She handed over her credit card and prayed it wouldn't be declined.

About four o'clock she popped in to have a quick cuppa with Mrs. M. She was back home, her daughter Geraldine looking after her.

"Merry Christmas," Stephanie said, handing her the parcel she'd wrapped in shiny silver paper and tied with fuchsia ribbon. Mrs. M. undid it with extreme care. "Shame to ruin such lovely paper." Inside was a pretty powder-blue sweater from Marks.

"Oh, now, that's really modern," Mrs. M. said, admiring the slash neck and three-quarter-length sleeves. "I love it, darlin'. I really do. Makes such a change from all the fawn cardigans my kids get me." Of course, she hadn't been able to buy presents for anybody and was feeling really guilty. "Will you tell Jakey I love him and that I'll make it up to him as soon as I can?" Stephanie told her to stop worrying and that Jake sent her a big kiss.

"I'll be back to work in no time, you know. Once I've

had my hip replacement operation I'll be sprinting like a teenager." A flicker of pain crossed Mrs. M.'s face.

Stephanie leaned over and gave her a kiss on the cheek. "I know you will, Mrs. M. I know you will."

She'd planned to let Jake stay up late. They would snuggle up on the sofa listening to carols, while the Christmas tree lights twinkled and the flames danced in the grate. Atmosphere-wise, she was going for a Perry Como Christmas special. Instead, Jake fell asleep in the car on the way home from her parents' and didn't even wake up when she carried him into the house.

"Come on, Jakey, don't you fancy some hot chocolate and marshmallows? And we haven't put out mince pies and sherry for Santa and the reindeer."

"Want lay-a-bel." She carried him upstairs, put a nappy on him—he still needed them at night—and then covered him with the duvet and placed his label in his hand. "Sing-sing," he mumbled, zizzing the label. "Sing-sing."

"Rudolph the red-nosed reindeer, had a very shiny nose . . ."

"No-no. Tomatoes one."

"But that's not a Christmas song, Jake."

"Sing-sing. Sing-sing."

"I went to the circus with my Uncle Jim / Somebody threw a tomato at him / Tomatoes are soft when they come in their skin / But this one half killed him / It came in a tin."

He woke about seven the next morning and came charging into her bedroom.

"Presents today?" he said. He looked the epitome of cute, standing there: eyes wide, one side of his face covered in pillow marks.

"Yes, sweetie. Presents today."

She thought he might ask if Albert was coming, but he didn't. She'd told him he couldn't make it and would come as soon as he could. Jake had seemed happy with that. Stephanie wasn't too happy with Albert, though. Not only wasn't he coming, the presents he'd promised to send by special courier for Jake hadn't turned up.

Usually he would come into her bed for a cuddle, but this morning he was tugging her duvet, desperate for her to get up so they could go downstairs.

He ripped the paper off all the books, puzzles and games, like some kind of wild animal. As she'd hoped, the present he loved most was the Bob the Builder tool belt. Their mutual joy was shattered, however, by the day's first tantrum.

Estelle and Harry had sent him a wading pool (for Hanukkah, rather than Christmas, but Stephanie had kept it until today for him to open). Why they hadn't come up with something slightly less season specific, Stephanie had no idea. She did her best to explain to Jake that they would have to put it away until the summer, but he could see no earthly reason why Stephanie shouldn't fill it with water there and then, so that he could splash around in the living room. In the end, unable to fight or reason with his screams and tears any longer, she gave in.

She covered the carpet in bath towels, blew up the pool and began carting saucepans of warm water from the kitchen into the living room. This was accompanied by Jake stripping off his clothes, dancing and clapping like a leprechaun on Ecstasy. When it contained perhaps an inch of water, she added some bath bubbles. Jake splashed around for a few minutes, maybe. Then he sat down in the bubbles and stayed there for the next hour and a half—serenely munching toast, biscuits and crisps, and watching his *Chitty Chitty Bang Bang* video.

"**What?** Albert didn't send anything for Jake?" Lizzie said, carving a cross into the base of a brussels sprout. She'd arrived just after ten to give Stephanie a hand. The three boys were in the living room (now minus the wading pool), where *Chitty Chitty Bang Bang* was playing for the second time.

"Nothing. I mean it's possible there was some mix-up with the courier company, but it's unlikely."

"Anything's possible at Christmas," Lizzie said, pincering a stray sprout leaf off her pink-and-white-striped rugby shirt. "Albert's a lot of things, but he's not mean."

"No, but he gets very tied up with his own life and forgets. I know he doesn't do it on purpose. It's just the way he is."

Lizzie wondered if it was too early for a glass of mulled wine. They decided it wasn't. Lizzie had transported it from her house in two giant orange juice bottles. Stephanie twisted off the top of one of them and poured the wine into a large spaghetti saucepan. It had just begun to simmer, giving off a glorious clovey, cinnamony aroma, when the doorbell rang. It was Estelle and Harry. "But, Mum, I wasn't expecting you two for hours."

"Your mother thought you might need a hand," Harry said.

"That's sweet, but I did say Lizzie was coming."

They came into the kitchen. Harry was carrying a Waitrose bag full of Belgian chocolates, truffles and packets of candy for the children. After they'd kissed Lizzie hello, Harry went into the living room to watch TV with the boys.

"I wanted to make sure you had everything under control," Estelle said.

"Oh, I think everything's fine, Mum."

Estelle went over to the turkey, which Stephanie was about to put in the oven. "No, no, darling. You can't leave it like that. You haven't greased the inside. What you need to do is gently pull the skin away from the meat. Then you slip your hand inside and smear it with butter. That way it doesn't dry out. Here, let me show you."

She took a large Sabatier knife from the drawer and rolled up her sleeves.

"Now then," she said when she'd finished, "shall I make the sweet-and-sour cabbage?"

"Tell you what, Mrs. Glassman," Lizzie said, oozing charm and tact, "the twins have been up since six and they're getting a bit stir-crazy. You and Mr. Glassman wouldn't take them for a walk in Highgate Woods, would you? I'm sure Jake would come too."

"Oh, God. Absolutely," Stephanie said. "Tell him he doesn't have to take his Bob the Builder belt off."

"Well, if you're sure you can manage. Remember to parboil the potatoes first and shake them afterward. Then the surface gets jagged and uneven and they crisp up better in the oven."

"Right you are," Lizzie said.

"You are a genius," Stephanie said to Lizzie after her parents and the children had gone. "They could use you at the U.N. Security Council."

After Harry, Estelle and the children got back from their walk, Harry went to fetch Grandma Lilly. They got back a little after one, just as Cass was pulling up in her Z4. Underneath her coat she was wearing a stunning acid green skirt and tight black silk blouse. She was carrying three bottles of champagne and a Harrods Food Hall bag: "Just some pâté and a teeny pot of Beluga."

Lilly presented Stephanie with a giant box of Milk Tray with a photograph of a Scottish terrier on the lid.

"Oh, and buy something nice for Jakey," she said, pressing a ten-pound note into Stephanie's other hand. She was suddenly transported back to all those childhood Hanukkahs and the whiskery old aunts.

The three friends had agreed on no presents for the grownups, other than edible contributions and small gifts for the children. But Lizzie, being Lizzie, had gotten presents for the adults, too. Kindling kits. Homemade. Everybody was handed a silver bucket covered in cellophane and topped with a red and green ribbon. Inside were a bundle of twigs neatly tied with more ribbon, corncobs, long matches, dried sage, orange peel and nutshells.

"My God, a Laura Ashley arson kit," Cass giggled, but only Stephanie heard.

Everybody oohed and aahed and said how clever Lizzie was—even Lilly, who thought it was some kind of trendy bouquet garni.

Cass bought the twins *Lamb's Tales from Shakespeare,* which Lizzie couldn't have been more thrilled about. The boys looked distinctly unimpressed until they started flicking through the books. A glistening fake dog poo fell out of one and a patch of gaudy plastic vomit from the other. Lizzie looked distinctly unamused, but the boys had hysterics. Estelle pretended not to have noticed.

"Oh, come on, Lizzie," Cass said, "it's Christmas. Lighten up. What did you and Dom get them, a glockenspiel each?"

"No, a puppet theater, actually."

"I rest my case."

Lizzie let out a slow breath. "Oh, I'm sorry. You're right. They deserve some fun. I think I'm more upset about Dom missing Christmas than I thought."

"I know, sweetie," Cass said kindly. Then she topped off Lizzie's glass with champagne.

Cass bought Jake police officer accessories, which included a working torch, handcuffs and a whistle. "I have to say, I nearly kept the handcuffs for myself," she cackled. Lizzie got him a sun-catcher kit. Jake ripped into the box, took out the clear plastic shapes, but didn't seem remotely interested.

"See, Jake, you paint them." Lizzie held up the paint box. "Then you can hang them in your bedroom and watch how they catch the light."

Jake still wasn't interested. Stephanie apologized on her son's behalf and said he was overexcited and probably needed a nap.

Lizzie also got him a plastic iron and miniature ironing board. Harry visibly blanched at this. He started to clear his throat to say something, but Estelle dug him in the ribs.

"Dougal and Archie loved their ironing board and Hoover when they were little. I think it's so important not to reinforce sexual stereotypes, don't you?"

"Absolutely," said Stephanie, thanking Lizzie and Cass profusely.

Apart from Dougal putting his dog turd on top of Lilly's gravlax, which didn't go down too well, and the twins disappearing to the loo during the main course and tipping all the goo from Jake's lava lamp down the bathroom sink, lunch went off without incident. Harry went on about his junk e-mail and lectured everybody on his theory that the Apollo moon landings had never really happened. Finally he decided to ask somebody else a question. Unfortunately it was Cass, who was pretty well oiled by then.

"So, Cass, how are things in the advertising business?"

"Oh, not bad. We've just taken on this new account. Fem-guard Tampons. We're trying to come up with a slogan. I'm thinking, 'Fem-guard Tampons—so natural you'll wish every day was that time of the month.' What do you think?"

Happy as Harry was to discuss penis extensions, he drew the line at women's sanitary arrangements. He turned crimson by way of reply.

"More cranberry sauce, Harry?" Cass said absentmindedly.

By four o'clock, Harry and Lilly were snoring at opposite ends of the sofa and the children were careening around the house and overdosing on refined sugars—today at least, Lizzie had given up trying to fight it. The rest of them were in the kitchen scraping plates and feeling bloated from too much food. They all agreed it had been the most sumptuous of Christmas lunches. Even Estelle was fulsome in her praise.

"Although it always helps when you have a good teacher," she said. "I taught her everything she knows." Stephanie put an arm around her mother's shoulders.

"Yeah, I know. Thanks, Mum." She gave her mother a kiss. Estelle positively glowed with pride. Just then the front doorbell rang. Stephanie looked up from loading the dishwasher.

"Who on earth could that be?" She wiped her hands on a cloth and went into the hall. As she opened the front door she was greeted by a tall male figure in biker leathers.

"Hey, *principessa!*"

Chapter 6

"Albert?"

"Er, I was when I last checked." His entire face was beaming. He threw his arms around her and wished her a merry Christmas.

"I don't believe it," Stephanie gasped. "Come in. Come in. Merry Christmas."

"So, how've you been?" he asked her.

"Fine. Really fine. Got a full house today, of course. Wow, you coming is going to be the best ever Christmas present for Jake."

"I can't wait to see him."

"But what are you doing here?"

"The Universal job fell through. So I hopped a plane."

"But why didn't you say something?"

"I wanted to surprise you."

"Well, you've certainly succeeded."

She asked him where he was staying. "Tom's apartment

in Kentish Town. He's away for the holidays. Loaned me his bike, too."

"Albert!" It was Estelle. "I thought I recognized the voice. Then I thought no, it can't be."

"Hey, Estelle," he said, hugging her and lifting her several inches off the floor. "Listen, is there something different about you?"

"I don't know. Is there?"

"I swear you've lost weight."

She blushed. Stephanie's eyes turned heavenward.

"Well, funny you should say that," Estelle said. "I've been on this special diet. You only eat protein and veg."

"Oh, that's real big in the U.S. Everybody is into the no-carbs thing. Anyway, it really seems to be working."

"You think so?" Estelle simpered. "You really think so?"

"Estelle, believe me. You look like a girl."

"And you are still a dreadful charmer," Estelle giggled.

"Come on, Albert," Stephanie said. "Let's go and find Jake. I think he's in the living room." He put his helmet on the hall table and took off his leather jacket. Underneath he was wearing a plain white T-shirt. It wasn't tight, but Stephanie couldn't help noticing the outline of his muscular body underneath.

"Dad, Grandma, wake up. Albert's here."

They both stirred on the sofa.

"Albert? Albert who?" Grandma said woozily.

"It's me, Grandma Lilly."

She sat bolt upright. "But we weren't expecting you."

"I wanted it to be a surprise." He bent over and kissed her.

"Albert, listen. Now that you're here, why don't you propose to Stephanie. You know you'd make such a lovely little family."

93

"Grandma!" Stephanie yelped. "Please."

By now Harry was on his feet, hand outstretched. "Albert. Great to see you. So, how's the stunt game?"

"It's good, Harry. Like falling off a log."

"So, what are you driving these days?"

"A fancy Honda Gold Wing. Borrowed it from a friend."

Estelle interrupted to offer Albert a cup of tea. "It'll help perk you up from the jet lag."

"I tell you what's good for jet lag," Harry said. "Char siu pork."

"Tea would be great," Albert said.

Estelle disappeared. "So, where's Jake?" Albert asked. Stephanie said she didn't know and suspected he might be hiding because of all the commotion. Harry said he'd heard the boys thumping around upstairs. As they climbed the stairs, they passed Dougal and Archie, who were charging down. Jake was in his room, bouncing on the bed.

"Hey, Jakey," Albert boomed. "How's my big guy?"

Jake carried on bouncing.

"Jakey," Stephanie said softly. "Look, Daddy's here."

Still no reaction.

"Jake, do you remember me? I haven't seen you for a while."

Jake landed on his bottom. Then he turned and looked at the photograph next to his bed. "My daddy?"

Albert came and sat next to him on the bed. "That's me. Mommy took that photograph the last time I was here. When we went to the zoo, remember?"

He grinned and nodded. "We went on da camel."

"Yes, Jakey, that's right. You and me, we went on the camel. Just the two of us."

"He was called Zebedee."

"That's right, Jakey." Albert shot Stephanie a broad smile.

"You remember. He was called Zebedee. Zebedee the camel." Jake giggled and let Albert swallow him in a great big bear hug.

"Oh, I've missed you, Jake. I've really missed you."

"Cass! Lizzie!"

More hugs—except Cass and Albert didn't so much hug as practically snog.

"God, you're beautiful," Cass purred, shamelessly running her hands over his torso. "Steph, I can't imagine why you let this man get away. You can always marry me, you know, Albert. I know a few stunt tricks of my own. I could show you if you like."

Albert grinned.

"Cass has been on the mulled wine all day," Lizzie explained. "It's great to see you, Albert. You're looking well."

"You too. How are the twins?"

"They're great."

"And Dom?"

"In Tokyo. Big merger thing."

"Same-ol', same-ol', then."

Lizzie smiled. "Yeah, same-ol', same-ol'."

Estelle and Harry left after tea because Lilly said she was getting tired. "Oh, by the way," she said to Stephanie before she left, "I found a tai chi class at the local community center. It's specially designed for the over-sixties. You know me, in for a penny in for a pound, so I booked a course."

Albert sat on the floor looking through dinosaur books with Jake and the twins. The three women were lolling on the sofas. "Oh, by the way," Albert said, "I'm sorry about

Jake's presents. I didn't forget. They're on their way. I asked my new . . ." he paused, searching for the right words, ". . . romantic interest to bring them over in a cab. She was taking a shower when I left, but she won't be long. I hope it's OK, her coming."

"Of course," Stephanie said.

"Oh, God, Albert," Cass said. "Not another romantic interest. I make lines of coke last longer than your relationships with women. And they're all the same—the lip liner, the pneumatic boobs, brains as thick as custard. If you closed your eyes, you'd never tell them apart." Albert just smiled. He liked Cass and never got offended when she challenged him.

Sunnie Ellaye was the usual Albert-type flake, although she was minus the lip liner, and according to Cass—who accidentally-on-purpose collided with her chest region within ten minutes of her arriving—the double Ds stroke Es were definitely her own.

She was more arty than brassy, though, with spiky tangerine hair and four-inch-high red platforms. She was, however, beautiful and very, very thin. Cass muttered something uncharitable about a spinal cord in flares, and then admitted she was just jealous. Stephanie immediately offered her a drink. "I've got champagne, mulled wine." Sunnie Ellaye said she didn't do alcohol. "So toxic. Say, do you have any guava nectar?"

"Er, don't think so," Stephanie said. "How about a cup of tea?"

"Ooh, that would be great. Green if you have it. It's so cleansing."

"Sorry, just Tetley's, I'm afraid."

Sunnie Ellaye opened her bag and took out a handful of tea bags.

Albert took one. "I'll do it," he said, patting her on the

behind. While Albert went off to make green tea, Stephanie led Sunnie Ellaye into the living room and introduced her to Lizzie and Cass. "You know, I love these London houses," she said. "They're so . . ." Several seconds ticked by, followed by several more. "Oh, God, what is that word?"

"Characterful?" Stephanie suggested.

She shook her head. "Nope."

"Charming?"

"Uh-uh. What is it? What is it?" Another beat or two. "No, I've got it . . . cute. That's it. Cute. And old."

Lizzie and Cass exchanged "We've got a right one here" looks.

"You're lucky you caught us when you did," Stephanie said. "We only just had running water installed."

A pause. "Really?" Then she burst out laughing: "You're joking, right? I geddit. This is that famous Briddish irony thing everybody talks about. Oh, God, this is so cool, my first Briddish irony. Hang on. Hang on. Let's see if I can do it."

Everybody waited. "Oooh, oooh. I goddit. I goddit. How's this? . . . Right-ho, Mary Poppins, let's jump into one of them there pavement pictures." By now Albert had come back. He was holding a mug of tea in one hand and a large plastic bag full of presents in the other.

"Isn't she just adorable?" he smiled. He was asking everybody, but his eyes were on Sunnie. He handed her the tea and kissed the end of her nose. "You know, when I'm with this woman all I ever do is laugh. But actually, sweetie, what you just did isn't irony, it's simply a very bad impersonation of Dick Van Dyke."

"So, Sunnie Ellaye, where are you from?" Lizzie asked. "I take it with a name like that, you were born in Los Angeles."

"No, Boise, Idaho. Actually, I'm one-sixteenth Russian,

one-eighth French, one thirty-twoth Irish and one-eighth Chinese acrobat."

"Which only adds up to eleven thirty-twoths." Albert laughed. "But what the heck?" He put the bag of presents down on the floor.

"And what do you do?" Cass asked her.

"I'm a trainee Reiki master slash lap dancer."

"Really?" Cass said without missing a beat.

"Lap dancing just pays my tuition." Cass nodded.

"Reiki, that's some kind of laying on of hands healing thing, isn't it?" Stephanie said.

"Yes. It's about channeling the universal life force into the body."

"So, getting back to lap dancing," Cass said. "How does it work? I mean, are you expected to . . ."

Sunnie Ellaye looked horrified. "Oh, my God, no. Although I get propositioned all the time. I dance and that's strictly it. Actually, it's how I met Albert."

"You've started going to lap dancing clubs?" Stephanie said, quickly adding: "Not that it's any of my business, of course."

He shrugged. "Bachelor night thing."

"But of course." Stephanie grinned.

"And I danced for you, didn't I, sweetie?" She sat down next to him on the sofa and began running her fingers, in tiny footstep motions, along the inside of his thigh. "And that was it. We felt this instant spiritual connection."

"I bet you did," Cass said as Sunnie and Albert began smooching on the sofa.

Eventually they stopped and Albert began taking presents out of the bag. "Steph, I got you this. I know you like it. It's not much. Just to say thank you for—you know. Everything."

It was a huge bottle of First by Van Cleef and Arpels, her favorite perfume.

"Oh, thank you, Albert. That is so thoughtful. There must be a gallon there." She went over and kissed him on the cheek.

By now it was past seven and Jake was beyond exhaustion. He was running manically round the room, making a loud buzzing sound. When Stephanie asked him what he was doing, he said he "be a buzzy beefly." After minutes of coaxing he finally agreed to sit on Stephanie's lap. He couldn't be bothered to open the presents, so Albert did it. The first was a baseball glove.

"See, Jake, I'll take you into the park and we can play catch."

Jake gave a serious nod, despite having not the remotest understanding of what Albert was going on about.

Then came the American football. Identical reaction from Jake. When it came to the toy cruise missile launcher, Lizzie's eyes began to bulge. When he produced the radio-controlled tank, she couldn't keep quiet. She cleared her throat. Stephanie muttered, "Lizzie, let it go. Just let it go." Cass sat grinning with anticipation.

"Call me quaint," Lizzie said, sounding like some lady bountiful tweedy type, "but the twins were into Peter Rabbit and Miss Moppet when they were Jake's age, not playing with imitation weapons of mass destruction."

Albert laughed and said kids didn't associate these toys with war. They were just fun.

"And you think death is fun, do you?"

"No. I'm not saying that. I'm just saying that children don't make that connection. They enjoy pushing buttons and making a noise."

"Lizzie," Stephanie whispered, "if you scale the moral high ground any higher, you'll have a nosebleed. Leave it. I'll deal with this."

"And a boy has to be brought up to be a boy," Albert went on. "If you know what I mean. No son of mine is going to read books about Miss Moppet."

"Or, God forbid, play with irons and ironing boards," Cass muttered, eyes gleaming with mischief. Stephanie dug her in the ribs.

"Oh, I love Miss Moppet," Sunnie Ellaye piped up. "I saw her in Vegas once. You really can't tell she's a man."

Albert helped Stephanie put Jake to bed after everyone left, not that much help was needed. He fell asleep virtually the moment his head touched the pillow.

"He's starting to look like me," Albert said, stroking Jake's cheek.

"Isn't he?" She smiled.

"I wish I could be here more. It tears me apart, not seeing him."

She put her hand on his shoulder. "I'm sorry."

"Hey, it's not your fault. So, what do you think of Sunnie?"

"I think she's very sweet," Stephanie said diplomatically.

"Yeah, I think so too," he said.

She switched off the bedside light and they went downstairs. Sunnie Ellaye was in the kitchen making another green tea. As soon as Albert walked in she draped her arms around him and began planting little kisses on his face. "Sunnie-Wunnie missed you," she said in a silly, childlike voice.

"Me too, babe," he said in between nibbling her lips.

"Right, food," Stephanie broke in, resisting the urge to put her finger down her throat. "You two haven't had a thing. How about I make some turkey sandwiches?"

"Great," Albert said. "But you sit down. I'll do it."

"I'd prefer some stir-fried tofu, maybe, if you have it," Sunnie Ellaye said. "I don't actually eat anything that had a parent."

"Actually, I'm fresh out of tofu," Stephanie said. Sunnie compromised on organic peanut butter on Hovis. While Albert made the sandwiches, Stephanie started unloading the dishwasher. Sunnie stood next to her, sipping her tea and chatting away.

"Ooh, what's that?" Sunnie said, picking up a three-inch piece of twisted stainless steel.

"Ah, funny you should ask," Stephanie said. "I'd never seen one before, either. It belongs to the chap who owns the house. Lizzie found it when we were preparing the turkey. It's a turkey lacer. You thread it through the skin and it stops the stuffing from falling out."

"Really? God, it's so . . ."

Long pause.

"Cute?" Stephanie suggested.

"No. That's not it."

"Useful? Brilliant? Inventive? Clever?"

"No. I'll get there. I'll get there."

Sunnie stood looking at it. "Interuterine! That's it. It's just so interuterine."

$\mathcal{S}$*tephanie* invited Albert and Sunnie Ellaye over for a fry-up breakfast on Boxing Day. In the end Sunnie didn't come because she wanted to catch up on her sleep.

"What I always wanted to know," Albert said, tucking into his streaky bacon, "is where a nice Jewish girl like you got the taste for pig?"

"Ah. Forbidden fruit," she said. "The smell used to waft

into our kitchen from our next-door neighbor's house. I re-member begging my mother to switch the fan onto suck."

Afterward they took Jake for a walk on Hampstead Heath. Except Jake spent most of his time on Albert's shoulders and screaming with delight.

"So, how's it working out with Mrs. M.?" Albert asked.

"Not so good." She explained.

"Your mother's looking after Jake? God knows I love Estelle, but she must be giving you hell."

"Not hell exactly." Stephanie smiled. "But close."

He didn't say anything for a moment. "Look, this may sound crazy, but think about it before you say no. I'm not working again until the middle of February. A few things didn't work out and so I decided to give myself a few weeks' break. Sunnie is only here for a few days because she's off to some Reiki conference in Cornwall, then back to L.A. I'd planned to take a trip to Europe, but I don't have to. Why don't I stay here and look after Jake? I'm desperate to get to know him. I've already missed so much of his growing up."

"Oh, it's a lovely thought, Albert. But I'm not sure it would work. I mean, you love playing with Jake for an hour or so, but what about when he makes a mess, throws temper tantrums? Children this age are so demanding. They need en-tertaining all the time and you can't let him out of your sight for a second. It's exhausting."

"But why don't I give it a try? Maybe there are bits of me I haven't discovered. I've got this feeling I might enjoy it. I'm bound to make mistakes, but I'm not an idiot, he won't come to any physical harm. I promise."

She looked at him. She could see in his eyes he really wanted to do this. And he was Jake's father. How could she say no?

"OK."

"We've got a deal?" he said, starting to laugh. She nodded. He turned his head up toward Jake, who was still
perched on his shoulders.

"Hear that, Jakey? We've just gotten ourselves a deal."

*O*n New Year's Eve, Cass had a party. The twins spent the
night at Stephanie's, and since Harry and Estelle never went
out on New Year's Eve on account of all the drunks and
tramps, they came to babysit.

The party was a housewarming as much as anything.
Cass had just bought a loft in a newly converted warehouse
near Camden Lock. Inside it was all white and steel and
installation-type artworks. The first time Lizzie saw it she'd
taken one look at the high metal-pronged kitchen stools and
blanched.

"Aren't they great?" Cass had said, purposely winding
her up. "You sit down and get a smear test at the same time."

Lizzie's verdict was that the loft was "all very arty, but not
exactly comfortable." She kept buying Cass huge bunches of
lilies, "just to soften the place up a bit."

Stephanie, on the other hand, adored it and was quite
open about being puce with envy.

The night of the party, the place was full of stoned advertising types and Sloaney PRs. The eats, which had been
done by some übertrendy Thai caterer, were sublime. Cass
was wearing a velvet dress in deepest plum, which was thigh
high and pretty much backless and frontless—or as Albert put
it: "pretty much pointless." Courtesy of a preparty line or
two, Cass was positively brimming with festive cheer. She
must have kissed everybody and told them how much she
loved them at least half a dozen times.

Most people were dancing in the "living space," which

was decked out in candles and trendy tubular fairy lighting. The rest were in the kitchen. Here Albert—draped in
Sunnie Ellaye (body glitter, fairy queen tiara)—was holding
court, telling stories and jokes. He was in particularly good
form and everybody was falling about—especially Lizzie. She
looked a bit frumpy, though, Stephanie thought—which was
hard with a figure like hers. She would have looked sensational in something short and clingy, but instead she was
wearing a chain-store floral skirt and little velvet-edged cardigan. It was pretty, just not sexy. Dom, on the other hand, was
looking severely cute in a dark navy suit with matching open-
necked shirt. But he seemed subdued. When Albert cracked
yet another joke, he barely reacted. In the taxi they'd shared
on the way over, Lizzie had been rabbiting away, but he'd
barely looked at her, let alone responded. His mind was
clearly elsewhere.

"Is Dom OK?" Stephanie said to Lizzie when they went
out onto the balcony to get some fresh air.

"Oh, you know, he's just exhausted. Not really in the
party mood. He's off to Hong Kong day after tomorrow,
poor love."

"You keep going on about it, but you two really do need
to get away together."

"I know. And he's promised we will. As soon as this case
is over."

A bit later Stephanie mentioned the Lizzie-Dom situation to Cass. She agreed there was something not right. She'd
noticed Dom disappearing into the bedroom a couple of
times.

"I'm pretty sure he was making calls on his mobile.
Couldn't hear anything. Probably business, though."

"On New Year's Eve?"

Cass agreed it wasn't very likely—even for Dom.

"You know what I think?" Stephanie said. "I reckon Dom's having an affair. You remember when we were over there just before Christmas. He seemed off with her then."

"I know," Cass said. "I've been thinking the same."

At midnight Dom was nowhere to be seen. Albert was at one end of the room snogging Sunnie Ellaye. Cass was at the other end, tongue down some seven-foot hunk. Lizzie and Stephanie looked at each other, shrugged and burst into giggles.

"Guess it's just you and me, then," Stephanie said.

"Happy New Year, hon," Lizzie said, hugging her friend tightly.

"Yeah, happy New Year," Stephanie said, returning the hug. When Lizzie pulled away she was smiling, but Stephanie was sure her eyes were glistening with tears. A few moments later Cass came over to wish them happy New Year.

"God, I need a man," she said. "Maybe having these braces fitted was a mistake. They're really putting them off, and I need sex. It's been weeks. I just get so cranky."

"But you were just snogging that amazing-looking bloke," Lizzie said.

"Oh, that's just Charlie."

"What do you mean 'just'? He's gorgeous."

"I know. Gorgeous and exceedingly gay."

"But he was tonguing your tonsils," Stephanie said.

"Only to be polite. He knew I didn't have a bloke."

"Oh, I've done things like that," Lizzie said. "I remember once, just before I met Dom, a chap named Freddie took me on this really romantic weekend to Paris. He wouldn't let me pay for a thing. On the way home he asked me to marry him. Of course I said yes. I didn't know what else to do. It seemed rude to refuse. Took me ages to pluck up the courage to tell him I wasn't really interested."

Stephanie got home just after three. She lay in the dark, hands behind her head, daring herself to imagine the excitement the new year might bring: a new agent, new opportunities. Oh, and a man. As she started to doze off, she imagined all kinds of scenarios—giving a brilliant lead performance in a West End show and the queen leading the audience in a standing ovation, bringing the house down at the Palladium. At the back of her mind, though, she couldn't help worrying about Lizzie and Dom. Christ, if they didn't make it, what hope was there for everybody else?

Chapter 7

By the end of the first week of January, Stephanie still had no offers of work. Albert popped in each day to see Jake. As she'd suspected, Albert was less than keen on Jake playing with an iron and ironing board.

"For crying out loud, Steph, you're turning my son into a faggot."

"Albert, that is nonsense. You can't *turn* a person gay. And even if you could, I'm sure the tank and cruise missile launcher will redress the balance."

She made it clear that if he insisted on her getting rid of the ironing board, she would also take away the toys he had bought. He didn't say another word.

In the afternoons he took Sunnie Ellaye sightseeing.

"Did you know that some of the dead people in Westminster Abbey were buried standing up?" Sunnie said after one particular outing. "Can you imagine what that does to their arches?"

Two or three times they took Jake with them on their

jaunts. Each time he came back in one piece and perfectly content, which Stephanie found remarkably encouraging. She also noticed that Sunnie Ellaye, despite her dippiness—or maybe because of it—seemed to particularly enjoy getting down on her knees and playing with Jake.

On the eighth, Sunnie left for her Reiki conference and on the ninth, Eileen Griffin rang with a job for Stephanie: playing the piano in the lounge at the Park Royal Hotel in Kensington. It was weekdays only, from three until eight. Tea to cocktails. Or as Stephanie put it: "Edelweiss" to "Moon River."

The hours suited her perfectly. She had the mornings with Jake, and since he was usually in bed by half past six, it meant Albert wouldn't have too strenuous a day. On top of that, Jake went to playgroup two afternoons a week, which made it even easier.

Albert arrived every day around lunchtime and went back to his flat every evening. By now Stephanie was confident that no physical harm would come to Jake, but it soon became clear that Albert had a hard time remembering the child was only two and a half. For a start, he let him pee into the loo—on his own. Of course it was much too high for him and when Stephanie got home each night, there were puddles of wee all over the floor.

"Albert, he has to pee into his potty and you have to hold it."

"What? I have to hold his penis?"

"No, you have to hold the potty. But sometimes he loses concentration, so, yeah, occasionally, you do need to point him in the right direction."

"Oh, man!" Albert also couldn't understand why Jake refused to sit still on the sofa with him and watch American football on Sky. Then he would feed him unsuitable food.

"I thought we'd have a treat, so I took him to Pizza Express. He didn't eat much, though."

"What did you order him?"

"Same as me—an American Hot. Except, of course, they're so small I had two."

She didn't know whether to laugh or to cry.

One night when she got home, there was no sign of them. The minutes turned into an hour. Then an hour and a half. She was starting to get really worried. It was hours past Jake's bedtime and she was convinced something dreadful had happened to him and that he was in hospital. She kept trying Albert's mobile, but there was no reply. About half past ten she heard Albert's key in the door. He came in cradling a sound-asleep Jake.

"Christ, Albert, where on earth have you been? I've been worried sick."

"Soccer game. West Ham was playing Arsenal, at home. West Ham won by three to nothing. Great match."

"Hang on. Let me get this straight. You took a two-and-a-half-year-old to a football match?"

"Sure. He loved it."

"Albert, how could you? And how could he love it? He's a baby. He must have been petrified. The crowd and the noise, for one thing. And West Ham's really rough. It's full of bloody hooligans. God, Albert, anything could have happened."

"But nothing did. We ate hot dogs and burgers—"

"Jake ate hot dogs? From a vendor? Have you any idea of the crap they put in those things? Christ, he could have bloody mad cow disease."

"Steph, calm down. He's fine. We had the best time. Now why don't you let me put him to bed."

And Jake continued to be fine. He displayed neither

emotional trauma from having gone to see West Ham nor even the remotest physical reaction to the food. Nevertheless, Stephanie did keep reminding Albert—purely to make him feel guilty—that it can take thirty years for the first symptoms of mad cow disease to appear.

When Stephanie mentioned to Lizzie that Albert's parenting skills weren't quite A-level, Lizzie volunteered to drop in on Albert for coffee from time to time.

"That way I can give him a few tactful pointers."

The transformation was remarkable. Lizzie turned up with her battered Penelope Leach, as well as *Fun and Games for Toddlers* and *Amazing Meals for Kids*. Instead of getting offended, Albert devoured the books. By the end of the third week, Albert had built a cardboard Wendy House, in which they would sit reading stories, or doing puzzles, Jake gobbling up Albert's "faces." These were organic oatcakes covered in low-fat cheese spread and finished off with smiley faces made from raisins and tiny bits of chopped up veggies. Fondant Fancies were long forgotten. By now Albert also knew Piaget's theory of child development by heart. One night Stephanie came home feeling especially tired because she'd had to wait nearly an hour for a train. Jake, who'd had a late nap and wasn't remotely ready for bed, came rushing up to her, desperate for her to do a puzzle with him.

"Oh, just a minute, Jake, I'm really exhausted. Let me sit down and have a cup of tea first."

Jake started to whine.

"Jake, give me a break. Please, poppet."

Albert picked him up, took him to the kitchen table and started doing the puzzle.

"You see, Steph," he said, "Jake is still at what Piaget calls the *preoperational* stage. As well as not yet being able to conceptualize abstractly, he remains totally egocentric and incapable of taking the perspective of the other person." Albert smiled at her. "I, on the other hand," he continued, "am not quite so egocentric. As a sensitive adult, I am able to appreciate you've had a crappy journey home and am happy to make you a nice cup of tea."

"You're really enjoying this whole daddy thing, aren't you?" she said after he'd finally put Jake to bed.

"Like you wouldn't believe."

"You don't know how happy that makes me," she said.

"Me too."

Then, out of the blue, he kissed her, briefly, on the lips. She stood there blinking with surprise, aware that if he'd put his arms around her and kissed her properly, she probably wouldn't have pushed him away.

Each night she came home to a perfectly contented Jake, but the kitchen and living room were always a complete mess. Albert never tidied up the toys and it never occurred to him to scrape dirty dishes and pans and put them in the dish-washer. He was now preparing Jake's supper each evening—chicken casseroles, vegetable moussaka. Wonderful as his food was, the chaos he managed to cause was staggering. Being an Italian son, he'd never cooked in his life. Back in L.A., he ate out. He put his newfound talent down to his mother.

"I guess it's in the genes."

Stephanie was desperate not to let Albert think she was ungrateful, but one night she came home to a particularly spectacular pickle, which she knew would take ages to clean up. She decided to say something. She was tactful, but firm.

"I know," he said. "I'm sorry. You see, Jake and I made cupcakes this afternoon." He nodded toward the counter. There were two lopsided cakes left, sitting on the wire rack, covered in runny blue icing and sprinkles. "Jake saved them for you. I did mean to tidy up, but then he asked me to play a game. And I think the playing is more important than a tidy kitchen." She looked back at the wonky cakes and her face broke into a smile. She could hardly believe that the man who couldn't bear the thought of his son owning an ironing board was now baking cakes with him.

"If Jamie Oliver can bake cakes, then I guess I can too," Albert said when she started pulling his leg about the cupcakes. "Start to worry when you find me and Jake bonding over our embroidery...Look, there's plenty of lasagna. Why don't we get Jake to bed and have a quiet dinner, just the two of us. I bought a bottle of Chianti."

"OK. Sounds good," she said. The food was delicious. After dinner they went into the living room. They sat there, finishing the bottle of wine and talking about Jake.

Eventually he said he ought to get going.

"I guess," she said. By now the wine was making her feel distinctly mellow.

They both stood up. A couple of beats, then: "We had fun in Verona, didn't we?" he said.

"Oh, yes," she said softly. "We had fun."

Then he put his arms around her. There was no kiss, just the hug. She found herself hugging him back, running her hand up and down his spine.

"You know, I sometimes wonder..." his voice trailed off.

"What? What do you wonder?"

"Oh, nothing. It's nothing...Listen, I'd better go. I'll tidy the kitchen tomorrow."

"You bet you will," she smiled.

By now she'd had five rejections from West End theatrical agents. They'd all sent identical "not-quite-for-us-regretfully-we-will-be-passing-wishing-you-every-success-in-the-future" letters. There was one she still hadn't heard from, but she wasn't holding her breath, since Ossie Da Costa was London's top agent.

"Oh, you never know," said Lizzie, ever the optimist. "Just hang on in there. No news is good news." In Stephanie's experience, the very opposite was true. When people had good news to impart, they imparted it, on the whole, by phone—not in writing—and very quickly.

Then, one lunchtime, just as she was about to leave for work, the phone rang.

"I'm calling on behalf of Mr. Da Costa," the female voice said. "He has asked me to tell you that he loves your CD and would like you to come in and see him. He was wondering if next Monday would suit you?"

"I've heard of Ossie Da Costa," Albert said when she told him about the call. "He's pretty big, isn't he?"

"Big? Ossie Da Costa isn't just big. He's huge. Colossal. Albert, we are talking mega here."

Chapter 8

"I'm really sorry, Mr. Da Costa's not back from his morning run," the girl in reception said. "He shouldn't be long, though."

Noticing Stephanie's puzzled expression, she added, "New Year's resolution. He's trying to lose a bit of weight, so now he goes out for a jog between meetings."

She suggested Stephanie wait in his office. "Cappuccino?" Stephanie said that would be lovely.

Ossie Da Costa's office was in a smart block just off Shaftesbury Avenue. It was pretty much as she'd expected: early nineties worn gray carpet, ditto the black leather sofa, walls covered in black-and-white photographs of his most famous clients. In front of a large picture window was an equally large, sleek desk, clearly designed to intimidate.

She'd just taken a sip of her coffee when she heard the door open. She sprang to her feet. Ossie Da Costa came bounding in, full of apologies. He was still in his running gear, rubbing his forehead with a towel.

OK, so how come she didn't know? Over the years there must have been umpteen newspaper and magazine articles that had mentioned it. Had she really managed to miss all of them? And ages ago, when she first mentioned to people in the business she was thinking about changing agents, the name Ossie Da Costa must have come up a dozen times. Why had nobody pointed it out? Not one person had said, "Of course you know Ossie Da Costa is a midget." Not that it mattered, of course. Stephanie wasn't the kind of person to judge people by their size, any more than she would have judged them by their color or race.

"It's just that when you meet somebody for the first time," she would say to Cass on the phone later, "it's helpful to know that they are three foot nine."

"Didn't you know?"

"You knew?"

"Oh, come on, sweetie. *Le tout Londres* knows Ossie Da Costa is fun size. He's famous for it."

"Well," he said as they shook hands, his head disconcertingly level with her midriff, "it's great to finally put a face to the voice." He was balding, fiftyish at a guess. There was a brief but broad smile. As he asked her to sit down, she detected a hint of a south London accent. With a pronounced rolling motion, he walked over to his desk and stretched to pick up the phone. "Sheila, hold all my calls; move Shania's people back to midday...All right, if they have a plane to catch organize a conference call from Heathrow." He was pacing up and down, still dabbing his face with the towel. "Oh, and Sheila, could you run out and get me a fried egg sandwich on white toast with extra ketchup? And when I say extra, I mean lots. Right?" He turned to Stephanie and asked if she would like something.

"I'm fine, thanks."

"You know," he said, letting out a long breath, "I do all this exercise, but afterward I'm bloody famished." She nodded in agreement. He sniffed under one armpit. "You see, what I don't understand is this," he went on. "They say it's healthy to lift weights, right?"

"Absolutely."

"OK, well, here I am, carrying a few extra pounds," he patted his fun-size paunch. "I mean, why isn't that exercise? By rights, fat people should be the fittest people around." He gave a loud laugh. She wasn't sure what to make of him. Although he was clearly the polar opposite of laid-back, there was a warm openness about his face, not to mention this rather appealing self-deprecation, which made Stephanie think that underneath all the bluff and bluster, Ossie Da Costa might well be a bit of a pussycat.

"I'm afraid you've got me there," Stephanie said, her eyes suddenly fixed on the fun-size bulge in his Lycra shorts.

"Sorry to go banging on. It's a bit of a hobby of mine. So, moving on to you. In your letter you said you've had some experience in musicals?"

Stephanie's eyes remained on the bulge.

"Yes, but no big roles, just small parts."

Her hand flew to her mouth, but Ossie didn't seem to have noticed the faux pas. By now he had turned to face his giant swivel chair. She watched him lift his stumpy leg up onto the seat and then, with a certain amount of effort, draw up the other one so that he was kneeling on the seat. It reminded her of the way Jake climbed onto the sofa. In a second he had maneuvered himself back round to face her and was adjusting the cushions underneath him. "Well, I have to tell you, Stephanie," he said, "you have an exceptional voice. And when I say exceptional, I mean exceptional. Exceptional with a capital E. I just can't understand why you're not bigger."

"You, too. No, sorry...I mean, my mum and dad say that all the time too. Why aren't you bigger? As in, you know, why aren't *I* bigger? Not you. You already are. Which is why I'm here. As it were."

Ossie managed to ignore this pile-up of verbal car crashes.

He asked a few more questions about her theatrical and musical experience. All the time she was desperate not to let him think she was remotely bothered by his size. The more she tried to forget about it, the more obsessed she became, and the more size dominated the conversation. She found herself using phrases she never normally used—the long and the short of it, broad as it is long. As she spoke, her mind became obsessed with height-related problems. If Ossie was in a tall building, there was no way he could reach the top buttons in a lift. What did he do if he wanted to go to the twentieth floor? Press ten or twelve, and walk the rest?

Eventually Sheila—late forties, toffee-colored tanning bed tan—came in with his fried egg sandwich and a cup of coffee.

"Perrr-fect," he said as she put it in front of him. "Oh, and Sheila, I've run out of sweeteners. Could you pop out and get me some more? And my shirts need picking up from the dry cleaners. If you wouldn't mind..."

She rolled her eyes. He responded by grinning and blowing her a kiss. Then he turned to Stephanie: "She's been with me for seven years. She loves me really." By now Sheila had disappeared through the door. He called out to her: "Don't you love me really, Sheila?"

"No," came the reply.

"Don't take any notice," he laughed. "She worships me."

117

Then he asked Stephanie if she'd ever done any film work. She said she hadn't.

"Godfather," he said, biting into his sandwich, so that a mixture of egg yolk and ketchup began dripping down his chin as if he'd just squeezed a giant zit. "Best film ever made."

"So they say," she said.

He wiped his chin with his towel and took another huge bite.

"OK," he said, mouth full, "what's your favorite film?"

"Oh, I'm not sure I have one." Actually, she did. It was *The Sound of Music.* She must have watched the video twenty times, and the scene with Julie Andrews and Christopher Plummer in the gazebo always made her cry. Since everybody she'd ever mentioned this to made fun of her, she wasn't about to risk telling Ossie Da Costa.

"Come on. Everybody has a favorite film."

Her mind was a complete blank. She could think of nothing intelligent to say. "OK," she said eventually. *"The Tall Guy."* She wanted the ground to swallow her up. "I love Jeff Goldblum," she said in an attempt to rescue herself. Then she blew it. "But my son—he's two and a half—he adores *The Wizard of Oz.* He knows all the words to 'Welcome to Munchkin Land.' "

"Really?"

Shoot me. Just shoot me.

He put down his sandwich. "Anyway, getting back to you. I think—correction, I *know*—you have a very bright future ahead of you. With your voice, that gorgeous face of yours."

She blushed at the "gorgeous face" bit. Judging by the grin on his face, he was clearly flirting with her. "OK," he said, slapping his palm on the desk, "I'm not going to beat around the bush. I have no doubts about representing you. How would you feel about that?"

She wanted to get up and hug him. "Great. Fantastic. Wow. God. Brilliant."

"I'll take that as a yes, then." He picked up a Cuban cigar—almost as long as him. Very slowly he put the end in his mouth and moistened it. Then he leaned back in his chair.

"You know, when you do those Peggy Lee numbers, you sound exactly like her. Has anybody ever told you that?"

"Yes," she said, laughing. "Once or twice."

"Well, I have a project coming up that I think might be just perfect for you."

"You mean it involves singing Peggy Lee songs?"

"I can't say any more just now. It's still at a very early stage of development. But I think this could be a major turning point for you."

Major turning point. Major turning point. The phrase wasn't just music to her ears, it was a full-on bloody symphony. She could practically hear trumpets playing.

He said he was in no doubt that she was right for the project. "But it's not just me you have to convince. Does the name Sidney Doucette mean anything to you?"

"What, the American theatrical impresario? Who hasn't heard of him?"

Ossie explained that "the project" was Sidney Doucette's brainchild and that if Stephanie was to become involved, she would need to audition for him. Apparently Sidney was due in London the next day. Ossie suggested bringing him along to hear her at the Blues Café.

"Great. My next gig's on Thursday."

"Thursday it is, then. You know, I have high hopes for you, Ms. Glassman. High hopes."

He grinned at her again. Then he picked up a match with his chubby little fingers, lit it and began drawing on the cigar. Anybody watching would have seen that he could

119

barely take his eyes off her, but Stephanie was far too excited to notice.

She virtually floated down Shaftesbury Avenue. She'd done it. Not only had she found a new agent—not just any old agent, but the best in the business—he already had what sounded like some pretty major singing role in mind for her. God, this time next year she could be . . . but she was too superstitious to continue the thought. The only thing denting her elation was the thought of having to sack Eileen Griffin. To give the woman her due, she hadn't been entirely useless. The gigs she'd found her may not have been the most prestigious or well paid, but she'd kept Stephanie in work, which in turn had meant she'd been able to keep the bank happy— just. She decided to play it safe and not do anything until after the audition. Assuming it went well, she would write Eileen a letter, thanking her profusely for all her effort and hard work and telling her as tactfully as she could that she now felt the time had come to move on.

It was still only eleven. What she wanted to do was stay up in town and buy something really expensive and frivolous to celebrate. But since her credit cards were all maxed out, she decided to pop home, say hi to Jake and get changed before she headed off to the Park Royal.

Because of her meeting with Ossie Da Costa, Albert had come over earlier than usual to look after Jake. When she got home, Albert was in the living room watching a video of the previous night's Liverpool versus Juventus game.

"Hiya," she said. "Jake having a nap?"

Albert didn't look up. "Oh, come on," he shouted at the screen, "that was totally offside. This ref's a complete fucking tosser."

Stephanie burst out laughing.

"By George, he's got it."

"What? What have I got?"

"British football-speak. You sound just like a native."

"I've been to so many games over the years. It just starts to rub off, I guess."

"Jake asleep?" she asked again.

"What? Oh, yeah. Been a bit cranky, so I put him down for a nap."

She went into the hall to take off her coat, just as the halftime whistle blew. He pressed the remote onto fast forward.

"So, I saw Ossie Da Costa."

He shot round to face her. "Oh, God. Shit. Sorry. How'd it go? Say, didn't I read somewhere that he's a midget or something?"

"Now you tell me."

"You didn't know?"

"Nope."

"I guess I should have mentioned it, but I just assumed you knew. So, has he agreed to take you on?"

"Yep. Isn't that brilliant? I'm so excited. My heart's still racing. This is the biggest thing that has ever happened to me."

"That's great, *principessa,* really great."

She told him about Sidney Doucette and the secret project.

"Sidney Doucette? Wow. Could be interesting." He was facing the TV screen again. "I wouldn't get too worked up, though. Nine times out of ten, these things don't come to anything. Happens to me all the time. It's the nature of the business."

"You know, Albert, until now I never had you down as a glass-half-empty person."

121

He shrugged. "I just don't want to see you get disappointed, that's all . . . Oh, that should so have been a free kick. Did you see that, Steph? Is this ref watching the same game? Steph, could you turn down the oven? Jake'll probably sleep for an hour or so and I don't want his lunch to burn."

She went into the kitchen and turned down the oven control. There were lumps of Play-Doh all over the table and floor, a pile of dirty pans in the sink. Liberace was wandering around, making tiny mewing sounds. He was clearly desperate to be fed. She went back into the living room.

"Look, Albert, I really don't mean to nag, but—"

"Oh, by the way," he broke in. "Take a look on the kitchen counter. I did some drawing with Jake today. He did his first-ever person."

"He did?"

Lying on the counter was a sheet of computer paper. In the middle, Jake had drawn a wobbly purple circle, from which there sprouted four stringy yellow limbs. Albert had added the face. Underneath, in neat lowercase letters, he had written *mommy.*

"Goal! Yesss!" Albert cried out. "Sorry, what were you saying before? I missed it."

"No, it's OK," she said, still smiling at Jake's picture. "Wasn't important."

It was Monday, so she should have been singing at the Blues Café, but it was closed for a private party and she had the night off. Cass had phoned and said she'd been invited to a gallery opening in Shoreditch and did Stephanie fancy coming. Since Albert had nothing planned and seemed perfectly happy to babysit, she said yes.

The gallery—a converted shoe shop—was tiny. The vast,

brightly colored oil paintings made it look even smaller. There were eight, maybe ten, all produced by an artist named Ed Blackwell, who was making quite a name for himself painting pictures of food. The ones hanging here were part of a series called "BritNosh." There was a plate of roast beef and Yorkshire pudding, egg and chips, beans on toast and one Stephanie particularly liked: a six-by-four-foot fry-up, complete with black pudding and a giant dollop of ketchup.

Not only was the gallery tiny, it was packed. It felt like being on the tube in rush hour, before they banned smoking. Stephanie couldn't help feeling sorry for the waiters who were finding it virtually impossible to fight through the crush with their trays of drinks and nibbles. The two women arrived late because Cass had been to a cocktail do earlier. By the time they got to the gallery, she was already a bit tipsy and desperate for a pee. As she went off to find the loo, a waiter appeared with a tray of champagne. Stephanie helped herself to a glass. Just as she was bringing it to her lips, she felt herself being jostled heavily from behind. The champagne shot out of the glass and down her shirtfront. She swung round and came face-to-face with Frank Waterman.

"Steph! Hi." Then he saw what he'd done. "Oh, God, I am so sorry. Don't worry, I'll pay for the dry cleaning." As she gave the wet patch a few futile flicks with her fingers, she smiled and explained that since she'd had Jake, she didn't buy anything that wasn't machine washable.

"I didn't know you had a child," he said.

"Yep, he's two and a half." She stepped back to let a woman squeeze past, treading on somebody's toe as she did so.

"Ah, the terrible twos," he said. "My nephew used to refuse to get dressed in the mornings. Once my sister actually carted him off to playgroup in his pajamas." Stephanie said she knew the feeling.

"So, you're married. I didn't realize. Funny, I just assumed . . ."

"No, his dad and I aren't together, but he's very much on the scene as far as Jake's concerned."

He gave an approving nod. She was just thinking that Frank Waterman really did have the sexiest of smiles. Not only that, but judging by his eye line, he appeared to be admiring her breasts. She instinctively glanced down at them. The champagne had spilled mainly onto the right side of her shirtfront. Since she was wearing only the flimsiest of bras, it had soaked through to the skin and her now cold, erect nipple was sticking out like a coat hook. She instantly slapped her hand across her left shoulder, so that her arm obscured the nipple. "So," she said, clearing her throat. She was about to ask him how all the wedding plans were coming along, when a bloke in a kilt and Yoko Ono windscreen shades pushed his way between them. After he'd gone they both started laughing and Stephanie forgot what she'd been about to say.

"Don't you think the paintings are brilliant?" Frank said. He explained that Ed Blackwell was a friend of his. "I'm probably biased, but I think he's really talented."

She agreed. "I like the fry-up best." She confessed her own talent for cooking fry-ups. "Of course, the secret's in the beans," she said. She must have gone on for a solid minute expounding her overcooked bean theory and its role in the quintessential English breakfast.

"You know," he said, when she finally finished, "you've given me an entirely new perspective on baked beans."

She realized she'd been rambling. "Sorry. I do tend to go on a bit."

"You weren't at all," he said. "I'd really like to try them."

He was looking at her in a way that made her think it wasn't just her baked beans he wanted to try. She looked down at her feet, not quite sure what to say next. Once again she decided to change the subject. "By the way, I've found an agent who's interested in taking me on." She'd just finished explaining about Ossie Da Costa, the secret project and Thursday night's audition, when Cass emerged from the crowd. She was holding a half-empty champagne glass. Stephanie could tell by her rather glazed expression that she was more than a bit tipsy now. Stephanie did the introductions. Cass took one look at Frank and went into full-on vamp mode, licking her lips and running her fingers over her cleavage and neck as she spoke. "And can I say how much I enjoyed your Hamlet," she said, her voice dropping at least twenty octaves. "I was spellbound. Utterly spellbound. I love a man in a codpiece." Even though she knew Cass couldn't help herself and always flirted outrageously when she'd had a few drinks, Stephanie couldn't help going purple with embarrassment. Frank simply grinned and said he'd never actually played Hamlet.

"You haven't? Then who am I thinking of?"

Just then a girl with fuchsia hair and thick black-rimmed glasses came over to say Frank's car had arrived from the BBC. He explained that he was taking part in a Radio 4 arts discussion program on government cuts in arts funding. "Boring, but worthy . . . I'll see you, Steph. Been great to catch up again." He kissed her on both cheeks and waved good-bye to Cass.

"Believe me," Cass said after he'd gone, "he so has the hots for you. Did you see the way he looked at you as he kissed you good-bye?"

"Cass, let it go. Frank's just a bit of a flirt, that's all."

"Really? Is that what you call it?" As she lit a cigarette,

Cass lowered her head and started squinting at Stephanie's bust. "Is it me," she said, inhaling sharply, "or do you have one nipple sticking out?"

The next day, when Stephanie got home from the Park Royal, Albert was in the bathroom standing in front of the full-length medicine cabinet mirror, stripped to the waist. Balanced on the edge of the bath was a tub of hot wax.

"Hey, hope you don't mind," he said. "I thought maybe I should lose the hairs on my back, so I borrowed your leg wax."

As he ripped a gauze strip from his shoulder, they both winced—him with pain and her with more than mild distaste. Urrgh, Albert had started depilating? In her book it was fine for gay blokes to do it. It was part of the culture, but when straight men did it, it was just so gold neck chain and tanning bed tan.

"God, now I know what women go through." His eyes were watering.

"No, Albert. Try waxing your balls. Then you'll have more of an idea of what women go through."

"Ow, that really stings," he said, rubbing the bright red patch that had now appeared on his shoulder. "I thought I might look better with a smoother contour, but I'm not sure it's worth the pain." Contour? When had Albert started using words like *contour*?

"Sunnie suggested I start waxing. She said she preferred men with smooth skin. What do you think? Would I look better without the hair?" Suddenly it made sense. *Contour* was such a Sunnie word. "To be honest," Stephanie said, "unless you're thinking of joining the Village People, I wouldn't bother."

"God, you're right. I wasn't thinking." With that, he threw the gauze strip into the bin and then stood in front of the mirror again. "You know, I really need to get to the gym," he said, sucking in his stomach and running his hands over what she considered to be a perfectly defined six-pack. "I'm starting to lose some tone."

She patted his stomach. "Albert, you look great. Believe me."

"Really?" He turned his body so that he was facing the mirror side-on.

"Really . . . So, Jake in bed?"

"I guess. He's spending the night at your mother's."

"How come?"

"Well, she offered and I said yes—which means, *principessa*, that I can take you out to dinner."

"Wow. What's the occasion?"

"Well, for a start, we should celebrate because you've found a new agent—and on top of that I thought it would be good for us to spend some time together."

"OK, I'd like that."

She went upstairs, touched up her makeup and put on her new denim skirt and pink gypsy blouse.

They took a cab to Hampstead. He'd booked a table at KN, a trendy new bistro that had just opened on High Street.

While they waited for their first course, they drank Campari and soda.

"It was you who got me into Campari," she said, "when we were in Verona." She stirred the ice around her glass. "Do you remember how it took me ages to get a taste for it?"

He nodded and leaned back in his chair. "I've finished with Sunnie Ellaye," he said.

"Oh, Albert, I'm sorry. She was great. Daft as a brush, but I really liked her."

127

"Yeah, me too. And she adored Jake."

"So, once again, you just got bored," she said.

He shook his head. "It wasn't like that. It was kinda mutual. Her last boyfriend got back in touch and wanted her to give their relationship another chance, and at the same time I felt I needed some space. Some time to get my head straight. You know, since I've been here with Jake, I've felt myself changing, mellowing. Does that make sense?"

She told him it had never occurred to her that he would take to fatherhood in the way he had.

Throughout dinner, Albert was quieter and more thoughtful than she'd ever seen him. When his salad turned up already dressed—rather than with the dressing on the side, the way he'd asked—instead of making his usual loud, big-shot American fuss, he said nothing. She wasn't even sure he'd noticed.

"You know what I really feel guilty about?"

"What?"

"That I missed seeing him come into the world."

"Oh, Albert, that wasn't your fault. I went into labor a month early. There was nothing you could have done."

When they got home, she went into the kitchen and poured them some more wine. She took it into the living room. The fire was burning in the grate. He'd dimmed the lights and put "Stand by Me" on the CD player.

"We danced to this in Verona," he said. "The first night we made love. Remember?"

"Of course I remember." They stood looking at one another.

"Hey, *principessa,* come here."

She hesitated a moment. He held out his hand. She put down the wineglasses and walked slowly toward him. She let him wrap his arms around her, felt his cheek against hers as they swayed gently in time to the music. She closed her eyes and rested her head on his shoulder as they danced.

"I always think of us when I hear this song," he said softly.

"Yeah, me too."

First he kissed her cheek. A moment later he was kissing her on the lips and she was kissing him back with the same deep, urgent passion she'd kissed him with that first night in Verona.

She felt him pull the low elasticated neck of her gypsy blouse down over her shoulder. He kissed her neck, the tops of her breasts.

"I've missed you," he whispered.

She began unbuttoning his shirt. As she looked into his eyes, she knew this was all wrong. Where was it leading? OK, she knew precisely where it was leading—to hot, steamy jungle sex. Whatever the rights and wrongs, she simply couldn't resist him. She began running her hands over his chest and down toward his belt. As she outlined his erection with her finger, his stomach gave a small quiver.

He pulled her blouse over her head, pulled down her bra straps one at a time and kissed her shoulders.

"Albert, stop a minute." He looked at her. "You really have finished with Sunnie, haven't you? You weren't lying back there in the restaurant, just to get me into bed?"

"I swear. It's over."

"OK." She let him unhook her bra.

"You are so beautiful," he whispered as he stood gazing at her breasts. The next second he was planting tiny kisses all over them, biting her nipples. She undid his belt buckle and started on his jeans buttons. Finally she pulled at the waistband of his boxers and trailed her finger over the tip of his penis. He responded by kissing her again, his tongue deep inside her. Somehow he'd managed to pull down the zip on her skirt.

"Take it off," he ordered gently.

He carried on watching her as she stepped out of it and began taking off her stockings.

"Now you," she said. She tugged at the tops of his jeans. He did the rest. His erection sprang out. She saw a tiny pearl of semen. He gave a soft moan as she rubbed it gently with her finger.

Finally he picked up a couple of cushions from the sofa and led her to the fire. As she lay down next to the hearth, bathed in firelight, he placed the cushions under her head.

"I want you," she heard herself say. "I really want you."

She felt his tongue moving up the inside of one thigh, then the other. Finally he ran his finger over the crotch of her pants.

"Oh, my God," he said. "You are so wet."

He helped her off with her pants. For a while he just looked at her. Then he opened her, slowly, carefully, as if she might break. When he pushed his fingers inside her, deeply probing, she gasped. When his tongue trailed over her and found her clitoris, she felt herself floating away, barely aware of her own consciousness.

"Please. Let me feel you inside me."

He moved himself up over her body. Soon he was pushing himself inside her, with slow, deep thrusts. Every so often he would stop to caress her with his fingers, changing the pressure, stopping completely when he sensed she was about to come. When he did this, she begged him to carry on, but he simply whispered to her that there was no hurry. Finally, as the caress between her legs became even more exquisite, he allowed her to come.

Afterward they lay on the rug, her head resting on his chest.

"Oh...my...God," Stephanie said.

"You called?" Albert replied, grinning. She bashed him playfully.

"You know," he said, "when I told you I'd missed you, I really meant it."

"You did? That's nice."

"Yes. Back home, I find myself thinking about you a lot." He began trailing a finger over her breast. "And these last few weeks I've found myself thinking about what Grandma Lilly said when I arrived on Christmas Day, about us making a lovely little family."

"Oh, Gran's such an old romantic. She's just thinking of Jake."

"I know, but I think she's got a point. And you and I have been getting along so well."

She sat up and looked at him. "What are you saying?"

"Don't you think we'd make a lovely family—you, me and Jake? I guess what I'm trying to say is, will you marry me?"

She sat blinking at him, not sure what to say. "Marry you? Wow, you certainly know how to surprise a girl. Look, Albert, I love you as a friend, as the father of my child, but I'm not *in* love with you. A child needs parents who are in love. We had a lot to drink tonight and we had sex, but don't let's start reading more into it."

"But you agree we get along?"

"Yes. We get on very well."

"And we both love Jake."

"Of course."

"And you find me totally irresistible."

131

"I do?"

His hand was stroking the inside of her thigh. "OK," he whispered, "tell me I don't make you horny."

"All right, I admit it. You are very sexy."

"Thank you. And I make you laugh."

"Yes. You make me laugh."

"And I'm learning how to be a real dad."

"You are. You're becoming a brilliant dad."

"And when I look at you I see this gorgeous, intelligent woman who is a wonderful mother. So, what else do we need to make it work?"

"Love."

"But we do love each other. I love you. You love me. What's the difference between being *in love* and simply loving? The whole in-love thing wears off in no time anyway. You know that. I love you, *principessa,* and I think we'd be good together."

"Albert, this is ridiculous—on a practical level if nothing else. For a start, you live in L.A.," she said.

"I'll move here."

"Don't be ridiculous, all your work's over there."

"I know, but I'm thirty-eight. I can't go on forever, punishing my body the way I do. And it's dangerous. I'm thinking maybe I should do something more low risk."

"Are you serious?"

He lay there, hands behind his head. "I have never been more serious in my life."

"OK," Stephanie said, "you do know that being married means being faithful, don't you? I mean, what's the longest relationship you've ever had?"

"I dunno. Three months. Four, maybe."

"I rest my case. So, apart from Sunnie Ellaye, are there any other romantic interests back home?"

"A couple maybe, but they don't mean anything. I've changed since I've been with Jake. My priorities are different now."

"Albert, one of the reasons I didn't let myself fall head over heels for you was that I knew what a womanizer you are. If we got married, you'd be cheating on me within weeks. Days probably."

"No, I wouldn't."

She lay there looking at him. "Albert, we have the greatest sex and I really care about you. My entire family cares about you. But marriage . . . that's huge."

"Would you at least think about it?" he said. "Take as long as you like."

She didn't reply.

"For Jake's sake," he went on. "Please. He needs to grow up with two parents who love him. I want him to be part of a family."

"He is part of a family. Him and me."

"Yes, but he needs a live-in father. So, will you think about it?"

"I don't know."

"Please?"

She shrugged.

"OK, I'll think about it."

What she really needed was for Albert to go home so that she could have some space to begin processing all this, but it was well after one and he'd had a lot to drink. She didn't have the heart to send him on his way. "Come on," she said, "we're both tired. Let's hit the sack and talk about it again in the morning."

Chapter 9

Albert dropped off almost immediately, his arms around Stephanie's middle. She barely slept. Was it remotely possible they could make a go of it? He wasn't the only one who wanted Jake to have two parents who lived under the same roof. She craved it more than anything.

She wanted Jake to have a dad who would be able to help him with his science homework, who would kick a football round with him in the garden, who would sit with him on rainy Sunday afternoons, building those miniature space rockets she'd seen fathers and sons flying in the park. In her imagination, she could see the three of them on Hampstead Heath. Jake is six or seven, his eyes dancing with excitement and admiration as his dad launches their first rocket. Of course it only goes up a few feet and gets caught in a tree, but in her fantasy, Jake doesn't notice and she and Albert convince him it has soared onward and upward through the Earth's atmosphere and is on its way to Mars. Afterward they drive to Mrs. Beeton's in the high street and eat crumpets and cream cakes.

The thought of Jake growing up with little more than an e-mail relationship with his father brought tears to her eyes. Could they...should they get married for Jake's sake? The wise, intelligent part of her knew this wasn't a sufficient basis for marriage. And what if Jake eventually found out that he was the only reason she and Albert had gotten together? How would he feel? Particularly if it all went wrong. Guilty, that's how he'd feel. Guilty and angry with her. Christ, he might never forgive her. But why did she assume it had to go wrong? What if it went right? Was it beyond the realm of possibility that she and Albert might even fall in love? She turned her head to look at him. He was lying on his back making chewing motions in his sleep, exactly like Jake. There was so much that was lovable about Albert, she thought. Looks and the stupendous sex aside, he was intelligent, funny, kind, and of course he adored Jake.

But Albert would never give up chasing women. She knew he lived for the chase. It made him feel alive. Working at a relationship bored him. And yet...and yet. She'd already seen him grow in a way she'd never thought possible. In a matter of weeks he had changed from simply being Jake's father into a real dad. She couldn't imagine anybody doing a better job. If it was true, if Albert really was going through some kind of emotional renaissance, it would be so easy for her to fall in love with him.

Her mind was still churning, well into the small hours. She woke up feeling just as knackered as when she went to bed, her thoughts just as confused. Albert was snoring softly beside her. She looked at the clock. It was past eight. She'd said she would pick Jake up from her mother's at nine and then Albert would have him for the rest of the day as usual. She threw back the duvet and headed into the bathroom to take a shower.

She came back wrapped in a towel. By now Albert was awake and sitting up in bed. "You look beautiful," he said, watching her trying to force a comb through her dripping hair.

"I do?" She sat down at her dressing table and carried on trying to detangle her hair.

"Oh, yeah." He got out of bed and came toward her. His broad chest was bare and there was a trace of a tan. Ditto on his legs, which looked firm and muscular in his boxer shorts. He kissed her on the shoulder. Then he lifted her hair and kissed the back of her neck.

"Albert, behave," she giggled. "I need to get ready. I have to get over to Mum's."

"Estelle won't mind if you're a few minutes late."

She put down the comb and turned her face toward his. As they kissed he pulled off the towel and began caressing her breasts. Then he took the towel away again and began trailing his finger downward over her belly.

Before she knew it she was on her feet and Albert was leading her back to bed. Even though she wasn't in love with Albert—not yet, at least—the truth was, nothing had changed since their time in Verona. She was still head over heels in lust with him.

"I'm going to make the duvet all wet now," she said as he pushed her down gently.

"No, I'm going to make you all wet now," he said, slipping his hand between her legs.

"Albert, there isn't time. I really do have to get going."

"Shh. Relax. Come on."

She tried to bring her knees together, but he swiftly

moved his body between them. A second later he was going down on her and, try as she might, she couldn't resist him. She closed her eyes, felt her breathing get heavier. The familiar floaty feeling began to overwhelm her.

"There you go," he said softly.

Then the phone rang next to the bed.

"Christ, who's that?"

"Leave it," Albert said.

"I can't, it might be Ossie Da Costa."

She wriggled up the bed. Albert followed her, his head still between her legs. She tried shoving him off, but he refused to budge.

"It's me."

"Hi, Mum."

"Listen, I just wanted to say—"

"Er, can you just hold on a minute?" She pushed Albert's head, but he was too strong for her. She covered up the mouthpiece on the phone. "Albert, will you stop?" she hissed. "I'm on the phone to my mother."

He looked up briefly, grinned at her and then carried on.

"Ooh, ooh. Oh, God."

"What?" Estelle said. "What's the matter? You all right?"

"Aaaah. Yeah, Mum, I'm fine. Bit of a toothache. Kept me up all night."

"You ought to see a dentist. Why don't you pop in and see your cousin Michael? He did my crowns. They're perfect. And he gave me a discount."

"Right. Mmmmm. Good idea."

"Have you tried oil of clove?"

"Oh, yes! Yes! Yes!"

"And it still didn't work?"

"Yes!"

"So, it did work?"

"Oh, God."

"If it was that good, why are you still in pain? Anyway, all I was going to say was, don't worry about collecting Jake this morning. If it's all right with you, your dad's going to take him to see the dinosaurs at the natural history museum. Is that OK with you?"

"Um."

"You sure?"

"Oh, yes. Oh, yes."

"Stephanie, you don't sound at all right. Look, why don't I ring cousin Michael and make the appointment?"

"No-it's-fine-I'll-do-it-bye." Click. "Aaah!"

Stephanie told Albert that she really needed to go shopping. "I have to buy a new dress for my big night at the Blues Café. And after that I'm meeting Lizzie and Cass for lunch."

He started kissing her breasts. "Hey, come on, don't be a spoilsport. We've got the morning to ourselves. Why don't we spend it fooling around?"

"I really can't," she said kindly. "The dress is important. And the girls are expecting me."

He gave an easy shrug. "In that case," he said, "I guess the only way I'm going to work off all this pent-up sexual energy is to head off to the gym."

Her search for the perfect dress took her to a vintage clothes shop in Camden that specialized in fifties and sixties evening gowns.

It practically leaped off the rack at her: strappy, full length, made entirely of peacock-blue sequins. It clung in all the right places, and the thigh-high split was sexy but not tarty. It even had long silk gloves to match and a pair of dyed silk slingbacks. The shoes were half a size too small, but once she had undone the tiny gold buckles and lengthened the straps, they were fine. The outfit was perfect.

She'd arranged to meet Lizzie and Cass at a little Greek place on Charlotte Street, just round the corner from Cass's office. She spent the entire tube journey there thinking about Albert. By the time she arrived, she was no nearer a decision. The only thing she knew for sure was that she and Albert shouldn't sleep together again until she'd sorted out her feelings. Sex would put pressure on her to say something she didn't mean. On top of that it would send Albert mixed messages, and that would be unfair and unkind.

When she took the dress out of the bag and showed it to Lizzie and Cass, they agreed it was fab and that Sidney Doucette would be bowled over.

"You know this really is a big deal," Cass said. "You auditioning for Sidney Doucette. I'd hang on to your hat, if I were you. Ossie Da Costa must have something pretty amazing in mind for you."

Lizzie agreed. "God, Steph, this time next year you could be really famous."

Stephanie said she couldn't bear to tempt fate and please could they talk about something else.

Over moussaka and a bottle of house red, they admired Cass's new handbag—Anya Hindmarch with a picture of a Jack Russell wearing a tiara—and discussed Lizzie's preparations for the twins' birthday party the following week: dinosaurs or *Thunderbirds* theme? They also deliberated over Albert's proposal.

"Go for it," Cass said. "Nobody in their right mind should walk away from such great sex. Sex like that feeds you, nourishes the soul. It energizes your whole being, makes you feel young, vital." By now she was gazing into the distance, warming to her theme. "It gives you a reason to carry on with this miserable, fetid existence we call life. Take him, Steph. Take him, do you hear? And hold on to him. Never let him go. Not ever."

"Bloody hell, we have got to find you a man," Stephanie said, laughing.

Lizzie was looking at Stephanie. "Unless of course you wait for Frank Waterman to make a move," she ventured.

"God, how many more times? Look, he's an actor. They all go in for that flirty, luvvie thing. It doesn't mean he fancies me. And even if he does . . ."

"There's no *even* about it," Cass broke in. "He does."

"OK, let's say he does. Where does that get me? I spend practically every waking moment trying to work out if I could have a future with Albert, and even if I couldn't, Frank's engaged. End of story."

Cass drew on her cigarette and looked as if she were about to launch into her the-only-way-to-get-what-you-want-in-this-world-is-to-take-it speech, but Lizzie got in first. "The way I see it, there's nothing as important as a child being with both parents. I mean, of course being in love is important, but Albert's right—the passion does wear off eventually."

Cass frowned and exchanged a glance with Stephanie. Then she turned to Lizzie. "But you and Dom still do it, don't you?" she said gently.

"Of course we do it," Lizzie shot back with what was clearly a nervous laugh. "All I'm saying is, we're not in that first flush anymore, and the sex isn't like it was. The twins wear me out. He's away all the time, and when he's home, he's exhausted. More often than not he'll sleep in the spare room if he comes in late, so as not to wake me. But that's normal. I mean, you ask any couple with young children."

Stephanie and Cass exchanged another glance.

"Lizzie," Steph said gently. "It's none of our business, but is everything OK between you two?"

Lizzie's body language was suddenly taut and defensive. She couldn't look either of them in the eye. Instead she was concentrating on running her finger round the rim of her wineglass.

"Don't be ridiculous. We're fine. Coping with Dom's job and bringing up kids is hard, that's all. Things will perk up soon. Once Dom stops traveling so much." There were tears in her eyes as she got up to go to the loo.

Cass lit an after-lunch ciggie. Then she turned to Stephanie and said it was perfectly clear that Dom was playing away from home. "What do we do?" Stephanie was in no doubt that they should do nothing.

"What," Cass said, flicking ash into the ashtray, "you mean I shouldn't tell her about Dom making all those phone calls on New Year's Eve?"

"Absolutely not," Stephanie said. "First, you can't be sure he was phoning a woman, and second, it's none of our business. Lizzie and Dom have to sort this out for themselves. All we can do is be there for her if she needs us."

Cass grunted. She was a natural confronter. When she faced problems in business, she never ran away. Her instinct was to tackle them head-on and find solutions. She was the same if she thought a friend was in trouble. She couldn't bear having to pull back. "It makes me feel so bloody useless. God, Steph, I just can't imagine Lizzie and Dom splitting up." Cass was looking quite distressed now.

Stephanie reached across the table and patted her hand. "No, nor can I," she said. "Nor can I."

Sitting on the tube on her way to the Park Royal, Stephanie realized just how worried she was about Lizzie. Much as she adored Cass, she had a special bond with Lizzie. They'd grown up together. Now they were both mothers. Stephanie would never forget the way Lizzie had dropped everything to come and take care of her after Jake was born. Lizzie had the warmest, kindest heart of anybody she knew. The idea of her being unhappy, even for a moment, was just unthinkable.

That evening, Estelle and Harry brought Jake home, put him to bed and waited for Stephanie to get back from the Park Royal. She'd made a special effort to be early because she knew they were going out to eat with friends at a smart new French place in town. Harry was fed up because he'd been made to put on a tie "to go and eat food I can barely see," and Estelle—who was debuting her brand-new "would you believe it I'm down to a size sixteen?" silk trouser suit—kept interrogating Stephanie about Grandma Lilly's gentleman caller. She was desperate to find out more about him. "But you know how touchy your grandmother is with me. The minute I say anything, she'll accuse me of interfering. Look, she talks to you. Maybe you could find out what's going on." Stephanie promised she would try.

Estelle was also upset because they weren't going to be able to make the Blues Café on Thursday. Harry's Masonic lodge was holding its annual ladies' night. "But we are so proud of you, darling. Believe me, this Sidney Doucette is going to snap you up."

"For once, I agree with your mother," Harry said. Then they both gave her a hug.

Before they left, Estelle took Stephanie to one side. "So, how are you and Albert getting on?"

"Fine." She hoped it had come out as laid-back as she'd intended. Anything that smacked of enthusiasm, like a "really well," would have Estelle on the phone to the caterers before you could say "phyllo parcels."

"That's good." A beat, then: "Just fine? I mean, fine's fine, but you know...I was wondering."

"What, Mum, what were you wondering?"

"Well, this is the longest you two have been together since Verona and I just thought, you know...that maybe there was something going on. I know I've said it before, but Albert is so lovely. He's good-looking, charming, witty—"

"He lives in California."

Estelle pounced, eyes gleaming: "Ah, so you have been talking about it?"

"About what?" Stephanie said, trying to deflect her now.

"About getting together?"

"Not really."

"What do you mean, 'not really'? Either you have or you haven't."

"Look, Mum, can we leave it? Albert said some stuff, that's all, but I don't know how I feel."

"OK, sweetheart," Estelle said, rearranging Stephanie's fringe. "It's your decision, but it would be so wonderful if you made a go of it. The three of you would be a proper family. Boys need dads. I know you are perfectly capable of taking him to football when he's older, or going with him to choose his first car, but believe me, it's his dad he'll want."

"Mum, I can't marry Albert just so that Jake has somebody to go to football with."

"Of course you can't, and you are a wonderful mother. If you decide to carry on bringing him up alone, I know Jake will never want for anything, least of all love, but I'm old-fashioned. I happen to believe that children should have two parents to love them, that's all."

She smiled at Estelle. "You know, that's the first time you've ever told me I was a wonderful mother."

"It is?" Estelle shrugged. "I suppose it just never occurred to me that you needed telling."

She wasn't too bothered that Harry and Estelle weren't going to be at the Blues Café on Thursday. They meant well, but their kvetching would only have made her more nervous. On the other hand, she felt it would be good to have some support. She decided to ask Albert to come. It was strange. She'd known him over three years and in all that time he'd never heard her sing onstage. "I know, *principessa*," he said when she brought it up, "and I'd really love to come. But who would babysit Jake?"

He was right. This was a problem. Estelle and Harry had the Masonic do, Lizzie was going to open house at the twins' school, Cass was out of town for a couple of days and poor old Mrs. M. had gone back into hospital for her hip operation.

"You know, perhaps I'll invite some of the guys over to play poker that night." Her stomach tightened. The rational part of her knew that Albert had to stay at home to babysit Jake, but she had this nagging feeling that he would rather be with his mates than come to hear her sing.

"Albert? You would come if you could, wouldn't you?"

"Hey, of course I would. What kind of a question is that? You feeling OK?"

"Yes, I'm fine. S'pose it's nerves. I shouldn't be nervous, though. It's only a bloody audition. I've done thousands without having my hand held."

"I'll be thinking of you, *principessa*. You know I will."

144

"I know you will. Thanks." Then she kissed him on the cheek.

That evening he stayed for dinner. Afterward, Albert scraped plates while Stephanie loaded the dishwasher. "So," he said, "where's your head at?" She knew he was talking about the "us" thing. She said she'd been thinking about little else, but asked him not to rush her. She could see the disappointment in his face. Albert was a bit like Cass. Once he made up his mind to do something, he wanted it settled there and then. Waiting didn't come easily to him. "So, I guess it's too soon to suggest moving in?" he said, handing her a pile of plates.

"Just a bit," she said gently. "I also think that maybe we should stop having sex while I try and sort out how I feel. Sex just feels like too much pressure and it's going to send you all the wrong signals."

"Oh, come on. Signals schmignals. I have a thick skin, I'll cope."

"Yes, but what about me?" she said with a soft laugh. "I won't cope. You'll end up wearing me down."

He shrugged and said whatever she wanted was all right by him.

After he'd gone she went upstairs to check on Jake. He was lying on his back, arms spread out, making little chewing motions with his mouth. The floor beside his bed was littered with his drawings. The landing light was shining and she could make them out quite clearly. She picked one up. There were three wobbly circles next to each other, each with the usual stringy arms and legs. Albert had labeled them: *Mommy, Daddy, Jake.* She looked back at Jake. "Oh, sweetheart," she whispered, stroking his cheek, "what should I do? What should I do?"

As she stood brushing her teeth, she decided to try and forget about Albert for a few hours and get a good night's sleep.

The blue dress was lying on her bed. Seeing it gave her another attack of nerves. She'd lost count of the number of auditions she'd done over the years, but she'd never done one as important as this, in front of a major hitter like Sidney Doucette. She knew that Cass and Lizzie were right. He wouldn't be coming to hear her if Ossie Da Costa didn't have something pretty remarkable in mind for her. OK, Albert might be right and it could all come to nothing, but whatever happened, the stakes had never been higher. She sat there, slowly running her fingers over the blue sequins. Then, daring herself to imagine what the future just might have in store, she picked it up, went over to the full-length mirror and stood, holding the dress in front of her. She could hear the music to "Paper Moon" in her head. Her body began swaying in time.

"...it wouldn't be make-believe if you believed in me..."

The next morning she phoned Grandma Lilly to say she would call in on her way to work.

When she arrived, the main door downstairs was open because somebody was making a delivery to another flat. Stephanie went in, took the lift to the third floor and rang Lilly's bell. No answer. She rang a second time, keeping her finger on the bell for several seconds. Still nothing. Stephanie bent down and pushed open the letter-box flap. From inside she could hear music. Correction: what she could hear was an apparently random selection of electronic atonal sounds, which sounded nothing like music. She screwed up her face and carried on listening. It reminded her of the stuff they played in her local health food shop—the kind of thing dolphins tapped their flippers to. She couldn't work it out. Lilly was into the big bands, Andy Williams, a bit of Ella.

Stephanie was in no doubt that had he been able to hear this racket from his watery grave, Glenn Miller would have done a 360-degree turn. "Gran," Stephanie called through the letter box, "it's me." No response. She decided the only thing to do was let herself in. Stephanie and Estelle both carried keys to Lilly's flat in case of an emergency. As she opened the door, she called out again to let Lilly know she was there, but all she got was more synthesized squawking.

She walked down the hall, the music getting louder. It was coming from the living room. "Gran! It's me! I let myself in. What on earth are you listening to?" The living room door was open. She knew she shouldn't have stood watching. Apart from being rude, she was going to frighten the life out of Lilly when she finally noticed her, but Stephanie couldn't resist it.

Lilly was standing, eyes closed, in the middle of her red-and-gold-swirly-carpeted living room, dressed in black silk Chinese pajamas. As the music played she turned slowly to the left, held out her right hand and gently rotated her palm downward. Then she turned to the right and repeated the action. She was clearly practicing her tai chi and, from what Stephanie could see, with more than a little grace. She carried on watching as Lilly shifted her weight onto her left foot, turned to the right and brought her hands in front of her, their backs touching. Then she lost her balance and opened her eyes. "Omigod, Stephanie," she gasped, slapping her hand to her chest. "You nearly gave me a heart attack. Why didn't you ring the bell?"

147

"I did. Several times, but you didn't hear me because of the music."

"Oh, I'm sorry. I was practicing the Thirty-Seven Postures of Cheng. That last bit was Embrace Tiger, Return to Mountain. I'm still not very good, but it's just so soothing and relaxing. I'm definitely becoming spiritualized. I can feel it. It's sort of bubbling up inside me."

"Maybe you need to take some Pepto-Bismol."

"Now you're teasing me. It is not indigestion. My entire body feels like it's being bathed in a deep inner calm. I tell you, taking up tai chi is one of the best things I've ever done. And don't you just love the music?"

"To be honest, Gran, I'm not keen. What is it?"

"Björk. Isn't she wonderful? Bernard, our tai chi teacher, recommended her. He thinks her music really complements the movements. I just love it."

"Omigod, my seventy-nine-year-old grandmother is into Björk?"

Lilly shrugged. "Why shouldn't I be?"

"No reason." Stephanie smiled, thinking that since her grandmother was into moments of ecstasy and tai chi, there was no reason why she shouldn't be into Björk.

Lilly asked her what she thought of the pajamas. She'd bought them at a Chinese gift shop in Covent Garden. Stephanie said she thought they were fab and highly appropriate.

"Maybe I ought to get changed. I don't want to ruin them. You sit down. I won't be a minute."

Lilly disappeared into the bedroom and Stephanie sank into an armchair. Her grandmother's living room was roughly ten feet by twelve. Before she moved in, Estelle had spent weeks trying to convince her to get rid of the furniture from her old house around the corner, on the grounds that it was big and old-fashioned and would swamp the new flat. Lilly had refused to listen. Her furniture was part of her. To give it away would be like giving away her memories. "Plus, nobody makes quality like this anymore." And that was that. Debate over. When Lilly moved, so did her furniture.

As a result the living room contained a bulky three-piece suite (faded green Dralon, tassels round the bottom), two nests of tables (dark rosewood), a forties' walnut sideboard ("Feel how solid it is. Go on, just feel") and a matching cocktail cabinet. Then there were all her "bits and pieces"—the silver photograph trees, the cut-glass vases of silk flowers, the Venetian glass sweets dishes and ashtrays.

Stephanie would never forget the day Lilly moved into her flat. She and Estelle came to help her unpack. One box contained seventy-five sherry schooners. "Mum," Estelle had pleaded, "this kitchen is minute. Where did you think you were going to find room for seventy-five sherry schooners?" It seemed she was holding on to them "in case people come," along with the nineteen tins of salmon and dozens of carrier bags and sachets of sugar and sweeteners. Nowadays the sherry schooners were collecting dust at the top of the airing cupboard and the sachets of sugar and sweeteners filled two kitchen drawers. Her shopping cart (a present from Estelle, which she never used because she said it made her feel like an old person) stood by the fire escape door and served as a receptacle for the carrier bags.

Lilly came back into the living room, cordless phone pressed to her ear. "Estelle, why do you keep asking me this?" She beckoned Stephanie to follow her into the kitchen. "Look, I don't know if I want to be buried or cremated," Lilly continued. "Surprise me."

"You know," Lilly said, putting the phone down on the counter, "your mother has been going through an odd phase

149

since her menopause. She's obsessed with my funeral arrangements. Sometimes I think she actually wants me dead. It's like
she's sixteen all over again." She shrugged and waved a hand
in front of her. "Still, I'm sure she'll grow out of it."

Stephanie said Estelle adored her and how could she even
think she wanted her dead. She made the point, as tactfully as
she could, that Lilly wasn't getting any younger and Estelle
simply wanted to get everything right when the time came.

It occurred to Stephanie that this was only partly true.
Estelle was probably finding it impossible to come up with
fresh excuses to phone her mother in order to pump her for
information about Maury Silverstone. Lilly began filling the
kettle. "Your mother told me about this big audition," she
said. "I'll be sitting here sending up a prayer." Stephanie
thanked her and said she needed all the help she could get.

"So, Gran, how are things with the Matzo Ball Mogul?"

"Oh, I finished with him before Christmas," Lilly announced, flicking the switch on the kettle.

"What? Why? You were having such a great time."

Lilly shrugged. "I was for a bit, but then I realized he
only wanted me for my body."

"I see," Stephanie said, surveying her grandmother's
birdlike seventy-nine-year-old frame.

"I need somebody who can appreciate me for my mind
as well. Somebody I can talk to. Maury was nice enough, but
he had no conversation. He would turn up, we'd have a couple of glasses of sweet sherry while I cooked him liver and
onions. Then after dinner, we'd go to bed. Sometimes we
didn't bother with dinner. I realized he wasn't so much a
boyfriend as . . . what's that modern expression? Fuck buddy?
That's it. Me and Maury were just fuck buddies."

Stephanie was having trouble working out if she was still
sitting in her grandmother's kitchen or whether she had

somehow stepped into a special senior citizen episode of *Sex and the City*. She pulled out a kitchen stool. "Fair enough," she said.

"Anyway, I've found somebody else. I've been seeing him for a while."

"Blimey, you didn't waste much time. Who?"

"Bernard, my tai chi teacher."

"Omigod, my grandmother's got a boy toy."

Lilly laughed and said he was about her age. "He thinks I'm such a natural that he's been giving me some extra one-on-one lessons to help me get in touch with my *p'eng* and *s'ung*—if you know what I mean." Then she dug Stephanie in the ribs and started cackling.

Chapter 10

The following night, before Stephanie left for the Blues Café, her parents, Cass and Lizzie all rang to wish her good luck. Albert said he was keeping everything crossed. She made some daft remark, prompted by nerves, about being careful or he could twist a testicle. For some reason this turned him on and he made her promise not to take off the blue dress until she got home, so that he could see how sexy she looked.

After giving her a quick good-luck kiss, he went over to the kitchen table and took off his jacket. As he hung it on the back of a chair she couldn't help noticing a postcard sticking out of the inside pocket.

"Ooh, who's been sending you postcards?" she said. He pulled out the card. It had a picture of the L.A. Kabbala Centre on the front. Was it possible that Albert corresponded with mystically inclined ultraorthodox rabbis?

"It's from Sunnie," he said, without the faintest sign of guilt or embarrassment. "She's into some more weird shit."

He laughed. There was a look of affection on his face, but nothing more. Despite Albert's history with women, it didn't really occur to her to be suspicious. Even though Albert was always attracted to flakes, Stephanie had thought from the beginning that Sunnie Ellaye was far too ditsy, even for Albert. He handed her the postcard. It was just a couple of lines to say hi, how you doing. She'd signed off "Love and hugs, Sunnie," and over the *i* in her name, there was a tiny heart instead of a dot. It occurred to Stephanie that she probably signed letters to the IRS the same way.

When she arrived at the Blues Café, her stomach was churning. Melody, the slightly dim manager with more curves than the Matterhorn ride at Disneyland, took one look at her and offered her a large brandy. When Stephanie declined because alcohol would only make her sleepy, Melody began rummaging around inside her trouser pocket. "Oooh, hang on. I think I've got a couple of Prozac left over from the other night when I went to see my mum."

"God, you need to take Prozac before you visit your mum?"

"Yeah. That way she can nag all she likes about why I'm not married and it just washes over me."

She brought out two white capsules and pressed them into Stephanie's hand. "Melody, these are coconut Jelly Bellies."

"They are? Oh, thank God for that. Here was me thinking I needed to increase my dose."

A few minutes later, she was standing in front of the full-length mirror in her dressing cupboard, repositioning her shoulder straps for the umpteenth time. She had to admit the dress could have been made for her, but maybe the sequins

153

were just a tad too Las Vegas. Perhaps she should lose the gloves. Her hand was in her bra cup, about to hoist up her bosom, when she heard a voice behind her.

"Wow! You look sensational."

"Frank!" Her hand sprang from her bosom and she turned round to face him. She couldn't believe how pleased she was to see him. "You know," she said, grinning, "that's the second time you've made me jump in two days. This has to stop."

"Sorry, but the door was open. I told the manager I was a friend."

"That's OK. Come on in." She noticed a slight tentativeness about him, as if he felt uneasy about coming into her private space. He leaned his body against the ancient Formica kitchen table, which was covered with her cosmetics.

"So, the dress really looks OK?" she said anxiously. "Not too much? What about the gloves? Be honest. I won't be offended."

He was holding her in his gaze, smiling. "They're perfect. You look perfect. Listen, I don't want to hold you up. I just popped in to wish you good luck. I thought I'd stay and see the show if that's OK."

"OK? I'd love it. You know I can't believe you remembered it was tonight I was doing the audition."

Just then Dennis popped his head round the door to say Ossie and Sidney had arrived and wanted to pop in and say hello. Frank said he should go. "I'll be sitting out there rooting for you," he said, kissing her on both cheeks. "Not that you'll need it. I know you'll be brilliant."

"God, I hope so." As he walked toward the door, she heard herself saying, "So, no Anoushka tonight?"

He looked taken aback. "I assumed you knew. It's been all over the tabloids. We split up. A couple of weeks ago."

"No, I didn't," she said, placing her hand on his arm. "Frank, I am so sorry." He said he was too, but it had worked out for the best. For a few seconds he seemed lost in his thoughts. Finally his face broke into a smile. "Do you fancy going for a drink after you finish tonight? After all the tension, I think you might need one. Unless of course you have other plans."

"No. No, I don't," she said. "I'd love to go for a drink."

She had imagined Sidney Doucette as sixty-something, short, with a camel coat draped over his shoulders Don Corleone style, a Rolex, and a paunch in a different time zone from the rest of him. When they were introduced, he wouldn't say much, just chew on his cigar and look her up and down as if he were inspecting a heifer at a cattle auction. When she started singing, he would sit there, one eyebrow raised, challenging her to thrill and astonish him. If he didn't like what he heard, he would simply get up and walk out.

"Stephanie, you decent?" Ossie said, tapping on the dressing room door.

"Yes, come on in."

"Not that I'd mind if you weren't," Ossie said, letting out a loud cackle. "Stephanie, may I present Mr. Sidney Doucette." Standing behind Ossie (whose head was turned up, his eyes glued to Stephanie's cleavage) was a tall, well-preserved chap in his midseventies, maybe, sporting a David Niven mustache and an exquisitely tailored gray suit. Underneath he was wearing a black silk-knit polo shirt.

"Miss Glassman," Sidney proclaimed joyously. With that he took her hand and planted an elegant kiss on the back of it. "Ah am enchanted. Truly enchanted." She recognized the Southern accent immediately. "Why, ah do declare," he went on, "aren't you just a sight for sore eyes? If you don't mind my saying, little lady, you are as perky as a ladybug's ears at planting time."

Resisting the urge to ask him if he had come to London on a 747 or in a surrey with a fringe on top, she said how do you do and thanked him profusely for taking the trouble to hear her sing.

"The pleasure is all mine," he said, finally letting go of her hand. "Ah have heard so much about you, little lady. Ossie here tells me you have the voice of an angel. Ah know it is going to be a pleasure and dee-light to hear you sing. Why, ah am as excited by the prospect as a possum up a gum stump."

Then he said he could do with wetting his whistle and where could a man get a drink around here. "What'll you have, Ossie? A short, I'll be bound." With that he roared with laughter. Hurt flashed across Ossie's face. It was the first time Stephanie had seen him drop his guard. For a moment he seemed truly vulnerable. But it didn't last. A moment later the smile had returned. "Actually, I'm a teetotaler," he said.

She couldn't help finding that odd. She would have put money on Ossie being a pretty hard drinker.

The two men turned to go. "Good luck, little lady," Sidney said with a wave. As she closed the door she could hear Sidney telling Ossie that he thought she looked as scared as a long-tailed cat in a room full of rocking chairs.

She walked toward the podium, her chest fit to burst because her heart was thumping so hard. Ossie and Sidney were sitting in the middle of the room. Sidney raised his glass to her. Ossie waved his cigar. Frank was sitting closer, just a few feet away. He was giving her a thumbs-up and mouthing something, which looked like: "You look great." She smiled back and picked the mike up off its stand. A moment later, the lights went down and the place fell quiet. She could still feel the pounding in her chest, the dryness in her mouth. The dress shimmered and twinkled in the spotlight. She turned to the band and took a deep breath. "OK, boys, 'I Enjoy Being a Girl.' " Ian, the drummer, gave her a matey wink. The intro began. She started moving to the upbeat tempo.

"I'm a girl and by me that's only great / I am proud that my silhouette is curvy . . ." She gave a Marilyn Monroe wiggle and ran her hand over her hips. What she couldn't have hoped to see was Ossie gazing at her, lips slightly parted, beads of sweat breaking onto his forehead.

Audience enthusiasm varied from night to night, and she was dreading a lukewarm crowd. But from the beginning she could feel they were with her. After that first song they clapped like mad. There were even a few whistles. Four numbers in, high on adrenaline and applause, she was having a ball. During her break Frank came up to tell her how brilliantly she was doing. Ossie and Sidney didn't budge from their table. She couldn't work out if this meant they were less than enthusiastic about her performance, or that they simply couldn't be bothered to get up because they were too busy talking and eating. Frank said it was undoubtedly the latter. "I mean, just look at them." Both men were plowing through the Blues Café's spectacularly large pizzas, but Ossie especially was concentrating on eating the way most people concentrated on filling out their tax returns.

She left singing "Fever" until the end. First came the gentle drumbeat. Then the bass kicked in. Her fingers clicked to the rhythm.

By the time she got to the "you give me fever" bit, she found herself looking at Frank. The instant she realized what she was doing and how it must look, she turned her head.

When she finished, the applause went on for ages. She even had to do an encore.

"**Well,** Miss Glassman," Sidney said afterward, as she stood at the bar sipping mineral water. "Ah think ah've heard all I need to." Her heart sank to her peacock-blue slingbacks. It was the phrase theater directors used after an actor or performer had given a mediocre audition. She'd heard it dozens of times. The audience may have loved her, but satisfying the likes of Sidney Doucette was another matter. She looked at Ossie. His face was positively contorted. It was only when he pulled a tube of Tums from his pocket and tore into the foil that she realized it was probably indigestion, rather than her singing, that had brought about the facial expression. She waited for Sidney to deliver the "not quite what I'm looking for" speech. Then she heard him say: "Ah do declare, Miss Glassman, that voice of yours sounds even better live than it does on your CD. Ah am in no doubt that we shall be meeting again very soon." Once more he took her hand and planted another elegant kiss. "Meanwhile you must excuse me. Ah have an engagement in St. John's Wood and ah am running late. Ossie, can you show me where ah can get a cab?"

Ossie, chewing on a Tums now, nodded and turned to Stephanie. "OK, my office ten o'clock Monday morning and I'll explain *exactly* what we have in mind for you." Then he grinned and did this Groucho Marx thing with his eyebrows. It didn't occur to her that this display was anything more than a joke on Ossie's part. The idea that he could possibly fancy her didn't even enter her mind.

Before she had a chance to pick herself up from the shock of the way the audition had gone, Ossie and Sidney were walking away, Ossie stifling a belch as he went. As he weaved his way between tables, a few people turned to stare at Ossie. He greeted each one with a smile and a wave. "That is one very brave man," she said to herself.

"Steph, you were fantastic out there." It was Frank. "No, you were more than fantastic, you were unbelievable. So, come on, what did he say?" In that instant the excitement kicked in. "He wants me," she said, flinging her arms around him. "Sidney Doucette wants me. I can't believe it."

Before she knew what was happening, Frank had picked her up and was swinging her round. "Wow! I knew it. I just knew it."

When he finally put her down she thanked him for coming. "You know, I really do appreciate it."

He told her he wouldn't have missed it. She could feel his eyes dancing over her face and for a moment she thought he might kiss her. Then Melody came rushing over, desperate to find out how it had all gone, and he didn't.

$\mathcal{S}$*tephanie* and Frank went to the pub across the road. When he asked her what she fancied to drink, she was in no doubt. "Ooh, a very large vodka and tonic, please." While he got the drinks she sat down at a table and wondered if she should ask him what happened between him and Anoushka. She decided against it, on the grounds that it was none of her business. In the end he brought it up himself. "Our backgrounds were just too different. I think what she really wanted was one of those posh city types. It's funny, I can do them onstage, but at home I'm still Frank Waterman from Watford, who likes brown sauce sandwiches. It was never going to work. I can't believe it took me eighteen months to see it." She told him that at least he realized things weren't right before they got married.

"You know," she went on, "I like them with those individually wrapped slices of processed cheese."

"What?"

"Brown sauce sandwiches." He made the point that then they became processed cheese sandwiches with brown sauce, rather than just brown sauce sandwiches. They argued for a minute or so, but finally she conceded the point. Somehow—maybe the vodka helped—the conversation went from processed cheese slices to Shakespeare. It turned out that Frank had just been offered a part in *Twelfth Night,* which was due to go into production in the late autumn. "I'm playing Orsino," he said. She didn't say anything. He gave her a quizzical look. "What are you thinking?"

"No, it's nothing."

"Yes, it is. I can see by your face." He was looking at her, smiling—head tilted slightly to one side. "All right," she said, "can I tell you something I've never told another living soul?"

"Absolutely."

She stared into her empty glass. "No, I can't. Forget it. You'll be offended." She was feeling really awkward now. She turned her face down. Frank reached across, put his hand under her chin and gently tilted it so that she was facing him again. For a few seconds their eyes were locked.

"I won't be offended. Promise." He took his hand away. Since she had been rather enjoying the feeling of his skin against hers, she found herself wishing he had left it there. "Go on," he said.

Gawd. She wished she hadn't started this. "OK, well, it's just that I think Shakespeare's comedies are a bit crap, really. Total absence of any good jokes, in my opinion."

He threw back his head and roared. "I agree."

"Really?" she said, utterly taken aback by his reaction. "You do?"

"Totally. I mean, all the cross-dressing and ridiculously unbelievable coincidences."

"Yeah," she said, "and those ludicrous lines like: 'He has not so much brains as earwax.' Like—hello, when exactly is the funny bit coming?"

By now she was warming to her theme, unaware that Frank was utterly transfixed. "I mean, I can understand that audiences found it funny four hundred years ago, but I just don't think people are being honest when they say it still works today. It's just the height of middle-class pretension, in my opinion. Oh, God, now I sound really arsey, don't I?"

"Only a bit," he said, still laughing. "But I do think you have a point. Ask me to choose between Shakespeare and Woody Allen and I know who I'd pick."

"Oh, I adore Woody Allen," she said. She said when she felt miserable she fried bacon and rented *Annie Hall*. She didn't have the courage to confess that when she was really miserable she watched *The Sound of Music*. She felt she'd already made enough of a fool of herself. "I love the lobster scene," she went on. He said his favorite was *Love and Death*.

Soon they got to chatting about their time in *Cabaret* at the Nottingham Playhouse. He reminded her of the time in the Trip to Jerusalem pub when she sang "My Melancholy Baby." "I had a bit of a crush on you after that." He started swirling the ice around in his glass. She could see his face was turning slightly pink.

"You did?" she said, desperately trying to conceal her shock. When she asked him why he never said anything, he said he had a girlfriend back in London. "It's ironic. After the show ended, I moved back to London and we split up."

She asked him where he lived now. When he said Muswell Hill, she couldn't believe it. His flat and her house were just a few streets away from each other. Neither of them could understand how their paths had never crossed.

They fell into silence. "Listen," Frank said, clearing his throat, "I was wondering if maybe you fancied . . ."

But she didn't hear him because Dennis and Ian from the band had suddenly appeared and were congratulating her on being taken on by Ossie Da Costa. "You were just great up there tonight, Steph," Dennis said. "Absolutely great."

After the kisses and hugs, she introduced Frank. "Och, no need for introductions," Ian said, smiling broadly and extending a hand toward Frank. "This man's famous. We know who he is, all right."

"Why don't you join us?" Frank said to the two men. "It's my round. What are you drinking?"

While Frank went off to get the drinks, Ian said how much they were going to miss her.

"Miss me?"

"Ah, well, with Ossie Da Costa managing you, you'll have your name up in lights in no time. You'll no' be hanging around the Blues Café much longer."

She said she wasn't so sure. "All depends what work Ossie finds me."

It was the first time she'd given any real thought to leaving. It suddenly hit her how sad she would be to leave. The boys in the band were almost family. She was in the middle of telling them how much she would miss them if she left and that she would always pop in to hear them play, when her mobile rang.

"*Principessa?* It's me. Listen, I'm really worried about Jake. He's been up for a couple of hours crying with stomach pains. He looks real pale and says he wants to throw up. The pain seems to be just on his right side. I'm worried it could be appendicitis."

She was already on her feet, reaching for her coat. "OK, just hang on. I'm on my way. If he gets any worse dial 999."

"Christ, what is it?" Dennis said. She explained, realizing that she was starting to shake. "Look, I'm really sorry to break up the party." They told her not to be so daft. Ian, the only one who'd driven in, offered to give her a lift. She said thanks but no thanks, since his car was parked in the garage miles away. It occurred to her that Frank might be able to take her home.

The area round the bar was heaving. She stood on tiptoe, trying to spot Frank, but couldn't. Then she realized he'd probably gone to the gents. By now she was starting to panic. Deciding that she had no time to hang around, she charged back to where the band was sitting. She told them she was going to get a cab and asked them to tell Frank what had happened.

Jake's suspected appendicitis turned out to be a severe case of broccoli-induced wind.

"You know how he loves it," Albert said. "He thinks he's eating baby trees. I guess I gave him too much tonight. Anyway, he let out this mega fart about ten minutes ago. He's fine now. Sound asleep."

Of course, Stephanie had to see for herself. She ran upstairs. Jake was lying on his back as usual, peacefully zizzing his label in his sleep. Gently, she pushed back his fringe and kissed his forehead. "Night-night, sweetheart. And no more frights, please, at least not for a bit."

It was only as she walked back downstairs that the panicky feeling fully subsided and she felt her heart rate come back to normal. In the kitchen Albert was gathering up curry cartons. "You know, you really do look amazing in that dress," he said. "That's not to say I wouldn't like to take it off, right now."

She smiled and gave him a kiss on the cheek. "Did Jake ruin your poker game?"

"Not really. I was already fifty quid down by the time he woke up. I let the guys carry on without me. So, come on, I'm dying to know, how did it go?"

"Great. Sidney wants me. I'm seeing Ossie on Monday and he's going to explain the secret project thing."

"See, what did I tell you?" Albert said, dropping a cigar butt into an untouched carton of raita. "I knew he would." Then he came over and hugged her and told her how proud of her he was.

Still high on adrenaline, she gabbled away about how nervous she'd been, how the audience had made her do an encore at the end. "And Sidney Doucette behaves like he's just stepped out of *Gone With the Wind*. Every time he spoke I felt I should be batting my eyes at him from under a parasol and telling him I was mighty obliged."

"Great. That's really great. Say, do we have any of those black plastic trash bags?"

"Cupboard under the sink," she said. Then she shot him a puzzled look. "I don't understand. What's great? Albert, have you heard a word I've been saying?"

"Sorry, *principessa,*" he said, pulling a plastic sack from off the roll, "I was miles away. Jake really wore me out tonight."

"I'm sorry."

"Hey, it's not your fault," he said, shaking out the bag. He held it open while she filled it with curry cartons. "Oh, by the way, one of the guys who was here tonight wants to sell his Harley. He's only asking four grand. For a two-year-old Harley, that's a bargain. What do you think? The thing is I'm starting to feel real guilty about borrowing Tom's bike the whole time."

She said it sounded reasonable to her and that he should go for it. "You can keep it garaged here."

"That's what I figured."

He put the rubbish bag down by the back door and came and stood in front of her. "You know, we really should cele-brate your success. It's been a bit of a night for both of us. I think we need something to unwind."

"Umm, a glass of wine would be nice," she said.

"I wasn't thinking of alcohol," he said, bringing her toward him and grinning.

"Ah."

He pulled down one of her dress straps and began kissing her shoulder. "So, who did you go to the pub with?"

"Oh, just Dennis and Ian from the band." She was aware that she hadn't mentioned Frank. Why? Nothing had hap-pened between them. He was just an old mate who'd come to hear her sing and taken her for a drink afterward, that's all. Then why hadn't she said anything and why was she feel-ing guilty? She knew exactly why. The excitement she'd felt when she thought Frank was about to kiss her was still with her. "Come on," she whispered, as he pulled down the zip on the back of her dress, "we both agreed sex would complicate things."

"No, *you* said sex would complicate things."

"Yes, but I thought you agreed."

"I just reneged," he grinned.

"You can't renege. Anyway, you just said you were tired."

"You know me," he said. "I'm never *that* tired." He lifted

off the other shoulder strap and began easing the dress down. She stepped out of it. He looked at her in her bra, stockings and high heels and gave a soft whistle.

"But I'm tired," she said, realizing that much as she tried to stop it, the moment she and Frank almost kissed kept gate-crashing her thoughts. "It's been a bit of a night and all I really want to do is sleep."

"Really?" he said, stroking her breast. "Are you sure that's all you want to do?" She let out a tiny whimper. Albert was like catnip: addictive and utterly irresistible. Finally he kissed her on the mouth. As she felt his tongue deep inside her, moisture began seeping from between her legs and thoughts of Frank started to fade.

"I love this bit of you," he said, stroking the back of his hand against her inner thigh, just above her stocking top. "It's so soft." She felt a delectable quivering in her stomach. He whispered to her to spread her legs. He pulled the crotch of her pants to one side. By now the blood was rushing through her ears. With a teasingly light touch he ran his fingers over her labia. She let out a soft moan. She was desperate for him to separate her, to find her swollen, aching clitoris.

"Please," she murmured.

He smiled and told her not to be in such a hurry. The gentle stroking carried on, him ignoring her tiny whimpers of frustration. When he finally parted her, she cried out in delight. As his fingers glided back and forth, they kissed again. Again he stopped. She let out another cry of frustration.

He told her to turn around. Gently he pushed her down over the table and pulled her pants down. There was a bottle of hand cream on the window ledge over the sink. He went over and got it. She heard him flip open the lid. A moment later she felt the thick, cold liquid drizzle onto her bottom.

Slowly he began massaging it into her skin. Then he brushed his fingers between her wet bottom cheeks toward her clitoris. She begged him to rub harder, faster, but he wouldn't. He simply carried on teasing her. Finally he stopped completely. She cried out as he pushed two fingers up hard inside her. As he explored her, he kissed the back of her neck, ran his tongue between her shoulder blades. By now her breathing had become slow and deep. She could feel herself floating, drifting away into a kind of trance. She was vaguely aware of him undoing his belt and pulling down the zip on his jeans. Instead of his fingers probing her now, she felt the warm tip of his penis. It was jabbing at her, stretching her, threatening to come inside her, but holding back. She pleaded with him to come inside her.

"Shh, just relax."

When it finally happened, the thrust was deep, almost violent. She cried out at the tiny, exquisite pain. He eased off. The thrusts became slower, more gentle. He found her clitoris again, his fingers sliding over it in firm circular motions. The quivering started to build up inside her like small bursts of laughter. She was frightened he would stop again, but he didn't. "There you go," he whispered. "There you go." She thought the sublime shuddering inside her would never end.

Albert gave one final, hard thrust. She could feel him holding his breath, digging his fingers into her buttocks. Finally he relaxed. He brought his lips to the small of her back and kissed her.

As they stood facing each other, Stephanie doing up her bra, Albert kissed her on the cheek. "You know, *principessa*," he said, "we really are great together."

She had to agree they were indeed great. She could tell by his expression that he was waiting for her to say he could move in and that she wanted the two of them and Jake to be a family, but she couldn't. Not yet. "I'm just not ready," she said. It felt so mean saying it, particularly as they'd just had such great sex. Why hadn't she shown some backbone and kept her promise about not sleeping with Albert until she'd gotten her feelings sorted out? Oh, and why had Frank suddenly popped back into her mind? "I know I'm stringing you out with all this. Do you think you can be patient for just a bit longer?"

"It's fine," he said, stroking her face. "There's no hurry."

Chapter 11

Estelle was on the phone first thing, to find out how the audition had gone.

"He wants you? Oh, darling, that's wonderful. Hang on, let me tell your father...Harry!" Stephanie jerked the phone from her ear a moment too late. "He can't hear me. He's on the other line talking to the people at London Online. He came home last night to nineteen junk e-mails, ten of them asking if he wanted his septic tank overhauled. Harry! Harry! You off the phone yet?" Stephanie winced and changed ears for a second time. "Harry!...He still can't hear me. Harry! It's great news. He wants her...What do you mean, 'Who wants her?' Sidney Doucette wants Stephanie...Your dad says brilliant and well done. You know, sweetie, we're so proud of you. So, come on, what is it he has in mind for you, this Ossie?"

Stephanie explained how he'd left the Blues Café before she'd had a chance to ask. "But how could you have let him go without telling you?" Estelle said in that familiar reproachful tone of hers. "You should have pinned him down, made him tell you what he has in mind."

Stephanie said everything had happened so fast. "One minute he was there, the next he was walking away."

"This would never have happened if your father and I had been there. I knew we should have come."

Stephanie took a deep breath and did her best to visualize her floaty ball. "So," she said, forcing a smile because she'd read in some magazine that "forcing the smile helps you feel the smile," "how was the Masonic do?"

Estelle said it had been a complete bore. The tedium had only been relieved by the grand master's tiddly wife—"You remember Sylvia Epstein, chin so pointed, she could use it to get pickles out of a jar"—crumbling Valium onto her crème caramel to give it some crunch.

"So," her mother went on, "did you manage to get anything out of your grandma yet, about this man she's been seeing?"

Tactfully avoiding the fuck-buddy issue, she explained that Lilly had dumped him. "But there's somebody else. Her teacher from tai chi."

Estelle was aghast. "What, some lad?" Stephanie explained that he was in his seventies. Estelle said that was all right, then. "When you think about it—teacher and pupil—it's all rather sweet, really."

Having to wait until Monday to find out precisely what the Da Costa/Doucette secret project involved was frustrating to say the least. Stephanie tried to reach Ossie all Friday morning but kept getting his voice mail. So what did he have in mind for her? Lizzie and Cass were still convinced she'd landed the lead in a West End musical.

She felt a rush of excitement. "God, suppose I have?" she heard herself say to Cass. "Can you imagine? It would be better than winning the lottery." Petrified of blowing her chances because she'd said too much, she decided to change the subject. "By the way, Frank turned up to hear me sing and we went for a drink afterward. But before that, there was one of those moments when I thought he was going to kiss me, but he didn't."

"And you're still telling me he doesn't fancy you?"

"OK, maybe I was wrong."

"And did you want him to kiss you?"

Stephanie's feelings of confusion were coming on strong now. "Yes, but it was probably just the excitement. Sidney Doucette had just told me he wanted me...and I'd just found out Frank's split up with Anoushka."

"Oh, my God," Cass said, sounding truly horrified. "He's split up with Anoushka? This is terrible."

"Yeah," Stephanie said, "he did seem pretty cut up about it."

"No, no, you don't understand. It's terrible for you." There was real passion in her voice. "If you're not careful, you're going to end up as his transitional woman. If you want him, you have to run like the wind."

"Hang on. If I want him, I have to run away?" Stephanie said. "Do you mind telling me what on earth you're on about?"

Cass explained she'd read this article in *Cosmo* about how men fresh out of a long-term relationship tend to fall for the first woman who offers them a shoulder to cry on. "Six months down the line, feeling much better because the transitional woman has spent night after night counseling him while he drinks himself into oblivion, he dumps her. Then he goes on the hunt again. If you've got your sights set on him, you have to wait until he's had his transitional fling."

171

Stephanie said that Cass knew perfectly well she hadn't gotten her sights set on Frank. "All I'm thinking about right now is whether Albert and I can make a go of it."

"Right, so you really don't have any feelings for Frank, then?"

"OK, yeah, I fancy him. But I fancy lots of people. It doesn't mean I have to act on it."

"True. But one day soon you could find yourself making love to Albert but thinking about Frank. That's the danger signal. Mark my words."

"You reckon?" Stephanie said, swallowing hard, remembering the way Frank had popped into her head last night while Albert was undressing her.

"Trust me," Cass said. "I've been there."

Of course, once Cass had gotten her going, she couldn't stop thinking about Frank—particularly how much she'd enjoyed chatting with him in the pub. Then about eleven, while she was getting ready to go to work, he phoned to see how Jake was.

"Dennis gave me your number. I hope you don't mind."

She said she didn't remotely mind. When she explained about the broccoli he seemed genuinely relieved.

"It used to have the same effect on Anoushka," he said, with an affection that Stephanie found rather endearing. "We'd go to bed and every five minutes there'd be these humongous blasts from under the duvet." Stephanie burst out laughing at the thought of the gorgeous Anoushka with her Fulham highlights, farting like an ocean liner docking in the fog.

"Look, I'm really sorry I ran out on you like that," Stephanie said. "I just panicked. All I could think about was getting home."

He said he completely understood and that he'd really enjoyed the evening. "When we were in the pub, I wanted to say that we should do it again, soon."

"I'd like that," she heard herself say.

OK, OK, she could handle this. Yes, she had feelings for Frank, but as she'd said to Cass, she didn't have to act on them. Her priority was to work out if she and Albert had a future. She was happy to be there for Frank, to offer him the occasional shoulder to cry on. Anything more would confuse things.

He told her he was going up to Manchester for the weekend to see some friends but promised to call her when he got back.

Over the weekend, she wrote and posted her letter ever so gently sacking Eileen Griffin, and did her best to stop thinking about Frank, but she couldn't. She didn't mean to, but she couldn't help comparing him to Albert. Frank hardly knew her and yet he had turned up to hear her sing. She knew that Albert couldn't be there because he was looking after Jake. But the more she tossed it around in her head— and, OK, she might just be paranoid—she couldn't help thinking that despite his protestations to the contrary, he hadn't really wanted to come.

What was more, when Frank found out that Ossie had finally agreed to take her on, he'd seemed almost as overjoyed as she was. Albert's reaction, on the other hand, had been pretty muted. Almost as soon as she had the thought, she was stricken with guilt. How could she be so selfish? Poor Albert had been pacing up and down with Jake for two hours, worried sick that he might have appendicitis. He'd been exhausted when she got home. What did she expect? If the roles had been reversed, if it was she who'd been tending to a sick Jake, her reaction would have been just as downbeat. Or would it? At the very least she would have given him a "well done" hug and she wouldn't have ignored him and gone on about buying new motorcycles. Again she pulled herself up. She'd always known Albert was self-centered, but he cared deep down; she was certain of that.

It was Stephanie's idea to skip breakfast that Sunday because Lizzie couldn't make it. It was the twins' birthday party that afternoon and she was going to be far too busy.

She was in the middle of cooking a fry-up for her and Jake, thoughts of Frank still center stage in her mind, when Cass rang to have a moan about having to go to the twins' birthday party that afternoon. She and Stephanie had been invited along to "liven things up."

"I mean, Lizzie's booked the customary pervy clown," Cass said. "Isn't that enough?"

Stephanie explained that she wanted them there to liven things up among the grown-ups rather than the children. "I think even Lizzie gets fed up, standing around with all those scrummy mummies, discussing house prices and school league tables."

"Yeah, I know," Cass said, clearly feeling a bit guilty now. "But what I really want to do is stay in and rent a movie. And my bush needs waxing. It's so overgrown they could hold the next *Celebrity Survivor* in it."

Stephanie couldn't help agreeing—about the birthday party, that is, not Cass's bush. Stephanie's perfect Sunday (assuming she was Jake-less and Cass and Lizzie weren't coming for breakfast) involved lolling on the sofa in her old toweling dressing gown, reading the papers and scratching. Every so often she would get up to make coffee or pluck the odd chin hair that she'd discovered while scratching, but that was pretty much it. Spending the afternoon justifying why Jake wasn't being prepped for preprep didn't really hold much appeal.

They drove over to Lizzie's in Stephanie's car, Jake strapped into his baby seat.

Cass seemed to be more down than ever about her lack of a love life and kept going on about what a huge mistake she'd made by having braces fitted on her teeth. The way she saw it, they were all that stood between her and a decent shag. "Seems like the only person getting any exciting sex is you— and your seventy-nine-year-old grandmother."

Stephanie made the point that the clear plastic was barely visible and that anyway, a man worth having wouldn't give a stuff. "And, just think, in a few months' time, you're going to have perfect teeth."

"Steph, I don't have a few months. The stress of doing without sex is really starting to get to me. I'm starting to forget things. On Friday night, I was at this really snotty Hampstead dinner party and everybody was talking about literature. The conversation got round to First World War poets and I said my favorite was Vidal Sassoon."

As Lizzie opened the front door, the noise of shrieking children charging around on the hardwood floors hit them like a blast of cold air. Lizzie was smiling gamely, but she looked drawn and weary. It didn't help that she wasn't wearing any makeup and that her hair, which looked like it could do with a wash, was hanging limp and lifeless around her shoulders. She screwed up her face in response to a particularly piercing screech. "I swear that next year I'm going to take the boys and a couple of their friends out for pizza and that will be that."

The three women kissed hello. Stephanie thought it strange that Lizzie looked quite so stressed. Not that she didn't have a right to, with dozens of seven-year-olds careening round her living room. It was just that Lizzie was so good at putting on kids' parties and she loved doing them. In the past, the noise and chaos had never gotten to her. Not that there had ever been much. Lizzie always had a strict timetable of games organized weeks in advance, which meant the children were constantly occupied and had no time to run wild.

The next moment Archie and Dougal came charging down the hall, yelling at the top of their lungs: "Look, more people! More people!" Stephanie and Cass took one look at the boys and exchanged amused glances. They were wearing miniature pith helmets and safari jackets.

"Boys, do calm down," Lizzie pleaded, taking a scrunchie off her wrist and drawing her hair back into a ponytail, "or we'll have to think about a time-out in your room." But Archie and Dougal took no notice. Instead they grabbed their presents, which Jake had been holding. Stephanie and Cass had gone in together and bought two copies of the *Guinness Book of World Records*.

"Love the outfits," Cass said, as the boys ripped off the wrapping paper.

"We're the chief explorers," Archie announced, puffing out his chest with pride.

"In the end the boys and I decided on a paleontology theme," Lizzie explained. "I was up until past midnight finishing off the jackets. I only did thirty papier-mâché helmets. I hope that's going to be enough." With that, she reached into her jeans pocket and pulled out a sticky label. She peeled off the back and pressed it onto Jake's sweatshirt. It read: Jake-asaurus.

In the living room, the *Flintstones* theme tune could just about be heard above the din. Stephanie and Cass stood admiring the party decorations while at the same time trying to ignore a gang of boys playing football with a pith helmet. Suspended from the ceiling were massive stegosauruses made out of kite material. With the help of a couple of slide projectors, the walls were covered in giant photographs of dinosaurs. In front of these stood tubs of giant palms and monstera plants.

"Hired them from the garden center up the road," Lizzie said. "Gives it that authentic Jurassic feel, don't you think?"

Both women agreed it did, that the effect was truly magnificent and that Lizzie was undoubtedly in possession of an awesome talent.

"Just wait until you see the cake," she said, her face brightening. At this point she noticed that the boys playing football had started a fight and were now piled in a heap, fists flying. Lizzie let out a long sigh. She looked exhausted, as if she just didn't have the energy to go over and break them up. Then, as if by magic, one of the nannies waded in and began hauling the boys off each other.

"I will never have children. Never, ever," Cass declared, her face positively contorted with distaste. "If I want to hear the pitter-patter of tiny feet, I'll put shoes on my cat."

By now the nanny was threatening to send the boys home if they didn't behave. Steph could tell she was a nanny because she was fat. Nearly all the nannies she'd met at local toddler groups and one o'clock clubs were overweight. Mothers clearly preferred them that way. Of course, it was easy to see why. Whose husband would want to shag the nanny if she had an arse the size of a mobile home?

"So," Cass said, "where's Dom? Shouldn't he be helping with crowd control?"

"Dom couldn't make it," Lizzie said, unable to look Cass in the eye. When Stephanie asked if the boys were upset about their father not being there, Lizzie just shrugged. Stephanie assumed Dom had been called away suddenly on business, and that he and Lizzie had had a bit of a domestic over it. This wasn't the time or place, Stephanie thought, to probe. Still, it explained why Lizzie looked so spent.

Stephanie decided to change the subject and ask what time the clown was due to arrive. Lizzie explained that in the end they'd decided against the clown on the grounds that he wouldn't stimulate the children's minds. Instead a paleontologist from the natural history museum was coming to give a talk about dinosaurs.

"A paleontologist?" Cass came back, her voice heavy with sarcasm. "Wow! Sounds like hours of fun." Lizzie said he did loads of children's parties and was apparently hugely entertaining. The only problem was she'd been expecting him at three and it was now half past.

Just then the nanny came over and offered to organize a fossil hunt. "Oh, would you?" Lizzie said, looking pathetically grateful. "That would be wonderful."

"All right, you lot," the nanny's voice boomed above the din. "Fossil hunt." Her announcement was met with deafening shrieks and cheers and demands to know what the prize was for the person who collected the most fossils. "Bet it's raisins," Stephanie heard an anonymous little voice grumble softly from under its pith helmet. "It's always raisins."

By now Jake had been adopted by a couple of motherly little girls and seemed perfectly happy to join the hunt for Lizzie's homemade biscuit fossils.

"Right, wine, I think," Lizzie declared, and led Cass and

Stephanie into the kitchen. Here, fifteen or so mums and a couple more nannies were standing around chatting in small groups, drinking Waitrose chardonnay. Stephanie caught snippets of conversation. It was mainly of the got-Magnus-into-a-wonderful-prep-school, needed-an-episiotomy, just-to-the-south-of-Tuscany variety.

"Anybody seen the corkscrew?" Lizzie said, moving things around on the worktop. Nobody had. She said she had a spare in the drinks cupboard in the living room and went off to fetch it.

As they helped themselves to nuts and crisps, Stephanie was aware of a silent, communal seethe coming from all the mummies. By now there wasn't one who hadn't seen Cass in her low-slung jeans and tight top. In a display of unprecedented mischief making, Stephanie said to one woman who was looking positively murderous with envy: "Doesn't she look wonderful? She just gave birth to twins, you know."

"Oh, stop it," Cass said to Stephanie, hamming it up for the woman's benefit. "You're embarrassing me." Then turning to the woman she said: "Actually, it was triplets." Stephanie and Cass giggled like a couple of mischievous nine-year-olds. Then to make matters worse Cass said loudly: "So, who's for an E?"

Several of the mummies seemed positively panic-stricken. "Just a joke," Cass said, holding out a handful of magnetic letter Es she'd just whipped off the fridge door. She reached into her bag for her cigarettes. "Better not," Stephanie said. "There are babies here." Cass rolled her eyes and snapped her bag shut.

At this point Lizzie came back brandishing the spare corkscrew. "Everything OK in here?" she said, totally oblivious to the withering looks the mummies were still giving Cass. While Lizzie opened a bottle of wine, Cass dug Stephanie

179

in the ribs. A woman in a rainbow-striped sweater was sitting at the kitchen table breast-feeding.

"Oh . . . my . . . God. Look at that."

"Come on, Cass," Stephanie said, "surely you've seen women breast-feeding."

Cass made the point that she had indeed seen women breast-feeding. "Breast-feeding *babies,* yes. Not children of three wearing CAT boots."

Stephanie shrugged and said these days it wasn't uncommon for women to breast-feed until the child chose to give it up.

"And look at all those blue veins on her boobs. She looks like she's got two slabs of Stilton on her front. And I bet she's got loads of loose stomach flesh. I'm never having children. Never. I mean it. Unless I can give birth through my kneecaps."

Lizzie handed them each a glass of wine. Cass was just about to put hers to her lips when she stopped. "Whoa, who is that man who's just walked in? He's absolutely gorgeous." The three women turned. He was tall and muscular, with trendy spiky hair.

"Oh, that's Alex," Lizzie said, giving the chap a hello wave. "I don't think he's quite your type, though."

"What, you mean because he's married?"

"Actually, he's not. His wife left him a few months ago. He gets the children at weekends."

"Right, well, maybe I can help get him over his grief." With that she was off.

"Cass, no," Lizzie hissed, making an urgent grab for her arm and missing. "Really, I don't think the two of you would have much in common."

"Lizzie, he's handsome and he has a pulse. That's 'in

180

common' enough for me." Cass turned away and started easing her way through the thickets of mummies.

Ten minutes later the paleontologist from the natural history museum arrived, full of apologies. Apparently the North Circular had been at a virtual standstill. Cass was severely disappointed that he looked nothing like Ross from *Friends*. The children, on the other hand, were more interested in his bag of fossils than his wispy beard and fawn cords that ended three inches above his ankles.

While Cass flirted with Alex and the mummies seethed even more, Stephanie offered to help Lizzie lay out the food on the long trestle table in the conservatory. The centerpiece was a truly magnificent erupting volcano cake, which Lizzie had spent days on. Sitting next to it were two giant plates of dinosaur-shaped sandwiches made from homemade bread (to which Lizzie had added green food coloring). Apparently these were to be followed by bronto burgers, pasta-raptor salad and vanilla Godzilla ice cream.

"You know, Lizzie," Stephanie said, "this entire party is utterly brilliant. You really ought to go professional, become a kids' party planner. What with that and selling all your candles and kindling kits, you could make a fortune. Dom must be so impressed."

"Well, he's not." With that Lizzie threw down the pile of paper dinosaur plates she was holding and started sobbing.

"Sweetheart, what on earth's the matter?" Stephanie said, putting an arm round Lizzie's shoulders.

"Dom's been having an affair," she wailed, tears rolling down her face. "It's been going on for months."

Stephanie wrapped her in a hug. "Oh, hon. I am so sorry."

"He said I'd gotten dull and boring and that I wasn't sexy anymore. Do you think I'm dull and boring?"

"Don't be ridiculous. You're not remotely dull or boring. And of course you're sexy. Lizzie, you are one of the most beautiful women I know."

"Yeah, but that doesn't make me sexy. I know I've gotten dowdy and frumpy. I've been too wrapped up in the boys. Oh, God, this is all my fault. I let this happen."

"Shh. No, you didn't. Dom just can't cope with domesticity and the chaos of having kids. Instead of confronting his problems, he's blaming you. On top of that he's decided to punish you by having an affair. There is no way this is your fault. So where's Dom now?"

"I told him to leave."

"Good for you."

By now the kitchen was empty. The mummies had gradually migrated into the living room to hear the paleontologist. Stephanie led Lizzie to the sofa, which was positioned against one wall of the conservatory, and sat holding her and rocking her gently. "Tell you what," Stephanie said after a few minutes, "how's about a nice cup of tea?" Lizzie took a tissue to her panda eyes, caused by her mascara running, and nodded. Stephanie put the kettle on and then went to fetch Cass.

In the living room, the children were kneeling on an enormous ground sheet, chipping away at a three-foot-high block of ice with plastic hammers and chisels.

"It's meant to be the polar ice cap," one of the mothers explained. "It's all Lizzie's idea. She's so clever. The child who finds the most mastodons wins a prize." Dom was such a prat, Stephanie thought. He had no idea what he had in Lizzie. She was beautiful, a wonderful mother, hugely talented. And she adored him. What more could he possibly want? Of course she knew the answer: a twenty-two-year-old firm-breasted innocent who wouldn't challenge him and laughed at all his jokes.

She virtually had to pry Cass off Alex. "Cass, I need you in the kitchen. It's really important."

On the way into the kitchen, Cass declared irritably that nothing could be more important than her trying to get laid. Then Steph told her about Lizzie. Cass's eyes filled with tears. "Not that it's come as a surprise," she said.

Cass went over and hugged Lizzie, which made her start crying all over again. Eventually they managed to calm her down and the three of them sat in the conservatory drinking tea. "Her name's Belinda," Lizzie said. "Belinda Olsen. Top honors from Oxford. She's doing articles at Dom's firm."

"God," Cass said, "her initials are B.O." Even Lizzie managed to laugh.

"So, how did you find out?" Stephanie said. Lizzie explained she'd overheard Dom on his mobile telling Belinda he loved her and couldn't wait to be with her.

"Just like Cass did." Stephanie had blurted it out before she could stop herself. Cass did a theatrical roll of her eyes.

"What? You and Cass knew?" Lizzie looked truly hurt. "And you never said anything?" Stephanie explained about New Year's Eve. "Look, blame me. Cass was all for telling you, but I persuaded her it was none of our business and that you and Dom had to sort it out. I don't think you would have thanked us if we'd blabbed."

Lizzie let out a heavy breath. "No, maybe not."

Eventually Lizzie said she wanted to get back to the party because the twins would be wondering where she'd gotten to. Stephanie asked her how much they knew about what was going on.

"Nothing," Lizzie said. "They think Dom's away on business."

Stephanie and Cass were worried about leaving her after the party, but Lizzie said she needed some space to think and that her mother had offered to have the boys for a few days.

"You know, you will get through this," Stephanie said. "And, whatever happens, we'll always be here."

"I know," Lizzie said with a tearful smile. "What would I do without the two of you?"

Jake slept most of the journey home. The two women didn't really discuss Lizzie and Dom. There didn't seem much to say other than that Dom was a complete tosser.

"I just hope he comes to his senses," Stephanie said. "If his marriage means anything to him, he'll get down on his knees and beg Lizzie to forgive him...So how did you and Alex get on?"

"Well," Cass said, "it's true. He isn't the type I'd usually go for."

"Yeah, I mean, you've never been out with a bloke who's got kids."

"Or a dog collar."

"Yes, you have. Don't you remember that kinky Gavin bloke you were seeing who bought you one with pink nylon fur and fake diamonds?"

"No, I mean a real dog collar."

Stephanie took a moment to process this. "Hang on. Omigod. He's a vicar? Gorgeous Alex is a vicar?"

Despite everything that had happened, Stephanie burst out laughing.

"So, I take it you're not planning to see him again."

"Well, you take it wrong. I'm seeing him tomorrow, as it goes."

"Where's he taking you?"

"His congregation is raising money for Oxfam and he's invited me to the church hall for a frugal lunch."

Chapter 12

Stephanie arrived at Ossie Da Costa's office the next morning exactly at ten. Sheila, his assistant, told her to go straight in and that she would be along in a minute with coffee. Ossie was sitting at his desk in his running shorts and T-shirt. He was eating a bacon sandwich and wiping post-jog sweat from his forehead, while at the same time carrying on a phone conversation that, for his part at least, was being conducted at a slightly high-pitched bellow.

"Look, Ed, with respect, I don't give a monkey's arse that you're the duke of Wessex." He stifled a belch and motioned Stephanie to take a seat. "I treat your company like I'd treat any other film company. If you want Branagh to do the voice-over for your documentary, then that's the fee. No discount...No, not even for lunch with Princess Michael of Kent..." It seemed that His Royal Highness, having given up the film business, had now relaunched his career with a documentary about the history of royal cutlery and china.

Just then Sheila came in carrying two cups of coffee.

"Buzz the intercom when he keels over with a heart attack," Sheila said, rolling her eyes to indicate that conversations like these were regular events, "and I'll phone for an ambulance." She handed Stephanie a cup of coffee and put the other one down in front of Ossie.

He was too busy shouting at Prince Edward to notice. He slammed down the phone, turned to Stephanie and grinned. "Ten minutes and he'll be back, offering the full amount, I guarantee it."

"Or he'll have you slung in the Tower," Sheila said, "and with a bit of luck they'll throw away the key."

"Oh, but you'd wait for me, wouldn't you, Sheila? And you'd bring me the occasional Havana to keep my spirits up?"

Sheila told him to dream on. Ossie responded by patting her on the bottom and asking her if she would mind putting what remained of his bacon sandwich in the microwave, as it had gone cold. Snorting and tutting, Sheila picked the plate up off the desk. Ossie waited until Sheila had closed the door. "It's her birthday tomorrow," he whispered. "I thought I'd surprise her." He pulled a small box out of his drawer, took off the lid and passed it over to Stephanie. Inside was a pair of large, exceedingly overstated gold and emerald earrings. "Lost track of how many times she's been thirty-nine, but I know for a fact she's fifty. I got them in Harrods' Egyptian department. Do you think she'll like them?" Stephanie said she was sure Sheila would love them.

Smiling, Ossie put the box back in his drawer. Then he looked up at Stephanie. The smile was still there, but she detected an uneasiness about his eyes. "You know, your performance the other night was outstanding. Quite outstanding. I have to say that Sidney is pretty smitten with you." She felt herself going red. "He's convinced you're perfect for what he has in mind."

187

"So what does he have in mind?" she asked, desperately trying to control her excitement. "I'm dying to know."

Ossie leaned back in his chair and tried to put his feet on the desk, but they wouldn't reach. He sat up again and began playing with the gold crucifix he wore on a chain around his neck. So, Ossie was a teetotaler and wore a crucifix. Was it possible that the loudmouthed, belching, "I don't give a monkey's arse" Ossie was religious? Surely not.

"OK. Sid is about to stage a new musical about the life of Peggy Lee. It's called *Peggy*." He brought his fingers together so that they formed a steep arch. "It opened on Broadway a couple of months ago to rave reviews. Then Holly Robbins, who was playing Peggy, had a stand-up fight with the director and they both walked out. Sid replaced them, but the magic had gone and they just couldn't get bums on seats and the show closed. Now Sid's bringing it to London with a completely new cast." She could feel what was coming. She could just feel it. "It's going to be the campest thing since his production of *Judy* a few years ago." As Stephanie nodded and said she'd read about what had happened in New York, she started to tremble. God, Sidney Doucette wanted her to play Peggy Lee. By now her pulse was racing. She'd lost count of the number of times she'd allowed herself to imagine being offered a part like this, but she never thought it would actually happen.

"It opens in a couple of weeks." Trembling with anticipation, Stephanie gave an eager nod. "It's fully cast. Katherine Martinez is playing Peggy."

The words *fully cast* and *Katherine Martinez* hit her like a wrecking ball. It took her a couple of seconds to regain her equilibrium. "Sorry, who did you say was playing the lead?" He repeated the name.

"Oh, right," she said, her excitement turning to numbness, "if it's opening in a couple of weeks, of course it's been cast." She could feel her eyes stinging with tears. What had she been thinking? Katherine Martinez was a Hollywood superstar. Stephanie Glassman played the piano in hotel lounges. How could she have imagined even in her wildest dreams that Sidney Doucette would bring in an unknown to play the lead? And now that she thought about it, with blond hair, Martinez would be the image of the young Peggy Lee. Stephanie could feel Ossie looking at her, taking in her expression. His face broke into a soft smile. "Stephanie, I know you're disappointed. It's my fault. I know I led you to believe that this was going to be something really big."

Desperate to give him the impression that she was a trouper used to getting knocked back, she told him it was OK and that he shouldn't worry.

"No, it's not OK," he said. "I'm as disappointed as you are. I swear to you, I thought Sidney was auditioning you for the lead. He has a history of taking gambles and casting unknowns. You may find this hard to believe, but until he and I left the Blues Café on Thursday night, I had absolutely no idea that Katherine Martinez already had the part. I'm furious with him for not being straight with me, and I've told him so."

"OK, but you mentioned that Sidney still has a part in mind for me."

"He does, but you're not going to like it." There was a long pause while Ossie lit up a cigar. "Katherine Martinez may have been given the lead, but there is one small problem." Stephanie gave a small frown. "The woman can't sing a note."

"I can see how that might be a problem if you're playing

189

Peggy Lee, yes," Stephanie said. Ossie cleared his throat. By now he seemed to be feeling even more uneasy. "That's where you come in," he said.

"Where I come in? I don't understand."

"OK, Sid is looking for somebody to record the songs and Katherine will lip-synch them on stage. He had a singer lined up, but she has come down with some virus that's affected her voice."

Stephanie sat processing this for a few moments. "But the singer gets the credit, right? I mean, her name is on the billboard alongside Katherine's."

Ossie took his cigar out of his mouth and flicked an ash into an ashtray. "Actually, no."

"What? You mean the whole thing's a con? The audience is tricked into believing Katherine can sing?"

"In a nutshell, yes. If you ask me, Sid's seen too many reruns of *Singin' in the Rain*. Anyway, the most important thing is that nobody must know. The cast and technical people have all signed confidentiality agreements."

Stephanie stared at Ossie and started laughing. "Sidney can't be serious."

"That's what I said, but I assure you he is—deadly serious."

"But he'll never get away with it. Everyone will see Katherine's lip-synching. You can always tell."

Ossie explained that, according to Sid, it had all been thoroughly thought through. The lighting was to be arranged in such a way that it would be hard for anybody not onstage to tell it wasn't Katherine singing. She suggested it might have made life a lot easier if Sidney had simply taken on somebody who could sing.

"Katherine's a huge star. She even looks like Peggy Lee. People will flock to this show. Having her in the lead is tantamount to Sid's company being given a license to print money. Look, I know the whole thing stinks. I've already told Sid I'm pretty sure you won't agree to do it—and I really wouldn't blame you."

"Too right I won't," Stephanie shot back. "For a start, it's dishonest. On top of that, why would I let Katherine Martinez take all the credit, when it's my voice the audience will be hearing? And what happens if it all goes pear-shaped and the press find out what's going on?"

"I have to say I don't think anybody will leak this. Not for the amounts Sid's paying them to keep quiet."

"Sorry, it makes no difference."

"OK, but I think I should tell you that he is offering you a thousand pounds for every week the show runs. I got him up from seven fifty. After all, you'd be carrying the show and getting none of the credit."

That stopped her in her tracks. "A thousand?...A week?"

Ossie nodded. "And Martinez has signed a year's contract." That meant the deal was worth fifty thousand pounds. Stephanie sat thinking about what she could do with money like that. She could get rid of her worn-out old VW, put down a deposit on a decent flat, take a holiday, and she would still be free to work on any other project Ossie found for her. She was aware she was sitting there with her mouth open, not saying anything.

"Look," he said, "don't make your mind up now. Go home and think about it. I want to make it clear, though, that if you go for it, I'm not going to take any commission from you. I can't say I approve of what Sid's doing, plus I gave you the impression this gig would be a turning point in your career. I feel I've let you down by offering you something this tacky."

Then he said he was in a hurry because he had another client due any moment. "Let's talk. And also, why don't you let me buy you dinner? Then maybe we could go on somewhere. A club, perhaps." His voice softened. "You know, Stephanie, you really are a very beautiful woman." Then he rolled his cigar in his mouth and did the Groucho Marx eyebrow thing again, just as he had at the Blues Café. It was only now that the light went on and she realized he fancied her.

It was too much to process at once: Sidney Doucette's insane plan, the thousand quid a week and now Ossie asking her out. He was clearly a fundamentally decent bloke, and judging by the earrings he'd bought Sheila, he wasn't without a tender, sensitive side. But she didn't remotely fancy him. He was still pushy and loud and he had the table manners of Henry the Eighth. Then there was the height thing. Was it politically incorrect to admit that men of three foot nine didn't turn her on? Either way, she couldn't possibly admit to Ossie that his size was an issue. It would have been too cruel. Of course, she could always tell him about Albert and how she wasn't interested in any romantic involvement right now. But she was certain that he wouldn't believe her. He was bound to assume that she'd rejected him because of his size. God, how did you turn down a midget who asked you out, without it looking, well, midget-ist?

"So, do we have a date?" Ossie prompted.

On the other hand, maybe he would respect her more if she was honest. "The thing is, Ossie . . . you see, the thing is." She shifted in her chair, groping for something tactful and kind to say. Of course, nothing came. "What I mean is . . . what I'm trying to say is . . . That sounds great. I'd love to have dinner."

"Excellent. I know this amazing Austrian place where you can sit and eat Wiener schnitzel until you think your name's Wolfgang."

"Wow. Great," she said, hoping her lack of enthusiasm wasn't showing. Just then the phone rang. "Ah, Your Royal Highness," Ossie said, giving Stephanie a conspiratorial wink, "I thought you might call back." Then he covered up the mouthpiece. "I'll call you," he said, puckering up his lips and making soft kissing noises.

She walked briskly toward Leicester Square tube, her head down against the bitter wind, cursing herself again and again for being stupid enough to think she might have been offered the lead. But she couldn't do what Sidney was asking. Not even for a thousand quid a week.

On the tube, a woman was sitting next to her, reading this month's *Vogue*. Stephanie peered over her shoulder, her heart sinking to her scuffed Faith boots as she stared at the razor-cheeked models draped in itsy-bitsy floaty things costing thousands. She yearned to treat herself to something pretty and just a bit extravagant. Not that she would have bought anything itsy-bitsy or floaty, even if she could have afforded it. She wasn't tall enough or sufficiently emaciated for either itsy or bitsy, and floaty made her look like a Druid. She carried on staring at the magazine, practically salivating at the La Perla underwear, the cutesy Lulu Guinness handbags, a particularly spectacular pair of green satin Jimmy Choo slingbacks. She began fantasizing about going clothes shopping with Cass, being able to have a massage or her highlights done, knowing she didn't have to panic or feel guilty about breaking the bank.

By the time she reached the Park Royal, her position on the Sidney Doucette offer had taken a distinct shift. Was there some way she could get past the dishonesty issue and accept it?

Since she was more than an hour early, she headed for the hotel coffee shop.

She sat scraping the chocolate off her cappuccino foam and thinking about Sidney's proposal. OK, maybe there was an argument that duping the audience didn't constitute such a major crime. As consumers, the audience would still be getting a decent product. An exceptionally decent product, even if she did say so herself. Plus, it wasn't as if anybody was going to get hurt. But what if it all went wrong and the press found out? Ossie had said it was unlikely, but he couldn't be sure. So, what would happen? Nothing—at least not to her. It wasn't as if anybody could destroy her reputation, since—let's face it—she wasn't famous and didn't have one to start with. It would be Sidney and Katherine Martinez who would end up taking the rap. What did she have to lose? Absolutely nothing. Yes, it meant handing over all the glory to Martinez, but for the kind of money Sidney was offering, maybe—just maybe—she could live with that.

She was pretty much convinced, but not quite. Maybe she was a wimp, but apart from the boob tube/ear-piercing incident when she was a teenager and taking the occasional dress back to Top Shop to get a refund after wearing it to a party, she'd never done anything dishonest in her life. It was bad enough that her bank account was permanently in the red. She knew perfectly well that the bank wasn't suffering, that it had vast piles of cash and that it made money out of the interest she was paying, but she still felt guilty, as if she were taking something that didn't belong to her.

She realized she needed reassurance, somebody to tell her she was overanalyzing the whole thing and that taking this job was the right decision. She dialed Albert on her mobile, but all she got was his voice mail. Cass couldn't talk because she was in Harvey Nicks, frantically searching for something to wear for her frugal lunch with Alex. "I'm due there in an hour and I've still got nothing." Stephanie suggested she might have more luck finding something appropriate in the Gap or Oxfam, but Cass said Harvey Nicks had just gotten in this wonderful selection of "previously loved" jeans, which she thought would hit the right sartorial note.

In the end she phoned Lizzie, but just to see how she was bearing up. She didn't think it was fair to burden her with any more problems. Lizzie said she hadn't slept and sounded pretty rough. When Stephanie asked if she'd heard from Dom, she said he'd phoned a couple of times, but she'd let the machine pick up. "I'm just not ready to speak to him." Stephanie offered to go round and keep her company that night, but Lizzie said she didn't feel up to it and would still rather be on her own.

She finally got Albert during her break, but he said he couldn't talk for long because it was his turn to be parent helper at Jake's playgroup and he was in the middle of chopping up fruit for the children's afternoon snack. "By the way, your mother called," he said. "She's desperate to see Jake. Is it OK if he sleeps over there tonight?"

"Fine," she said. "Listen, I saw Ossie this morning and found out about this project. It's all a bit complicated and I could really do with some advice. Do you fancy coming to supper?"

"Sure, but only if you wear the blue dress," he said.

She giggled and told him to behave. "Look, it's been completely dead here the last few days. I'm going to see if I can get off early. Tell you what, I'll cook. How do you fancy Thai curry?"

She managed to get away just after six. By half past eight, having sprinted round the Muswell Hill Sainsbury's picking up chicken breasts, curry paste, coconut milk, rice wine and all the other herby, spicy bits she needed, she was standing in front of a smoking wok, stir-frying strips of chicken. She took a glug of wine. Albert would be there any moment. Twenty minutes later, there was no sign of him. She wasn't particularly bothered. Knowing Albert, he'd gotten caught up in something and misjudged the time. She decided to put the food in the oven to keep hot and check her e-mail. Among all the junk there was one from Jimmy, who owned the house. She assumed it was just to say hi and check how she was getting on. Only it wasn't. Jimmy was coming home. Apparently Brian, his ex, had followed him to Thailand and they'd gotten back together—exactly as Cass had predicted. "We're planning to travel around for another couple of months and then we'll be coming back. Sorry, Steph, but I'm going to need the house back sooner than I thought."

She sat, eyes closed, rubbing her forehead. Even though the news hadn't come as a complete shock, she'd been hoping Jimmy would stay away for a few more months at least. Since she didn't have the money for the rental deposit on a new flat, she would have no choice but to move in with her parents. Oh, great. Unless, of course, she bit the bullet and accepted Sidney Doucette's offer.

Another half hour passed. Still no sign of Albert. She tried him on his mobile, but all she got was his voice mail. Ten o'clock came and went. First she was cross, then she started to worry. Just before eleven, as she was starting to really panic, the phone finally rang.

"Albert, you OK? I thought you'd had an accident."

"Listen, *principessa,* I can't talk, I've got hardly any battery left." In about ten seconds he explained that he'd completely forgotten she was expecting him for dinner and that he'd driven to Wandsworth to look at the Harley this poker pal of his was selling. "Then we went to the pub to seal the deal. I am so sorry. I know you wanted to talk. Can we do it tomorrow?"

It seemed so childish to make a fuss. He hadn't meant to upset her. He'd simply forgotten. It happens. OK, it happened to Albert more than most, but it was still no big deal. "Yeah, fine. No problem," she said. "See you tomorrow." But there was no reply. His battery had clearly given out. She put down the phone and sat at the kitchen table, raking her hair with her fingers. Yes, she could reheat the curry tomorrow night and they could talk then, but try as she might, she couldn't help feeling hurt. The point was, tonight hadn't been unusual. She'd done her best to ignore it, but as the weeks went by she was realizing that despite what Albert had said about really caring for her, his first concern in life—apart from Jake—was Albert. She'd had a glimpse of her future with him and it felt lonely.

When the phone rang a second time she assumed it was Albert ringing from a call box to offer more apologies. When she answered, her tone was distinctly downbeat.

"Stephanie, that you? Have I gotten you at a bad time?"

It was Frank. Her spirits lifted immediately. "No, I was just watching some weepy chick flick on the telly."

"Oh, right. Listen," he said. Then he paused. "God, is it really eleven? I had no idea it was this late. You sure I haven't woken you?" She said she was positive. "OK, it's just that I was wondering if you fancied going out for dinner on Saturday."

She hesitated, but only for a moment. "That would be great." She was vaguely aware of some kind of mechanical noise in the background. "Where are you?" she asked.

"Actually, I'm sitting in the launderette round the corner. My washing machine's broken, and I just realized I'd run out of socks."

She started laughing. "Look, I don't suppose you're hungry, are you?"

"Starving. I haven't eaten since lunch. I was going to pick up fish-and-chips on the way home."

"OK, stay where you are. I'll be there in five minutes. You do like Thai green curry, don't you?"

"Love it."

She wasn't surprised when passersby gave her strange looks. After all, it was half past eleven at night and she must have looked a strange sight, walking down the street wearing oven gloves and carrying a large orange Le Creuset casserole. In addition, dangling from her wrist was a Sainsbury's carrier bag containing two of Jake's red plastic Bob the Builder beakers, a bottle of Jacob's Creek and a corkscrew. Eagle-eyed pedestrians might also have observed the two forks sticking out of her coat pocket. She realized that any sensible person would have suggested they have dinner at her place, after he'd finished doing his laundry, but somehow the idea of the two of them sharing Thai curry in the launderette seemed like more fun.

"Grub up," she announced as she walked in, grateful that he was the only person in the place. She put the Le Creuset down on the long Formica table. Then she handed him the bottle of wine and a corkscrew.

"You know, I've never met anyone like you before," he said, smiling and kissing her on the cheek. He poured the wine into the Bob the Builder beakers. "I thought glass would break," she said by way of explanation. He said she'd been very sensible. As they clunked beakers they both started to laugh.

"Come on, dig in before it gets cold," she said, producing

the two forks from her pocket. They ate perched on the table, the Le Creuset between them.

He declared the curry to be wonderful and said he hadn't had this much fun in ages. The truth was the curry was a bit dried out from being in the oven so long, but she appreciated the compliment and thanked him.

"It's me who should be thanking you," he said. There was something about his smile, the way his eyes had met hers, that made her think he was referring to more than just the food. Maybe she was reading too much into it, but it was almost as if he were thanking her for having walked into his life. "So," he went on, "did you see Ossie today?" She took a mouthful of wine and told him the tale. "Blimey, Sidney Doucette must be pretty sure this is going to work. His technical people must have really thought it through. So, what are you going to do?"

She said she'd pretty much decided to do it. "Thing is, I just find it so hard to be even slightly dishonest. Does that sound really wimpy?"

"Nah," he said, stabbing another piece of chicken. "It's a girly thing." She felt herself feeling defensive and turned on at the same time. "So, you've got a criminal record as long as your arm, I suppose."

"Not exactly, but I came pretty close to getting one." He explained that when he was in high school, he and some of his mates broke into their school one night and painted "HM Prison" in twelve-foot-high letters on the roof. "We had this appallingly sadistic headmaster, and by the time we were seventeen we decided we'd had enough. The police never got involved, but the story made the local paper and we were expelled."

"Wow, I'm impressed," she said. "But you were doing it for a good cause. All I'd be doing it for is the money."

"Is that such a bad thing?" he asked. "I mean, how much do you need it?"

She shrugged. "I've got to get out of my house in a couple of months because the bloke who owns it is coming back. I don't have enough money to pay the deposit on a flat and no prospect of raising it in time. I suppose I could borrow it from my mum and dad, but rents have gone up since Christmas and I'm not sure I'd even be able to earn enough to cover the rent on a new place. On top of that my car's knackered and I haven't had a holiday in years. If I took the Doucette job, I could actually start thinking about buying somewhere."

Frank told her he thought she was making the right decision. He made the same points she had about the audience not really being shortchanged, since she had a fabulous voice and that reputation-wise it was Sidney Doucette and Katherine Martinez who were taking all the risk. She drained her beaker. "It's what I needed to hear," she said. "Thanks."

The next thing she knew her fork was sliding off her plate. She and Frank both made a grab for it, but she got there first and his hand ended up on top of hers. Instead of taking it away, he let it rest there for several seconds. It felt strong and warm and she wondered what it would be like to be wrapped in his arms.

For the next twenty minutes, while Frank's underwear went round in the tumble dryer, they sat chatting about his weekend in Manchester, his rehearsals for *Twelfth Night*. When the dryer stopped he went to empty it. He came back with a load of hot dry underwear and socks, which he put on the Formica table. They carried on chatting while she helped him bundle his Paul Smith socks into pairs. It seemed a bit forward to start folding his underwear, but she noted they were boxers—mainly black and gray. A faint smile must have

crossed her lips because he said, "They meet with your approval, then."

"Oh, God. No, sorry. I didn't mean . . ." But he told her
he was only teasing. "You know," he said, "I can't believe I've
had such an entertaining evening at the launderette."

"Neither can I," she replied.

"And thanks for the curry. It was wonderful."

It began as a hug. But all the time Stephanie stood there
wrapped in his arms, patting him gently on the back, she was
aware of his body next to hers, her breasts pressing against
him. He moved his head to look at her. She felt his eyes scan-
ning her face. He ran his finger down over her nose to her
mouth and she smiled up at him. As he cupped her face in his
hands and brushed her lips lightly with his, she breathed in
his warm heavenly smell. She felt his lips part. Hers followed
suit. She closed her eyes, melted into him as his tongue—
hard, pressing, urgent—found hers. He tasted of wine and
smelled of Snuggle.

Chapter 13

As she lay curled up in bed, eyes closed, Stephanie must have relived Frank Waterman's head-swimmingly glorious kiss twenty times. Again and again she felt his arms tight around her, his skin against hers. She could smell him, taste him. More than anything, she realized she would have happily ripped off her clothes in the middle of the launderette and let Frank take her on the Formica table among the abandoned odd socks and tea towels.

Of course, there was no knowing where their relationship would lead, but she was certain she needed to find out. She also knew she owed it to Albert to be straight with him, to explain that she'd been having serious doubts about their future and that there was somebody else. There was no way she was prepared to see Frank behind his back. Telling him would be one of the hardest things she'd ever done.

She fell asleep just as it was getting light. The next thing she knew she could hear Albert calling up from the hall. Barely awake, she reached out from under the duvet and groped for the alarm clock. It was half past eight. "Hang on. Won't be a minute." Her eyes red and puffy from lack of sleep, her hair looking like a family of starlings had been nesting in it, she pulled on her dressing gown. She shuffled into the kitchen, still doing up the belt. Albert was standing by the kitchen table, looking frantically under old newspapers and letters.

"Wow, you look like you've been up all night. Are you OK?" Albert said, looking up briefly. Stephanie yawned and ran her fingers through her hair. "I didn't sleep very well. Things on my mind. Listen, Albert—"

"*Principessa,*" he said, interrupting her, "you seen my wallet? I think I've lost it." She shook her head. While Albert carried on rummaging, she opened the fridge door and took out a carton of orange juice. "But you must have had it last night when you paid for the bike." He said he and his poker friend had agreed on a price, but he hadn't actually paid for it. "I need to get to the bank to get some cash." He went over to the counter and began hunting among the jars and dirty dishes. "And get it to him before twelve. He's going out of town."

Just then Albert's mobile started vibrating. Irritated, he flipped open the top. It was Lois, his agent in L.A. "God, Lois, what's so urgent? It must be one in the morning there . . . No, I already told you. I can't do it. I'm looking after my little boy for a few weeks. And I'm not a model. I do stunt work, for chrissake. Look, I'm sorry they can't find anybody else, but that's really not my problem . . . OK, speak to you soon. Bye."

Stephanie asked him what she wanted. "Some director just called her. Apparently Michael Douglas is filming in Berlin. He's doing these nude sex scenes and he needs a butt double."

Stephanie burst out laughing. "Michael Douglas needs a butt double?"

"Yeah. Apparently his buns have gotten real crepey and they need somebody toned, but not too young. Lois and I got drunk one New Year's and slept together, so she knows I have a great butt."

Stephanie stood there shaking her head and smiling. "Do it," she said.

"I can't," he said. "Who'll look after Jake?"

"I'll sort something out. Come on, it'll be paying a fortune and you haven't had a break for weeks. Phone Lois back and say you've changed your mind."

"You mean that?" She nodded. "I love you, *principessa*. I really love you." He began punching out Lois's number. "Lois, it's Albert..."

It turned out he had to be at Heathrow by three at the latest. "I'll just make it," he said to Stephanie, "if I can find my damn wallet." In sheer desperation he went over to the fridge and started moving containers around.

"Don't be ridiculous, it's not in there," Stephanie said, laughing. "Think. Where did you last have it?"

He decided it might be in the living room. She followed him. She knew she couldn't have picked a worse moment, but she couldn't help it. She just had to tell him about Frank. To let him go to Berlin still assuming they had a future just wasn't fair.

"Albert," she said, swallowing hard, "I've been thinking about stuff—you-and-me stuff—and I think we really need to talk."

He picked up a cushion, swore and threw it back down on the sofa. "*Principessa*, please. Now is not a good time. Shit. Where is it? Where did I leave it?" His face was starting to turn pink. "Maybe it's upstairs." He darted into the hall. She followed him. "You see, the thing is," she said, trotting up the stairs behind him, "I'm just not sure you and I . . ." He disappeared onto the landing.

"Got it!" By now he was standing in the loo, waving his wallet victoriously over his head.

She stood there, watching him. "Do you mind telling me, who takes their wallet to the loo?"

"I was on my cell booking tickets for a soccer game."

"While you were on the loo?"

He shrugged. "I multitask." Then he kissed her on the cheek.

She asked him if he had time for a quick coffee.

"OK, so long as it's real quick."

As she stood spooning coffee into the cafetière, he came and put his arms round her waist. "Listen, I just wanted to say I'm sorry about last night. Do you know what else I love about you, *principessa*?" She shook her head. "That you are so totally un-needy. I mean, practically every other woman I know would have been pissed with me when I didn't show up." Then he gave her another kiss. "So, I forgot to ask. How did it go with Ossie?" He took an apple out of the bowl and bit into it. She told him the tale.

"Well," he said when she'd finished, "seems like you managed to make the right decision without me. If nobody stands to get hurt, why would you turn down that kind of money? I mean, it would be a total no-brainer."

She asked him what he knew about Katherine Martinez.

"K-Mart?" he said with a soft laugh.

"That's what you call her? K-Mart?"

He shrugged. "Everybody loathes her. I worked with her on a movie a few years ago. It's the usual Hollywood diva deal: she swans onto the set four hours late. The director's too intimidated to say anything. She's too snooty to socialize when she's not filming and spends her time holed up in her trailer with her sushi chef and tarot reader." Just then his mobile went. It was the chap selling the Harley.

"OK," he said, looking at his watch. "I can probably just make it in an hour." He flipped the top of his phone and stood up. "Gotta run, *principessa*. I'll e-mail to let you know when I'll be back."

"Albert, hang on. We really do need to t—" But he was already out the door.

As soon as Albert left, she phoned Estelle to ask her if she would mind hanging on to Jake for the week. Stephanie was feeling desperately guilty about how much the poor little mite had been shunted around since Christmas, but if she was going to take the Sidney Doucette job, asking her mother to look after Jake was her only option. Of course Estelle couldn't have been more delighted. "Listen, darling," Estelle said after Stephanie had said how guilty she felt about neglecting Jake, "you're trying to make a go of your career. That's never easy for married women, let alone single parents. Come on, stop beating yourself up. And he's always with Albert or me and your father. You know how much we all adore him."

"I know. That makes me feel better."

"So," Estelle went on, "how did you get on with Ossie yesterday?"

"Look, what I'm about to tell you is top secret, right?"

"Darling, you know me, my lips are sealed."

Stephanie told her about being the voice for Katherine Martinez. "So, it's not a real part, then?" Estelle said, barely disguising her disappointment at not being able to show off at the next Masonic ladies' night. Then she started to panic and go on about repercussions, although when Stephanie asked her what repercussions there could be, she couldn't actually think of any. Estelle put Harry on the line, clearly thinking that since he'd been a lawyer his legal brain would be able to think up the repercussions she couldn't. Harry listened closely and agreed with Stephanie that she probably couldn't do herself any harm by taking the job. "On the other hand, this Sidney Doucette character is obviously as bent as a twelve-bob note. I don't think you can trust him. If you ask me, a thousand quid a week seems far too good to be true. Just make sure you get it in writing."

"Of course you'll have it in writing," Ossie assured her when she phoned to tell him she was accepting the offer. "But how come you've changed your mind?" She told him she still wasn't happy about it, but she couldn't walk away from the money.

Ossie told her that the show's director wanted to start recording on Monday. Apparently, it was imperative that it was finished that week because the press night had been scheduled for the following Friday and Katherine would need time to practice lip-synching Stephanie's voice. Until now, in rehearsals she had been using CDs of the real Peggy Lee.

Stephanie decided that rather than take the week off from the Park Royal, she would tell them she wasn't coming back. The Blues Café on the other hand was anxious not to lose her and offered her a month's sabbatical, which she accepted. She wanted a break and, more important, to spend some time with Jake. Once the recording was over, with the first thousand-pound check in her account, she could afford to take it easy for a bit.

Ossie also told her that she would be expected to sign the same confidentiality agreement that everybody else involved with the project had signed. "Of course," she said, realizing she'd already told Frank, Albert and her parents. Plus, there was also no way she was about to lie to Cass and Lizzie. But what the heck, she couldn't keep this thing entirely to herself. She just couldn't.

"So, are we still on for dinner?" Ossie said. "How's about Monday night after you've finished in the studio?" She had to admit she'd been praying he'd forgotten. "Of course. Wiener schnitzel. Monday's fine. I'll look forward to it."

Naturally, when Estelle had said her lips were sealed, this was only partially true. The moment Stephanie put the phone down from Ossie, she had Lilly on the phone. She then proceeded to have the identical "repercussions" conversation she'd had with her mother.

"So, Gran," Stephanie said eventually, desperate to change the subject, "how are things with you and Bernard?"

"Fantastic. And you know what? He's also a wonderful tai chi teacher." Lilly then launched into an exhaustive and meticulous account of how much more aligned her body had become since Bernard had begun teaching her how to move harmoniously. This in turn was making her feel so much more emotionally centered. Stephanie had to admit that her grandmother was a truly remarkable woman. While the rest of the elderly population seemed happy to totter over the hill into dotage valley, here was Lilly, busy having moments of ecstasy and balancing her chi.

"Anyway," Lilly went on, "the reason I rang was to say that Bernard's coming over in an hour or so, and I was wondering if you'd like to meet him."

"Ah, so, it's getting serious between you two, then?" Stephanie said. Lilly laughed and offered a cryptic "maybe."

"I'd love to come," Stephanie told her. Then she said she was calling in to see Mrs. M., who'd just come out of hospital after her hip replacement, and she'd come on afterward. "But I can't stay long. I have to be at work by lunchtime."

Mrs. M. answered the door, her weight resting heavily on a three-pronged aluminum cane. She looked tired and a bit pale, but she insisted that she was in no pain. "See, the limp's almost gone," she said as she led Stephanie down the hall. "A bit stiff, that's all. Just you wait, I'll be sprinting in a few weeks."

"Course you will," Stephanie said brightly, knowing full well that even with her new hip, Mrs. M. would never be able to chase after Jake and that there was no way she could give her back her old job.

"So, how's my little man? I've still got his Christmas present here, you know, all wrapped up. Tell you what, why don't I come over for a cuppa when I'm feeling a bit better and give it to him then? Do you think he'll mind waiting?" Stephanie said she was sure he wouldn't.

On the coffee table in the living room was a dainty bone china coffeepot and matching cups and saucers. Carefully arranged on top of a doily-covered plate were slices of poppy-seed cake and Battenberg sponge cake. "Oh, Mrs. M., this looks lovely."

"My daughter Geraldine did it," Mrs. M. said. "You just missed her. She popped over to Brent Cross Marks to buy a corselet." With that she let go of her cane and sat down heavily on the sofa, letting out a breathy oomph as she went.

"These are for you," Stephanie said, presenting her with a big box of Belgian chocs and a selection of the month's glossies.

"Ooh, darlin', you shouldn't. You really do spoil me. Oh,

now then, will you look at that?" She was staring at the front cover of *Hello!* "Isn't she a beauty?" How she'd missed it, Stephanie had no idea. There was Katherine Martinez, all strapless red satin, perfectly color-coordinated pout and itty-bitty ski-jump nose. Stephanie read the headline: "Hollywood Legend Katherine Martinez Speaks Candidly from Her Beverly Hills Cottage about Her Upcoming London Stage Debut as Peggy Lee."

"Mrs. M., do you mind if I just have a glance at this article for a sec?"

"Not at all, darlin'," she said, passing Stephanie the magazine. "You're like me. Nothing like a bit of escapism."

Mrs. M. poured the coffee and Stephanie flicked through the pages of *Hello!* Of course, the Beverly Hills cottage turned out to be a sprawling hacienda, which looked like it had been done up by a gay gaucho. But there was no doubt K-Mart looked stunning languorously draped over various bits of antique furniture.

"You can see she's got that kind of fresh-faced look Peggy Lee had," Mrs. M. said, sliding a cup of coffee along the table toward Stephanie. "Oh, look, it says her 'mellifluous velvet voice has been rigorously honed during the last year by daily singing lessons.' You know, whatever you say about these Hollywood stars and their egos, you have to admire their dedication."

"Oh, absolutely," Stephanie said, practically biting into her tongue to stop herself from blurting out the truth.

Lilly had forgotten to mention on the phone that she'd pulled a muscle in her back. Her walking was barely an improvement on Mrs. M.'s.

"I'd just done Step Back to Repulse Monkey," Lilly

explained, "and was about to move into Golden Cock Stands on One Leg, when I felt this sharp pain. It's already better than it was. I'll be fine in a few days."

Stephanie offered to take her to a chiropractor, but Lilly insisted that she was on the mend. As they sat down in the living room to wait for Bernard, Stephanie suggested that Lilly was overdoing the tai chi, but her grandmother wouldn't hear of it.

"By the way," Lilly said, "there's something you need to know about Bernard. I didn't see any point telling you before because I wasn't sure until recently that he felt the same way about me as I do about him. The thing is, Bernard isn't just my tai chi teacher. Years ago, long before I met your grandfather, he and I were an item."

"You're kidding."

Lilly shook her head and explained that they used to go along to the same youth club in Hackney. "He was my first love," Lilly said wistfully. They had gone out for six years, but when they decided they wanted to get engaged, her parents forbade it because Bernard wasn't Jewish. "Then he was called up for his national service, we lost touch and eventually I met your granddad, Norman. Don't get me wrong, I loved your grandfather, but I always carried a torch for Bernard." By now Stephanie was so moved she had tears in her eyes. She asked Lilly if Bernard ever married. "Yes, but his wife died about ten years ago."

"Wow, Gran, that's a bit of a story. So, I take it the spark is still there?"

Lilly laid her hand on Stephanie's: "Like you wouldn't believe," she said.

Even though she knew it wasn't her grandmother's style, for some reason Stephanie had gotten it into her head that

Bernard would be a tiny, whippety aesthete with a stringy goatee who would sit on the floor in the lotus position drinking herb tea and quoting Zen proverbs. She couldn't have been more wrong. Bernard Dixon wasn't remotely whippet-like. He was a great bear of a man with a gentle, open face and hod carrier's arms. With his trendily cropped gray hair, loose tai chi trousers and T-shirt he also didn't look a day over sixty.

"Excuse the getup," he said to Stephanie as they shook hands. "I've just come from giving a class." The voice was big too. There was nothing remotely frail about this man. It occurred to her that Albert would be like this when he got older. The thought was only reinforced when he winked at her and said she was "a real Bobby Dazzler, just like your grandmother." He offered to make coffee so that Lilly could rest her back, but Lilly wouldn't hear of it. "You two stay here and get to know each other," she said.

In the five minutes it took Lilly to make coffee and open a packet of chocolate digestives, Stephanie heard about Bernard's five grandchildren, the building company he'd set up in the sixties (which his sons now ran), how it took thirty years to become a tai chi grand master (which he now was), how he'd met his wife on a blind date, that she'd died ten years ago from cancer and how, even though he'd loved her to bits, he'd always kept a photograph of Lilly. He took it out of his wallet and handed it to Stephanie. The small black-and-white print was faded and battered. "It's your grandmother at a Christmas dance. Doesn't she look beautiful?" Lilly, who couldn't have been more than eighteen, did indeed look beautiful. Thick, lustrous curls tumbled down over her bare shoulders. Her dark lips formed a perfect bow-shaped pout. "Of course, I had a hand-span waist in those days," Lilly said, coming in with a tray. "It was the year Bernard got his first job, as a bus conductor."

"That's right," he said, leaping up and taking the tray from her. "And when I was on late shifts you used to spend the entire evening on my bus."

"The 123 from Ilford to Tottenham."

"All you ever cost me was a fourpenny ticket," he said, laughing. "Talk about a cheap date." He wrapped his arms around her. They looked so incongruous, Stephanie thought: the bear and the little bird. Lilly looked up at him and giggled. "Ooh, I could stay wrapped up in here all winter." Her head was resting on his chest, which she could barely reach.

"What's the weather like down there, Titch?" he asked. Lilly pulled away and bashed him affectionately on the arm. If ever a woman was in love, Stephanie thought, then Lilly was.

The three of them sat chatting, mostly about how Lilly was a natural at tai chi. "You know, she's got such wonderful structure and balance."

Lilly said that all the years she'd spent dancing must have paid off. Eventually Bernard went into the kitchen to make everybody more coffee.

"You know," Lilly said, "it's like we were never apart. And you wouldn't believe the sex. When Bernard makes love to me, it's pure magic. That man may be eighty, but he plays me like a violin."

"Really?" Stephanie said, desperate to be spared any further details of her grandmother's sexual congress with Bernard. "That's wonderful . . ."

"Actually, I've been having these—you know . . ." she had lowered her voice to a whisper, ". . . multiple moments of ecstasy." She nodded her head several times as if to underline

213

the statement. Stephanie swallowed hard. *"Multiple?"* she said, clearing her throat. "Wow, Gran, I'm impressed."

"And I tell you, we are talking more than two here."

"More than two?" Stephanie repeated, desperate to change the subject.

"So, do you want to know how many it was?"

"Gran, it's not really any of my business."

"OK, if you push me. It was six."

"You had six multiple moments of ecstasy with Bernard? Blimey! That's amazing."

Lilly broke off a small piece of chocolate digestive and put it in her mouth. "Stephanie, Bernard has asked me to live with him."

"Live with him? God, Gran, it's a bit soon, isn't it? I mean, you've hardly had any time to get reacquainted."

"Look, at our age, when something feels right, you don't waste time."

Bernard was back now, handing around the mugs. "Your grandmother's right. We haven't got our lives stretching out in front of us."

"I can see that," Stephanie said. "But I'm worried about you rushing into things."

"There's something else," Lilly said, exchanging an anxious glance with Bernard.

"I know . . . you're pregnant."

"Damn, you guessed," said Bernard, laughing.

"No, you daft ha'porth," Lilly said, "but it would mean moving."

"Out of London, you mean?" Stephanie said.

"Way out."

"What, to the coast?"

"In a manner of speaking," Lilly said. Another exchange of glances.

"How do you mean?"

"Well, it would be on the coast, all right—the Florida coast." Stephanie was too stunned to speak.

"But why Florida? What's wrong with Bournemouth?"

"I've been offered a job," Bernard said. Stephanie swiveled round to face him. "What sort of job?" What she wanted to say was "Who offers jobs to men of eighty?" but she was too polite.

"Teaching tai chi to the elderly in Miami. Old people react better to teachers of their own age. And tai chi isn't just a martial art, it's relaxing, it keeps people fit and mobile. The job even comes with a free apartment."

"And the block's fabulous," Lilly said, positively bursting with excitement. "It has two pools. *Two* pools. Can you imagine? And then there's all that sun. Imagine waking up every day to blue sky and sun."

"But you're not sure?" Stephanie said.

"I'd miss you and my only great-grandson like mad. And I know your mother would never forgive me."

Bernard admitted that his children were none too pleased about the idea either. "But it's such a wonderful opportunity. We can't pass it up." Stephanie found herself raising objections, such as what Lilly would do if she got ill, had an accident or realized she'd made a mistake.

"They do have hospitals in America," Lilly said. "And if I'm unhappy, I'll come home."

Stephanie still had her doubts, but she was starting to see it from Lilly's point of view. "Maybe at your age," she said to them, "it's time to stop thinking about everybody else. There are planes. We'll visit." Then she took Lilly's hand and gave it a squeeze. "Mum will get used to the idea. Just you see."

Lilly shrugged. "I'm not so sure. Look, I'm really nervous about telling her. I'm frightened she'll start ranting and raving and putting her foot down. Would you tell her for me?"

"Gran, I think maybe it would be better coming from you."

"Please."

Oh great, Stephanie thought, why do I get all the best jobs? "OK, if you really want me to, I'll tell Mum. No problem."

Cass was on the phone next. She was disappointed for Stephanie that she hadn't landed the lead, but she was certain that accepting Sidney Doucette's offer was the right thing to do. "Blimey, take the money and run. That's what I say. Plus if Ossie really does feel guilty about all this, he'll be making an extra effort to look out for something really decent for you. You're bound to hit the jackpot soon." She had to rush into a meeting, so they didn't have time to discuss how the frugal lunch had gone.

"Why don't you pop round after I get back from the Blues Café?" Stephanie said. "I'll do a fry-up." Cass said that sounded great.

Stephanie was just about to phone Lizzie to see if she felt up to coming, when Lizzie rang. "So, what happened with Ossie?" It was so typical, Stephanie thought. No matter what she was going through, Lizzie still thought about other people. Stephanie wasn't sure how she would react when she told her that she'd accepted the offer. Whereas Stephanie was merely neurotically honest, Lizzie was wildly, fanatically so. An overdue library book practically had her handing herself in at the local police station. But even Lizzie could see Stephanie didn't have much choice. "Look, I'm not as daring as you and if it were me, I'd probably wimp out, but you need the money. Nobody is going to get hurt. Go for it."

Stephanie knew she didn't need Lizzie's approval, but it was good to have it all the same.

"So," Stephanie said, "how are things with you? Any news from Dom?" Lizzie said he'd phoned last night in tears, saying the affair was over, that it had been a huge mistake, that he was missing her and the boys like mad and begging her to let him come back. "So, you going to let him?"

Lizzie let out a long breath. "I guess—eventually. He's even suggested we go to counseling. The thing is, I'm so angry with him. I can't ever remember feeling this angry. I did something quite appalling yesterday, I was so furious." Stephanie imagined Lizzie, incandescent with rage, cutting up his Nicole Farhi suits, e-mailing a photograph of him in thong Speedos to all his colleagues at the law firm or at the very least cleaning skid marks off the loo with his toothbrush. "You know that handbag he got me for Christmas? I took it back to Harrods and got a refund."

Stephanie's instinct was to say "Wow. Alert the First Wives' Club. They're bound to offer you a lifetime's free membership." She held back because she knew how hard Lizzie found it to show anger. Returning the bag—which she'd adored—was, as far as Stephanie knew, the nearest her friend had ever come to demonstrating real fury.

"Did taking it back make you feel better?" Stephanie asked kindly.

"You have no idea."

"Good for you. Look, Cass is coming round tonight when I get back from the Blues Café. Why don't you come too? We can talk."

"Great. It'll do me good to get out. You two can help me think up ways to get my own back on this B.O. hussy."

"Fine. But I'm assuming we're going more for mild name-calling than bare-breasted mud wrestling."

"OK, OK," Cass said, dipping sausage into runny fried egg yolk. "I know we're here to talk about Lizzie, but I simply cannot hold back. I just have to tell you how the frugal lunch went." She sat chewing for a few seconds. Then she swallowed. "Girls...it has finally happened. I am in love." Apparently Alex was gentle, so unmaterialistic, a wonderful listener, and really cared about the poor and the future of the planet. "He raises thousands for Oxfam and every year he spends two months in Africa working in this tiny village school."

"But, Cass," Stephanie said, "he's also a Christian. No, he's more than that. He makes his living from being a Christian."

"OK, I admit, he's not perfect. But if I can date blokes who wear corduroy, I'm sure I can cope with a Christian."

"But you have nothing in common," Lizzie said. "First, there's the religion thing. On top of that, you are the most materialistic person I know. And you don't give a stuff about the planet. You still think the ozone layer is something that comes off during a chemical peel."

"That's not fair," Cass came back, pretending to look hurt. "I think I'm very environmentally friendly."

"Cass," Stephanie piped up, "shagging a gamekeeper once at a country house weekend does not count as environmentally friendly."

"Well, I'm a great believer that opposites attract. Plus Alex has got a body like a condom full of walnuts."

"My God," Lizzie said, "you slept with him on the first date? I mean, he *is* a vicar. They're not meant to have sex outside marriage, let alone on the first date."

Cass shrugged. "We couldn't wait. He felt guilty, but

218

while he was going down on me I sang 'Jerusalem.' So are you pleased for me? Say you're pleased for me."

Stephanie and Lizzie got up from the table, hugged her and said of course they were pleased for her. "I know it's early days," Cass went on, "but I know this is going to lead to something. I just know it."

The conversation turned to Lizzie. "You know, I've been thinking," Stephanie said. "I'm not sure revenge is such a good idea. At least not in the way you mean it. The point is that Dom wants to come back and you know that eventually you'll take him back. I can see that flogging his golf clubs or slashing B.O.'s car tires might make you feel better in the short term, but I don't think it's really going to solve anything."

Cass said she agreed. In her opinion, something far more dignified was called for. "What you have to do," she said, "is turn the tables. At the moment you are the victim. You need to reclaim the power. Dom must be on his knees, begging you to have him back." She began opening a new packet of Marlboro Lights.

"How do I do that?"

"Easy. Has Dom got any company dos coming up?"

"Yes. His firm's annual dinner at Eden."

"Perfect," Cass said, pinching a cigarette from the packet. "You simply turn up looking like Cameron Diaz, on the arm of some seven-foot steel-torsoed hunk. That won't be a problem. I know dozens. That way Dom is reminded of how absolutely stunning and sexy you are and that you have men lusting after you. Believe me, he will be eaten up with jealousy."

Lizzie sat processing for a few moments. "I'm just not sure I'm brave enough. And Cameron Diaz? I look more like Camilla Parker Bowles these days."

Cass asked if it would help if she took her shopping. "We'll buy a fabulous dress, get your hair and makeup done. Come on, it'll be fun."

Lizzie started giggling. "And we'll put it all on Dom's credit card."

"You bet," Cass said.

"And you two will come with me for moral support?"

"Sweetie, we wouldn't miss it for the world," Cass grinned. Then she turned to Steph to get her reaction.

"Count me in," Steph said. Then she got up and opened another bottle of wine to celebrate. She was on the point of telling them she'd kissed Frank and that he had asked her out, but she pulled back. Cass would only go on about the dangers of being a transitional woman and Lizzie, feeling vulnerable because Dom had been cheating on her, would make her feel guilty for seeing Frank behind Albert's back. Just now, she didn't want to hear it.

Chapter 14

Stephanie turned off the light and lay in bed staring at the moon shadows on the wall. She didn't need Lizzie to make her feel guilty about seeing Frank behind Albert's back. She already felt it. From time to time, the roller blind stirred in the breeze and knocked gently against the window frame. Then the shadows would start to dance.

Why had she let Albert run out on her yesterday? She should have chased after him, insisted he stay just for a few minutes and listen to what she had to say. It would have been painful, but at least everything would have been out in the open. Of course he would have been distraught—not about losing her, she suspected, but about losing the family he wanted so badly. Albert adored being a father, and he was happy enough being a boyfriend. What he didn't want was to be a husband. She thought about phoning him in the morning and immediately decided against it. No, she had to speak to him face-to-face. She owed him that much.

By morning, a hard red zit the size of Krakatoa had

appeared on the side of her nose. Not satisfied that she was already deeply troubled about the date with Frank, God had clearly decided to push the point home.

She was thinking about phoning Frank to call off their date, when he called to tell her he would pick her up at seven thirty. The moment she heard his voice her spirits soared and she realized how much she wanted to see him. He said he'd booked a restaurant in a village on the Thames, just outside Oxford. "I hope that's OK. The drive will give us time to talk and I thought it would be good to get out of London for a few hours."

She said it sounded perfect.

From then on, her guilty feelings didn't so much recede as find themselves overtaken by excitement. She decided to wear the deep pink halter-neck dress Cass had given her a few months ago. "I bought it in a rush without trying it on. Sod's law, it's turned out to be miles too big, but I know it'll look perfect on you."

"Gee, thanks," Stephanie had said, feeling like a pregnant ewe. She asked Cass why she didn't take it back to the shop. Cass said she'd lost the receipt and she couldn't be bothered.

Of course Cass was right. The dress looked wonderful. Stephanie's angular shoulders were one of her best features and it showed them off to perfection. Over the top she would wear the pretty pink faux Chanel coat she'd bought in Kookai last year.

Every couple of hours she found herself standing in front of the bathroom mirror, assessing the zit situation. It reminded her of being sixteen again. How many Saturdays had she spent in tears, wailing to her mother that she couldn't possibly go to the party, club or whatever with a face full of boils. Estelle would tell her not to be silly, that she only had a few tiny pimples and you could hardly see them. "Yeah, right," Stephanie would say. "Where, from Fiji?" Of course, she always ended up going, albeit with her face covered in patches of supposedly flesh-colored acne cream, which was so orange that only a satsuma could carry it off. Somehow, Estelle had always managed to convince her that nobody would notice in the dark.

Today, though, she was in luck. There was no need for the satsuma acne cream. By evening, the zit was looking considerably less livid and it had stopped hurting. Nevertheless, she still spent ages dabbing it with concealer and adding extra blusher to draw the attention away from her nose. Then, of course, she realized that the blusher made her look like a cheap tart and she had to take it off again. By twenty-five past seven, she'd only just finished her makeup. Realizing the time, she bolted into the bedroom and got dressed in three minutes flat. She was putting on her earrings and at the same time slipping her feet into her slingbacks when the doorbell rang.

"Wow, you look absolutely stunning," Frank said, kissing her on the cheek. "You don't look so bad yourself," she smiled, taking in the expensive gray suit and pale lavender open-neck shirt and thinking how truly handsome he was.

The journey must have taken well over an hour, but for Stephanie it seemed to pass in minutes. As usual they didn't stop talking. She learned that his parents had retired to Eastbourne, where they were stalwarts of the local lawn bowling team, that he had a dotty, tree-hugging sister who lived in Cornwall with a Buddhist clown and that his favorite book was the *Boys' Bumper Book of Magic Tricks,* which he'd been given for Christmas when he was nine. "I'm really starting to get the hang of some of the tricks now," he said in mock seriousness. She burst out laughing, realizing how much she loved this funny, self-deprecating side of him. She didn't mean to compare him to Albert, but it wasn't hard to see that Frank was so much less tied up with his own ego.

He seemed particularly keen to hear about Jake. "Managing on your own must be hard."

She told him how difficult it had been when he was a baby and he didn't sleep. "But my friends and Mum and Dad have been great. Jake's dad lives in L.A., but he comes over when he can."

She prayed he wouldn't ask her any more details about her relationship with Albert. If he knew they were involved—albeit about to become uninvolved—he might well run a mile. There was no way that a kind, decent man like Frank would want to come between her and the father of her child.

The restaurant was part of a Georgian manor house. It was set back from the road, at the end of a sweeping gravel drive. "Oh, this is so beautiful," Stephanie said, gazing at the grand floodlit facade. Beyond the house, she could see the jet river twinkling in the moonlight.

The place was pleasantly full, but not crowded. In the bar a coal fire burned in the marble fireplace. Frank ordered two glasses of champagne and Stephanie went to the ladies' room to check on her zit. It was fine. All you could see under the concealer was a slight bump. God was giving her a break after all.

Back in the bar, she sat down next to Frank on one of the squidgy chintz sofas. They clinked glasses and sipped the champagne. He moved closer to her so that their bodies were touching. At one point his thigh brushed against hers and her whole body was filled with tiny prickles of excitement.

He let his finger trail over her collarbone. "Has anybody ever told you that you have the most beautiful shoulders?"

"Oh, maybe once or twice," she said with a coquettish grin.

As they carried on chatting and laughing, she was struck, not for the first time, that whenever she was with Frank, she felt as if she had come home. It was beginning to dawn on her that she was falling in love.

Soon a waiter arrived and handed them each a menu. He was tall and possessed what Stephanie decided was a rather imperious, Jeeves-ish bearing.

She and Frank both agreed that they couldn't resist the beef Wellington. When the waiter returned to take their order, Stephanie became aware that he kept glancing at her feet and smirking. Her legs were crossed and at first she thought he was admiring them. It took her a few seconds before she realized what he was really looking at. Her eyes locked onto her feet. On one she was wearing a pink suede slingback, which perfectly matched her dress. On the other was a peacock blue one, which perfectly matched the dress she'd worn for the Sidney Doucette audition.

"Stephanie?" Frank said, looking perplexed. "You with us? The waiter is asking how you'd like your beef done."

She uncrossed her legs and sat trying to arrange things so that the pink shoe obscured the blue one by resting on top of it. Of course, this simply drew Frank's attention to her feet. Without missing a beat, he said: "You know, Steph, I've been meaning to say, those really are great shoes." She looked up at him. He was clearly struggling to stifle his laughter. "Vivienne Westwood is so witty, such a risk taker."

Taking her cue from Frank, Stephanie turned to the waiter and said, very pointedly, "Yes, isn't she?"

The waiter's expression turned to embarrassed confusion. He finished taking their order and practically ran out of the bar. Frank was almost weeping with laughter. Stephanie, of course, was almost as embarrassed as the waiter. Avoiding the zit issue, she explained how she'd been rushing to get dressed.

"Stephanie, please don't worry. The shoes look brilliant."

"No, they don't," she giggled. "They look completely and utterly ridiculous. But thank you for saying so. And thanks for putting that waiter in his place."

"My pleasure," he said, leaning in and kissing her gently on the mouth.

The elegant cream dining room was bathed in candle-light. On each starched-linen-covered table there were wine-glasses the size of fishbowls and a tiny crystal vase full of snowdrops. They were shown to a table next to tall French doors. Stephanie peered through the glass. In the moonlight, she could see a couple of swans swimming sedately down-river.

"Wonder what they're doing out after dark," she said. Frank gave a soft laugh and said they were probably going to a late movie.

"They mate for life, you know, swans," she said, feeling awkward and wondering what on earth had prompted her to say that.

He smiled back at her. "I thought that was penguins," he said. She watched him stroke the tablecloth, wiping away imaginary crumbs. "Do you know when I first realized I wanted to get to know you again?" She shook her head. "When Anoushka and I bumped into you in Debenhams."

"What, in that Mrs. Claus outfit? I nearly died."

"You looked amazing. It's funny, but I think I knew there and then that Anoushka and I were never going to make it."

Each course was more glorious than the last. The beef melted in the mouth, the bread-and-butter pudding—which they shared because they were so full—was a heavenly com-bination of crispy toasty topping and smooth custard laced with nutmeg and cinnamon.

By the time the coffee came, they were exchanging their

favorite jokes. These eventually got sillier and sillier. When he asked her how you know if you pass an elephant, she said in her best music hall voice, "Aye don't know, how do you know when you pass an elephant?"

"You can't get the loo seat down." They laughed and snorted so much they started getting disapproving looks from the other diners.

As they walked back to the car after dinner, he put his arm round her and she snuggled into him. On the drive home they listened to Sinatra. "I've had a wonderful time tonight," he said, resting a hand on her thigh. She told him she had too.

When they pulled up outside her flat, he switched off the car engine and turned to face her. They sat locked in each other's gaze for a moment or two. Then he began stroking her face. Finally his fingers went to her lips. "I really love the corners of your mouth," he said. She felt herself go red and asked him why. "Because they're always slightly turned up—as if you're about to smile." The next thing she knew he was kissing her. She melted into him, her body aching for him. As she felt his hand brush over her breast she desperately wanted to invite him in, but she couldn't do it. Her mind was filled with a vision of Albert. Try as she might she couldn't get rid of it. She couldn't make love to Frank until she had ended it with Albert. She just couldn't. It would be too cruel.

As they pulled away and her hand edged toward the door lever, she could see a cloud of disappointment pass over Frank's face. But it only lasted a moment. "Maybe we could get together on Monday after you've finished at the studio," he said. His smile had returned, which made her feel much easier. He probably just assumed she had a no-sex-on-the-first-date rule.

Then she remembered her date with Ossie. As she

227

explained, Frank couldn't disguise his amusement. "So, what are you going to tell him?" She shrugged and asked Frank how offended he would be if he were a midget and she told him in the most sensitive way possible that she didn't fancy exceedingly short men. "On a scale of one to ten?" he said. She nodded. "Ooh, about 197, I'd say. Clearly, your only option is to marry the man."

"Gee, thanks. You're a big help."

Then he smiled and said he was just teasing. "If you do it tactfully, I think he might really appreciate your honesty."

"That's what I thought," she said, "but it's just not going to be easy."

Frank wished her good luck with Ossie. She told him she was going to need it. Then she thanked him again for a fantastic evening. After giving him another quick kiss on the lips, she opened the car door.

She practically floated up the garden path to the house. The night air was bitter and her coat was only draped around her shoulders, but she didn't feel a thing. She was falling in love. She hadn't felt this happy in years.

She woke up on Sunday morning desperate to see Jake. There was no reason her mother needed to have him today. Perhaps she would take him to the natural history museum. "Actually, that suits me brilliantly," Estelle had said. She explained that her deep freeze had just broken down, that the repairman had pronounced it a goner and that she and Harry needed to get to John Lewis to order a new one. "It'll probably take all morning. Jake is going to be bored stiff if he comes."

Stephanie offered to collect him, but Estelle said she and Harry would drop him off. "And maybe I can put a few bits in your freezer." Stephanie said that was fine, since her freezer was practically empty.

Her parents arrived just after ten. Stephanie scooped Jake up into her arms and hugged him.

"Hi, poppet. How are you?"

"Better," he said. Then he wriggled down and ran off to find his digger.

Her father, red faced and looking fit to burst, was speaking into his mobile in this strange strangulated tone. He dropped two M&S carrier bags full of frozen food by the fridge.

"No, don't you dare put me on hold again. You will not put me on hold. I demand to speak to your supervisor." He looked sharply at Estelle. "Can you believe it? They've put me on hold."

"He's on to the London Online call center in Rawalpindi," Estelle explained. Apparently, not only hadn't the junk e-mails stopped, but she and Harry were now getting them through the post. "That postman's such a gossip," she said, lowering her voice. "Now the entire neighborhood thinks my husband suffers from…" She mouthed the words *erectile dysfunction.* "I can't look anybody in the face."

Estelle opened Stephanie's deep freeze and began filling it with food from the carrier bags.

Harry turned toward the two women and raised a hand in front of him to indicate somebody had come back on the line and they should be quiet. "Look," he said, rubbing his forehead, "time and again, you've promised these e-mails would stop, but they're just getting worse. On top of that, these companies are now sending me this obscene junk through my letter box… How have they gotten my address?… What's my name? You have my name. I must have given it to you fifty times. What?… No? I am not Mr. P. Enis Extension. I am Harry Glassman. Oh, God, what's the use?" He laid the phone down on the kitchen table and flopped onto a chair.

"Come on, Dad, calm down," Stephanie soothed. "I'm sure this whole thing will get sorted out eventually. Look, why don't I make us all a nice fry-up?" She told them that Cass and Lizzie weren't coming because they'd gone shopping. She didn't mention—because it would have been of no real interest to her parents—that this wasn't any old shopping spree. It was the first stage in Lizzie's grand makeover.

"Now you're talking," Harry said, cheering up.

"Come on, Harry, be sensible," Estelle said, closing the freezer door and starting to fold the carrier bags. "You know all that cholesterol's not healthy. You had your low-fat yogurt and muesli before we left."

Harry turned to Stephanie. "Do you mind telling me what I have to live for? She wonders why I read *Final Exit* in bed at night." Estelle finished smoothing out the carrier bags and told Stephanie to take no notice. Stephanie persuaded them to at least stay for coffee. While she put the kettle on, Harry went to check on Jake.

"Mum," Stephanie said, swallowing hard, "I need to talk to you. You know this chap Grandma's been seeing?"

"The tai chi teacher."

Stephanie nodded. "His name's Bernard. Does that mean anything to you?" Estelle thought for a minute. "Vaguely," she said. "Yes. I'm pretty sure she went out with a chap called Bernard before she met my father. Her parents put a stop to it because he wasn't Jewish." She was silent for a moment. Then she started to frown. "Are you telling me that this is the same man?"

"Yes. And they appear to be head over heels in love."

"You're joking. I don't believe it. Mum's in love with him? With a man she knew nearly sixty years ago?"

230

"I've met him," Stephanie said, "and he's lovely, a real charmer—a bit like Albert. You'll like him." Estelle's antennae were on full alert. She'd clearly picked up on Stephanie's underlying anxiety. "OK, why am I suddenly getting a bad feeling about this? I mean, how come you're telling me all this and not my mother? And how come you've met him and I haven't? Something's not right here. There's a problem, isn't there?"

"Mum, maybe you should sit down."

"No, I'm fine. I don't need to sit down. Just tell me."

Stephanie let out a long breath. "OK, Bernard wants Gran to move to Florida with him. They're going to live together and teach tai chi to the elderly."

Estelle practically fell onto a kitchen chair. "Florida? He wants her to move to Florida?" By now her voice was trembling. "What are you saying? He wants her to live there permanently?" Stephanie said that was the plan. "But that's outrageous. I've never heard anything so absurd. The woman's almost eighty years old, for crying out loud. She's got a heart condition. Who moves continents at eighty?" Estelle was back on her feet, pacing. "And why would he want to tear her away from her family? What does he want? Her money? I'll give him bloody Florida when I get hold of him."

Stephanie managed to convince her that Bernard wasn't remotely interested in Lilly's money. "From what I can tell, he's a good, kind man, he's pretty well off himself, and they're really in love." Estelle told her not to be so ridiculous.

"They're eighty. People of eighty don't fall in love. Stephanie, I can't let my mother go to America with some man she hardly knows. It's preposterous. I don't care what you say, he could be a dangerous criminal, for all we know. And even if he's not, what if she gets ill or has an accident? I can't let her fend for herself at her age. I just can't. I have to talk to her and make her see sense."

"OK," Stephanie said, "but when you do, just keep calm. There's nothing to be gained by losing your temper."

"I am calm!" Estelle shot back defensively. "I'm always calm. When am I ever not calm?"

When Stephanie suggested going to the natural history museum, Jake didn't seem particularly excited. He was far more keen on the two of them sitting on the living room floor, doing puzzles and looking at books. After what must have been the ninth reading of *Fatapillow,* Stephanie suggested they make meringues. Jake adored using the electric whisk. It made him feel grown up. He also loved the noise and the magical way the egg whites expanded and changed into a thick glistening mass. She'd barely finished asking the question before he was tearing off into the kitchen to find the whisk. She rolled up his sleeves and tied a tea towel round his waist to serve as an apron. "Now remember, hold the whisk with two hands and keep the beaters low down in the mixture like this. If you don't, it'll fly all over the place."

He gave a solemn nod. She flicked the switch on the handle. The whisk buzzed and made delicious sloshing sounds in the egg white, which made him giggle. Stephanie stood watching him for a minute or so. Deciding he had the whisk reasonably under control, she went to find the sugar. Her back couldn't have been turned for more than twenty seconds, but it was time enough for Jake to lose concentration and for substantial amounts of the thick egg white to end up on the counter and the wall tiles. Of course, he thought this was great fun, and the more the egg white splattered in his face and hair, the more he squealed with pleasure. Stephanie couldn't get cross. She stood behind him, watching him having fun and realizing just how much she was going to miss him this week.

She made bacon and eggs for lunch. Afterward, Jake said he wanted to watch a video. She brought his duvet down from his bedroom and they spent an hour or so snuggled up under it, watching *Aladdin* and eating the meringues, which made a terrible mess on the sofa. About half past two she suggested they go for a walk. Jake was less than keen and would have been happy to sit watching videos all day, but she insisted they needed some fresh air. "Tell you what, you can take your tricycle. And afterward we'll get crepes. How's that?"

"Chocolate?" he asked, head on one side.

"Absolutely."

Just then the phone rang. It was Lizzie, sounding as high as a kid on artificial food colorings, to say that she and Cass had had *the* most fantastic morning shopping, how she couldn't believe Dom's credit card hadn't gone into meltdown, and could they pop in for a cup of tea to show off their purchases. Stephanie said she was just about to go out for a walk with Jake. "I promised him pancakes. Tell you what, why don't you meet us at the crepes place in an hour or so?"

It was twenty minutes before they left the house. Stephanie couldn't find her mobile phone. Like so many people, she felt naked going out without it. It should have been in the bag she'd used last night, but it wasn't. After looking down the backs of chairs and sofas, under beds, in drawers and cupboards, she finally gave up. Jake swore he hadn't touched it. Maybe her mother had picked it up by mistake.

It was one of those gloriously bright but arctic winter afternoons with a Pepsi-can–blue sky. Jake pedaled happily for a good half hour. Then he got tired and said his fingers and toes hurt. Stephanie brought his mittened hands to her mouth and breathed warm air onto them, but it didn't do much good. In the end he announced that he wasn't going to pedal anymore and demanded that she carry him. "Jake, I can carry the bike, but I can't manage you as well."

Jake had just started to whine when she heard a male voice behind her asking if she needed a hand. She turned round to see Frank. The collar of his suede jacket was up against the cold and he was wearing a thick black woolen hat pulled down to his eyes. He looked supremely sexy. She instantly became aware of her lack of makeup, the two fleeces she was wearing one on top of the other and her ancient, baggy joggers. But her discomfort was fleeting. There was something about the way he was looking at her that made her feel as if she were dressed up in her full Peggy Lee regalia.

"Couldn't quite face making a start on this lot," he said, nodding at the stack of Sunday papers under his arm, "so I thought I'd take a stroll through the woods." Then he noticed Jake and bent down. "So, you must be Jake. Hi, I'm Frank. That's a great bike. I bet it goes really fast." The arrival of a stranger had made Jake cheer up. "A million fousand miles an hour," he said, nodding and stretching his arms wide to emphasize the point. "You want a go?"

"I think I might be a bit too big," Frank smiled, "but tell you what, why don't you get back on and I'll pull you along so's you don't have to pedal." Jake looked up at Stephanie as if to ask whether that was OK. She nodded and he climbed on.

"How come he wouldn't do that when I suggested it?" Stephanie said.

"Simple," he said, "you're his mother." She told him they were heading for the crepes place and asked if he fancied joining them. "I'd like that," he said. "Oh, by the way, I found your mobile in my car. It must have fallen out of your bag."

"Oh, thank God." She told him how she'd been turning the house upside down looking for it. They agreed she would pick it up later, after she'd dropped Jake back at her mum and dad's.

La Crêperie was packed and they had to queue for a table. It wasn't more than ten minutes or so, but long enough for Jake to get irritable. Stephanie picked him up and he began pinching her face and laughing. "Hey, Jake, stop that. It really hurts."

"Jake," Frank said, "do you like magic tricks?" Jake's face immediately brightened and he began nodding. Frank reached behind Jake's ear and produced a pound coin. "Wow, look what I found." Wide-eyed, Jake burst into fits of giggles. " 'gen. Do it a-gen." Frank obliged. Then he made the coin disappear, which enthralled Jake even more.

"He's a lovely kid," Frank said, once they'd sat down.

"He likes you. He's not usually so forthcoming with strangers."

"You know," he said slowly, stirring his cappuccino, "I didn't get much sleep last night."

"You didn't?"

He shook his head. "I kept thinking about how much I'd enjoyed being with you." He reached out and took her hand. It occurred to her he might be about to say he loved her.

"Me too," she said.

"Hi, you lot." Stephanie looked up to see Cass. Lizzie was standing next to her, unable to take her eyes off Frank. The two of them were loaded down with bags. "You won't believe how much money we spent," Cass went on, shoving bags under the table. "Dom is going to go absolutely ape when he finds out."

"Frank, you remember Cass," Stephanie said, her smile belying her desire to throttle her friends for barging in at that precise moment. "And this is Lizzie." He reached over and shook Lizzie's hand. She said how do you do, but she was blushing like a starstruck fourteen-year-old. Frank didn't seem to notice, though. He stayed and chatted for twenty minutes or so, Lizzie gradually relaxing in his company. Then he said he had to get going because he had to finish reading a film script.

"The director wants to know by tomorrow if I'm interested in auditioning for a part and I'm barely halfway through." He turned to Jake, did the pound coin trick again and said good-bye to Cass and Lizzie. Finally he bent down and kissed Stephanie on the cheek. "See you about eight. I should have finished the script by then. We'll get a takeaway." She nodded and said she'd be there.

"Cass told me you and Frank had dinner last night," Lizzie said, a slightly pinched expression coming over her. Stephanie nodded. She was half expecting a lecture from Lizzie about persevering with Albert for Jake's sake, but she knew lectures weren't Lizzie's style. "I just hope you know what you're doing, that's all." She raised her eyebrows, making it clear that she was worried it was all going to end in tears and Jake would be the one to suffer.

Stephanie looked at Jake, who was busy stuffing handfuls of crepe into his mouth and at the same time smearing his face in chocolate sauce. She began wiping off the worst of the sticky mess with a napkin. Then she turned back to Lizzie. "You know I want the best for Jake, but I'm falling in love with Frank. I can't just ignore that." Lizzie gave an "If you say so" shrug, which Stephanie couldn't help finding irritating. Later on, as she walked home, she considered her reaction to the shrug. Why had she let it get to her? Why had she felt so challenged? Of course, she knew the answer. Lizzie had sensed that deep down Stephanie wasn't as convinced as she made out that choosing Frank over Albert would be best for Jake.

"God, that's two of us in love," Cass piped up excitedly. "Maybe we should think about a double wedding." Stephanie made the point that Frank hadn't even said he loved her yet and that Cass had only been seeing Alex for five minutes. "I know," she said, a wistful look in her eyes, "but I'm certain Alex is as in love as I am. I can just feel it."

Stephanie could see that Lizzie was becoming increasingly upset by all this talk of falling in love, so she decided to change the subject. "So, come on, what's in the bags?" she said. "I'm dying to see."

Her face brightening, Lizzie pulled out half a dozen tight-fitting tops, a couple of tailored jackets, hipster jeans, pointy suede boots and a fabulous cream coat. "Oh, and we also bought this dead-sexy silk dress for Dom's do on Tuesday night, but it's being shortened."

"God," Stephanie said, holding up a tan suede miniskirt. "If it's anything like the rest of this stuff, Dom is going to be on his knees begging you to take him back."

Frank answered the door wearing jeans and a white T-shirt. His feet were bare, which Stephanie found immensely sexy.

"Hi, you," he said, pulling her to him and kissing her on the lips. His body felt deliciously warm, as if he'd just come out of the shower. He led her into the living room. This had been knocked through into the kitchen to make one large space. She took in the wooden floor, the white walls, the Conran sofas, the fire burning in the minimalist white fireplace, the perfect low lighting. Ella was singing softly in the background.

"So, how was the script?" she said.

"Excellent, but the part they had in mind required some muscle-bound hunk. Not quite me, really."

"Oh, I don't know." She smiled, running her hand over his chest. He kissed her again. "You know, this really is a lovely room," she said. She decided it combined artistic flair and general tidiness with the perfect amount of bloke-ish mess. Although Stephanie had no time for men who lived like slobs (Albert veered perilously in this direction), she could never see herself hooking up with a man who ironed his briefs and filed his herb jars in alphabetical order. In Frank's case the mess consisted mainly of books, CDs and the Sunday papers strewn about the place. The dining table was awash with bits of model airplane. Frank told her it was going to be a radio-controlled glider. "I'm making it with my nephew, the one whose father's a Buddhist clown. Poor lad comes to stay when he gets sick of playing Zen glove puppets." Stephanie laughed. She only stopped laughing when he wrapped her in his arms and told her he couldn't remember the last time he'd felt this happy. "Whenever we're together it just feels so natural and easy, so right."

"I know." She smiled. "I feel the same." Then a thought occurred to her. "Frank, are you sure our relationship isn't some kind of rebound thing for you? I mean, this isn't just some kind of transitional thing, is it? I'm not just filling in the gap until you find somebody you really care for?"

He started laughing. "Christ, where did that come from?"

"Cass read this article in *Cosmo*. Apparently I should run a mile now and wait until you've had your transitional relationship and only then should I make my move."

He grabbed her arm. "Stephanie, you are going nowhere. Understand?"

"Yeah. Got it." It occurred to her that this might be the

time for her to tell him she was falling in love with him, but aware that she didn't want to put too much pressure on him or come across as even more needy than she'd probably just appeared, she held back.

By now he had started kissing her. Her body quivered as he slipped his hand under her top and she felt his warm skin on hers. "I want you," he whispered urgently. She wanted him too. Desperately. But she knew she couldn't sleep with him. Not yet. Not until the Albert situation was resolved.

"Look," she said, pulling away slightly, "there's something I should tell you." Her own sexual frustration aside, she wasn't too bothered about telling him the reason why she couldn't sleep with him. Frank would understand. After all, she was only asking him to hang on for a few more days. Maybe she could even sell it to him as prolonged foreplay.

"Oh God, you're going to tell me I've got halitosis or something."

She laughed and said he knew perfectly well he didn't have halitosis. "You remember ages ago when you asked me about Jake's father?" He nodded. "Well, a few weeks ago he asked me to marry him." Frank stood frowning, gathering his thoughts. "I'm assuming you said no."

"Not exactly."

"Ah," Frank said by way of understatement.

"No, no. You don't understand." God, she was messing this up. "I'm planning to say no. It's just that I haven't quite said it yet. It's complicated." She explained about Albert being in Berlin thinking there was still a possibility she was going to agree to marry him and how it wouldn't feel right sleeping with Frank until she'd told Albert the truth. "He'll be back in a few days. I'll tell him then and everything will be fine."

"Will it?" he said. She could feel the hurt in his voice.

"Of course. Why shouldn't it be?"

He went over to the sofa and sat down, making her feel strangely abandoned. "It seems to me that you haven't sorted out your feelings for Albert. If you had, you wouldn't have let him go to Berlin without getting this thing sorted." She explained that she'd tried, but Frank wasn't impressed. "And now you're stringing both of us along." She was so shocked by the suggestion that she didn't speak for a few moments. She sat down next to him on the sofa. "Frank," she said, "I am not stringing you along." Her voice was soft and steady. She was determined to make him believe her. Then the most appalling thought occurred to her. She asked him if he was finishing with her. He shook his head and managed a half-smile. "No, of course I'm not," he said. "That's the last thing I want to do. On the other hand, I think you need to take some time to sort out how you really feel. We can't be together until you're certain."

"But I am certain," she pleaded. "You have to believe me." He looked back at her. She could see by his face that his mind was made up and that there was no arguing with him. She stood up to go. She felt like a child being dismissed from the headmaster's study with instructions to go away and reflect on her wrongdoings.

"By the way," he said as she reached the door. "Good luck for tomorrow."

"Thanks," she said, her voice trembling.

Chapter 15

Stephanie lay in bed, cursing herself for being so stupid and naive. Frank was bound to think she still had feelings for Albert. It was the most logical thing to think. Anybody looking at the situation from the outside would come to the same conclusion. And he would be right. She did still have feelings for Albert. The point was, of course, that those feelings didn't come close to what she felt for Frank. She knew she should have stayed and forced Frank to hear her out, but she had been so shocked by his reaction that her mind hadn't been functioning properly.

Two hours later, still wide awake, she got up and made some hot milk. Then she remembered she had some herbal sleeping tablets in the medicine cabinet. Although they looked like hamster food pellets and smelled strongly of cheesy socks, she managed to get a couple down with the milk. Miraculously she dropped off.

The second she woke up, she thought about phoning Frank to have another go at persuading him that he'd gotten it all wrong, but she knew it would do no good. She absolutely refused to be defeated, though. In a few days Albert would be back, they would have the big conversation and everything would sort itself out. She just had to hang on.

Chalk Farm Studio, where she was recording the songs for *Peggy*, was in a converted warehouse near Camden Lock. She arrived dead on eight, as per Ossie's instructions. She was almost as nervous as she had been for the audition. Over the years she'd been in umpteen recording studios to do backing vocals or advertising jingles, so from a technical point of view she knew what to expect. On the other hand, this would be the first time she'd performed solo with a full-size orchestra. Everybody, from the musicians to the producer and engineers, would have his attention fixed on her. That was the scary bit.

A blade-thin girl with spiky blue hair and bum cleavage showed her into the control room. Ossie and Sidney Doucette were already there, sitting next to each other on a leather sofa. Ossie's legs were stretched out in front of him, his tiny brogues barely reaching the edge of the seat. The two men were drinking coffee out of Starbucks cups. Behind the console, an engineer with a voice to match his huge beer gut was twisting back and forth on his swivel chair, apparently telling Ossie and Sidney his life story. "And after I stopped working for Motorhead, I spent five years as a roadie for Anal Wig."

Sidney, who was displaying more than a little Southern discomfort at the mention of anal wigs, seemed particularly relieved to see Stephanie. He leaped up to greet her. "Well, pick my peas, Miss Stephanie, aren't you as perty as a speckled pup?" Then he strode over, ostentatiously took her hand and kissed it.

"Hi, Mr. Doucette."

"Now then, young lady," he said giving the back of her hand a couple of avuncular taps, "we don't stand on ceremony here. It's Sidney. Please."

"OK, Sidney." She waved hello to Ossie. Then Sidney introduced her to the engineer, whose name was Graham. Just then Sidney's mobile went. He excused himself and went outside to take the call.

She sat down next to Ossie, who was pulling a sheaf of papers out of a large brown envelope. It was her contract. "I've been through it. Sid's signed his bit. All we need is your signature and maybe Graham here could witness it."

A few minutes later she'd signed the contract along with the confidentiality agreement and Ossie was assuring her that the first thousand-pound payment would be in her bank account by Friday. It was a huge relief. She'd gone well over her overdraft limit this month and it would spare her having to make yet another cringing call to Kevin at the bank, begging him to give her time to get her account straight.

"I'm really looking forward to dinner tonight," Ossie said after Graham disappeared through the connecting door into the studio. What with the confusion and emotional havoc caused by the Albert/Frank situation, Stephanie hadn't given much more thought to her date with Ossie until she was driving to the studio. She'd toyed with the idea of telling him that her personal life was desperately complicated just now and that there was no possibility of her starting a new relationship. In the end she'd decided that telling him the truth was her only option. This, of course, was far easier said than done. What was the kind, tactful way of saying "I don't fancy you because you're three foot nine"? Somehow between now and tonight, she had to find one.

"Me too," she said.

"Great. Fantastic." She was aware that he seemed slightly fidgety and nervous. The realization that Ossie had a great deal of emotion invested in this date made her feel even worse about what she had to tell him.

Through the glass partition she could see the studio starting to fill up with musicians. She felt her stomach tighten as she watched them unpacking their instruments. There were blokes with saxophones, trumpets and trombones, and a couple of slightly drippy girls tuning their violins. In the middle of the studio stood a shiny grand piano. At the back Graham was helping to set up some drums. "God," Stephanie said, "how did Sidney convince all these people to go along with this scam?"

"Look at them," Ossie said. "Not one of them is over twenty-five. They're all young and hungry."

"But what about Katherine? Why did she agree to it? She's hardly hungry."

"That's where you're wrong. Her career's in the toilet. Nobody wants to work with her. She's just thrown one tantrum too many. On top of that, she's made some bad financial investments and she's in debt. You know she and Sidney are an item?" Stephanie said she had no idea. "Between you and me, I think she's just after his money, but Sidney's convinced it's true love, daft old bugger."

Just then Sidney came back into the control room, followed by a spindly chap with splayed gappy teeth and Art Garfunkel hair. Ossie winked at Stephanie and whispered: "See what happens when cousins marry."

"Who is he?"

Ossie explained that he was Konstanty Novakovitch, the

show's musical director, who would be overseeing the recording. "Same deal as the musicians. Talented, unknown. Although he's very big in Banja Luka."

"Where's that?"

"Bosnia."

"Bosnia? You are joking. God, I knew this whole thing was doomed from the start. First, the average age of the band is twelve and a half and now the director has barely set foot outside the Balkans. Does he know anything about this kind of music?" Since she'd had her back to the two approaching men, she was unaware that they were now standing beside her.

"Actually, I know gret dill about this musics," Konstanty Novakovitch said, looking distinctly offended by her remarks. "I am studying American jazz and blues five years at conservatory in Sarajevo. Miss Peggy Lee came to geev master class. Ver' beautiful and talented woman." Then he handed her a list of show songs and walked away in a huff.

"Don't mind him." Sidney laughed. "Artistic temperament. You'll get to like him."

Ossie said he had to get to the office and would meet her at the Jägerhütte in East Finchley at eight. After he'd gone, Sidney sat Stephanie down, patted her knee and thanked her for agreeing to take part in "mah little project." Having just signed her contract, she wasn't about to lecture him on the dishonest and deceitful nature of his little project. Instead she just smiled back at him. "You are a very talented singer, Stephanie," he said. "You will get your proper reward one of these days. Mark mah words."

Just then the bum cleavage receptionist came in with more coffee, pastries and a selection of newspapers. Sidney picked up the *Daily Mail*. K-Mart was beaming out from the front page. Stephanie watched Sidney's face getting redder by the second. "Sidney? You OK?" He responded by throwing the paper onto the coffee table. Stephanie picked it up. It seemed that Katherine Martinez had thrown another of her famous tantrums. According to the article, she had taken one look at her dressing room at the Duke of Kent Theater, where *Peggy* was being staged, declared it shabby, filthy and dilapidated "like this whole goddamn country," and demanded new carpet, furniture, and that it be repainted in soothing pastels. On top of this she insisted that the theater provide an ayurvedic masseur as well as a cranial osteopath. Apparently she had been so abusive to the theater manager that he had walked out on the spot.

Stephanie looked up to see Sidney stabbing at the numbers on his mobile.

"Oh, now then, sugar, what is all this ah've been reading? You know you only have to come to Daddy and ah will fix everything. Just tell me what you need and ah will see that it's done...OK, you just stay calm now. ah will be right with you. Of course ah still love you, sugar. Of course you are beautiful. You are the most ravishing, radiant creature in the cosmos. Why, when ah looked at you in bed this morning, ah said to myself, 'This woman's beauty could charm the morning dew off the honeysuckle.' "

Sidney picked his coat up off the back of a chair. "She just gets a bit feisty when she's nervous, that's all." He kissed Stephanie's hand once again and said that even though Konstanty was Bosnian and uglier than a lard bucket full of armpits, he had every faith in him.

After he'd gone, Stephanie began looking over the list of songs Konstanty had given her. It was the first time she'd seen it. There were fifteen, ranging from the simpler arrangements like "Fever" to the big orchestral numbers like "Alright, OK, You Win" and "Big Spender."

"You can manage them?" She looked up to see Konstanty standing by the engineer's console, holding a cup of coffee.

She smiled. "Yes, I think so," she said. "Look, I'm sorry I was rude with you before. I just don't feel particularly at ease with this whole enterprise, that's all." Konstanty shrugged, giving her the impression he felt the same, but wasn't prepared to discuss it.

Throughout the week she would run up against this attitude with all the musicians. Everybody knew that what he was doing was wrong, but nobody was prepared to admit it or talk about it, even among themselves. The truth would hang around the studio like some huge pink spotted elephant that everyone refused to acknowledge.

Konstanty sat down next to her and explained that they would run through each number at least three times and that the recording shouldn't take that long, since the orchestra wasn't actually being recorded.

"I don't understand," Stephanie said. "Why wouldn't you record the orchestra?" He explained that the musicians couldn't lip-synch and had to perform live onstage. Consequently it was only her vocal track that was needed. "The orchestra ees only here today to guide you, yes?"

An hour later everything was set up and she was standing at the mike as the trumpets and double bass kicked in with the intro to "Why Don't You Do Right?" She must have sung it more than a hundred times at the Blues Café. Closing her eyes and trying to imagine it was just Dennis and the boys standing behind her, she felt the music and went with it.

As Sidney said she would, she found herself coming to rather like Konstanty. For a start, he really did seem to know his stuff. He stopped her if he thought a phrase was too clipped or he felt she'd breathed in the wrong place. He encouraged her to come to grips even more with "thee smoky yet laid-back sexualitee" of "Fever." His criticism was always constructive, though, and he took care not to eat away at her confidence. As a result, by half past six they had laid down four tracks and decided to call it a day.

Along with everybody else, Stephanie had switched off her mobile during the recording session. As soon as she was outside the studio, she turned it back on. She had thirteen messages—all from her mother. It immediately occurred to her that something had happened to Lilly or, God forbid, Jake. She was just about to play the first one when Estelle phoned again. "Oh, thank God I've got you," she said. Stephanie could practically hear her mother slapping her chest with relief. "I've been trying to get you all day." Stephanie explained she'd had her phone switched off. "So, it all went OK?"

"Great. No problems. Mum, is everything OK?" Stephanie pulled her coat tightly across her against the wind and started walking to her car.

"Not really, no. I went to see your grandmother today. Anyway, when I arrived, Bernard was there." Stephanie asked her what she thought of him. "Oh, he seemed nice enough on the surface, I suppose."

"So you brought up the Florida thing?"

"Of course. That's what I went for."

"Don't tell me you lost your temper and blew the whole thing."

"No, I didn't."

"You didn't?" Stephanie said, opening the door of her car. "I'm amazed."

"I waited until he'd gone. Then I lost my temper and blew the whole thing."

"Ah."

"I forbade her to go. She told me I couldn't tell her how to live her life and then she said I should leave. Now we're not speaking and your father's furious with me. I know I should have handled it better, but she's my mother. She's old and I want to protect her." Apparently, after the confrontation Estelle had been so distraught that she'd blown her diet by buying half a dozen cheese Danish and eaten the lot in one sitting.

"Don't worry," Stephanie soothed. "I'll have another talk with Gran." She gently revved the car engine to encourage the heater to come on. Then she dialed her grandmother's number.

"Look, darling," Lilly said, when Stephanie brought up the Florida situation, "this man is giving me the chance of a few years' happiness. Aren't I entitled to that?"

"Oh, Gran, of course you are. But we love you and worry about you. And we're all going to miss you."

"I'm going to miss you, too, especially Jake."

"Mum knows she shouldn't have lost her temper, but she's really frightened about what might happen to you."

"I know she is, but I'll be fine. I'll have Bernard looking after me. I may be getting on, but I'm not senile. If Estelle loves me, then she has to let me make my own decisions, and so do you." It was clear that Lilly was declaring the subject closed.

$\mathscr{S}$tephanie managed to get home, change into trousers and a shirt, which were smart rather than sexy—so as not to give Ossie the wrong idea—and make it to the restaurant by just after eight.

As she parked the car, she could feel herself starting to get nervous. She knew she had to tell Ossie the truth, but she was still struggling to think of the words that would let him down gently. She was also aware that telling the truth wasn't getting her very far lately.

The Jägerhütte, with its stuffed deer heads on the wall and general *bierkeller* rusticity, looked like the kind of place Hitler would have chosen to hang out after a hard day's annexing. Stephanie was greeted by a waiter sporting lederhosen and a three-foot-long pepper grinder. As he took her coat, she could see Ossie sitting at the table. His head was down and he was swirling the ice in his soda. He looked edgy, she thought, just as he had this morning. He clambered down from his chair when he saw her coming toward him. She bent her knees so that he could reach up to kiss her.

"So," he said as they sat down, "did I tell you, they do the most wonderful schnitzel here?"

"Yes, you did mention it." He really wasn't himself, she decided. When the waiter appeared she ordered a spritzer. He asked for another soda. While they waited for their drinks he asked her how her day had gone.

"Great. No problems. And I'm really starting to like Konstanty."

"Good. Very good. I'm pleased." He looked up to see what had happened to their drinks. "Look," he said, clearing his throat. "I'm going to come straight to the point. I've got something really important I'd like to say to you." In her general panic it occurred to her he was about to announce that he was in love with her. She absolutely had to say her piece first and stop him. "Actually, Ossie, I'm glad you said that, because there's something I need to say to you too."

"Do you mind if I go first? I've been up half the night preparing what I was going to say." Gawd. He really was about to declare his undying love. "The thing is," he said, "I know we're going to have a great professional relationship and I think we're going to be great friends, too, but I don't think we're quite going to make it together as, you know, an item."

Whoa. Hang on. He couldn't go out with *her*? "We're not?" she said. "Why not?"

He shook his head. "Look at us. We're just so different."

She let out a long breath. "Oh, God, Ossie. I'm so glad you found the courage to say it. I've been dreading bringing it up in case I offended you."

"How could you offend me? It's nobody's fault."

"No, no. Of course it isn't."

"I mean," he continued. "You're Jewish and I'm a moron."

"Ossie, that's ridiculous," Stephanie exclaimed. "You're a highly intelligent man."

Ossie smiled a patient smile. "I didn't say I was a moron. I said I was a Mormon. I'm a member of the Church of Jesus Christ of Latter-day Saints."

"Get out," she said, throwing back her head and laughing loudly. Then she saw the expression on his face and realized he was deadly serious. "So, how come you've never mentioned it?"

"Stephanie, unless you're Donny Osmond, being in show business and a Mormon doesn't exactly go down well."

"Now I get it. That explains the crucifix and the no alcohol. But you still smoke, you swear, you sleep with women."

He shrugged. "OK, I struggle with my faith. That doesn't make my intention any less serious." She supposed she just about took the point. "You're a beautiful woman, Stephanie,

251

and I know you'll find the right man someday. It's just not me. I know you feel hurt and rejected right now, but it will pass."

"I hope so," Stephanie said, praying that she sounded sufficiently wounded.

Ossie was staring into his glass. "I think I ought to tell you that Sheila and I have sort of got it together."

"Sheila? She hates you."

He laughed. "No, she doesn't hate me. She really does adore me. And I think the world of her. The point is neither of us could admit it."

"Why?"

He explained that he'd originally met Sheila through his church and that he'd offered her a job when her husband left her. "She was married for twenty years to this bastard who was constantly playing away from home. My problem was that I've always had this thing about being seen with beautiful young women. I wanted to prove to the world that although I was short, I could still date. Of course, those relationships never went anywhere, but I was so obsessed. I couldn't see what was under my nose. Anyway, on her birthday I took Sheila out for dinner and I gave her the earrings. We got pissed and she ended up telling me she'd always had a thing for me, but her husband walking out left her feeling very insecure and she has been too scared to say how she felt about me in case I rejected her. Thinking back, I've probably always loved her."

Stephanie nodded. "I hope it works out for you, Ossie," she said, placing her hand on top of his. "I really do."

"So, you're OK? You wouldn't believe how worried I've been."

"I will be," she said, keeping up the wounded act.

"You'll still stay and have dinner, though, won't you?

The sauerkraut they do here has to be tasted to be believed."
She said that of course she would stay.

"Fantastic." He grinned. Then he tucked his napkin into
his collar. "So, Stephanie, have you ever thought about allow-
ing the Holy Spirit into your life?"

To her enormous relief, Ossie's question was only a tease.
Proselytism, he assured her, wasn't his style. Puzzled that a
man like Ossie had found God, she asked him what the at-
traction was. He shrugged. "Sometimes being this size isn't
easy. You need something to get you through." She wasn't
surprised to find out he had been taunted mercilessly as a
child. "Walking through the school gates every day was like
going into a war zone," he told her. "There was never anywhere to hide. The bullies always found me. I soon learned
my only option was to tough it out. Then, when I got home,
I used to send up a little prayer. It got me through. I'm not as
hard as I appear, you know."

"I'd worked that out," she said gently. She was finding
him so easy to talk to now that she was soon telling him about
Albert and Frank.

"It's funny," he said, "so often, we try to do the right
thing and we never get it right."

"Tell me about it," she said, managing a smile. "Thanks
for listening." He told her it was his pleasure.

She'd just finished saying good night to Ossie and was
walking back to her car when her mobile went off.

"Hi, it's me." It was Cass. She sounded distraught.

"Sweetie, what on earth is it?"

"Alex has just dumped me."

"Dumped you? But yesterday you were about to walk
down the aisle."

"I know. I can't believe it. Look, I realize it's late, but can you come over? I could really do with somebody to talk to."

Stephanie looked at her watch. It was past eleven. If she didn't get a decent night's sleep she would be a wreck in the morning. "All right, hang on," she said. "I'll be there in twenty minutes."

Chapter 16

"Can you believe it?" Cass's slurred voice was heaped with indignation. "Me, of all people. An oat." She carried on pacing, virtually empty Scotch glass in one hand, cigarette in the other. "Help yourself to a drink."

Stephanie said she was fine. "I don't understand. How do you mean, an oat?"

"A wild oat." She tipped back her head and drained her glass. "Alex confessed tonight that he and his wife had been childhood sweethearts, that he'd never slept with anybody apart from her and now he's sowing his wild oats. I can't believe he just used me for sex. He actually told me I meant nothing to him. I feel so humiliated." That was the essence of it, Stephanie thought. Cass had never been dumped in her life. And to be dumped in such a callous way was doubly cruel. Her heart would mend, but her pride would take longer to recover.

Stephanie went over to the window where Cass was

standing, gazing out at the city lights. She put an arm round her. "Bastard," she said.

"You won't tell a soul, will you?" Cass said, flicking ash into an empty glass. "I couldn't live it down if it got out that I was an oat. I'd be a laughingstock. I mean, we can tell Lizzie, but nobody else must know." Stephanie gave her a squeeze and promised she wouldn't say a word. Cass wiped her nose on a ball of tissue. "So, how are things going between you and Frank?"

Stephanie hadn't planned to say anything, since Cass was so upset. "Not so great, since you ask." She told the tale.

"It's funny," Stephanie said, letting out a long breath. "Before I told him about Albert, I almost told Frank I loved him."

"What, *before* having sex? How quaintly old-fashioned."

"What do you mean?"

"What I mean is, the man might turn out to have a really small penis. Then what would you do?" Stephanie said she was sure they would be able to work through it together. "How big are his ears?" Cass went on. "It's a scientific fact that men with big ears have big penises." Stephanie said she'd never really noticed Frank's ears. Cass picked the whiskey bottle up from the coffee table and poured herself another drink.

"Do you think I've lost him?" Stephanie said. Cass shook her head and said that he might take some convincing, but if he loved her he would come round. They sat talking for another twenty minutes or so, Cass repeatedly topping off her drink. Finally her eyes started to glaze over and her speech was starting to slur more. "Come on, you look exhausted," Stephanie said. "Let's get you to bed." Cass stabbed out her cigarette in the whiskey glass and nodded. Then she let Stephanie make her some chamomile tea.

"Oh, by the way," Cass said as she sat in bed, sipping the

tea. "I didn't find an escort for Lizzie for tomorrow night. I couldn't believe it. Every one of my contacts was busy or out of town. I tried a couple of agencies, but all the decent blokes were booked. What are we going to do? Lizzie's plan totally collapses if we don't find somebody."

Stephanie hadn't the faintest idea what to do. Conjuring up hunks at a moment's notice wasn't exactly her forte. "Don't worry," she said, patting Cass's hand. "You get some sleep. I'll phone Albert in the morning. He's bound to know somebody."

It was past one when she left Cass's flat. She really was going to be knackered tomorrow. She could only hope that her adrenaline would kick in and keep her going. When she got in there was an e-mail from Albert asking how the recording had gone and saying he would call in the morning. The e-mail came as a surprise. She'd assumed that Albert, being Albert, would have forgotten about the recording.

She fell asleep almost as soon as her head hit the pillow. A couple of hours later she woke with a start, heart thumping in her chest. She'd been dreaming that she was living with Frank and he was trying to persuade Jake to come into the garden and play football. Jake, who looked eight or nine in the dream, was punching him over and over again and screaming, "I won't. I won't. You're not my dad. You'll never be my dad." Then Jake turned to Stephanie and burst into tears. "Why did you send my dad away? I hate you." On her way downstairs to get some water, she kept telling herself the dream meant nothing, that her brain was overtired and it was playing tricks. Nevertheless, it had managed to tap into the guilt and fear she was already feeling about depriving Jake of his father and leave her shaken.

Albert called her the next morning from the hotel restaurant where he was having breakfast.

"So, is Michael Douglas's arse really crepey, then?" she said, toweling her hair, which was still wet from the shower.

"As a matter of fact, not at all," he laughed. "I've no idea why they needed me. But, hey, how did the recording go?" She told him so far, so good. He sounded genuinely interested and pleased it was going so well. "I've been speaking to Jake every day," he went on. "You wouldn't believe how much I'm missing him. You know, when I get home we really need to sort out where we go from here. Being apart from you two has made me realize just how much I want us all to be together."

"I know, Albert," she said, her voice quiet and thoughtful as images of last night's dream filled her head. "I know . . . Listen, you don't happen to know any hunky blokes, do you?"

"Hey, come on, *principessa*. Hang in there. I'll be back in a few days."

She explained that the hunk was for Lizzie. Albert said he knew plenty, but they were all in L.A. Just then he broke off from their conversation to say hi to somebody. "You'll never guess who's here—Sunnie Ellaye. I bumped into her last night. She's here with her boyfriend, Brad. He's the guy she went back with after we split up. Anyway, Brad's a set designer on the film and she came along for the ride . . . Hold on, she wants to say hello."

"Stephanie, hi," Sunnie squealed. "Can you believe this? It's such a . . . I mean, it really is . . ."

"A coincidence?"

"I was gonna say *weird,* but I guess it's a coincidence too. You know, I never told you how much I enjoyed spending the holidays with you. And I so miss Jake. He's such an adorable little boy." Then she lowered her voice. "And I'm so glad you and Albert have got it together. I have to tell you, he doesn't stop talking about Jake. They need to be together. The three of you need to be together."

Dippy as a fondue she might have been, but there was no getting away from it, Sunnie really was a sweetheart. Stephanie barely had a chance to say how much she appreciated the thought, before Sunnie was saying she had to go. "A friend of mine from L.A. is throwing a martini and manicure party at the Hitler Bunker and we still need to pick up cuticle cream and olives."

Albert came back on the line. "Don't even ask," he laughed. "That woman just cracks me up." Then he said he'd be home on Saturday.

The moment she got off the phone, Stephanie's thoughts returned to Lizzie's lack of a hunk. She was beginning to panic. She couldn't let her friend down. She just couldn't.

When she arrived at the studio, Graham and another engineer were having a problem with one of the mikes. While the orchestra sat around chatting in the studio, she and Konstanty stayed in the control room going over her songs and drinking coffee. "So, Konstanty, how are you getting on with Katherine Martinez?" He shrugged.

"She is pussycat so long as I geev her the compliments all the time." Stephanie said it sounded like exhausting work. "It is. You know, I wouldn't have taken thees job if it hadn't been for theater."

"Theater? I don't understand."

"In my hometown of Banja Luka, the theater was destroyed during the war. I am trying to raise money to rebuild it. Just a few more thousand dollars and we will have enough.

I thought it was worth taking reesk and doing something a leetle deeshonorable for good cause. What do you think?"

"Oh, I think you did the right thing, Konstanty. Absolutely the right thing." He asked her why she had agreed to be Katherine's voice. She explained about being a single parent with a massive overdraft, Jimmy wanting his house back and the fact that she didn't think she'd be able to afford to rent anything decent on what she could hope to earn.

"I think you do right thing too," he said.

Since Graham was still fooling with the mike, they carried on chatting and for some reason she found herself telling him about Lizzie.

"Don't suppose you know any dishy blokes, do you?"

"As happen, I do," he said. "My brother."

"Get away," she laughed. Then, realizing that her great fat mouth had completely disengaged from her brain, relaying her thoughts about the impossibility of a man as aesthetically wanting as Konstanty having a good-looking brother, she turned instantly crimson.

"Deeferent father," he declared solemnly.

"Oh, no, I didn't mean . . . I mean, I wasn't suggesting."

Konstanty laughed, showing off a mouthful of splayed gappy teeth. "Eet's all right. I know I'm no George Loony." He explained that his brother Igor was one of Bosnia's top male models, that he was visiting and would probably be more than delighted to help out.

"Oh, no, Konstanty, don't worry," Stephanie shot back, certain that Igor would look like a Polish Mafia boss. She could see it all—the mullet, the white jacket with sleeves pushed up to his elbows and the mirror sunglasses. "I'm sure we'll find somebody." But Konstanty refused to take no for an answer. Ten minutes later it was all fixed. "OK, he understands eexactly what he has to do. But I warn you, he speaks very leetle English." That was the least of her worries, Stephanie thought. She decided that all she could do was sit tight and pray that he would be vaguely presentable.

Sidney didn't come into the studio that day. According to Ossie, whom she chatted to briefly on the phone, he was too busy pandering to K-Mart's ever-increasing demands.

Stephanie's second day in the recording studio turned out to be much more demanding than the one before. Konstanty kept finding fault with her. She couldn't work out if she was making more mistakes because she was tired after last night, or because Konstanty was simply being more critical than the day before. In the end she lost count of how many times he said: "No, no, no. I can hear tiny extra breath in third bar. We try it maybe just one more time, I theenk." Then the orchestra would start to huff and puff and get generally pissed off, which undermined her confidence even more.

By seven o'clock, just as Stephanie's inner trouper was seriously considering going AWOL, Konstanty took off his headphones and declared that he was happy. They had finally managed to lay down five more tracks, each one free of extraneous breathing.

Lizzie and Cass were due at half past eight. Igor arrived at ten past. The second she heard the doorbell, her stomach did a nervous flip. "Please, God, let him be gorgeous. Please, God, don't let him look like some Wham reject." She finished doing up the zip on the pink halter-neck dress she'd worn on her date with Frank and ran downstairs.

When she opened the door, her jaw fell practically to her chest. Igor wasn't merely gorgeous. Igor was a babeski. He was about six two or three with dark blond swept-back hair and deep blue eyes. Unlike his brother, he had perfect, gleaming white Chiclets teeth. He looked a lot like Dom, she decided, only broader and more muscular. He was wearing a black, slightly shiny suit, but it wasn't shiny in a naff Banja Luka way; it was shiny in a classy Hugo Boss–sheen way. Underneath he was wearing a white open-neck shirt. Stephanie's face broke into a huge smile. Oh, this was so going to work. She invited him in. He smiled and gave an eager nod. "Tenk you," he said. She took him into the kitchen and offered him a cup of coffee. "No, tenk you." Stephanie did her best to make conversation, but Igor's English was pretty limited. In the end she excused herself and went to do her makeup.

When she came back, Igor was looking at the newspaper. She gave him another smile, tapped her watch and tried to explain that Cass and Lizzie wouldn't be much longer. Then she bent down and began stacking the dishwasher. "Ah, you haf lovely pussy," Igor declared. Stephanie's back shot into an upright position. "Excuse me?" she said.

"Your pussy. Eet ees lovely. It ees boy or girl?" It was then that Stephanie noticed Liberace nuzzling Igor's ankles and purring.

"Ah, you mean my cat," she said. "He's a boy." Just then the doorbell rang. "Excuse me. I think my friends are here."

Cass looked gorgeous in a black dress that wasn't so much little as antimatter, but Lizzie looked stunning. "Oh . . . my . . . God" was all Stephanie could manage as she gazed at the clingy low-cut cream silk dress. Her hair had been newly streaked and cut into a layered, choppy bob. Draped around her shoulders was a sheer wrap, dotted with sparkly flowers.

"Doesn't she look fab?" Cass said, grinning.

"You mean it?" Lizzie asked with genuine uncertainty. "I really look OK?"

"Lizzie," Stephanie said, "you look breathtaking. Utterly breathtaking. I just can't wait to see Dom's face." They stood in the hall for a few moments, the girls demanding the low-down on Igor. When Stephanie explained that he was a Bosnian model, Cass looked horror-struck. She was clearly envisaging the Wham-reject scenario. Lizzie being Lizzie said she was sure he would be perfect. Stephanie merely gave them a smug look and led them into the kitchen. The moment he saw Lizzie and Cass, Igor leaped to his feet. "Hello, preety ladies."

"Blimey," Cass whispered. "I wouldn't mind nibbling his *knublewurst*." Stephanie was so surprised and delighted that Cass had recovered from Alex's rejection so soon that she didn't bother pointing out that *knublewurst* was Polish rather than Bosnian. Not that it would have mattered to Cass, since anything east of Sloane Street was all the same to her.

Lizzie was already shaking Igor's hand and doing her best to explain that he was her escort for the evening. Igor was clearly smitten. He couldn't take his eyes off her. Stephanie felt uneasy. She hoped Konstanty hadn't given him the wrong idea about what was required of him tonight.

Since parking was bound to be a nightmare, they had decided to take a minicab into town. Stephanie had booked it when she got home and it was due any minute. "Oh, by the way," Lizzie said. "I have news." The smile on her face couldn't have been any bigger. She explained that two gift shops, one in Hampstead and one in Richmond, had bought her kindling kits, soaps and candles. "The managers said if they sell well, they'll put in regular orders. I still can't quite believe it."

Stephanie and Cass threw their arms around her, practically knocking her off balance. "You mentioned before Christmas that you were thinking of doing it," Stephanie said. "Why didn't you tell us you were going ahead?" Lizzie explained she hadn't wanted to say anything in case nothing came of it.

Cass said they should open a bottle of champagne, but since Stephanie didn't have any, they had to make do with toasting Lizzie's success with flat Appletize. Igor seemed utterly bemused by the jollity. This became even more apparent when Lizzie sat him down at the kitchen table and tried to explain, with the aid of paper and Jake's crayons, what kindling kits were. Poor Igor was still scratching his head when the doorbell went.

"Cab for Glassman?" the driver grunted. He was six six, with a wrestler's build, a gold hoop earring in each ear and closely cropped hair. The only thing missing was a tattooed message across his head informing members of the male population not to mess with him unless they wanted to end up between two halves of a burger bun. Normally, Cass, who always went weak at the knees at the sight of "a bit of rough," would have taken one look at him and started making *wuurrrgh* noises, or hoisted up her boobs and suggested he wasn't the only one who gave rides. Tonight, though, she only had eyes for Igor. Not that Lizzie was letting her anywhere near him. As they left the house, Lizzie put her arm firmly through Igor's. Judging by his expression, this seemed to delight him no end. Then she turned to Cass, who was a couple of paces behind, and threw her a look, which made it clear she should keep her hands off.

Cass insisted on sitting in the front. Since Igor was out of bounds, she was beginning to show some interest in the driver. Igor sat in the back between Stephanie and Lizzie. They couldn't have been going for more than a few seconds when Stephanie noticed the lucky black cat hanging from the driver's mirror. Then she saw it catch Igor's eye. She watched him lean forward and tap the driver on the shoulder. "You have very nice—" Before he could get the word out, Stephanie let out a loud scream. The driver slammed on the brakes, throwing them all forward in their seats. "Bloody 'ell," the driver muttered. "What the fuck's going on?"

"Sorry," Stephanie said meekly, "I thought I saw a fox run out."

The Eden, off Piccadilly, was the usual metal-and-glass minimalist deal. It was packed with thirty-something admen in sharp suits and spindle-legged women carrying handbags so tiny they could barely accommodate a tampon. Stephanie couldn't help thinking that after a late night she had eye bags bigger than these things. The people from Dom's office were having loud predinner drinks at one end of the long, mirrored bar.

Lizzie's plan was to go up to Dom, feign wide-eyed surprise at bumping into him and pretend she'd completely forgotten this was the venue for his office party. She would then introduce Igor. On the way over in the cab the women had done their best to explain to Igor that he should keep his hand on Lizzie's bum at all times. "No problems," he'd said, clearly thinking his boat had come in. After a couple of minutes, Lizzie would say they had a table waiting and she and Igor would saunter in to dinner, pausing once for an affectionate kiss. They decided this should be on the lips, but strictly no tongues. Dom, of course, would be left seething with jealousy. Stephanie and Cass, having watched the meeting from a safe distance, would join Lizzie and Igor at their table a few minutes later.

They were waiting for the girl at the desk to hand them their cloakroom tickets when Lizzie spotted Dom. He was standing at the bar with a young woman with whom he

265

seemed to be engaged in a significant amount of eye contact. "Omigod, that's her," Lizzie whispered. "That's bloody B.O. He said he'd finished with her. Lying bastard. Right, I'm going to sort her out." Before she had a chance to move, Stephanie and Cass each grabbed one of her arms.

"Don't be ridiculous," Cass hissed. "You'll just make a scene and ruin everything. Never forget, dignity is power." Cass and Stephanie exchanged anxious glances. They'd never really seen Lizzie angry.

She appeared to be calming down. Then, when Dom disappeared—presumably to the loo—leaving B.O. on her own, the fury overtook her again. She marched off toward the bar. Cass and Stephanie were behind her trying and failing to catch hold of her. Igor picked up the cloakroom tickets and stood watching from a few yards away, bemused as ever.

Lizzie approached the woman from behind and tapped her sharply on the shoulder. The woman spun round. "I'm Lizzie, Dom's wife. Or maybe he didn't mention he had a wife and two children."

"Er, no, actually he didn't."

"I might have guessed," Lizzie said acidly.

The woman gave Lizzie a puzzled frown, but clearly feeling the need to be polite, extended her hand. "Pleased to meet you, I'm—"

"What you are," Lizzie declared, "is a tart." Then she picked up a large glass bowl from the bar, turned it upside down and anointed the woman in guacamole. Green gloop poured down her face and onto her black suit jacket. The woman sat there gasping and blinking, unable to take in what had happened. People nearby stood in embarrassed silence.

"That's for sleeping with my husband, you . . . you floozy."

The woman wiped some guacamole off her forehead and flicked it onto the floor.

"I see," the woman said. "Well, for your information, I'm not a floozy, I'm the restaurant manager and I had never met your husband before this evening."

"Yeah, right," Lizzie shot back. "I saw the pair of you when I came in. You couldn't take your eyes off each other."

"We were going over the menu for your husband's company dinner tonight," the woman said. At this point one of the barmen handed the woman a towel and confirmed she was telling the truth.

Lizzie stood there, lost for words. She picked the towel up from the woman's lap and began making feeble, hopeless dabs at her hair and jacket. "Omigod, what can I say? I am so sorry. Look, go out and buy a new suit and send me the bill."

"You bet I will," the woman snarled, snatching the towel from Lizzie. Then she got up and bolted toward the ladies' room. Everybody watched as she almost collided with Dom, who was coming out of the men's room. A few moments later he came running over. "Lizzie? What are you doing here? The girl who runs the restaurant said you just poured guacamole over her head."

"I did," Lizzie said, almost in tears, "but I didn't mean it. I thought she was the woman you've been seeing." If they weren't already, the crowd was now completely hooked. You could hear a pin drop.

"Lizzie," Dom said, ignoring the onlookers, "I told you. It's all over. I love you. I made a terrible mistake. I'm just desperate for you to forgive me."

"Of course I forgive you. Oh, Dom, I'm so sorry. It was partly my fault. I got all boring and mumsie."

"Lizzie, you could never be boring and mumsie. Look at

you in that dress. You look so beautiful. I don't think I've ever seen you look so beautiful." He whispered something in her ear, which was clearly of an intimate nature because she turned red and started to giggle. Then he took her in his arms and kissed her thoroughly on the lips. There were *aah*s and gentle applause from the crowd. This was just dying down when Igor appeared, looking more confused than ever.

"So," he said to Lizzie, "you still want I should make fuck with you?"

Chapter 17

For a couple of seconds it looked like Dom was going to take a swing at Igor, but once Lizzie had managed to calm him down and explain that the whole Igor thing had been a setup to make him jealous, he took it in good stride and admitted he probably had it coming.

Igor's reward was dinner with Cass. "It's the very least he deserves," she purred, running her hand slowly down his shirtfront. She invited Stephanie to join them, but the offer was only halfhearted. Stephanie knew when she wasn't wanted. She said she had an early start the next day and should probably call it a night. "You absolutely sure?" Cass said, looking positively gleeful.

Dom decided to skip the firm's dinner. Instead he and Lizzie took a cab home. The last thing Stephanie heard was Dom asking Lizzie again if she could forgive him. "Of course I can, you silly old Domkin."

"Oh, Lizzie-Lumpkin," he replied, running his fingers through her hair, "I really do love you."

When Stephanie got home there was a message from Frank to say he was off to Paris for a few days to make a Renault commercial. He still sounded hurt, she thought sadly.

Cass rang first thing in the morning, sounding pretty miserable. She'd gotten nowhere with Igor because he'd genuinely had the hots for Lizzie. She also said she was off to the orthodontist to have her braces removed.

As soon as she put the phone down, Lizzie called to say she and Dom had made love practically all night and that he was home to stay. She'd also told him about the deals she'd pulled off with the gift shops. "I thought he might pooh-pooh the whole thing, but he didn't. He was just so proud and said he'd never had sex with an entrepreneur before. Isn't that sweet?"

Of course, Stephanie was overjoyed that Lizzie and Dom were back on track, but part of her couldn't help feeling envious. While Lizzie's life was sorting out, her own was becoming more and more confused. She kept thinking about Jake and the dream and wondering if he really would become bitter and resentful when he found out she had refused to make a home with his father. And as she'd already admitted to herself, it wasn't as if she felt no affection for Albert. Yes, he could be selfish and insensitive, but despite that she did care for him. She cared for him a great deal. But she didn't connect with him the way she connected with Frank. And when she was away from him she didn't feel the body-wrenching ache that she felt for Frank. The same ache that she was feeling right now.

The recording, which had been scheduled to last all week, was finished in three days. Konstanty was ecstatic. "You have worked so hard, Stephanie. You know, a magneefi-cent talent such as yours deserves so much more than thees."

Then he kissed her on both cheeks and wished her good luck.

"You too, Konstanty. I hope the show goes well." Then she said she hoped he would understand if she didn't come and see it. It was one thing knowing that Katherine Martinez was stealing all the glory; watching her do it was quite another.

"I understand," Konstanty said. It was hard saying good-bye. Although Konstanty's incessant quest for perfection irritated her, she had developed a considerable respect for him. Just as she was about to leave, Konstanty called her back and asked if she could possibly do him a favor. The songs Stephanie had recorded had been burned onto three CDs. Now that they knew they were ready, the sound engineers at the theater were crying out for them. "I can't take them because I am going to BBC to do TV interview. I phone bike-company, but they het nobody available for three hours. Could you take them, maybe?" Since Stephanie was free that afternoon, she said she was only too happy to oblige.

When she arrived at the theater, the lobby was full of TV cameras and reporters. Apparently K-Mart was about to arrive to give a press conference. Stephanie had no desire to hang around and meet her. The woman was hardly going to greet her with any affection.

"OK, everybody," a skinny guy in a radio headset announced, flapping long, feminine arms to get some quiet, "Miss Martinez's car has just drawn up outside." He pressed the earpiece against his ear. "I am informed she is now getting out of the car." At this point he realized nobody was paying him any attention. "Please, everybody," he said again, clapping this time. Finally there was a semblance of quiet. "OK, Miss Martinez is making her way to the main entrance. May I remind you that you are not to address Miss Martinez until she gives the signal that she is ready for the press conference to begin. You are asked to refer to her as Miss Martinez and she also requires that nobody make eye contact with her."

K-Mart glided in, oozing poised glamour and a fixed, blood-red smile. She was in full *Peggy* costume and makeup. Her hair, which had been dyed a soft honey blond, was piled into a bun on top of her head. She was wearing a full-length scarlet empire-line evening dress. Diamonds winked at her ears and wrists. Naturally, the photographers ignored the German "diktat" not to address her and were all calling for her attention. She stopped just once to pout for the lenses. Amid more shouts of "Over 'ere, Kathy, love, over 'ere," the chap in the headset drew her away from the photographers and guided her to a long table, which had been placed in the center of the lobby. He pulled out a chair for her. Ignoring him, she lowered herself onto the seat. She took a few seconds to smooth out the creases on her skirt. Finally she lifted her head and proffered a regal smile to indicate she was ready to begin.

"Kathy," the first reporter kicked off, "when did you discover your voice sounded so much like Peggy Lee's?" She grimaced at the familiarity, but answered haughtily.

"Oh, ever since I was a teenager, and younger. I sang in my high school jazz band. Teachers were always pointing it out and saying what a great range and power I had. I would probably have been a great singer, but you know, the acting thing came along..."

Stephanie couldn't bear to hear any more. She decided to find the theater manager, hand over the CDs and leave. He was on the phone when she went into his office. He broke off from his conversation and looked up. "These are the CDs the sound people have been waiting for." As she put them down on the desk, he gave her the thumbs-up. "Oh, by the way," he said, covering up the mouthpiece on the phone, "you couldn't drop these in Katherine Martinez's dressing room, could you?" He nodded his head toward a vast bunch of lilies and white roses lying across the seat of a chair. "You have to pass it on your way out."

"Fine," she said acidly, picking up the flowers, but her lack of keenness was lost on the theater manager, who went straight back to his phone conversation.

Stephanie opened the door of the dressing room and put the flowers down on a table. She was turning to go when an emerald satin gown draped over a chair caught her eye. She couldn't stop herself. She picked it up, held it against her and looked at herself in the full-length mirror. "Why couldn't it have been me?" she muttered to herself, aware that she was feeling like Cinderella abandoned to a basement kitchen full of pumpkins with no hope of rescue from a fairy godmother. She couldn't have been standing there for more than a minute when the door burst open. She swung round, half expecting to see a kind, elderly woman in a crinoline and a mobcap. Instead it was K-Mart. The smile had gone and had been replaced by an irritated scowl. "You took your time," she snapped at Stephanie.

"I'm sorry?" Stephanie said, taken aback by the statement. K-Mart took the dress from her and started examining it. "I'm assuming you managed to get the stain out." It was obvious she thought Stephanie was from a dry-cleaning company.

"I—I don't know," Stephanie stammered. "I just delivered these." She nodded toward the flowers. "Actually, I'm Stephanie Glassman." K-Mart frowned with surprise. She didn't speak for a moment. Instead she just stood there, looking Stephanie up and down.

"So, you're the voice," she said eventually. Stephanie nodded and watched her pinch a cigarette out of a packet

273

with two highly polished, blood-red talons. "OK, what do you want?" She lit the cigarette with a gold lighter and took a long, urgent drag. "Hasn't Sidney paid you enough? Are you after more? If you're thinking of blackmailing me I think I should warn you—"

"Katherine, I don't want anything. I delivered some CDs and the manager asked me to drop these flowers off."

"Well, now you've done that," K-Mart sneered. "Close the door on your way out."

At that moment Sidney appeared. When he saw Stephanie was with K-Mart, the smile left his face. "Well, ah do declare," he said, looking as if he expected the eye scratching and hair pulling to begin in a matter of seconds. "My two most favorite ladies . . ." K-Mart told him to cut the crap.

"Sugar, are you OK? You look a little pale. Maybe ah could get you something. How's about a massage? Or ah could call your clairvoyant. That always calms your nerves."

"I'll be fine," K-Mart barked, "as soon as Miss Glassman has gone." As Stephanie walked past her, K-Mart let out a plume of smoke through her nostrils. Sidney offered her a feeble wave. She closed the door as instructed. OK, what did she expect? The woman was hardly going to fall all over her with gratitude. On the other hand, a simple thank-you might have been nice.

Stephanie went home to pick up her car and then drove over to her mother's to collect Jake. As she pulled up she noticed one of those American-style motor homes parked across the drive. It wasn't the biggest she'd seen, but it still looked massive and lumpen in the narrow suburban street full of station wagons and hatchbacks.

As she walked down the path, her mother's neighbor, Jean,

a thin, pinched Jehovah's Witness who always gave the impression the aliens had forgotten to remove her anal probe, called out to her: "Stephanie. A letter for your father came to us by mistake." Stephanie was just about to take the letter from Jean, when Estelle appeared from nowhere and grabbed it instead. Even in the half-light Stephanie could see quite clearly that it was addressed to Mr. P. Enis Extension. Jean shot Stephanie a pitying look, which said, "If I had known what was going on when you were growing up, I would have called in social services—what your poor mother must be going through."

"Thank you, Jean," Estelle said in a tone that indicated that would be all and Jean could go back inside now. Jean turned away in a huff.

Estelle stood there, tearing up the letter. Apparently there had been three other letters that week addressed to Mr. P. Enis Extension, which had gone to Jean by mistake. "They'll drum us out of the neighborhood, I just know it," Estelle said, voice clenched.

Stephanie was just about to ask her mother what she was doing out of the house, when Lilly and Bernard appeared. They had clearly been visiting and were now leaving. So, Lilly and Estelle were speaking again. That was a relief. Harry was standing in the doorway holding Jake. "Wave bye-bye, Jake," he was saying. "Wave bye-bye." Jake appeared to have gone shy and had his head buried in Harry's shoulder.

"You two off home, then?" Stephanie said to her grandmother and Bernard.

"In a manner of speaking, I suppose," Lilly replied with a smile. Stephanie returned the smile with a perplexed frown. "Your grandmother has a new home," Estelle announced, her voice brimming with sarcasm. "Why don't you ask her to show you?"

"I don't understand," Stephanie said. She watched Lilly

275

and Bernard exchange uneasy glances. "Bernard and I can't teach tai chi in America because we couldn't get work permits. They said we were too old. So, instead we're going to offer classes to the elderly in this country."

"All over the country, to be exact," Bernard butted in. "Starting in Devon. Hence the camper bus." He explained that so far eight old people's day centers in the South West alone had booked their specially designed one-week courses.

"Omigod, so that's yours?" Stephanie said, turning toward the motor home. "You're going to live in it?"

Bernard and Lilly nodded. "Isn't she a beaut?" Bernard enthused. "Of course she's not brand-new, but she handles like a dream."

"My God," Estelle muttered, lifting her head heavenward, "it isn't enough the whole neighborhood knows my husband receives porn in the post, now they know my mad mother's run off with a gypsy."

"Ignore her," Harry called out from the doorway. "Give her a few days. She'll get over it."

Lilly and Bernard insisted on giving Stephanie a tour of the camper. The vehicle itself couldn't have been more than two or three years old, but the oppressively brown and beige interior was a monument to the seventies. "Genuine teak veneer," Lilly said, rubbing her hand over one of the cupboard doors in the minuscule kitchen area. "Feel the quality." Then she opened the cupboard, which was packed with tinned salmon, tuna and Heinz Cream of Tomato soup. She insisted that Stephanie sit on one of the benches, which were upholstered in brown and orange stripes. Stephanie couldn't place the fabric, but suffice it to say that as she touched the metal edge of the wood-effect Formica table in front of her, she received a sizable static shock. Bernard lifted up the table to demonstrate how the benches unfolded to make a double bed. "Cozy," Lilly said, winking and digging Stephanie in the ribs. "There's even a shower and a loo."

"So, you two are really serious about this?" Stephanie said. They told her they were. Deadly.

"Stephanie," Bernard said, "your grandmother and I don't know how many years we've got left, but for now we've got our health and we want to make the most of it. And we love each other." He put his arm around Lilly and kissed her cheek. "This is going to be such an adventure," he went on. "We're going to help people as well as see a bit of the country."

"Well," Stephanie said, seeing the excitement dancing in their eyes, "if it's really what you want, then I couldn't be more happy for you." She stood up and hugged them both.

By now, Estelle had gone back into the house. Lilly and Bernard wanted to pop in again for a final good-bye. Stephanie followed them. As they walked into the kitchen, Estelle was sitting at the kitchen table hugging Jake as if to say "At least I've got you."

"Come on, Estelle," Harry said, sitting down next to her, his hand on her shoulder, "you should be glad you've got a mother with so much get-up-and-go. And at least she's not leaving the country now."

"Harry's right," Lilly said. "What do you want me to do all day, sit around watching *Family Fortunes* and dribbling?"

Estelle looked up. Her eyes were threatening tears. "I just worry about you, that's all. I don't want anything to happen to you."

"Look, it probably won't." Lilly sat down at the table and put her hand on Estelle's arm. "But if it does, at least you'll know I died happy, right?" Estelle shrugged a noncommittal shrug. "Now come here," Lilly said, "and give your old mother a hug."

They finished their good-byes in the street. Harry and

Bernard exchanged handshakes. Then Harry bent down to kiss his mother-in-law. "You're a good boy, Harry," Lilly said affectionately. Harry mumbled something under his breath about his mother-in-law waiting until he was nearly seventy to finally tell her he was a good boy.

"You make sure you look after my mum," Estelle said to Bernard, her eyes filling up now. "And phone from the first campsite, just to let me know you're OK." He nodded and kissed her on the cheek. Lilly hugged Stephanie one last time. A few moments later, Bernard gave a couple of loud honks of the horn and they were gone.

As they walked back into the house, Estelle turned to Stephanie and said, "So, do you reckon they—you know—*do it?*"

Stephanie suggested that she, Jake and her parents go out for dinner to cheer themselves up, but Estelle said she was still feeling a bit emotional. "I think I'd rather just stay in and watch TV with your father."

In the end, Stephanie took Jake for pizza. Since she'd spent three days at the studio pigging out on doughnuts and bacon rolls, she decided to have a prawn salad. The mayonnaise tasted slightly bitter, she thought, but not enough for her to send it back.

Next morning she was feeling a bit nauseated and she could feel the beginnings of stomach cramps. She took a couple of Diacalm and hoped it would go away. It didn't. Then, to make matters worse, a dispatch rider turned up at lunchtime with a letter from Sidney Doucette's lawyer saying an injunction had been taken out against her, preventing her from going within half a mile of Katherine Martinez. The letter wasn't exactly threatening, but she was left in no doubt that her career would suffer if she started making trouble by asking for more money or if she tried to sell her story to the press. Indignant and fuming, she got straight on the phone to Ossie. "I told Katherine I didn't want any more money. And I'd never go to the press. If I did that I'd have to own up to my part in all this. Where would that get me?"

"I know," Ossie said, "but the pair of them have started to panic. The nearer they get to the first night, the more scared they are of the secret being blown." Then he called Sidney a slimy, evil bastard and told her there wasn't much they could do. "Take my advice. The injunction is totally unfair, but it's not worth fighting. Just keep your head down and bank the money. The first check should reach you any day."

She got the point. Sidney was a powerful man. She couldn't take him on. The only thing she could do was to try and let it go. Of course, she was well aware she had no real right to the indignation she was feeling. After all, she was practically as guilty in all this as Sidney and K-Mart. The only difference was that her motivation had been financial desperation while theirs had been greed.

By now the cramps were getting worse. On top of that, Jake, who had missed her these last few days, was demanding her full attention. "Mummy do painting now?" he said after she'd spent an entire morning reading and doing puzzles. "OK, poppet," she said, rubbing her stomach, "painting it is."

They were sitting at the kitchen table doing finger painting when Stephanie heard the key in the door. "Albert?" she called out.

"No, Fidel Castro. Of course it's me."

"My daddy," Jake squealed. A second later he had scrambled down from the table.

"Jake, your hands are covered in paint! Come back!" But she was too late. Jake had practically collided with Albert, who scooped him up and threw him in the air. Jake screamed with delight. "Hiya, big guy," Albert said, kissing him. "I have so missed you. So, how've you been?"

"Better." Jake nodded solemnly. "My doing painting. Come and see."

As Albert carried him back to the table, Jake started smearing his father's face in red paint. Albert realized but didn't seem to mind in the least. "Hi, *principessa.*" He bent down and kissed Stephanie on the cheek.

"Welcome back." She smiled, returning the kiss. She was aware that she felt genuinely pleased to see him. Albert stood back, looking at her. "You OK? You look really pale." She told him about last night's prawns. He suggested she go to bed while he took care of Jake. She told him that Jake was really excited at having her back and that she was sure she could make it until bedtime. On top of that, Mrs. M. was popping round later to give Jake his Christmas present.

"Oh, by the way," she said, picking up the letter from Sidney Doucette's lawyer. "This arrived a couple of hours ago." He took the letter and started reading. "Christ, what did you do to bring this on?" She explained.

"That man really is a miserable slimeball," he said. Then he made much the same point as Ossie had about how she couldn't fight him and that she should take the money and run.

While Albert took Jake into the living room to open the present he'd bought him, Stephanie made coffee. When she went in a few minutes later the carpet was strewn with bits of cardboard packaging and Albert was showing Jake how to work a radio-controlled Jeep. He was far too young to master the controls and he kept crashing it into the furniture. Then Albert would put his great big hand gently over Jake's and show him how to guide the joystick. "That's it, Jake. Easy does it... See, you did it! Good job." Jake would then insist on doing it on his own. Of course he would crash it again and Albert would patiently take his hand again. Stephanie stood in the doorway, holding two mugs of coffee, watching all this. When he saw her, Albert looked up. "I know," he said. "Let's see if Mommy can do it." Stephanie protested that she was hopelessly uncoordinated, but Albert got up, took the mugs from her and pulled her down onto the carpet with them. To entertain Jake, she made out she was even more hopeless than she really was and crashed the car into the hearth.

"Silly Mummy," Jake said to Albert, clearly feeling she was so useless that she was beyond help.

"Girls," Albert whispered, shaking his head. Then the pair of them started laughing conspiratorially and Jake pushed Albert onto the floor and began crawling over him. Seeing them together like this brought tears to her eyes.

"Now Daddy's turn," Jake cried.

As they watched Albert guide the car skillfully around the room, Jake climbed into Stephanie's lap. "You love having your daddy here with us, don't you?" she said, bringing her cheek next to his. Jake started nodding.

"My daddy come and live in my house now?"

She hugged Jake to her and felt the lump in her throat getting bigger.

Albert said he had to go back to his flat to check his post, but he promised he would be back in time to help bathe Jake and put him to bed. Mrs. M. arrived just as Albert was leaving. He was his usual flirty charming self and she was clearly smitten. "Now then, isn't he just gorgeous," she said after he'd gone. "What a lovely little family you make." Before Stephanie had a chance to say anything about Albert moving in, Jake came tearing in. He looked at Mrs. M. and suddenly went shy, burying his head in Stephanie's lap. But Mrs. M. soon got around him with the Play-Doh food factory she'd bought him for Christmas. Soon it was as if she'd never been away. Stephanie couldn't help noticing that Mrs. M.'s limp, although much improved, was still very much with her. "The doctors said the hip replacement has been a partial success," she confided. "They said at my age I shouldn't expect miracles." She paused and looked at Stephanie and then at Jake, who was kneeling up at the kitchen table with his food factory, trying to make Play-Doh spaghetti. Stephanie could see a sadness creeping into her eyes. "I've decided to move back to Ireland."

"Oh, Mrs. M."

"The thing is," she said, forcing a smile, "I'm not getting any younger and the doctors reckon this is about as good as my hip is ever going to get. My kids think I need looking after. On top of that, I miss my grandchildren." She picked up a piece of Jake's Play-Doh and began kneading it between her fingers.

"We are going to miss you," Stephanie said, getting up to give her a hug.

"I hope you don't think I've let you down. I know how much you were depending on me."

"We were," Stephanie said, excusing herself a white lie. "But you mustn't worry. I'm certain you're doing the right thing. Albert and I will work something out." Stephanie had never seen Mrs. M. look so relieved. "I'm going to rent out my house. So, I'll be back for visits."

As Stephanie sat sipping her tea, she was gripped by a particularly viselike cramp. Mrs. M. must have seen her wince.

"You're not well, are you? I thought you looked under the weather when I arrived." After Stephanie had explained what was wrong, Mrs. M. insisted on phoning her daughter Geraldine and getting her to come round with a bottle of Collis Brown mixture. "The old-fashioned remedies are always the best," she declared. "It'll sort you out in no time."

Geraldine was a plump jovial soul, a lot like her mother. She had just arrived when the phone rang. It was Ossie.

His tone was controlled panic. "Steph, we've got a situation. One of the CDs you brought round to the theater yesterday has gone missing. It's the press night tonight. They need you to come in and sing a couple of songs live onstage."

"What? How on earth am I supposed to do that?" He explained that the idea was to hide her behind a pillar and K-Mart would still lip-synch as planned. She burst out laughing and said the idea was preposterous. "And by 'they,' " she went on, "I presume you mean Sidney. Sorry, I refuse to do any more to help that man. Anyway, even if I wanted to, I can't. He took out an injunction against me. Remember? I can't come within half a mile of K-Mart."

"It's been lifted," Ossie said. "Listen, you're not doing this for Sidney. You're doing it for Konstanty. I just had him on the phone. He's desperate."

"But why can't Konstanty get the studio to make some copies of the CD?"

"He tried, but they're refitting the place and they've closed for a week."

"Great."

"Look, I don't know how these CDs got lost, but I really think you should do this. The last thing you want is for Sidney to stop paying you, and I promise you, he's quite capable of it."

She let out a long, slow breath. "God, why is it Sidney always gets what he wants? . . . OK, what time do I need to be there?"

"Now. They're sending a cab."

Mrs. M. and Geraldine said they would look after Jake until Albert got back. Dosed up on more Diacalm and Collis Brown mixture, she climbed into the cab.

When she got to the theater Sidney was waiting for her in the lobby. "Well, missy, don't you look like a magnolia petal on a dewy summer's morning." He was all innocent smiles, as if the injunction hadn't happened. She gave him a cold stare. "I'm not doing this for you, Sidney. I'm doing it for Konstanty." Sidney's smile turned to steel. He said he didn't care who she was doing it for, just as long as she did it.

Konstanty hugged her when he saw her. "I don't know how to thenk you," he said. The Collis Brown was doing little to stop the cramps, which were now coming every couple of minutes. "Stephanie, you look as eef you're een pain? Are you OK?"

"Bit of a tummy bug," she said. "Don't worry, I'll be fine."

"You sure?"

"I'm sure," she said with a reassuring smile.

"OK, come, I take you onto the stage and show you what to do." As they worked their way through the backstage corridors, Stephanie asked him what songs he wanted her to sing. " 'I'm a Woman' and 'Big Spender,' " he said.

On top of feeling ill, Stephanie was starting to feel real fear. She'd never performed in a proper theater before, albeit from behind a pillar. Hundreds of people, including every theater critic in London, would be out there, listening to her. The stage, which had been transformed into a glitzy New York nightclub circa 1940, seemed vast. There was a grand Ziegfeld Follies staircase, a vast crystal chandelier and lots of red plush. At the back of the stage was a shiny black and silver two-tier platform where the band would sit. In front was a small podium and one of those old-fashioned chunky metal microphones.

Konstanty explained that Peggy Lee's entire life story, from her childhood with the stepmother who beat her, to her marriage to an alcoholic guitar player named Dave Barbour and her final performance at the Hollywood Bowl, where she was too frail to stand, would be told from this set. "You see Grecian pillar at side? Ve will mike you up and you can sing from behind, yes?"

"I guess," Stephanie said with a shrug, "but do you think we're really going to get away with it?"

"Once sound boys hef everything sorted out, nobody vill know, belief me."

"If you say so," she said, feeling too rough to raise any more objections.

Stephanie wasn't due to do her bit from behind the pillar until after the intermission. The first half of the show was relayed to her through speakers into the theater manager's office, where she had been allowed to camp out. She couldn't believe how well the scam appeared to be working. Nobody was even remotely aware that K–Mart was lip-synching. After each song the applause was deafening. Theater critics were the hardest audience in the world to win over, and yet they couldn't have been more enthusiastic. She didn't know whether to laugh or to cry. By now the medicine had taken the edge off the pain, but she was running to the loo every fifteen minutes or so. Each time she went, she felt sick and light-headed, as if she were about to pass out. When Konstanty came in during the intermission, she almost told him she wasn't up to singing, but he seemed so desperate and so re-lieved she was there that she just didn't have the heart.

As soon as the curtain came down after the first half, Konstanty and a sound engineer took her onto the stage. She was focusing so hard on how ill she was feeling that any nerves she'd had an hour or so ago completely disappeared. The soundman gave her a handheld mike and explained that her voice would be heard from speakers at the front of the stage, exactly as if the CD were playing. "Eet ees only two songs," Konstanty reassured her. "Ve will sneak you off vhen stage lights go down between acts."

"OK," she said, desperately hoping she could hold out for twenty minutes without going to the loo.

As the audience returned, she could feel herself begin-ning to burn up. "Please, God, just get this over with. Please." She had never felt less like singing in her life. Konstanty had explained there would be five minutes of dialogue, then she would hear the intro to "I'm a Woman."

The curtain was still down. From behind the pillar she watched the band come onstage and take their places. Several smiled and gave the thumbs-up. As the curtain went up and the stage lights came on, her nerves finally kicked in. On top of everything else, she could feel herself shaking. Hidden behind the pillar she didn't see K-Mart come onstage. All she was aware of was the dialogue. Since the band was behind her and she had to stand facing the pillar in front of her, there were no visual clues from the band that the first number was coming up. She had to wait. Finally she heard the intro. Somehow she managed to come in on cue:

"I can wash up forty-four pairs of socks and have them hanging out on the line . . ." She could hear the words coming from her mouth, but she felt disconnected somehow, as if her voice wasn't coming from her, but from somewhere way off in the distance. By now the nausea really began to overtake her. She could literally feel the blood draining from her head. Still singing, she leaned against the pillar. " 'cause I'm a woman, W-O-M-A-N . . ."

It was then that the world started to spin and turn a strange shade of green. The audience full of theater critics looked on aghast as Stephanie lurched from behind the pillar, wobbled for a few seconds and then collapsed spectacularly onto the stage, microphone in hand, mumbling "I'm a woman." Then she threw up.

Chapter 18

Stephanie was too busy being sick over one of the double bass players who had rushed to her aid to be aware that the curtain had come down and that K-Mart was standing over her screaming, "You selfish bitch, how could you do this to me?" Or that Sidney Doucette had to pull her off and drag her into the wings, where they stood spitting and cursing and making plans for a swift exit to South America. Nor did she have any idea that the theater critics, who at first sat in shocked silence along with the rest of the audience, would soon be congregating in the bar laughing their heads off and screaming into their mobiles to their respective news editors that there hadn't been a scam like it since *Singin' in the Rain,* when Debbie Reynolds's character, Kathy Seldon, pretended to be the voice of Lina Lamont. For anybody privy to the commotion, it was clear that the *Peggy* debacle was about to hit the headlines big-time and that the search was now on to identify the voice behind K-Mart.

One of the girl stagehands helped Stephanie to the loo

and stayed with her while she carried on throwing up. At one point, while she was having a break from puking and was instead sitting in the locked cubicle diarrhea-ing, she heard Konstanty's voice. He asked her if there was anything he could do to help. "Oh, Stephanee, I am so sorree. I could see you veren't well. I shouldn't haf made you go through vith it. Ve should haf just dropped the missing songs from the show. Now ve are all in the sheet."

"Yeah, but right now," she said, gripping her stomach, "some of us are just a bit more in the sheet than others." She asked him if he would phone Albert and ask him to come and get her. She knew it would mean bringing Jake, but she didn't think she had much choice. She couldn't go home in a cab and risk chucking up over the upholstery.

She didn't dare leave the ladies' room. After about twenty minutes Albert appeared at the cubicle door. By now she was kneeling in front of the loo again, puking. "Don't come too close," she said, looking up at him. "I've got sick in my hair."

"Don't worry about that," he said, bending down and rubbing her shoulders. "Do you think you can make it to the car?"

"I don't know. I'll try." Since all the hacks were camped out at the main entrance and stage door, they had to leave by a tiny side exit. Albert had parked her car on double yellow lines outside. She sat slumped in the back holding a Waitrose carrier bag to her mouth. "Oh, God," she said as he started the engine. "Who's with Jake?"

"Shh, don't worry. I called Mrs. M.'s Geraldine."

When he got her upstairs to the bedroom, Albert put towels over the pillows so that she wouldn't get sick on them. Then he sat on the bed gently wiping her face with a warm flannel. She carried on throwing up for the next couple of hours. He stayed with her, holding her head. Whenever the

289

stomach cramps came and she needed the loo, he guided her across the landing in case she fainted again. Then he waited outside until she'd finished and took her back to bed.

Also that night, the press got to work and managed to worm their way in among the cast and the band and get various members to talk. By the next morning the story was all over the papers. The headlines were pretty predictable: "Martinez Sensation," yelled one tabloid; "Star in Voice Swap Con," screamed another. The broadsheets devoured the story too; old stills from *Singin' in the Rain* appeared on several front pages. The day after that, pictures appeared of K-Mart and Sidney fleeing their hotel, their heads hidden under blankets as they were smuggled into a limo with blacked-out windows, apparently bound for Heathrow.

The doctor came and diagnosed food poisoning—as if she didn't know—and told her to drink plenty of fluids. Albert immediately went out and bought a dozen bottles of Gatorade. She managed a little that first day without bringing it up, but mostly she slept. In the evening Albert helped her into the bath and washed her hair. For the next three days he ran up and downstairs, shopped, cooked for Jake and kept him amused. She couldn't have asked for more, particularly as the keeping-Jake-amused bit was particularly hard. There was a thicket of reporters permanently camped outside the front door, and whereas Albert was prepared to go out alone and shoulder his way through the mob, he wasn't prepared to risk Jake being traumatized. The upshot was that Jake didn't go out for nearly a week and as each day passed he became more and more stir-crazy.

Cass, Lizzie and her mother phoned each day, but she wouldn't let them visit because she didn't want them being set upon by the reporters. They wouldn't have been able to handle them the way Albert did. He'd become adept at barging his way through the crowd, refusing to make eye contact with any of the reporters or answer questions. And when a woman from the *Sun* started calling through the letter box pretending to be from Interflora, Albert was wise to the ruse, thanked her sweetly and swiftly closed the slot.

However badly Albert had behaved toward her before he went to Berlin, he had certainly made up for it now. Whether or not this change in him would be permanent, she didn't know. Somehow she doubted it. But there was no getting away from it: while she was ill the three of them had become a proper family. Yes, she was passionately in love with Frank; of that she was in no doubt. And before they had said good-bye at his flat he had made it clear he still wanted her. And yet . . . and yet.

As the days went by and she got stronger physically, doubts began forming in her mind. She would lie in bed remembering what Albert had said to her the first time he asked her to marry him: "The whole in love thing wears off in no time. You know that." Maybe she did. Time and again, her thoughts returned to Jake. She couldn't forget the image of him and Albert playing together with the Jeep, the way her small son had climbed into her lap and asked her so sweetly if his daddy could come and live with them. Her heart ached as she heard his voice in her head. Part of her felt like a tragic Jane Austen heroine, torn between duty and true love. Then she would realize how self-indulgent she was being and snap out of it. Her position wasn't remotely tragic. Tragic heroines were forced into loveless marriages. She, on the other hand, did love Albert. And it was Albert, not Frank, who was the father of her child.

"You know," she said to Albert one morning as he leaned

her forward in the bed and plumped her pillows, "I really don't know what I'd have done without you these last few days. Thank you." When he'd finished, he sat down on the bed. She reached out and took his hand. "When I watched you and Jake with the Jeep the other day, it almost made me cry. You were wonderful with him. He adores you. I know he wants us all to be a family...and I think I do too. When I'm better I don't want you to go home."

"You sure?"

She nodded. "I'm sorry it's taken me so long to make up my mind."

"Wow, *principessa,* that's fantastic." He was saying the words, but the expression on his face seemed muted, as if deep down he wasn't sure.

"You are pleased, aren't you, Albert? This is what you want?"

"Yes. Yes, of course it is. I couldn't be happier. I'll go over to the flat tonight and pick up my stuff." She couldn't quite put a finger on it, but he suddenly seemed distant, disconnected from her somehow. He carried on being a bit quiet for a day or so, but afterward he went back to his usual self. She put it down to his being exhausted from looking after her and Jake and thought no more about it.

Each day another letter would arrive from a newspaper offering Stephanie money for her story. Albert would bring them to her. They were all of the "We just want to give you the chance to tell your side of the story" variety.

Of course, she knew that as soon as she was fully recovered she would have to speak to the press. The story was refusing to go away and it was the only way to get the journalists off her back. She also knew they were unlikely to show her any mercy and that it was possible she would never work again.

Konstanty attempted to come to her rescue. He gave an interview to the *Mirror* ("Director in *Singin' in the Rain* Scandal Speaks Out") in which he confessed his part in the scam and said he was deeply ashamed. He said he'd only done it to raise the money to rebuild the theater in his hometown, but he admitted that was no excuse. When asked about Stephanie, he said she was a deeply talented, struggling singer and single parent who only accepted Doucette's offer because she was about to lose her home. The next day's headline read: "Martinez Exploited Refugee and Social Security Mum."

Of course, Stephanie had never been on state benefits in her life and the encamped journalists could see perfectly well that she lived in a large house in a middle-class neighborhood. None of this seemed to be important, though. Instead, the newspapers turned the real story into something resembling a plot for a silent screen melodrama starring Sidney Doucette as the evil, wax-mustached baron, Katherine Martinez as his ruthless, cold-blooded but beautiful sidekick and Stephanie as the innocent, impoverished peasant girl on whom they prey.

Grateful as she was to Konstanty, Stephanie felt compelled to set the record straight.

The press had been stationed outside her house for four days when she decided to go out and speak to them. Still feeling weak and shaky, she blow-dried her hair, put on some makeup and pulled on a pair of jeans and a ribbed polo neck. The second she opened the front door the flashes opened up like an electric storm. There were probably no more than a dozen reporters there, mainly young women, but they all started bombarding her with questions and pretty soon it felt as if there were hundreds. "Stephanie, how do you feel about the way Katherine Martinez exploited you?"

"I wouldn't say she exploited me, exactly. I was fully aware of what..."

"Stephanie, how do you keep your figure so trim?"

"Well, personally, I find vomiting and diarrhea works pretty well."

"So, better than the Atkins Diet? That's interesting."

"How would you describe your feelings toward Martinez? You must be experiencing a sense of deep anger."

"I'm not sure I would put it quite that strongly . . ."

"Will you be getting counseling?"

"I don't think so."

"Do you think Katherine has had breast implants?"

"Look, I can't see how that's relevant."

"So, that's a yes?"

Since none of the reporters seemed remotely interested in hearing what she had to say, she told them she still wasn't feeling very well and hoped they would understand if she called it a day. As she turned to go, the reporters all surged forward, clamoring for her to answer "just a couple more questions."

When Albert showed her the article in the following morning's *Daily Mail,* quoting her as saying: "Silicone-breasted Martinez made me bulimic," she threw the paper across the bed. Albert told her to take it easy and that she should be grateful the press wasn't tearing her to shreds. She supposed he was right, but she couldn't get away from the feeling that being torn to shreds was what she really deserved.

"Well, your wish has been granted," Ossie said when she told him how the lack of punishment was bothering her. "Sid's refusing to pay you a brass farthing." Apparently Sidney had phoned Ossie from Brazil, where he and K-Mart were hiding out until the heat died down, saying that since the game was up, he could see no reason to pay anybody anything.

"What?" Stephanie said. "Nobody? Not even the band?"

"Nobody."

"Bastard."

So, here she was, penniless, jobless, about to lose her home and yet deep down she couldn't help feeling she'd gotten what she deserved.

Stephanie had hardly eaten for a week. Then, on the eighth day, she woke up starving. Albert, who had been sleeping with Jake (he'd become a bit clingy since Stephanie got ill), asked her what she fancied to eat. "Don't mind," she said. "Just as long as there's lots of it."

"Wow," he said. "Somebody is on the mend." He said he would bathe Jake and then, as they didn't have much in, the two of them would go shopping. At that point, as he had every day, Jake started campaigning to go to the park. Since the reporters had disappeared after having gotten their interview with Stephanie, she insisted Albert take him. "I haven't eaten for a week. I can hang on for a couple more hours."

She had a shower and went downstairs to check the post, which had been piling up since she got ill. It was mostly bills. The only letter was a curt, two-line note from Eileen Griffin saying she was sorry to lose her and grudgingly wishing her well. It was pretty much as she'd expected. As she put it in the bin, she noticed that the kitchen phone was unplugged. Albert had disconnected it when the press started phoning incessantly. She pushed the plug back into the socket and dialed her voice mail. As she suspected, most of the messages were from newspapers offering her ludicrous amounts of money for her story. She still had absolutely no intention of taking any of them up, but a bit of her—the out-of-work, about-to-be-evicted, penniless bit—was tempted. There were also several messages from seedy-sounding men asking if she would be interested in doing glamour modeling. One bloke even wanted to know if she would consider giving hand relief. Then Frank's voice came on.

"Hi, Steph. I've been trying to get you for days and I've lost your mobile number. Where are you? Are you OK? Look, I just wanted to say I've been doing some thinking about us. There's loads I want to say. Let's talk when I get back. Should be home tomorrow." He sounded so upbeat, so hopeful. She felt a momentary surge of joy, which instantly turned to sickness. She walked upstairs slowly, partly because her legs still felt weak and partly because she was dreading having to tell him about her decision to be with Albert.

Unable to think of anything that didn't sound clichéd and trite, she switched on the TV at the end of the bed. A couple of transsexuals were discussing whether it was OK to be bridesmaids if they still had penises. She never did find out whether or not it was, because the front doorbell rang. She pulled on her dressing gown, trekked downstairs again and opened the front door.

"Frank! You said you weren't getting back until tomorrow."

"This is tomorrow," he said brightly. "I left that last message yesterday."

"Oh, God, yes. Sorry." She stood back to let him in.

"Listen," he said, putting his arms around her, "I want to apologize. I overreacted when you told me about Albert. I should have trusted you when you said there was nothing going on." Oh, God, why did he have to say he was sorry? Now telling him that she and Albert had decided to make a go of it would be doubly hard. She couldn't work out if she was finding it hard to breathe because of all the guilt she was feeling or because he was holding her so tight. As he began kissing her on the lips, she turned her head away.

"Steph? You all right?"

"The thing is, I haven't been well," she said. He'd only just walked in. She couldn't start telling him about Albert while he was practically still standing on the doorstep. He put his hand to her face.

"God, you don't look too good. And you've lost weight. What happened?"

"Ah, so you haven't seen the papers, then?"

"No, I didn't bother to get them when I was in Paris."

She took him into the kitchen, put the kettle on and told him the saga. "What a nightmare. So, how you feeling now?"

"Still a bit feeble, but I'm getting there."

"Anyway, at least K-Mart and Doucette got what was coming to them. But what about you?"

She shrugged and said the press had gone easy on her. "But Sidney's buggered off to Brazil until the heat dies down and is refusing to pay any of us. I just hope Ossie can find me some more work soon."

Just then the doorbell rang. Convinced it was Albert, she turned white. Then she remembered that Albert had a key.

"I think I know who that is," Frank said. He was smiling a cryptic smile. He told her he had a surprise for her and that she should go and wait in the living room. "A surprise? What sort of a surprise?"

"Just do as you're told," he said. She trotted off into the living room.

A couple of minutes later two deliverymen in overalls appeared. Each of them was holding one side of what was clearly a canvas, a very large canvas covered in a white sheet. Frank asked them to prop it up against the wall. Then he thanked them, handed them a couple of quid each for their trouble and they took their leave.

"Why don't you see what it is?" Frank said.

She looked at him, still perplexed. Then she began pulling at the sheet. "Oh, Frank. I don't believe it. You bought this for me?" It was the Ed Blackwell *Full English Breakfast* painting she'd admired at the gallery in Shoreditch. She gazed at it, tears in her eyes, her fingers skimming the giant puddle of ketchup, the fried eggs, the brownish-purple rashers of streaky bacon. "I wrote you a note," he said, handing her a small envelope. "Open it later, when you're on your own."

"OK," she nodded. "Frank, it's beautiful. It's the most wonderful present I've ever had."

"It's my way of saying I love you."

"You do?"

"Of course I do. It wasn't until I went away that I realized just how much."

She began fiddling nervously with the envelope. "I don't know what to say."

" 'I love you too' would be a start."

She looked into his happy, expectant face. In a few seconds she would shatter every ounce of joy he was feeling. "I do love you . . ."

"Blimey, do I hear a *but* coming on?"

She slipped the envelope into her dressing gown pocket. "I can't let you give me the painting," she said.

"Why on earth not?"

She suggested they go and sit on the sofa. "The thing is," she began, looking down at her hands and then up at him.

"What?"

"Oh, God, this is so difficult . . . The thing is, Albert and I have decided to try and make a go of it."

"What? You're not serious. After everything you said?"

"Frank, please try to understand. At the end of the day, he's Jake's father and I think Jake deserves a proper family."

298

"But you and I could be a proper family."

"It wouldn't be the same."

He began rubbing his forehead. "Do you love Albert?"

"I have feelings for him."

"That's not what I asked."

"No, I'm not in love with him, if that's what you mean."

"So, you're prepared to sacrifice your happiness—our happiness—in order to live with a man you're not in love with."

"I want what's best for Jake."

"What's best for Jake is that he lives with two people who love each other. Do you think Jake wants a martyr for a mother?"

She bridled. "I'm not being a martyr. I told you I have feelings for Albert. And you wouldn't believe how he's looked after me these last few days. He's been wonderful."

"So, that's it. Albert holds your head while you're chucking up and you're his."

"Stop it." Her voice was raised now. "There's more to it than that. Much more."

She watched his face start to soften. "So, when I do this..." Gently he pulled her dressing gown off her shoulder and started kissing the top of her breast. "It means nothing." She ran her hand over the back of his head. The next moment he was cupping her face and kissing her, his tongue deep inside her. For a few delicious seconds she kissed him back.

Somehow she found the strength to push him away. "I can't do this."

He stood up. "So, that's it?"

"I'm so sorry." She turned her head toward the canvas. "I'll arrange for somebody to pick up the painting and deliver it to you."

"I don't want it. Keep it." His voice was icy. He began

walking toward the door. Then he turned around briefly. "Say hi to Jake for me," he said.

"Frank . . ."

She heard the front door open and close. Tears tumbling down her face, she pulled Frank's envelope out of her dressing gown pocket. Her hands were shaking as she opened it. " 'When you put your arms around me, you give me fever that's so hard to bear.' All my love forever, Frank." She fell onto the sofa and sobbed.

Eventually, realizing that Albert and Jake would be back any minute, she pulled herself together. She went into the kitchen and put on some more coffee. The kettle had just boiled when Albert came in, Jake trotting behind him chomping on a Waitrose gingerbread man. Albert was loaded down with supermarket bags.

"What's with the painting in the living room?" Panicked and completely taken off guard, she said it was a get-well present from Cass.

"Must have cost a fortune," he said.

"Oh, well. You know Cass. She saw it, the whole breakfast thing reminded her of me and she just had to buy it." He said he wasn't sure he liked it. "I do," she said. "I love it. It's bold and colorful."

"So is a freshly severed artery. That doesn't mean I'd hang it on my wall. Personally, I'd have preferred a landscape." His not liking the painting didn't really matter, but at that moment it seemed to her to symbolize the gulf between them. He told her he'd bought bagels for breakfast. "I hope you've still got an appetite."

"You bet," she said, wondering how she could possibly eat when the lump in her throat was so painful.

Chapter 19

Over the next few days Stephanie tried valiantly to put Frank out of her mind and focus on the three of them being a family. Even though she hadn't completely regained her strength, she threw herself into domestic activity. She cooked shepherd's pie and roast beef; she organized outings. One Sunday morning, bundled up in fleeces, hats and scarves, they went to see the deer in Richmond Park. There had been a heavy snowfall overnight, so they stopped off at a petrol station to buy a toboggan.

The park was full of daddies and children having hysterics as they careened down the snowy slopes. The deer remained aloof, ignoring the commotion, while the mothers busied themselves with their camcorders or dusted off and comforted little ones who had taken a tumble in the snow. As Stephanie watched Albert and Jake come off the toboggan for the umpteenth time and roll gleefully in the thick white carpet, she threw back her head and laughed, but at the same time, she was fighting the great ball of sorrow in her chest.

The next day they took Jake to see a puppet show on a barge at Camden Lock. Afterward they went out for pizza and Albert tried to teach Jake how to count in Italian. She watched Jake's little face, frowning with concentration, as he struggled to get his tongue around the strange sounds. "Way to go," Albert declared, beaming, when Jake finally made it to five without help. Stephanie was cheering him on, too, but as she took a sip of wine she found herself staring off into the distance. Even though she, Albert and Jake were finally a family, she couldn't help feeling desperately alone. She had given Jake the father he needed, but like a fool, she had sacrificed her own needs. Loath as she was to admit it, Frank had been right. She was being a martyr.

Letting Frank go had been a catastrophic mistake. All she could think in her defense was that her decision had been due in part to her having been ill, and as a result, her judgment had been wildly off. Every bit of her ached for Frank. No matter how much she wanted it to happen, it was never going to be possible to build a relationship with Albert based merely on affection and the love they shared for Jake. Deep down, she supposed she'd always known it.

They hadn't made love since Albert moved in. Stephanie convinced him that she still wasn't feeling 100 percent better, and for the time being, at least, Albert, who was still fairly distant and withdrawn, seemed happy not to push her.

"Oh, by the way," he said one night, over dinner, "Sunnie is leaving Berlin tomorrow and stopping off in London on her way home. I thought I might ask her to stay for a few days if it's all right with you."

"Sure," Stephanie said. "She and Brad can stay as long as they like. They can have the spare room."

"Actually, she'll be on her own. Brad has to stay on in Berlin."

Sunnie was her usual confused dippy self—going to the supermarket to seek out no-fat double cream, choosing what to wear each morning by dowsing, demanding to know why they built Windsor Castle so close to the airport. She was delighted to see Jake, whom she'd bought Tibetan prayer bells, which he went round the house tinging incessantly.

It was obvious she made Albert laugh and the two of them still clicked. Stephanie didn't see it, though. She was too lost in her thoughts about Frank to notice.

"You know what, Albert?" Sunnie said one morning over her green tea. "I just found a chin hair. I feel so ancient suddenly."

"*You* should worry. A few months ago I found my first gray pubic hair."

"Oh, how awful."

"You're telling me. It was in an egg roll."

The two of them roared. Stephanie barely reacted. Albert asked her if she was feeling OK.

"Fine," she said, aware she sounded vague and a bit off.

"I thought I'd take Sunnie and Jake to Brighton for the day. Why don't you come with us? The sea air will do you good." She shook her head and said she'd rather stay at home.

It wasn't until the following weekend that she finally caught up with Lizzie and Cass. Lizzie phoned on Saturday morning to invite her over for morning coffee. She said Cass was coming. "And I'm sure Jake would love to see the new weaving looms we just got for the twins."

As she and Jake walked up the front path, Dom was coming toward them. He was wearing a baggy sweater and beaten-up jeans. His face seemed far less strained than usual and he was actually smiling. "Don't tell me," she said, "you're on your way to the office, but it's dress-down Saturday."

"Nope. As it happens, I'm on my way to the garden center to buy a couple of topiary bushes. Did you know that doing topiary can be very emotionally soothing?"

"I can see that," she said, watching Jake run up to Lizzie's front door and start banging on it to be let in. "Listen, Dom, I don't want to worry you, but I have this feeling that when the aliens abducted you, they severely messed with your head. The Dom I know definitely doesn't do topiary."

"Ah, you knew the old Dom," he said. "The new Dom is a changed man. You see, Lizzie and I talked. She made me realize that if I carried on working like I have been, I would make myself ill. But more than that, she showed me that I was missing the boys' growing up. So, I bit the bullet. I went to my boss and said I would resign unless I got weekends off. You know, I never quite realized how much the firm valued me. He didn't even argue."

"Good for you. That's brilliant."

"By the way," he said, "I'm sorry about what happened— you know, the show and everything, you getting ill. I hope it all works out."

"Yeah, so do I," she said, managing a smile. By now Lizzie was standing at the door calling at her to come in because having the door open was letting out all the heat.

As she and Jake stood in the hall taking their coats off, Stephanie's mobile rang. Lizzie said she would take Jake into the living room to find the twins.

"Hello, Miss Glassman?" It was a male voice. Youngish. Rather posh, she thought.

"Speaking."

"This is Edward Windsor."

"Sorry?"

"Prince Edward. I have been having a conversation with Lord Lloyd Webber and we are very interested..."

"Hang on. You are His Royal Highness, Prince Edward?"

"Yes."

"Yeah, right, and I'm the Duke of Edinburgh's secret love child. Good-bye." She flipped the phone shut, not before she'd muttered "fucking cranks" loud enough for the caller to hear.

Lizzie came back into the hall and asked her who had been on the phone. "Oh, just another lunatic call. I've had two or three this week." She told her about the hand-relief bloke.

Lizzie and Cass both agreed that she was still looking a bit peaky. Lizzie said she needed fattening up and insisted on making hot buttered crumpets. "Don't do that," Cass said, "you'll undo all the good the food poisoning did."

"The good?" Lizzie said, horrified. "Sorry, I'm not with you."

But Stephanie was. "I think she's referring to me having lost a few pounds."

"Too right," Cass said. "I mean, weight loss is definitely the upside of getting ill. Forget dieting. Just eat raw chicken, or even better, go to India for a week. That way the weight falls off and at the same time you gain a suntan." Lizzie said that she hoped Cass never had daughters because she would set such a terrible example for them. Then Cass said at least no daughter of hers would ever own a weaving loom.

Just as things looked like they were about to get heated, Stephanie noticed Cass's braces had disappeared. "Cass, the braces are gone!"

"Aha, there's where you're wrong. I found this new ortho-dontist and he's fitted me with the latest type of brace that fits behind the teeth so you can't see it. Look! Isn't it incredible?"

Stephanie and Lizzie peered into Cass's wide-open, bleached-tooth mouth and agreed the hidden wires were in-deed incredible.

"And it's not just the braces that are incredible. I have to say the orthodontist is severely cute. It's partly the gloves. The smell of latex really turns me on. Anyway, I ended up giving him my card and asking him to call me if he felt like it."

"So, has he phoned?" Stephanie asked.

"Not yet, but I just know he will."

It was Lizzie who finally got round to asking how things were going with Albert now that he'd moved in. "Not bril-liant. Actually, I'm going to ask him to move out." Lizzie and Cass exchanged shocked glances. Lizzie asked her what had gone wrong.

"Well," she said, after Stephanie had explained, "if you're really sure you can't make a go of it, I suppose you've got no option. When are you going to tell him?"

Stephanie said as soon as she could find a time when Sunnie was out of the way. "The whole thing's just such a mess. I've hurt Frank and now I'm going to hurt Albert. Then there's Jake. I just can't bear the thought of what it will do to him if Albert leaves. You know how much he adores him."

"And he'll go on adoring him," Cass said, patting the back of Stephanie's hand. "That won't change."

Lizzie was sitting there biting her lip.

"What?" Stephanie said.

"Presumably," Lizzie began tentatively, "you're going to ask Frank to have you back."

"I think I've got to give it a try, don't you?"

"Oh, God, absolutely." She paused. "The thing is...I mean, I'm not saying this is going to happen, but it might. Suppose he doesn't want to take you back?"

Stephanie had thought about this over again and each time the pain was unbearable. But it almost didn't matter, since what she had been feeling over the last few days was equally unbearable. She swallowed hard. She could feel her hands beginning to tremble. "I think I'd rather be alone than stay with Albert and live a lie," she said.

Jake had lunch with the twins and then said he wanted to go with them to the butterfly museum. Dom, who had returned from the garden center with two topiary bushes and a pair of shears, said he would drop him home after supper.

Stephanie had told Albert she was going shoe shopping with Jake after she'd gone to Lizzie's. Since that wasn't going to happen, she decided to go home and see if by any chance Albert was alone.

As she opened the front door, she heard what sounded like frantic scrabbling and shuffling coming from the living room. "Albert? That you?" she called out, walking toward the living room where she was sure the noise had come from. She stood in the doorway. Albert was desperately trying to scramble into his boxers. Sunnie Ellaye was sitting on the sofa, naked and rigid with fear. Her hands were clamped to her breasts, her mouth was open, her eyes were aghast. She looked like a Pompeii hooker a millisecond after the hot ash hit. Stephanie stood there for a few seconds, blinking in disbelief.

"The hole usually goes at the front," she remarked to Albert, who was bending down in his boxers, his rear end facing her, trying to find his jeans.

"Principessa," he said, turning to face her, "I didn't mean for you to find out like this. I am so sorry. Look, we need to talk."

"You think?" she said. Part of her wanted to laugh. Talk about ironic. A few minutes ago she'd been telling Cass and Lizzie how guilty she felt about hurting Albert, when all the time he had been shagging Sunnie.

"Oh, God," Sunnie piped up, "this is so. I mean, it's just so . . ."

"Embarrassing?" Stephanie said, maintaining her faux casual air. "Humiliating? Mortifying? Shameful? Crushing?"

"Yes, it's all those things," Sunnie said, reaching out, grabbing her shirt and holding it to her front. "But it's also unforgivable. Albert and I have been cowards. I'm sorry." Unable to look Stephanie in the eye, she picked up the rest of her clothes. "I think I should get dressed and make myself scarce for a while."

"I think that would be a very good idea," Stephanie said icily as she moved to one side to let her through the door. Then she went over to Albert, who was pulling on his jeans. "So, when did you two get back together? Berlin?"

"We realized there was still chemistry, but nothing happened, I swear. Not then. It's just been these last few days. Sunnie and Brad have split up and we just . . ."

"I see. It all makes sense now. That's why you weren't exactly over the moon when I said you should move in."

He placed his hands on her shoulders. "Until the last couple of days, I really thought you and I could make a go of it for Jake's sake," he said.

She laughed softly, pulled away from him and sat down. "Me too. You know, if this whole thing weren't so sad, it would be comical."

"How do you mean?"

"I was coming back to tell you it wasn't going to work between us."

"Really?" he said, clearly taken aback. Stephanie nodded. "I haven't been honest with you, Albert. There's somebody else. He's been around for a while. His name is Frank. We went out while you were in Berlin. It was also Frank who bought me the painting, not Cass."

"Christ. I wasn't expecting this. So, have you been sleeping with him?" She shook her head. "Hey, well, at least one of us managed to do the decent thing."

"So you and Sunnie are really in love?"

He nodded. "She and Brad realized it wasn't working because she still had feelings for me. This woman really adores me. And she kinda looks up to me. I guess I'm one of those guys who needs to be adored and looked up to. You know, what with my ego."

She let out a soft laugh. "Yeah, I know," she said.

"So, what about you and Frank?" She told him there was no her and Frank. "I sent him packing because I thought you and I had a chance together."

"Christ, what a mess."

She shrugged. "I did what I thought was right at the time. So what now?" she said. "Will you go back to L.A.?"

He looked shocked. "And leave Jake? You have to be kidding. There's plenty of work to keep me going in this country and in Europe. In a year or two I might think about setting up an agency for stunt artists."

"And Sunnie?"

"I think she'll stay on too. Apparently there's a serious Reiki master shortage in this country."

Stephanie laughed and told him she was glad he was staying. "I couldn't have faced telling Jake you were leaving again."

309

"I'll get a place a few streets away. Promise." He pulled on his shirt and started doing up the buttons. "I'll be over every night to help put him to bed. He'll hardly know I don't live here. And on weekends he can stay with me."

"That would be great. Hang on, your shirt buttons are all crooked." She reached out and started redoing them. "And tell Sunnie Ellaye no hard feelings and she's a very sweet girl. You know, I do love you, Albert." She kissed his cheek.

"I love you, too, *principessa*."

"Now, that's what I like to hear!" Albert and Stephanie shot round to see Estelle and Harry. "The door was open," Estelle said. "Oh, congratulations, you two." Before they could say anything, Estelle was kissing and hugging them both.

"Mum, no, you don't understand." But Estelle was too excited to listen. "And your father's got some fantastic news. That's why we're here. We didn't want to tell you over the phone."

"Actually," Harry began, "we have two bits of fantastic news. First, I have found a way of stopping the junk e-mail once and for all." He started going on about something called a spamming program. Estelle rolled her eyes. "It means that whenever a company sends me junk e-mail, I can send them back hundreds of thousands of junk e-mails of my own. Isn't that a hoot?" He started chortling and slapping his thigh. "It's guaranteed to stop them in no time."

"All right, Harry," Estelle said, taking a deep breath, "that's all very interesting. Now get to the point and tell Stephanie the really good news."

"OK. You won't believe what came in the post this morning." Harry handed Stephanie a letter. It was from one of the companies that had been e-mailing her father, offering to overhaul his septic tank.

Dear Mr. P. Enis Extension:

You won't believe what good fortune this letter brings!!! You are a Grand Draw WINNER*!!!! You have been selected from all your neighbors in* LONDON *to win a two-week holiday to Barbados with Mrs. P. Enis Extension and three additional members of the P. Enis Extension family. Not only will you have a chance to relax on some of the finest beaches in the world, you will also be taken on privileged tours of properties with our revolutionary new Turdaway™ luxury septic tank system! Imagine how envious all your friends and neighbors in* EDGWARE *will feel when they see the P. Enis Extension family on their way to* EDGWARE *airport and a holiday to Barbados. (Terms and conditions apply, see attached document.)*

"I phoned the company to check it all out," Harry said. "It's completely genuine. They're paying for all five of us— you, Albert and Jake count as additional family members. We spend half a day doing the septic tank tour with some PR girl and the rest of the time is ours. They'll never know we don't actually need a septic tank in Edgware."

"Look, Mum, Dad. This sounds wonderful, but before you get too carried away, there's something I need to tell you."

"Maybe I should go," Albert said.

Estelle in particular was desperately upset that Stephanie and Albert had split up. "Are you absolutely sure? I mean, couldn't you try counseling or something?"

"It wouldn't work. Albert and I both realize that it was only Jake keeping us together. A child needs parents who are in love. If we'd stayed together it would have been out of

311

duty. That wouldn't have been fair to Jake. Anyway, Albert's got somebody else and what you don't know is that I have too. At least I did have. It's a long story, but I've messed him about because of this whole Albert thing and I don't know if he'll still want me."

Estelle hugged her. "If he loves you, he will. Don't you agree, Harry?"

Harry was sitting in the armchair, rereading the letter from the septic tank people. "Definitely. And he can come to Barbados instead of Albert. Or, if you're being very modern and civilized, Albert can come too. And he can bring his new lady friend. Let them all come. Of course they'd have to pay for themselves. You know, every room has its own terrace and plunge pool. We'll have to watch out with Jake." Estelle shot Stephanie a look, which said "He means well."

"So, come on," Estelle said, "what are you waiting for? Off you go and tell this Frank of yours that you love him."

"What, now? Right this minute?"

"Can't see any reason why not. Can you?" She was shaking at the thought, petrified of his rejection. She managed to say that she supposed not. It was Saturday afternoon, so there was a strong possibility he would be at home. "I love you, Mum," she said.

"And I love you, darling," she said, hugging Stephanie.

Stephanie had reached the front door when she heard her father say, "What about me? Don't I get the chance to tell my daughter I love her?"

"You had your head buried in that stupid letter."

"It won't look so stupid when you're sitting at the hotel bar, sipping piña coladas."

"OK," Estelle said, "but the moment reception pages Mr. and Mrs. P. Enis Extension, I'm leaving. Understand?"

Trembling, Stephanie rang Frank's doorbell, but there was no answer. She tried his mobile, but it was switched off. She was walking back down the path, desperately wondering what to do next, when Ossie phoned.

"Stephanie, did the queen's youngest son happen to phone a while ago, and did you happen to tell him to get lost?"

"No, some nutter rang pretending he was the queen's youngest son and I told him to get lost."

"No, actually it *was* His Royal Highness you told to get lost."

"Oh, don't be so ridiculous. Why would Prince Edward be phoning me?"

"Because he and Andrew Lloyd Webber are taking over the *Peggy* production. Edward, it seems, is branching out beyond films. And guess who they want for the lead?"

"Who?"

"Oscar the Grouch."

"What?"

"They want you, Stephanie. You. At least they did want you until you sent HRH packing."

"Oh, God. Shit. What should I do?"

Ossie laughed and told her not to worry. "I told him you've been getting some crank calls. He understood. I've set up a meeting with him and Andrew on Monday. But it's only a formality. They're desperate to have you. And guess what? They want Konstanty to direct."

For a few moments her spirits soared and she felt like dancing. "Wow, Ossie. That's amazing. I can't believe it. I'm going to be a star. Me. Omigod." Then she realized that the one person in the world she wanted to tell, she couldn't. She must have gone silent for a good while, because Ossie asked her if she was all right. She brought him up to speed with the Albert/Frank situation. "I've no idea where Frank is."

"I do." He told her that Frank had just accepted a job in Australia for ten weeks before he starts rehearsals for *Twelfth Night*. "I know his agent. We had dinner last night. He happened to mention Frank was going off to do *Taming of the Shrew* in Sydney. Stephanie, I'm so sorry."

"That's OK," she said, fighting the urge to curl up into a ball and sob. "Not to worry. Tell HRH and Lord Lloyd Webber I'll be there on Monday."

She couldn't face going back to an empty house, so she decided to pick up an *Evening Standard* and go and sit in Starbucks with a grande espresso. Miserable as she was feeling—her incredible professional break aside—she couldn't help smiling when she read that life wasn't going well for Sidney and K-Mart in Brazil. Since Sidney had put all his money into the *Peggy* show, he had now declared himself bankrupt, and Katherine, who was already in dire financial straits, had been forced to accept a role in a Brazilian soap. The paper also made the point that it somehow seemed fitting that, as she could only speak English, Katherine's part would be dubbed into Portuguese.

Stephanie's spirits weren't lifted for long, though. Soon tears were streaming down her face. Starbucks was opposite the launderette where Frank had first kissed her. She stared out the window remembering how they'd sat there on the long table, laughing, drinking wine and eating slightly dried-up Thai curry. She closed her eyes and felt the kiss, the way he'd held her, the way he'd looked into her eyes.

She didn't know what made her do it—maybe some masochistic part of her needed to feel the pain even more intensely—but she decided to walk across the road to the launderette and look inside.

The traffic was particularly heavy. As she stood trying to get across the road, her mobile went off.

"Steph, it's Cass. Guess what? My sexy orthodontist called. We're going out tonight. He's taking me to the Ivy. I'm dashing out to find something to wear. God, I feel like a teenager. I'm just so excited."

"Great. Good for you."

"Christ, what's up?"

Stephanie told her what had happened. "And now I find out Frank's gone to Australia to forget about me."

"Sweetie, I am so sorry. Look, come over. I don't have to go out."

"No, it's OK. I'll be fine."

"Well, if you're sure." Stephanie didn't say anything. She was now standing outside the launderette, and as she peered inside, something, or to be more precise, somebody had caught her eye. He was sitting down and he had his back to her, but she was pretty sure it was Frank.

"Stephanie, say something. Look, are you really all right? I'm worried you're going to do something stupid. Stephanie, speak to me."

"I've found him."

"Who?"

"Frank. I've found him."

"No, darling, you haven't. It'll be somebody who looks like him, that's all. Listen, where are you? Maybe I should come and get you."

When he stood up, she knew for sure it was Frank. She watched him take his laundry out of the washing machine and load it into the dryer.

"No, it really is him. I can see him quite clearly. He didn't go to Australia. He's here."

"Steph, are you sure?"

"Positive."

"OK, but just one word of warning. If he takes you back, please remember you haven't slept with him. I'm still worried about the possibility of him having a small willy. Just keep in mind what I said about the relationship between ear size and penis size. Do not commit yourself until you've taken a look at his ears. Promise me."

"OK, right, whatever. Bye, Cass."

"No, that's not a promise—"

Stephanie flipped off her phone and walked toward the door of the launderette. She almost collided with a bustling elderly woman who would never see five feet, pushing a wicker shopping cart full of neatly folded bed linen. "Bloomin' soap dispenser's playing up," she grumbled to Stephanie. "I lost two fifty-pence pieces before it gave me any powder. I've left a note for the manager. They say this place is managed, but there's never anybody here. Blinkin' disgrace if you ask me."

Desperate to get through the door, Stephanie was virtually jumping up and down with frustration. "I know, it's awful," she said, trying to work out a way to step over the shopping cart. "The thing is, if I could just get by—"

"And another thing," the woman persisted, steadfastly blocking the doorway. "Look at the state of the floor. Covered in dust and filth. The only way to clean a floor properly is to get down on your hands and knees and scrub. Of course, no-body can be bothered these days. Whole world's gone bone idle if you ask me."

"I'm sure you're right. If I could just squeeze—"

But the old biddy wasn't listening. She was looking past

Stephanie toward the bus stop. "Ooh, that's my bus. Excuse me." She barged past Stephanie and trotted off to the stop.

Frank, who appeared to have heard none of Stephanie's exchange with the woman, was sitting with his back to her reading a magazine.

"So, washing machine still not fixed, then," she said, her voice shaking. She made him jump. He turned to face her. Once he'd gotten over the shock of seeing her, an awkwardness overtook him. "No," he smiled, folding up the paper. "Repairman said I need a new one. Haven't gotten round to buying one yet."

"Right," she replied, returning his unease now. "I thought you were in Australia."

He shrugged. "Decided I couldn't face all those jolly Aussies when I was feeling so miserable." She nodded.

"Mind if I sit down?"

"Help yourself."

She sat down next to him. "Prince Edward and Andrew Lloyd Webber are taking over the production of *Peggy* and they're pretty sure they want me in the lead. I'm meeting them on Monday."

"Wow, Steph. That really is fantastic news. I couldn't be more pleased for you." She stared down at a dust ball on the floor. The old woman had been right. The floor really was pretty grubby. Stephanie didn't say anything for a few seconds. "By the way, Albert and I are finished."

"I'm sorry."

"Thanks."

"So, what happened?"

"After you left the other day," she said, "I couldn't stop thinking about you. I realized I'd made a mistake and that Albert and I were never going to work. I adore Jake, but I

317

couldn't sacrifice my happiness for him." Frank nodded. "And anyway," she went on, "you can't marry someone when you're in love with someone else." Despite herself, her face broke into a ridiculous smile.

"What?" he said.

She told him she'd just realized she was quoting Christopher Plummer's line from the gazebo scene in *The Sound of Music*. "You know, that bit where he tells Julie Andrews he's ditched the baroness."

"I've never seen *The Sound of Music*," Frank said.

"Oh, you should," she said, relieved to have a chance to witter on about something inconsequential instead of having to explain why she was really there. "People laugh at it and make fun, but it's got everything: music, romance, comedy, Nazis. You can borrow my video."

He nodded without showing any emotion and she knew she couldn't avoid the real issue any longer. "Frank, I know I've treated you very badly, but..." Her sentence trailed off.

"But what?"

"OK, it's probably ridiculous, but I was wondering if there was any hope of us getting back together."

He stared at her. "What? And have you change your mind again? I don't think so."

"But I won't. I promise."

"How do I know that?"

"I guess you don't. I suppose I'm asking you to trust me. Anyway, Albert's got somebody else."

"Oh, I get it," Frank said, springing up and walking toward the line of washing machines. "Albert walks out and so you come looking for me. Good old Frank, he'll come running."

"No, that's not how it was," she cried out, her voice full of hurt and indignation. But she could see his point. By now she was on her feet too. He had his back to her. "Frank, look at me." He turned round to face her. "I'd decided to end it with Albert before I discovered he was seeing somebody else. And that's the truth. I swear on Jake's life. Ask Lizzie and Cass if you don't believe me."

He looked at her, his eyes boring into her. It seemed to go on forever. "I love you, Frank. That was never the issue. You know that. This was always about me trying to do what I thought was best for Jake. I got it wrong. You told me and I ignored you. Please forgive me."

"I love you too," he said finally. "I never stopped loving you. Not for a moment." He allowed his face to break into a smile. "Come here," he whispered. She practically threw herself into his arms, which he wrapped so tight around her she virtually couldn't breathe. "And thinking about it," he went on, "I really could do with somebody who knows about washing machines to come with me to choose a new one."

"Oh, absolutely," she said, looking up at him. "I mean, if you fancied, we could go on a trial date to the John Lewis white-goods department. You know, see how we get on."

"I might be up for that," he said.

"So, am I forgiven?"

"You're forgiven," he said, giving her another squeeze. "Although I'm not so sure about this weird fascination you have with *The Sound of Music*."

"Believe me, you'll love it." She grinned.

"I'll try anything once," he said, clearly amused.

"Good. So, before we go on this trial date, could we maybe go back to your place and . . . you know."

"People usually go out first and have sex afterward," he said.

"Yes, but technically we have already been out on a date."

"I suppose," he said. The next moment he was kissing

319

her on the mouth. By now her back was resting against one of the washing machines. As their kissing grew more urgent, the machine lurched into a violent, almost earthquakelike spin. Her back and hips shook as if she were performing some wild erotic dance. "I don't know about you," she giggled "but I think somebody up there is trying to tell us something."

Frank grinned. "OK, c'mon, let's go."

"What about the washing?" she said. "It's still in the dryer."

"Sod the washing."

They got to the street. "Oh, Frank, by the way, there's just one thing."

"Oh, God, what now? Don't tell me you're having second thoughts again."

"Absolutely not. But would you mind if I just took a quick look at your ears?"

"My ears? Why?"

"I'll tell you later."

He presented his head for her inspection. She examined one side and then the other. "Perfect," she announced. "Absolutely perfect."

DON'T MISS

Sue Margolis's

Other Hysterical Novels

NEUROTICA
SPIN CYCLE
APOCALIPSTICK

All available as Delta paperbacks

NEUROTICA

If He *Always Has the Headache,
Why Should You Suffer?*

Tabloid reporter Anna Shapiro can pinpoint the day, three years ago, when she and her husband, Dan, last had great sex. Anna would be grateful if something as ordinary as a mere headache were her husband's excuse; Dan's hypochondriacal terrors include brain tumors, tropical diseases, and spontaneous combustion. But now an assignment for a racy tabloid exposé inspires Anna to go where no journalist has gone before, to answer some questions that suddenly seem very important: What is the perfect outfit for committing adultery in? Is it beyond the pale to pick up a man—no matter how sexy—at a funeral? Yet the most crucial question is one Anna never expected: Is she willing to give up her marriage and children for the biggest gamble of her life?

> "Taking up where *Bridget Jones's Diary* took off, this saucy, sexy British adventure redefines the lusty woman's search for erotic satisfaction.... Witty and sure.... A taut and rambunctious tale exploring the perils and raptures of the pursuit of passion."
> —*Publishers Weekly*

> "Screamingly funny sex comedy...the perfect novel to take on a holiday."
> —*USA Today*

SPIN CYCLE

Her Husband Left Her for Another Man.
Her Boyfriend May Be Cheating.
Her Mother's Got a Secret.
Is Everyone Having Great Sex but Rachel?

Lately, stand-up comic Rachel Katz's life has begun to resemble a not-so-funny comedy routine—the kind where nobody laughs and everybody inches toward the door. It began when her husband cheated... with another man. Now she's raising a ten-year-old son who's fixated on Barbra Streisand and wondering if her dentist boyfriend—who won't stop flossing long enough to make love to her—is having an affair.

Enter Matt Clapton, a wickedly sexy washing machine repairman who likes Rachel's jokes and makes her feel like a woman for the first time in ages—maybe in her entire life. With her mother busy planning a wedding Rachel isn't sure she wants, her son dead set on inviting Barbra to the reception, and the groom-to-be in South Africa working on someone else's oral hygiene, the question is: What's she going to do about it? Especially when fame and fortune beckon in a comedy contest that could put her on the map and change her life forever.

SPIN CYCLE tells a wickedly funny, shamelessly erotic story of lovers and liars, exes and children, parents and other strangers. This hip and hilarious novel features a heroine who never loses her sense of humor and who discovers, somewhere between the rinse and spin cycles, that love—and laughter—can truly conquer all.

APOCALIPSTICK

A Wickedly Funny Novel About Sex, Romance, Wrinkles... and Other Natural Disasters

When it comes to men, beauty columnist Rebecca Fine always seems to be on the scruffy end of the mascara wand. But all that changes the morning she meets Max Stoddart, her new colleague at the *Daily Vanguard*. With his upscale suit, Hugh Grant hair, and obscenely good looks, he's a single woman's dream come true. But is Max the catch of the decade—or just a major babe magnet?

Meanwhile, Rebecca's old high school nemesis has resurfaced, a former blond bombshell called Lipstick who is now engaged to Rebecca's widowed dad. And it's good-bye to articles on toe cleavage when a hot tip sweeps Rebecca to the center of the Paris cosmetics world, where a miracle antiwrinkle cream is about to be launched. That is, until she blows the whistle on a scandal that could set the beauty business—and the future of world peace—reeling. Will Rebecca win the recognition—not to mention the Pulitzer—she yearns for... and get the man of her dreams? Stay tuned.

"Sexy British romp... Margolis's characters have a candor and self-deprecation that lead to furiously funny moments.... A riotous, ribald escapade sure to leave readers chuckling to the very end of this saucy adventure."
—*USA Today*

"[An] irreverent, sharp-witted look at love and dating."
—*Houston Chronicle*